Crowned Heads . . .

"is a terrific read, engrossing, scary, and richly, superbly entertaining." —COSMOPOLITAN

"ANOTHER WINNER. HORROR, NOSTALGIA, SUSPENSE, AND MORE WILL STEADILY KEEP READERS' ATTENTION."
—LIBRARY JOURNAL

"Thomas Tryon's newest novel *CROWNED HEADS* is outstanding. . . . Stunning, sad, and best of all a piece of reality about a world built around make-believe." —HOUSTON CHRONICLE

"BRILLIANT. . . . THE MARK OF A MASTER CRAFTSMAN." —FORT WAYNE JOURNAL-GAZETTE

Thomas Tryon . . .

"writes with hyp⟨...⟩invention."

Fawcett Crest Books
by Thomas Tryon:

THE OTHER

HARVEST HOME

LADY

CROWNED HEADS

CROWNED HEADS

BY

Thomas Tryon

A FAWCETT CREST BOOK

Fawcett Publications, Inc., Greenwich, Connecticut

CROWNED HEADS

Main Selection of the Literary Guild
Selection of the Reader's Digest Condensed Book Club

Grateful acknowledgment is made to Warner Bros. Music for permission to reprint lines of lyrics from "Blues in the Night," lyrics by Johnny Mercer music by Harold Arlen. Copyright © 1941 by Warner Bros., Inc., copyright renewed. All rights reserved. Used by permission.

Chappell & Co., Inc.: Lyrics on page 106 from "LOOKIE, LOOKIE, LOOKIE, HERE COMES COOKIE." Copyright © 1935 by DeSylva, Brown & Henderson, Inc. Copyright renewed, assigned to Chappell & Co., Inc. International Copyright Secured. All rights reserved. Used by permission.

ABC Music Corp.: Lyrics on page 356 from "California Dreamin'" by M. Gilliam and J. Phillips. Copyright © 1965 by American Broadcasting Music Corp., Inc. Used by permission. All rights reserved.

This book is for
Arthur and Edward.

Uneasy lies the head that wears a crown.

Henry IV, Part II

Fedora

Fedora was dead, and who could talk of anything else? Including the entire staff of *Good Morning USA,* whose producer wanted a twenty-minute air-time recap of the actress's illustrious career, with "fresh angles" and "a new slant." Marion Walker wondered what there was to say about Fedora that hadn't already been said. As hostess of *the* morning network TV show, Marion helped the nation get started every day, its matutinal mixture of brains and beauty. Though she had interviewed Kissinger and Teddy Kennedy, she had never interviewed Fedora; few in the world had. Its most celebrated screen actress, Fedora was also its Great Enigma, but Marion knew someone who supposedly had talked with her recently, Barry Detweiller. Barry knew everybody: Sinatra was a crony, so was John Lennon. He drank with Teddy White, lunched with Jackie, dined with Clare Luce. His credentials were impeccable. He'd had a highly regarded by-line with *Life,* had published several books, including a novel, his name meant an important story, and he was a good news reporter. Marion knew if anyone could help her it was Barry. She telephoned him at home, where he was reputed to be holed up, finishing a new book.

"Barry . . . Marion. I want to talk about Fedora."

"Sure thing, Marion. Go ahead."

"I mean I want *you* to talk to *me* about Fedora."

"What do *I* know about her?" Barry asked innocently. Marion's reporter's instinct told her it was an innocence born of knowledge.

"You saw her recently, didn't you, on Crete? There must be a few sidelights you could give me, couldn't you?" Marion was using her most persuasive tone. In her line of work it seldom hurt to be a woman, nor was she a woman to take no for an answer.

"Well, let's see," Barry said. "Which sidelight do you want? Sidelight A—Fedora uses Camay soap for the look of beauty? Sidelight B—Fedora sleeps in the nude? Sidelight C—"

"Barry, I want something for a story. A fresh angle, a new slant."

"Oh, slants and angles you want. How about the triangle? Mother, son, Fedora. Or the other triangle—son, wife, Fedora? Or how about the sinister Dr. Vando, who looks like Lionel Atwill and gives her injections of sheep semen in his mysterious laboratory?"

"*Barry*, I haven't time, I really haven't. . . . I want a story."

"*Oh*, a *story*. I see. . . . Well, let's think a minute here—there must be a good one somewhere. Yeah, I think I've got one. Sure, okay, fine. Come along to me for drinks about seven. We'll have dinner—"

"I can't."

"You can't? I thought you wanted a story."

"I do, but—" She was checking her desk calendar; ending her list of many appointments was: *"8:00 p.m./Sills/Siege of Corinth."* "Beverly's singing at the Met. I've got to hear her; she's coming on the show next month. How about lunch tomorrow?"

"No dice. I'm flying to London. But I'll tell you this—" He lowered his voice confidentially. "It's a terrific story."

"*Really* terrific?"

"*Really* terrific."

"I'll be there." Beverly Sills and *The Siege of Corinth* would have to wait; Marion would switch her tickets. Fedora didn't die every day of the week.

Barry's apartment was in the East Seventies, and the garrulous taxi driver who took Marion there that spring evening was swift to point out in his hearty Brooklynese that Fedora had once been his passenger, and had she "evuh seen huh in *Ophelie?*" Yes, Marion had seen *Ophelie;* not the silent version—she was too young—but being one of Fedora's best-loved films, the sound remake was often on the *Late Show.* "Huh foist talkie—I seen it in '29, an' I seen huh last in '69. Whadda bomb—dey killed huh wit' bad pitchuhs. But howdya figure—forty yeahs on the screen an' still a lookah?

My old lady nevuh looked dat good at thoity. Don't tell me dat Vando guy didn't do numbuhs on huh."

Exactly what "numbers" the mysterious Portuguese doctor had "done" on Fedora was only one among the items Marion wanted to quiz Barry about. Though the actress had been hidden from its sight for many years, the world seized on any scraps of news concerning her, and all anyone could talk about was her death yesterday in Menton, France.

"You liked her?" Marion asked the driver.

"Lady, I woishiped huh."

"Why?"

"Class. She had class. I don't care what no one says about huh, whatevuh crazy things she done. I loved huh. Ev'ybody did." Thus spake the man in the street.

To show that celebrity makes itself felt even among its staunchest decriers, the cabby had fixed a rose over his rear-view mirror as a floral tribute, marking how infinite and long-lasting was the power of her name, the magic of her art. Neither the cabby nor Marion had ever known a world in which there was no Fedora. Marion considered the fact: George Washington had refused a crown (the wisdom of this was debatable to some), but given that America's true royalty is crowned from the court of Hollywood, then in that ersatz monarchy Fedora was queen; she had outshone all and outlived most, though whether by purely natural causes remained as yet undiscovered.

Barry's living room was what she expected: hardly neat, but a man's place, a writer's place, lots of shelves with books, magazines, newspapers, manuscripts, file drawers; a few handsome touches, good antiques mixed with sturdy but comfortable pieces, and over the mantel, unmistakably, a portrait of the lady in question, Fedora herself. Barry was easy and relaxed and prepared to be a good host. He suggested some wine, she accepted. The bottle was produced, cooling in a bucket. Vouvray *pétillant,* he announced, a naturally semi-sparkling, dry white, and Fedora's favorite.

"Oh?" Marion stabbed him with a quick look. "How do you come by that information?"

"She told me herself."

"And the portrait?"

"That's another story."

Marion put on her glasses and examined the painting closely. "It's her to the life. Who did it?"

"As you see, it's unsigned. But it was painted in the Dakota." The Dakota was one of New York's venerable landmark apartment buildings. Barry explained that he had known the girl who had owned the painting two decades earlier; it had hung in her apartment until at her death it had passed into his hands. Now, reframed and dramatically lighted, it formed the focal point of the room. Technically, it was not particularly well painted, but Marion recognized immediately how, like Fedora herself, it manifested an aura of mystery and romance. She was posed on a gold-and-black-striped couch of faintly Empire design, one hand resting against a hip, the other supporting the head. The background was an almost *grisaille* rendering of a large apartment interior, room after room receding dimly, each elaborately decorated with bombé chests, crystal chandeliers, candelabra blazing with candles. Fedora's costume was a many-ruffled, high-collared white peignoir; Marion remembered it as the one Cyril Leaf had designed for *Ophelie*, which Leaf had personally loaned for the Diana Vreeland exhibition at the Metropolitan Museum, "Romantic and Glamorous Hollywood Design."

Marion said it was Fedora to the life, though the features were heavily stylized, the nose was too long, the eyes were too large, too heavily lidded. They gazed past one with an idle, almost vacant stare; but it was Fedora's hauteur, all right. The mouth was thin and darkly red, not sensual but provocative—the renowned "Mona Lisa" look. The hair was arranged carelessly, but with a sense of period, the way Fedora had worn it in the movie.

Barry pointed out above the table serving as a bar a small framed document. Aged and important-looking, with an embossed official seal, it proved to be a note in Italian, addressed to Fedora, professing admiration for her talent and beauty and hoping she would one day visit Rome, where the author would have the privilege of meeting her personally. It was signed "Mussolini."

"It must be worth a lot of money," Marion said, awed in spite of herself.

Barry laughed. "Exactly what the person who gave it to me said."

"Fedora?"

"Mrs. Balfour."

"Ahhh—the ubiquitous Mrs. Balfour." Like most people, Marion was acquainted with the name. Mrs. Balfour had been the inseparable companion of Fedora for many years. "She *gave* it to you?"

"For services rendered. A bribe, actually."

12

"Where and to whom?"

"That's two too many questions for openers. You sound like a lawyer."

"I'm only asking."

"I last saw Mrs. Balfour on Crete, at the countess's villa."

"That would be old Countess Sobryanski?"

He nodded, and reached for the wine from the bucket. He filled their glasses and held the bottle of Vouvray so Marion could read the label.

"Fedora told you it was her favorite?"

"One of them. Did you recognize the music on the hi-fi when you came in?"

"No. What was it?"

"The Baltic Symphony—a particular favorite of Countess Sobryanski. As a matter of fact, it was being played a lot at the villa when I was there. . . . Wait a minute, I've got some noshes in the fridge." While he went back to the kitchen, Marion stole a look at the table where a typed manuscript lay, bound by an elastic band, but without a title page. Surreptitiously she leaned and read the first line: "She was called the Perfect Work of Art—" Marion straightened as Barry returned with a tray of hors d'oeuvre. She adjusted her glasses, took out a pad and pencil, and struck a business-like attitude on the sofa.

"Your new book?" she asked, glancing at the manuscript as if for the first time. Barry smiled, nodded, offered her a canapé and a napkin. "Nonfiction or a novel?" she continued casually.

"My editor says it's both, but that it has too much romance for anything since the Brontë sisters. Actually it's about Fedora."

"Oh? You've been writing about her, then? Another biography?"

He chuckled. "There *are* a lot of them, aren't there?"

"Is it juicy?"

"Of course."

"A scandal?"

"Some might think so." He picked up the manuscript, hefted it, then dumped it into Marion's lap. "Why don't you just take it home and read it? It'll save me a lot of talking."

"*May* I?" She looked again at the top page.

He grabbed it back and returned it to the table. "No, you may not. And you won't need to take notes."

"I always take notes."

"Not this time." He had gone to the window and stood

looking out at the garden; an ailanthus was turning a feathery green, and shrubs were bursting with white blooms. Marion put aside her pad and pencil, took off her glasses, and waited. He said nothing, seemingly lost in thought. She felt a growing exhilaration and excitement at the prospect of the disclosures he was about to make, and yet she could sense that he wanted to prolong the effect of his big moment. It was something like knowing the whereabouts of the bones of Peking Man, or holding the key to the fourth dimension.

Which in a way it was, dealing as it did with time. Anyone acquainted with the merest facts of Fedora's history must realize, as Marion certainly did, that in some vague and strange way "time was of the essence." Where fiction had become fact and fact fiction no one was any longer able to tell—unless it was now to be Barry Detweiller—but the single obvious fact was that Fedora's career had spanned a period lasting from silent pictures well into the age of wide-screen stereophonic films. She had remained at the height of her artistic powers, her beauty, her youthfulness, for half a century; not an impossibility, except for the fact that she had not aged to any noticeable degree. Dr. Vando was said to be at the bottom of this mysterious yet essential fact, yet just as essentially, no one had ever been able fully to explain it.

Of her early contemporaries and peers, as Barry now pointed out, who was there still living? Lillian Gish. Gloria Swanson. Janet Gaynor. A handful of others. Joan Crawford had still been Lucille Le Sueur, an unknown Charleston cup winner, when Fedora was a star in silents. When Stanwyck matured to an old lady in *So Big* (with Bette Davis as the tender ingenue), it was Barbara's eighth feature; Fedora had shot over a score by then. Davis made her first film at Universal in 1931, a studio not even in existence when Fedora was a leading lady at AyanBee. Carole Lombard was only a Sennett bathing beauty when Fedora had played in four pictures. Harlow was dead in 1937 after a career spanning less than a decade. Swanson, perhaps Fedora's nearest contemporary, did only eleven sound pictures, Fedora three times that number. Dietrich was "box office poison" when Fedora was packing houses with a major success a year. Garbo left the screen at thirty-six and never returned, while Fedora was still playing leading romantic parts into the late 1960s.

Barry had turned and was staring musingly at the manuscript on the table; to prompt him on his way, Marion asked:

"What began it all? Your fascination with her? You *are* fascinated, you know."

He shrugged and took the club chair. "I don't know, really; it just . . . started."

"When was the first time you ever saw her?"

"I was about seven, I think. And it wasn't in the movies."

"In person?"

"Who ever saw Fedora in person in those days? Not in Villanova, Pa., you didn't see Fedora in person. It was an ice cream parlor, where they'd taken me after Sunday school. We got Dixie cups, and I wanted chocolate. I pulled off the lid, which was covered with chocolate ice cream, and licked it, and who appeared from beneath my tongue but Fedora. It was a still from *Tsarina*—you know, Catherine the Great? Someone said, 'Oh, you have Fedora,' and I said, 'Who's Fedora?' I'd never heard of her. But I liked the way she looked. When *Madagascar* came to town I told my mother I wanted to see it. She said no, it was a grownups' picture. I carried on until she finally agreed to take me to a matinee, but I never got to see the end of it."

"Did you walk out?"

"Not exactly. When I came across Fedora years later, I told her the story. We were talking about her films and I mentioned that I'd liked *Madagascar,* but hadn't seen the last part. She asked why not. I said, 'Remember the scene with the native uprising, and you and Willie Marsh were about to be slaughtered?' 'I remember,' she said. 'Well,' I said, 'you were both in this room at the top of some stairs—I think it was in a plantation house—and the natives broke in below and they were brandishing clubs and axes and spears. Then they went charging up the stairs and started breaking down the door and setting fire to the place. You were behind the door.' 'Yes,' she said, waiting. I said, 'I got so scared I wet my pants and my mother had to take me out.' "

Marion shrieked with laughter. "You didn't tell that to Fedora!"

"I did. She wasn't amused. But I didn't do it intentionally. I thought it was a funny story. I wasn't thinking about the age thing at all."

"What did she say?"

"She gave me that narrow-eyed look and said loftily, 'I see. You must have been ver-r-ry youn-n-ng,' dragging out the words in that Russian drawl. My mother told me I wasn't going to see any more movies like *Madagascar*. Then *La*

Gioconda came to Philadelphia. Kids didn't go to see Fedora movies, usually, they were too sexy, but Mona Lisa was 'historical' and they took our whole class out of school, stuck us on a bus, and sent us to the movies. When it was over we were supposed to go to the Fels Planetarium to get more culture, but some of us hid in the dark and sat through the co-feature, a B comedy with Florence Rice, and then we saw Fedora again.

"There was a poster stand in front of the theater and when we left I tore the poster off and ran with it. You've seen the shot?"

"The Da Vinci painting with Fedora's face superimposed, wasn't it?"

Barry nodded. "I tacked it on my bedroom wall. It stayed there for I guess about ten years, until I went in the service. My mother threw it out then. But at some point a friend had taken a crayon and drawn a mustache on it. It made me so goddamn mad."

"It sounds like you fell in love with her."

"We were always falling in love with movie stars then. My brother wrote Lana Turner's name in wet cement after the cellar drainpipe was excavated. But Fedora—you didn't fall in love with just her face. You fell in love with all of her— her voice, her body, her talent, her gestures, everything about her that is so familiar, but so . . ."

"Enigmatic?"

"Clichés? From you, Marion?"

"Sorry." She tossed back her hair with the gesture that was probably more familiar to more viewers than all Fedora's gestures in all her films. "But she *was* an enigma, and you must have solved it, or you wouldn't be writing one more book about her."

"I never thought I'd be writing about Fedora. Then after I began writing magazine pieces, it became a kind of dream to do one on her, but I didn't want to do it without interviewing her, or someone who knew her really well."

Marion glanced again at the manuscript. "You must have finally gotten your interview. That's more than a magazine piece."

"I got my interview, but not the way you'd think."

"Did you get all the answers?"

"All the ones that matter, at any rate."

Marion leaned eagerly to Barry, quickly raising a flood of questions, names, events. Was Dr. Vando a quack? Was it true about the sheep cures? Did he operate on her eyes to make them larger? What was the Hollywood gossip concerning Count Sobryanski, and his mother, the dowager countess, who had been with Fedora so much? Did Barry subscribe to the monkey gland theory? Was it true she became addicted to hashish at the count's home in Morocco? . . .

Barry waited for the tide of questions to ebb, then asked soberly:

"Marion, you really want the story? The whole story?"

"I *want* it."

"Then I'll give it to you."

"Nice Barry."

"Nice Marion. But let me preface it by telling you three things. You won't believe it all, even though my facts are unassailable. You'll be flattered, because I've never told another person. And you'll be very angry, because you can't use it."

"Can't use it?" Her nostrils widened; she tossed back her hair again. "Then what good is it to me?"

"I haven't any idea. You asked me for Fedora stories, and I'm willing to give you a great one. But only here, and only now. Afterward you have to forget it. Otherwise you'd scoop my book."

Deflated, Marion drew back against the pillows in ill-disguised frustration. "Why tell me at all?"

"I thought, out of the whole thing, you might glean a few little things you could use, the kind of 'sidelights' you were talking about. If we're friends—and I hope we're friends—I'm going to use you as my patsy. A dry run, if you like. Only a few people other than my editor know anything about what's in this manuscript, and he thinks I made most of it up. Come on, don't look so disappointed. You want to hear or not?"

"I am disappointed—and yes, I *do* want to hear. Go ahead. Start."

"In twenty-five words or less—right? It's not quite that easy. How much do you *really* know about her?"

As a good newsperson, Marion thought she had done her homework well, having spent the afternoon going through the files her staff had brought in for an initial survey. "Well," she began, "I know her father was a grocer and her mother was a milliner—"

"Wrong on both counts. He was a schoolteacher, she was a washerwoman. Fedora told me so herself."

"On Crete?"

"No. At the Louvre, thirty years ago."

"You've known her that long?"

Barry nodded. "Right after the war. She was living in Switzerland with the Sobryanskis until after V-E Day, then she stayed in their Paris house, the one Cole Porter used to have, in Rue Monsieur. I was living around the corner, in Rue de Babylone, and I used to see her sometimes. One day she spoke to me in the Louvre. I never learned why, really. She'd come to see the 'Mona Lisa.' What does this line mean to you?" He quoted: " 'Rien d'ailleurs ne rassure autant qu'un masque.' "

" 'Nothing provides as much assurance as a mask.' Colette, isn't it?"

"Very good. Colette, yes. Fedora quoted it to me. That was her, you see; she, too, had a mask."

"You mean her need for privacy?"

"I mean her whole life."

"What *was* true about her?"

"Very little, actually."

Marion had the sense to realize that in Fedora's case facts were of little consequence. For two reasons. First, it was not the reality of Fedora that mattered; nobody was ever much interested in her vital statistics. What was interesting was the myth, and few myths are made of facts. Second, the facts were mostly wrong to begin with. To prove the point, Barry went over the list he had taken from the New York Public Library, biographies ranging from ho-hum to what-else-is-new? They raked over the old stories and rumors—the double love triangles and mysteries, the character of the sinister Dr. Vando, the seemingly eternal presence of Mrs. Balfour, Fedora's friendship for the Sobryanskis, mother and son, wife and husband—all relying heavily on early studio biographies based on information supplied after her meeting with Maurice Derougemont, and as he himself had later admitted to Barry,[*] they were as much a figment of his imagination as were the plots of the numerous pictures they made together.

The one book doing any sort of justice to its subject was the well-known Arthur Tole biography,[†] a carefully written and annotated work with a good sense of place and time, and even of the woman herself. It was published the year following Fedora's last, never completed, picture, *The Dying Summer,* and appeared to be as accurate as possible, at least regarding her films. Barry's hard-cover copy was well worn,

[*] Barry Detweiller, "My Ten Years with Fedora," an interview with Maurice Derougemont, *Life,* August 12, 1968.

[†] *Fedora, The Woman and the Legend* (New York: Guild Books, 1970; reprint Hammond House Press, 1972).

and from it he now drew out and handed to Marion a type-written page, which reproduced the biographical material concerning Fedora's films that is found at the end of the Tole book.

It read:

FEDORA FEDOROVNYA (Maria Katrin Fedorowich)
Born November 7, 1895, Tiflis, Georgian USSR

GERMAN-LANGUAGE SILENT FEATURES (Impro-Berliner Films):

Der Grimme Sensenmann (released in USA as *The Grim Reaper*), 1916; *Der Heirats-antrag (The Proposal)*, 1916; *Die Zuchthäuslerin (Prison Woman)*, 1917; *Zigeuner (The Gypsy)*, 1917; *Auf Schlittschuhen (On Ice Skates)*, 1918.

ENGLISH-LANGUAGE SILENT FEATURES:

Zizi (A&B 1919), *The Phantom Woman* (A&B 1920), *Palmyra* (A&B 1920), *Sorry She Asked* (A&B 1921), *Rumored Affair* (A&B 1921), *The Fatal Woman* (A&B 1921), *Thaïs* (A&B 1922), *Sins of the Mother* (A&B 1923), *Without Remorse* (A&B 1924), *Judith and Holofernes* (A&B 1924), *Impératrice* (A&B 1925), *Queen Zenobia* (loanout, Par. 1925), *A Woman's Past* (A&B 1926), *Madame Bovary* (A&B 1926, abandoned), *Ophelie* (A&B 1927).

ENGLISH-LANGUAGE SOUND FEATURES:

The Sorrows of Marta Lange (A&B 1928), *The Red Divan* (A&B 1929), *Adrienne Lecouvreur* (A&B 1929), *Aphrodisia* (A&B 1930), *Theodora of Byzantium* (A&B 1930), *The Daughter of Olaf Ruen* (loanout, MGM 1931), *Elizabeth of Valois* (A&B 1932), *Tsarina* (A&B 1932), *Madagascar* (A&B 1933), *Andromeda* (A&B 1933), *Sappho* (A&B 1934), *Espionage* (A&B 1934), *The Travesty* (A&B 1934), *The Player Queen* (A&B 1935), *La Gioconda* (A&B 1935), *Tsigane: A Gypsy Story* (A&B 1936), *The Voices of Joan of Arc* (loanout, RKO 1936), *The Mirror* (A&B 1937), *The Three Sisters* (A&B 1937), *Madame de Staël* (loanout, MGM 1938), *Night Train from Trieste* (A&B 1938), *The Duchess from Dubuque* (A&B 1938), *The Miracle of Santa Cristi* (Samuel L. Ueberroth Productions, released through UA 1955; cameo role), *The Blue Nile* (Samuel L. Ueberroth–Carlo Umberti–Illumina Productions, released by J. Arthur Rank 1957), *Madeleine Pomona* (MGM, filmed at Elstree Studios, London, 1959), *From the Shores of the Caspian* (Universal-International 1961), *Ophelie* (remake, Warner Bros. 1963), *Mother Russia* (Crown Films Ltd. 1964), *The Lynx* (Sagittarius Productions 1966), *Monte Carlo Lady* (Fox 1968), *For Lovers Only* (Columbia 1968), *The Swag* (Columbia 1969), *The Dying Summer* (MGM 1969, uncompleted).

Marion hazarded that this information seemed accurate,* and that the book was a notably honest attempt to render a true picture of Fedora. Barry agreed only partially: the discovery that she was born not in Russia but in the Georgian Caucasus near the Black Sea was a clever piece of detective work on Mr. Tole's part, but it still fell rather short of the mark. To hint at the quality of the other books, Barry pointed out that one listed her as a Pole, another as a Latvian, while a third gave her birthplace as Smolensk. So wide was the variance of "facts" concerning Fedora.

The more realistic ones now offered by Barry were those, he said, he had ferreted out during his stay on Crete, this only fourteen months earlier. As he had stated, Fedora's father was not a grocer but a schoolmaster, nor was her mother a milliner, but a laundress whose unfortunate illness and subsequent aging caused Fedora so to fear the ravages of time. True, the family was poor, but the young daughter never totted up accounts payable for cheese, as screen-magazine articles had reported. Nor was her name ever Fedorova or Fedorovskaya or Fedoro; it was Fedorowich. This was changed by the German film producer Improstein when he brought her to make her first films in Germany.

Barry took exception to another oft-reported "fact." It was not the famous director Derougemont who gave her the name Fedora. She was known as Maria Fedorovnya when she worked for Improstein in Berlin, but it was she herself who thought up Fedora as a first name. Derougemont's only part in the matter was to suggest that she drop Fedorovnya, which people had trouble both pronouncing and spelling, and find a better marquee name.

True, Barry said, that she went to St. Petersburg in her early teens, untrue that she began as an actress at the Bureinsky Theater there. She was engaged not as a player but as a "helper of wardrobe," as such people were called, and with

* Film historians seem to disagree concerning *Tsigane* (A&B 1936) and whether it was a remake of her earlier German film for Improstein, *Zigeuner* (Impro-Berliner Films 1917). No known print of the latter still exists.

the Peterhof Company. It was with them that she made her stage debut.

Her German pictures, unfortunately, with the notable exception of her first, *Der Grimme Sensenmann,* have been lost or destroyed, but movie stills of the time show her as pudgy and sulky, with no more hint of the splendid creature she was to become than the caterpillar gives of the butterfly before spinning its cocoon. Improstein, who saw her at the Peterhof and encouraged her to come from Moscow to Berlin, said in his memoirs * that she was a docile cow, but one who gave sweet milk. She never, however, became one of that notorious stable of girls he maintained in the Tiergarten Allee—which was sportingly referred to as the "Augean Stables" because of both its ample size and the inability of the authorities to clean it out—but occupied quarters of her own choosing and financing while she undertook her first screen role, that of the barmaid in *Der Grimme Sensenmann,* released in America as *The Grim Reaper.*

Barry showed Marion the photographs from this period, painstakingly assembled for the Tole biography, and she could easily trace the early emergence of the dainty butterfly from the stolid caterpillar. Fedora was no sylph, but little by little the fatty tissues disappeared, the eyes lost their puffiness, the mouth its rather ridiculous fruity shape. Improstein, presumably, had paid to have her teeth capped.

"If you check the early fan magazines," Barry noted, "they say she'd met Vando by that time. He was working on his experiments at the Bagratian Clinic outside Moscow, and it's possible he'd already had something to do with the physical alterations."

"Did he operate on her eyes?"

"Come off it—of course he didn't. That's the kind of show-business gossip that always attaches itself to people like Fedora."

The story of her next move, from Berlin to New York, was so at variance with reality that in talking about it Barry first reiterated the published "facts" and then told Marion the truth as he later had it from Fedora herself.

"Actually, all the biographies agree in this, but none is correct. Here's the way they tell it. After the Armistice, Derougemont arrives in Germany from France and goes to a party at Improstein's house, where *Zigeuner* is being screened. He sees the lovely Maria Fedorovnya, offers on the spot to buy her

* O. E. Improstein, *My Years with UFA* (Berlin: Schwelgren Editions, 1935).

21

contract from Improstein, who agrees to sell it to him. If you read his memoirs, Improstein says he later considered it the rashest and most ill-advised act of his career. Despite the fact that through his movie earnings at UFA he was later able to help finance the Weimar Republic, he was at the moment in financial trouble and he actually did sell her contract; but not to Derougemont, who had never been to Berlin at that time, and who, by the way, was not even the Frenchman he claimed to be."

"Maurice Derougemont wasn't French? What was he?"

"Hold your horses—that comes in a minute. Back to the fan mags. With the agreement in writing, Derougement goes whooping off into the street, buys a fur coat and a dozen roses, presents himself at Maria's door, flashes an engraved card and a dentist's smile, and lays the coat at her feet, the roses in her arms, and the contract in her hand. He tells her to be ready and packed on the morrow, he books passage, first class, but with discretion, mind you—the staterooms are on different decks. There follows a merry transatlantic whirl. La Fedorovnya is a sensation on the dance floor and a celebrated guest at the captain's table. She arrives in New York harbor gazing starrily up at the Statue of Liberty and doing cheesecake poses for a mob of press and photographers against the mahogany rail of the *Hohenzollern*—same coat, same contract, new roses.

"She has a gay old time in Manhattan, including a trip to the zoo, where she wants to see 'zee polar-r bear-r-rs—they remind me so uf home,' then a nifty drawing room on the train and the trip to sunny Cal. Add more roses, more executives—the coat seems already to have been Hollanderized and gone to cold storage; no doubt the change in climate—and the script of *Zizi* is tucked into her little pink mitts. Buzz buzz buzz, and off to the studio for make-up and wardrobe tests and interviews, then into production, then to preview in Glendale, then to stardom, and there you have Fedora, born if not bred."

"None of that is true?"

"A fiction from start to finish. Now I'll tell you about Derougemont. Maurice Derougemont, you see, dear Marion, was not French at all, as he claimed to be, but American. He came from San Francisco and his name was Moe Roseman. When he met Fedora he was a two-bit shill in front of a burlesque theater in downtown Los Angeles. Sam Ueberroth, who later became Samuel L. Ueberroth, producer, was his sidekick, and with straw hats and snappy bow ties they hawked the charms of hula-skirted lovelies to be discovered inside. Moe was at that time seeing a good deal of Sam's sister, Viola, who was a secretary at Ayan-Bee, and it was through her that he first encountered Maria Fedorovnya. By the time Sam was making major films, Viola had attained a position of eminence as an important agent."

Barry had known Viola for years, and though she was occasionally faulted for her sharp tongue, he had found her profoundly loyal to her friends. He had importuned her to talk to him about Fedora, and she had adamantly refused. She did, however, recall for him the precise details of her and Moe Roseman's initial encounter with Fedora. It had been on a Sunday, and Vi had expressed the wish to go to the beach. She and Moe caught the Venice Short Line from downtown; the car was hot and smelly, and bore only three passengers: a young couple and Fedora. Fedora was crying, and feeling sorry for her, Viola moved beside her to discover what the matter was. She met with a stream of what sounded like gibberish, but Moe recognized it as Russian. He could speak a little and thus a line of communication was opened. During the trip they talked, and he learned that she was an actress who had come from Berlin, where Abe Bluhm of AyanBee studios had offered her a contract. It was Bluhm who bought her contract from Improstein, and he then had left Berlin for Vienna, telling Maria to get to New York on the next boat. Which she did, but hardly in the manner described earlier. She traveled third class on the *Kronprinzessin Carolina*, was terribly seasick, and arrived sans fur coat and sans roses, to be taken in tow by a member of AyanBee Pictures' office staff, who checked her into a cheap midtown hotel, where he left her for two days. She spoke hardly any English and the city terrified her.

With the same paucity of fanfare, she was met in Pasadena by a man in a secondhand roadster, in which he drove her to a hotel—little more than a rooming house, really—on Melrose Avenue, and deposited her. A dapper fellow, the man wore a gray flannel suit and spats, which Fedora found odd, considering the hot weather. He also sported a gray felt hat with a natty silk band, the brim turned rakishly up on one side and down on the other. "What kind of hat do you call that?" she asked him in her broken English. "That?" he replied. "That's a fedora. Why?" She shrugged and tilted her head critically to one side. "I like it," she replied.

No one at the studio seemed to know who she was or what was to be done with her. She languished for endless weeks, picking up her salary check on Fridays with the secretaries and the grips, and believing she had made a dreadful mistake. She had never seen the Pacific Ocean and made up her mind one Sunday to go unaccompanied to the beach. On the train she was drowned in a wave of self-pity and homesickness. Enter Moe Roseman and Viola. His American tongue fumbled over the Russian syllables of her last name and he said, half kidding, that she ought to get another one. "I have," she said. "What?" he asked. "Fedora," she said. "Fedora's a hat," he said. "I know," she said. "I want to be a high hat."

So she had the name before she had anything else, except the face. Later, the "high hat" remark was misinterpreted as meaning that she wanted to be snooty, but at the time she meant only that she wanted to be important, famous. It did not take long, and both Moe Roseman and Viola Ueberroth were pivotally involved. Moe had been peddling a scenario around the studios, one which in fact Sam Ueberroth had written. It was titled *Zizi*, and since "Fedora" had been put under contract personally by Abe Bluhm, Moe thought he sniffed possibilities at AyanBee. He and Vi tricked Fedora out in a glamorous outfit, borrowed some furs, a large dog, and an important-looking car. Sam, in a chauffeur's uniform, drove Moe and Fedora to AyanBee, where Viola had telephoned down to the gate to have them passed onto the lot; the pass read "Madame Fedora and Maurice Derougemont." Bluhm was still in Europe, and his partner, one Jake Amsteen, was minding the store, though the right hand of Bluhm never let the left one of Amsteen know when it was washing, or what. Though he knew nothing of Fedora, Amsteen was impressed. Moe used the French boulevardier's accent he later became famous for, Fedora was charming, Amsteen was conned. "Derougemont" encouraged the mogul to look over the *Zizi* scenario, and a month later the picture went into production, Fedora starring, Moe directing. When Bluhm returned from Europe he was furious, since none of these proceedings had been made known to him, but when the picture was played in test dates, everyone started asking who Fedora was. They shortly found out. The picture made some money and its star created public interest, receiving sufficiently good notices to be given the important role in *The Phantom Woman*, which was directed by Moe Roseman, now known professionally as Maurice Derougemont. Together they did a number of her early American films. She rose to stardom at the same time as Talmadge and Normand, she was vamping along with Theda Bara and Valeska Suratt, she played Thaïs soon after Betty Blythe did *Queen of Sheba,* which Fedora far outgrossed, she worked cheek by jowl with Swanson, she beat Norma Shearer into talkies by one year. Barry now showed Marion some interesting documented facts in the Tole book. Shearer was listed as being seventy-four when the book was published. Swanson was seventy-seven. Normand had died forty-six years before at thirty-one, Talmadge had retired twenty-seven years before at thirty-three. Fedora's birth date in the available studio biographies was given as June 1895; the date had been verified in yesterday's obituaries.*

"Are you implying the date's not correct?" Marion asked.

"I'm implying nothing, I'm merely stating so-called facts. What actress doesn't lie about her age? But you have to remember, she was a patient of Vando's. Now, here's a little sidelight for you: I once heard some movie people talking about casting a part in a picture, that of an old courtesan. The name of Swanson came up; she would be perfect, they said—that brace of bared teeth, all those wrinkles. . . . A quiet voice from another corner, a woman friend of Swanson's said, 'She hasn't got them, you know.' 'Hasn't got what?' 'Wrinkles.' And she hasn't; or damn few. It's a remarkable quality about that face, and the tone of the flesh, that age hasn't mangled it as it has so many other faces of equally famous but younger beauties. But if at seventy Swanson looked, say, fifty, what of Fedora, who at almost eighty looked forty!"

Barry asked Marion what she thought of this, and all she could do was shrug, hold out her empty glass for more wine, and tick off on her fingers the items that had been repeated for years. Vegetarian diet, organic foods, no drinking, lots of sleep. Swanson subscribed to this regimen to guarantee her own agelessness. Dolores Del Rio was said to have maintained her youthful looks by various means, all probably fictional: eating gardenia petals; having wax injections under her skin, which required her being strapped to the bed so she couldn't move or roll over, which would have made her face lopsided; sleeping until four and keeping herself supine when possible; avoiding sun and other strong light. As for Fedora, there was the obvious vote for a series of face-lifts, but a woman can go only so far with the plastic surgeon before she looks embalmed. Then there were the other theories, resulting from her connection with Dr. Vando. Sheep semen, monkey prostates, the Swiss sleep cure. Vando, they said, for years

* *New York Times,* April 21, 1975.

smuggled her biannually into his Basel institute, where she would be put to sleep by injection for periods upward of a month and a half, and fed intravenously, after which she would arise from her bed newly rejuvenated, a rebirth of Venus. But how many rejuvenations over the decades would it have required for Fedora to maintain her agelessness?

Barry refilled Marion's glass and then his own, carrying it to the window. The twilight had waned, the lights of the apartment beyond the garden wall had gone on, oblongs of orange in the gathering dusk. Barry held his glass up, squinting at the wine against the light. "Lovely color, this Vouvray."

"Indeed." Marion sipped, waiting; Barry was thinking again. She gave him a verbal nudge. "Was it at the Louvre that she told you she liked it?"

Barry nodded, and turned from the window. He switched on some lamps, then sat again. "Are you famished?"

"I'm getting there."

"There's a little French place around the corner—"

"Wait, wait. I want to hear about the Louvre first."

"You have to understand about that meeting. It wasn't anyone else's Fedora then, just mine."

"How d'you mean, 'just' yours?"

"I mean you don't bump into Fedora every day; she doesn't just appear and start talking to you—"

"Why did she talk to you?"

"Impulse, perhaps. Maybe she wanted to speak with an American—we were still popular in Paris after the war. She'd been cooped up in the Sobryanskis' château for six years, she was tired of Switzerland—said they were trying to make her fat. But the way I saw her that day, she might have been just anybody. And the remarkable thing was I liked her, I really liked her. It was this way:

"When the war ended in 1945, I was twenty. I'd been in the Army for three years. They were about to send me back to the States on a troopship, but I thought I wanted to stick around Europe awhile. I had myself transferred onto the staff of *Stars and Stripes,* which I'd been doing some minor pieces for, and a year later I was mustered out. I thought writing was okay, but I wanted to try painting, too, and I made tracks for Paris. I spent a lot of money on brushes and paints, an easel, and I settled down to be a great artist, with a girl I'd met in one of the cafés on the Boul Mich.

"One rainy afternoon—this was in March and it was quite cold—I went off to the Louvre to sketch, and Denyse—that was her name—was to meet me there at four. We were going to see *Les Enfants du Paradis,* which Carné had made during the Occupation, but I'd never seen. It was playing on the Champs Élysées.

"I was sketching in one of the sculpture galleries. You know the Canova at the top of the stairs at the Metropolitan? A similar figure, but smaller, less heroic. It was about a quarter to four and the light was getting bad, and I thought the drawing was, too. A young French couple had come by and they were studying the statue. Neither of them seemed to know much about art, but they appeared interested, so I told them what I knew about the figure, that it was a representation of the Greek hero Perseus, and the grisly snake-crowned head was Medusa, the Gorgon, whom he'd slain before he won the beautiful Andromeda.

"We chatted awhile, they thanked me and wandered off among the statues. I thought the place was empty, then I heard a woman's voice, but not Denyse's. She said in English, 'What makes you think you know so much?' Not harshly, but with this frank directness and a kind of ironic humor. I recognized her right away. She was chic in a simple Chanel suit, a long wool coat, no hat, and dark glasses, which on her were as revealing as her naked eyes would have been. Seeing my expression, she laughed, that same movie laugh I thought I'd heard a hundred times.

" 'You recognize me?'

" 'Certainly.'

" 'Too bad.' She adjusted her dark glasses. 'I should have worn my mask. *"Rien d'ailleurs ne rassure autant qu'un masque."* You know that line?'

" 'Yes; Colette.'

" 'Very good. I am dining with her tonight.' She asked me if I'd seen her movie *Andromeda,* and her expression seemed to take for granted that I had. 'Did you like it?' I said yes, but that I'd liked others better. Which? That's when I told her about the Dixie cup cover and the chocolate ice cream, and then about wetting my pants at *Madagascar* and my mother taking me out. I saw that I'd made a faux pas, that she didn't like being reminded of her age, and I tried to make a recovery. I said one of my biggest favorites was *The Player Queen* and that I'd seen it at least ten times. She took that as being perfectly natural on my part, as if everybody would want to see *The Player Queen* ten times—"

"Barry, that's not a good film, and you know it," Marion protested. "It's pure schmaltz."

"I don't care. I like it and I said so. Find me a better job of a woman playing a man playing a woman."

"It's clever, that's all."

"What's wrong with clever? . . . Then she sort of jutted out her jaw at me and said, 'Well, *do* you know anything about art?' I would have hidden my sketch pad, but she'd taken it out of my hands and was holding it away from her with a critical attitude, turning the page this way and that.

" 'Not a bad thing,' she said grudgingly, as if she didn't really want to compliment me. 'But one doubts you'd make a good artist.' She handed back the pad and dusted the charcoal from her fingers on the sleeve of my shirt—I'd got it only a few weeks before. She stared around at the statuary, looking, but not really interested. 'This place,' she said, 'it's like a marble graveyard. A bad anatomy lesson—stone parts of human beings who will never live, never have lived. I think people worship ancient things too much. Like me, you see.' First came the famous movie pout, followed by the ironic smile. 'You shouldn't be drawing in here; you should be out in the street, watching people, where the life and the blood are. You are lucky—you can go there and not be troubled by your fellow creatures. What else do you do besides draw?'

" 'Not much.'

" 'Then you'd best get on with something different, or you'll soon be *sta-a-ahrvin-n-ng*.' She really relished the word.

" 'Ahr-r-rt is hahr-r-rd,' she said, like Duse or Bernhardt, the deep tragedienne voice, causing me to believe that if anyone ought to know the truth of that statement, 'Art is hard,' she should. She gave me another look. 'Do you live alone? No, you're not the type, I see that. Who is she?'

" 'Just a girl . . .'

" 'Aren't they all? You would be better keeping cats; they are cheaper and you can leave them for the weekend.' She stabbed my chest with her finger. 'Heart or art. You cannot have them both, you know—eventually you must choose.'

" 'Why?'

"She shrugged. 'You would have to take the matter up with a wise person, not me. I only know it's true. They are like oil and water—each repels the other. I know nothing of either. I have no heart and I have no art. I only work work work; that is all I have done in my life—work.' She lifted her shoulders and sighed. 'I have been successful in my life, but my life is not a success.'

" 'When are you going to make another picture?' I asked.

"She gave me a surprised look. 'You want me to?'

" 'Everybody does.'

" 'Too kind—everybody. I hope you appreciate this. That I am doing you the favor of talking to you. I don't usually. I never talk to strangers.'

" 'I'm flattered,' I told her.

" 'You should be.' She was looking at the statue again, and she said a word I didn't understand."

"What word?" Marion asked.

" 'Callipygian.' "

"It means—"

"I know what it means—now. But not then. She laughed. 'It means he has a beautiful ah-h-hss. If one likes ah-h-hsses. How do you look without your trousers? No, I don't mean your ah-h-hss. Do you have legs, good ones? I have always admired men with good legs. I once had a friend, he had awfully good legs. Do you know Willie Marsh?"

" 'No.' I said I didn't know any celebrities, which I didn't in those days. Years later I interviewed Marsh about the Bobbitt pictures, and I told him what Fedora said. I guess he was pleased.

"Fedora gave the place a final look; she raised her hand with a weary, encompassing gesture. 'All this. Those Gr-r-reeks didn't have it. I have spent much time there, and I know. They just didn't have it. Not then, not now.'

" 'You don't like Greece?'

" 'A land of goats and ruins. Nothing but veal and Ionic columns. And I dislike the wine. Give me a good Vouvray *pétillant* every time. Do you have one or two moments for me?'

"Did I have one or two moments for her? I was aware that her look amounted to a survey, long and calculating. My insides were churning. I felt drawn to her, physically moved, hypnotized even. Almost dumbstruck. She was ineffable, she had this winning impudence, a kind of daring—not toward me, who was nobody to her, but a daring of her position, her stardom. As if she were pitting both her power and her vulnerability against a stranger. I felt that I was her instrument. I would have done anything for her, been anything, gone anywhere. As it happened, she only wanted to go to another part of the museum. 'Come along,' she said. 'There's something I want to look at.' I went with her, carrying my sketching things, and remembered only as we started climbing the staircase under the 'Winged Victory' that Denyse was already late and would be looking for me.

"'I'm supposed to meet someone,' I blurted out, and she made a noise, something halfway between a sniff and a snort.

"'I, too,' she said. 'Never mind, they will find us. People can always manage to find me. Somehow.' She said it so ruefully that I laughed, but she found it no laughing matter. 'Ver-ry funny, you think. You would find it otherwise if you were I.'

"We got to the top of the next flight of stairs and she headed for the lobby, saying she wanted a cigarette. She didn't have any, so I offered her one of my Camels. She said she liked the taste, and pocketed the whole pack."

"Just like that?"

"Just like that. No thank you, nothing. She smoked and puffed and watched me—a real examination—then she grabbed my sleeve again and felt the material.

"'Where do you get a shirt like that?' she demanded. It was a wool lumberjack shirt with the tails out. I told her my mother had sent it to me from Abercrombie's in New York.

"'It's very red,' she said.

"'Hunter red, they call it.'

"'You are a hunter? You shoot little animals?'

"I laughed. 'No. It's just what they call it, hunter red, like in hunting coats.'

"'Ahhh. I see.' She nodded, but she was still looking me over. Then she reached out and turned my head from side to side. 'Who do you have chop your hair off like that?' I explained that I went to an Army barber, and she said, 'If you let the Army cut your hair you deserve such a butchering. I know a good barber; you should go to him.' When I asked who the barber was, she couldn't remember. 'Write your number,' she ordered, and I gave it to her. 'I will call you,' she said."

"I bet she didn't," Marion interrupted.

"I bet she did. I had the hunter-red shirt dry-cleaned, and brought it in a bag to the Sobryanskis' house around the corner in Rue Monsieur. I handed it to the butler and said to take it to Madame Fedora."

"You gave it to her?" Marion asked. Barry nodded. "Did she thank you?"

"Two days later the phone rang and a voice said, 'Is that you? His name is Jérôme; he's at the Crillon. Get you hair cut.' Then she hung up."

"Without mentioning the shirt?"

"Not a word. I figured the butler probably kept it. . . . Anyway, we finished our cigarettes, then passed through a number of galleries, mostly the Italian masters, but nothing interested her much until we got to the Dutch and Flemish school, where one caught her eye. It was a Hals, a portrait of an old woman, and she stopped, staring at the wrinkled face with a disdainful expression. 'She looks like a washerwoman, I think. Can you believe I was once a washerwoman? Yes, it's how I began my life, washing other people's clothes. And my mother before me.' I said I thought her mother had been a milliner, and that's when she set me straight; about her father, too. 'Hear my laugh——' She put her head back, her hands knuckled on her hips, and let loose with that laugh. 'That,' she said, 'is a washerwoman's laugh. Don't be deluded by the movies.' She looked back at the Hals and became grave, almost melancholy. "It must be dr-r-readful to get old like that. One would rather be dead.'

"'Would you honestly?' I thought she was trying to make an effect, but decided she wasn't.

"'If it came to that, I would.' Then she did an odd thing. She opened her coat and held it out away from her body. 'How do you think I keep my figure?' 'Admirably,' I said. She laughed. 'I have lived in Switzerland all through that damned war and I tell you they did not starve, the Swiss. Neither did I, but I did not get fat. The Duchess of Windsor says one cannot be too rich or too thin; the Duchess of Windsor is right. I am dieting anyway. It is the curse of a woman's vanity.'

"Personally, I thought her vanity was serving her well. She looked almost like my own contemporary, but she must have been thirty years older, at least."

"Vando's work, of course," Marion interjected.

"I was certain it was. We walked along and she talked about herself and her work. She said, 'I do not practice an art, I practice a trade, like any journeyman. Like a plumber or a carpenter—that's what I am.'

"We'd come to the entrance of another gallery when she suddenly turned again and spoke sharply to someone who'd come up behind us. 'Ah, Balfour, there you are, I've been waiting.' She said it with such irritation and grandeur, rather like a queen who had been kept cooling her heels by a footman—but of course she hadn't been waiting at all. Obviously her friend had been scurrying all over the place, looking for her. She was a wispy little thing with sensibly arranged hair and a plain face, which said she was surprised to see Fedora talking with mere me. Fedora turned back and again felt the fabric of my shirt. 'Good wool. Hunter red. Abercrombie's.' She seemed to be filing the information. Then she stepped away from me, with an expression that was almost blank, as if she didn't know me or didn't care to. I thought it was an act for her friend's benefit. I said quickly, 'Since you did me the favor of talking with me, would you let me return it?'

" 'How?'

" 'Let me take you to dinner some night while you're in Paris. There are some swell bistros in—'

" 'Saint Germain; I know.' She gave her throaty Slav's laugh. 'I thought you'd get around to that.'

" 'Maybe I could even try a painting of you, if you had the time.'

" 'Young man.'

" 'Yes?'

" 'Do you know what they paid me in Hollywood? By the hour?'

" 'No . . .'

"She laughed again, outrageously, too loudly for the Louvre, and said, 'Neither do I. But it was a lot. More than you could afford. Besides, no one will ever paint this face—at least not the way one wants it painted.' She turned to her companion. 'This poor young man saw *Madagascar* when he was a baby. The natives frightened him and he wet his diapers. We must run that movie sometime; it's been yea-a-ars. Come along, Balfour.' Without another word to me, she went off. Her friend gave me a sniff and trotted after her.

"I followed them both at a distance. By that time I'd completely forgotten about poor Denyse, who was probably doing some scurrying of her own. There was a crowd gathered around a painting, which was roped off by velvet cords on stands, and it was difficult to get near it. I saw that it was the 'Mona Lisa.' Fedora was standing against the far wall, using a pair of opera glasses on it. She had removed her dark glasses, and when she brought the binoculars away from her face I saw it in all its simple beauty. She wore hardly any make-up —lipstick and some penciling of the eyebrows. It was a strange and exciting moment, watching her looking at the actual portrait of the woman she had played in *La Gioconda*. Don't tell me comparisons are odious. They favored each other in the strangest way. A case of art copying nature as nature had copied art. They were undoubtedly the two most often reproduced women's faces in the Western world. I was mesmerized again. I thought how both of them epitomized the un-understood enigma of all womanhood. The older, Italian one was far from any modern standards of beauty as shown in *Vogue* or *Harper's Bazaar*, and the other, the movie one,

was the apogee of them. Taken together, I thought they em-
bodied the most subtle mystery and power. I could see why
some publicity guy dubbed her the 'Mona Lisa of the screen,'
and the 'perfect work of art.' She really was just that, a perfect work of art.

"I felt a touch on my arm and there was Denyse. I had no
idea how long she'd been standing there, but she'd seen me
staring at Fedora, and she was mad, all right. She was even
madder because now we'd missed the start of *Les Enfants du
Paradis*. I couldn't resist looking again when Fedora moved
back to the entrance. As she passed me, she didn't slow her
step, but said behind her hand, 'Your little friend is jealous.' "

At the Reynard Intrépide, a small, cozy, candlelit restaurant
on Fifty-eighth Street, it was late for dining. There were few
people, and service was prompt. Barry ordered a plain Bibb
lettuce salad with the meal, then asked for oil, vinegar, and
lemon, and insisted on making the vinaigrette dressing himself. He'd had the recipe from William Marsh, who'd got it
from Noël Coward; the trick was a couple of pinches of sugar
and dry mustard.

"I mentioned that I interviewed Willie once, during the
Bobbitt craze. Do you know him?" Marion had never met
him. "Little Willie," as he was known affectionately, was one
of the real gentlemen of Hollywood. He was a fine actor, he
had once had a good baritone, he was a graceful dancer. He
was debonair, thoughtful, and kind. Everyone in the business
loved him. He'd enjoyed all his successes, the earlier ones on
the musical-comedy stage, then in pictures. His wit was dev-
astating, his style elegant; he was the last of a great old line,
most of whom were dead: Coward, Chevalier, Clifton Webb,
Jack Buchanan.

In the thirties Willie Marsh had made a number of pictures
with Fedora, and he had spoken fondly of her to Barry. This
was in the fifties, after Willie's star had risen again and he
was playing Alfie, the butler, in the Bobbitt series. He and
Bee Marsh had had a large party, honoring the child star,
Bobby Ransome, who played "Bobbitt." Barry was invited,
along with most of Hollywood; the following day he'd interviewed Willie at the Polo Lounge at the Beverly Hills Hotel,
which was where Willie had mixed the salad dressing. Bee
Marsh was having a portrait done, and she had with her a
present Fedora had given Willie when they were making *The
Player Queen*: a hand mirror, reputed to have belonged to

Catherine de' Medici. The goldwork was said to have been Cellini's, and it was a museum piece, worth thousands of dollars.

"Where did Fedora get it?"

"Lord Beaverbrook gave it to her, I was told. Countess Sobryanski must have been intrigued by it: she later wrote a scenario around it and they copied the mirror for a prop; but the picture was a disaster."

"You mean *The Mirror?*"

Barry nodded. "Fedora never should have played Catherine de' Medici. Too unsympathetic. I remember Willie's line that day at lunch—I don't think he originated it, but it was appropriate, since we were speaking of Fedora. Tossing the lettuce, he said, 'Legend is the salad dressing of history,' and I guess in her time Fedora has dressed lots of dinner salads."

"Do you think it was true he fell in love with her?"

"I couldn't say; the subject didn't come up. Remember, Bee was there at lunch, too." Certainly he must have been infatuated with Fedora, however; the papers had been full of stories at the time, including reports that unbeknownst to Bee, Willie had tried to arrive at some arrangement with his old co-star, ". . . though why he should have waited until she got so temperamental and difficult to want to marry her, I couldn't say," Barry continued. "He did point out that in the thirties she'd been gay and charming, and that on the set she was always a total professional, letter perfect in her lines, open to suggestions from her director, compatible with the other actors. She was idiosyncratic about a lot of things, though— wouldn't ever wear green, wouldn't touch chocolate, shellfish, or cucumbers, wouldn't work after five o'clock. She always insisted on sitting at a left corner of a table, unless it was round. Willie said it was one of her Russian superstitions. Bee Marsh argued that it was because she was left-handed and wanted her eating hand free; which was probably more likely, though God knows she was superstitious. Willie said she was totally dispassionate about her work; once a part was done it was done. Viewing her performance later, she often used the third person, which I guess indicated a certain objectivity. 'She' did this or that, 'she' looked thus and so, or more imperiously, she used the indefinite 'one.' 'One' didn't like Chinese food, 'one' never dared eat oysters, 'one' detested red chiffon.

"But it was only after her comeback, during *Santa Cristi,* that she became difficult."

Marion remembered the stories well. After her comeback

she'd indulged in temperament and fits of hysteria, holding up production for days, having people fired, refusing to play scenes as written, all the dismaying and surprising traumas of that part of her life.

"What did you like most about her, that day in the Louvre?"

Barry thought a moment before replying. "It seems to me that the real stars, the truly marvelous people in the world, hold two essentials in common. They're basically simple, and something of the child remains in them. I liked that about Fedora."

"And did she still have it the last time you saw her?"

"Oh, yes. But in quite another way."

"But—what was she *really* like?"

"Dunno."

"But you knew her."

"Not at all. Nobody ever knew her, I don't think, unless it was Mrs. Balfour. It was a waste, really. It took years to create the public figure, the mythical image—the legend. The 'salad dressing.' She allowed it; that was probably her mistake. She was only the counterpart, the shadow. And it was the shadow that fled the press, fled people, fled the world. She really had few friends other than Balfour, the Sobryanskis, Willie Marsh, and Viola Ueberroth. Her mirror was her only intimate, and she wanted its reflection to be the single most important statement she cared to make."

Both Willie and Bee Marsh had indicated to Barry that Fedora was extraordinarily vain about her looks. Her fear of losing them, a not uncommon characteristic in women, became in her a deepseated paranoia. The Ueberroths, Derougemont (if Moe Roseman was ever to be believed), more particularly her own make-up man and hairdresser, all had attested at various times to this preoccupation with her looks. It was her greatest flaw.

"Did you ever meet Vando?"

"He was in Europe while I was living there, but I never met him. I saw him, though."

"What did he look like? I've never even seen a picture of him."

"To my knowledge he never let any be taken. Nobody ever saw him much, but he was always there in the background, at least as far as Fedora was concerned."

"Was he sinister?"

"Actually he was a very ordinary-looking man. Short, portly, rather bland. They say he used to have a little mustache, although when I saw him he'd shaved it off. But sinister, not at all."

Hardly more was known of Emmanuel Vando now than at the time, and few facts had come to light since his death. Fedora had always been inclined to surround herself with "types" —colorful, amusing, even bizarre (Derougemont easily fitted this category). But to outward appearances Vando seemed nothing more than what he claimed to be, a doctor of gerontology. He was a Portuguese, born in the Algarve, and claiming degrees at the University of Lisbon and the Neurasthenic College in São Paulo. He had a wife he had never divorced but didn't live with, and children whose fates remained obscure. There was little doubt that he was to a large degree a charlatan, yet there was never any doubt in the public mind that it was he who was responsible for Fedora's continuing youth.

It was, if indirectly, Vando who had initiated the German mogul Improstein's discovery of Maria Fedorowich at the Peterhof Company in St. Petersburg. She was already under consultation to the Portuguese, who was at Moscow's Bagratian Clinic, and in order to catch himself this big rich fish, Improstein, he baited his hook with a prime example of his theories, an older actress in the company. Improstein was less impressed with her than he was with Maria, whom he subsequently brought to Berlin. As for Vando's work at the clinic, it was not until the early thirties that he made anything known concerning his discoveries about the preservation of human tissue and the intricate processes he had devised for the retardation of age effects.

"What were those stories about the Nazi business?" Marion asked.

"That came out at the Nuremberg trials. Testimony given by one of the defendants, a man named Fritsche, tied Vando into having treated several high-ranking Nazis during the war. The Portuguese government evidently had already gotten wind of things, which is why they revoked Vando's passport before the war. In any case, his reputation was destroyed, he had to close his clinic, and the only patient he continued seeing was Fedora. He died a ruined man."

"I remember reading an interview Rudi Kramm gave back in the sixties. He said he'd never photographed a face like that; he called Vando a genius."

"Do you think Kramm was as good a cameraman as King?"

"I don't know; I suppose so. Kramm was the first one to

shoot her in color, wasn't he? She'd never made a color picture before *Santa Cristi.*"

"That was her first."

"Which did she prefer?"

"She never said. I don't imagine Kramm ever topped 'The Queen's King,' though."

Since *Ophelie,* Fedora had had only one cameraman, Walter King, hence the sobriquet "The Queen's King." People said he couldn't have managed it without Vando, but Walter King was an artist, and he discovered new things in Fedora's face that as she grew to increasing maturity only intrigued her viewers more.

But what, Marion wanted to know, was his secret? How had he done it?

"Ever see Corinne Griffith in *Black Oxen?* No, too young, and they don't show *that* on the *Late Show.* It's from a Gertrude Atherton novel. Fedora's story isn't dissimilar—a woman's physical youth is restored by gland treatments, and so on. But if Vando was a charlatan, as they say, would she have continued going to him for all those years?"

"She was always sneaking in and out of his clinic, wasn't she?"

"She spent her life sneaking in and out," Barry said, pouring more wine. It was true; Fedora's had been the great disappearing act of the century. It seemed her natural habit, like the fox's of going to earth, and while at first the newspapers and radio played it up importantly, the more often it happened, the less likely they were to make anything of it. There'd be a small paragraph buried among inconsequential items, mentioning that Fedora had not been seen since last May, the studio had no clue as to her whereabouts; then would come the follow-up item: she had surfaced in some unlikely outpost, once in Samoa, once aboard the Ranee of Sarawak's yacht, once in the Yucatán jungle while visiting the Mayan ruins.

In the mid-twenties she had completed a number of pictures in a row: *Without Remorse, Judith and Holofernes, Impératrice,* and in the autumn of 1925 she was loaned to Paramount to begin the spectacle *Queen Zenobia.* She returned to AyanBee early in 1926 to do *A Woman's Past,* which was to be followed later that year by Flaubert's *Madame Bovary.* She was fatigued, and as she often did to rest between pictures, she left Hollywood for Europe. It was known that also on board her ship was Jan, or John, Sobryanski, who was from then on to figure so importantly in her life. Heir to a large lumber fortune, only scion of a venerable Polish name, John Sobryanski was cultured and sophisticated, and though some years her junior, obviously smitten with the famous star. By the time the ship docked at Le Havre, the entire passenger list was speculating on the romance. Subsequently they were seen together in Paris, watching the races at Longchamps, then in London, at Ascot, where they were formally invited to meet their majesties in the royal enclosure; Queen Mary was a close friend of John's mother, the countess Sobryanski.

Subsequently they toured, *à deux,* on the Continent, in a well-photographed maroon Hispano-Suiza, journeying eventually to Kraków, to the ancestral estate, where Fedora met Countess Sobryanski. Later they went to Berlin, where Vando's clinic was then located. Improstein had introduced the doctor to many wealthy and influential Germans and his work was still enjoying considerable patronage. Following Berlin, the couple went to Switzerland and pictures of them boating on one of the lakes in pastoral calm made the papers, worldwide. Count Sobryanski was later to buy a small château in Montreux, at the end of Lake Geneva, prior to the loss of the Kraków estate in the war, but it was perhaps merely coincidental that a short time later Vando opened another clinic at Basel, only several hours away.

The idyll was eventually interrupted when Fedora was required to return to Hollywood for wardrobe fittings and tests for *Madame Bovary.* She had wanted to play Emma for a long time. Unfortunately, production difficulties were encountered, then script problems, and the film was twice delayed. Louella Parsons described her as chafing under the enforced wait, and quoted her as having let it be known that she would rather be back in Europe for the winter season. Then, just before she was to begin the film, she collapsed. The cause given by Parsons: Vando's regimen. The picture was finally abandoned altogether, but instead of returning abroad, Fedora sequestered herself in her Beverly Hills house.

Next, a broker disclosed that the property was up for sale. People came to inspect the vacated premises, but it added little to the legend of their goddess to discover that the house was unpretentious, that she lived modestly and used toilet paper like anyone else.

Then a San Francisco paper printed a photograph of a Spanish-mission-style domicile, with a banner line offering the tantalizing question: "FEDORA'S NEW HOME?" The building was the Convent of Santa Margarita up in Monterey, and word had leaked that the actress had got herself to a nunnery and was "in retreat" behind its walls, resting after her collapse. She found little rest. Newsmen marshaled in squads, manning posts at the main door and at salient points about the grounds. Photographers attacked the rear walls, where they were confronted by outraged nuns, who demanded they leave the premises. One enterprising reporter attempted an assault over the wall, where his intrusion among the outraged sisters was sufficient for him to verify that yes, Fedora was within. He had glimpsed a woman sitting in the garden and he had not the slightest doubt that it was she whom he sought. Rumor became rife that she intended taking vows.

The siege turned into something of a carnival, with assorted vehicles parked helter skelter at the entrance, radios playing, food being consumed, and litter strewn about.

Fedora remained invisible. Then suddenly all the hoopla proved fruitless, since its object had mysteriously reappeared in Hollywood. No one had seen her leave the convent, but a limousine arrived at the Bel Air Hotel, where the star was now registered; she was driven to the studio, where she lunched with various notables in the commissary, photographs were taken to mark the occasion, and a new movie was announced. Such furor did the actress Fedora occasion and thus were her comings and goings noted by an eager and curious world.

She completed *Ophelie,* one of her most beloved silent pictures, that year. She received her first Academy nomination for *The Red Divan,* but lost to Norma Shearer. Her films were released with almost unvarying regularity through the following decade. During this period it seemed she had given up her penchant for travel; she seldom left Hollywood or its environs. She preferred her new house in Pacific Palisades, with its view of the ocean. The property was enclosed by a high stucco wall, over which could be glimpsed only the tops of banana trees, and few visitors were admitted. Her housekeeper-companion was an Englishwoman, Mrs. Balfour, the widow of a Scot who had raised alfalfa in the San Fernando Valley. After his death she moved to Encino, and it was Viola Ueberroth who found her and brought her to Fedora.

Then, in the middle thirties, the Sobryanskis, mother and son, arrived unexpectedly in Hollywood, and their itinerary was diligently recounted by the papers. They visited Shirley Temple in her bungalow at Fox, lunched with L. B. Mayer at Metro, and at AyanBee they came on the set to watch

Fedora and Willie Marsh shooting *The Player Queen*. Everyone knew the reason they were there: Sobryanski was hoping to persuade Fedora to marry him. Despite their wide acquaintance with notables, neither Barry nor Marion had ever met the count. What details there were were most accurately reported in the Tole biography (Tole had himself secured several interviews with the count, who was still living in Menton, while the countess spent most of her time on Crete). His mother was the countess Maria Yvonne Lislotte Chernieff Sobryanski. She seldom went to movies and initially had never seen Fedora on the screen. Of the old nobility, she hardly approved of her son's involvement with an actress—and an "older woman"—no matter how beautiful or famous. The reasons for her change of heart were as obscure as other details of the story, but the fact was that the two women did afterward become exceptionally close friends. Though the three were the object of considerable speculation in the press, no one had ever accurately divined the true relationship. But at the time, lacking the success he sought with Fedora in Hollywood, the forlorn count returned with his mother to Europe.

It was further noteworthy that the link between Fedora and Countess Sobryanski was more closely forged during the war, when Fedora sought refuge at the château in Switzerland, and that she was later a frequent guest at their other residences—the Paris apartment, their horse ranch in the Camargue, and the villa on the island of Crete. Just before the war John had finally married and produced the heir required to ensure the title, and his wife seemed as much in evidence—and as good friends with Fedora—as was his mother. By then the family estates had been wrested from the Nazis by the Russians, but since Countess Sobryanski had been outspoken on the subject of Communism, she was not permitted to return to Poland, and spent her time exiled on Crete. Barry recalled for Marion the *Life* (September 23, 1946) photographs of Fedora and the countess exploring the labyrinth at Knossos and other excavated sites. Lislotte, always a regal figure, was now white-haired, if trim and spry, a somewhat younger version of Mary, dowager queen of England, whom she had known as plain May Teck, and with whom she shared an affinity for fine needlework, porcelain snuffboxes, and cameos, one of which Mary had bestowed on her friend.

But before all this, Fedora's long Hollywood career continued. She revealed her finest artistry with the production of *The Voices of Joan of Arc*, and again she was nominated by the Academy, and again she lost, this time to Luise Rainer for *The Great Ziegfeld*. This was followed by the unfortunate *The Mirror*, from a story written by her friend Countess Sobryanski; two successes, *The Three Sisters* and *Madame de Staël*; then two dreadful flops. One, *Night Train from Trieste*, took advantage of the war-scare headlines, while another, her last Hollywood film, *The Duchess from Dubuque*, in which she again co-starred with William Marsh, was a badly conceived attempt to convert her into an "American princess," a formula plot already a screen cliché, which kept the customers away in droves and hastened the decline of not only her own career but that of Marsh as well.

She completed her contract at AyanBee, stunned the world by announcing that she would make no more films, then disappeared again. She sold her house, flew to Halifax, and boarded one of the last ships taking passengers to Europe before the outbreak of the war. She arrived eventually at the Sobryanskis' Montreux château, where she remained sheltered and in seclusion until peace came six years later. She never returned to America.

After V-E Day, when she was again seen, it was sometimes in Paris or London, sometimes in Athens, en route to Crete, in the company of the Sobryanskis. Publishing more photographs, *Life* (July 23, 1951) noted that the countess was aided in her ascent up the gangplank by a cane; she had fallen from a horse at the Camargue ranch. Tourists who came to Crete with cameras to get snapshots of their goddess were disappointed, and found themselves confronted by only another high wall; though there was a fine view of the Aegean, there was none to be had of Fedora. She kept virtually out of the public eye for almost another ten years, during which time it remained a matter of conjecture whether she really would never make another film.

There was little doubt that one of the Stories of the Decade was Samuel L. Ueberroth's production of *The Miracle of Santa Cristi*. And since Fedora's was an unbilled appearance, the surprise was the more astonishing. Marion remembered it well. Beatrice Marsh had found a book, *The Miracle of Santa Cristi*, which she gave to Viola Ueberroth to read. Viola agreed it had movie possibilities and turned it over to her brother. Sam, now Samuel L. Ueberroth, arranged to produce it independently of Columbia, where he had been under contract. Ueberroth shocked the industry by casting his girlfriend, an ex-baton twirler from Santa Monica, who until his liaison with her had made only B pictures; this was Lorna

Doone, whom he later married, and still later divorced, and whose career had had so many quirky and passionate ups and downs. Lorna played the American girl touring in Italy, where she meets a young boy who becomes a miracle worker through the intercession of the Holy Virgin, who appears to him in the local church.

The boy, Bobby Ransome, later famous as the star of the Bobbitt films, was discovered by Viola Ueberroth. The problem casting was that of the Virgin. She appeared with the child in five scenes in the church interior, and the major requirement was that she be classically beautiful. Sam Ueberroth had flown with Viola to Tel Aviv, where they located an Israeli girl and signed her for the part. Locations were shot at Rocaillo, a small hill town about eighty kilometers outside Rome; the interiors were to be done at Cinecittà. The Israeli girl had completed only two days' shooting, however, when Ueberroth looked at the rushes, didn't like her, and ordered her replaced. Viola had a private meeting with Sam and the director, then she went south to Morocco. When she returned from Tangier, she was accompanied by a second party, incognita, who was smuggled into the Grand Hotel through the kitchen entrance. The following week Fedora began her comeback on the screen.

The Miracle of Santa Cristi was premiered in New York ten months later. Cannily, Ueberroth had made no announcement of Fedora's unbilled appearance, nor was she listed in the credits. He waited for word of mouth and gossip to do their work. Pins could have been heard to drop in the theaters as the boy knelt in the darkened church and saw the radiant vision emerging from the shadows of the sacristy. She stood there, robed in white, with a blue mantle, a girdle of gold, the Crown of Heaven on her head, surrounded by a blinding nimbus of shimmering light, through which could be discerned a face. But whose? Whom did it look like? It looked like Fedora. But no, they said, it couldn't be. Then, yes, they said, it was. Finally Ueberroth called a press conference and "confessed" that indeed it was Fedora. But oh, they said, they'd tricked her close-ups, shot her through gauze, burlap, even linoleum. It couldn't possibly be her; this was seventeen years later. It was a cheat; they'd used dazzling light to disguise the wrinkles and sag. It scarcely mattered. Her slaves rejoiced in being tricked; their goddess could do no wrong. She spoke no lines, it was all pantomime, but her brief scenes electrified, if frustrated, the audiences, and the line at the Roxy reached almost from Seventh Avenue to Fifth.

The picture itself proved far from satisfactory, but Fedora's presence in only five short scenes was sufficient to ensure its success. Having thus aroused the world anew, she once more disappeared. The fox had gone to earth again and, like hounds, rumor, conjecture, and supposition went sniffing in her wake. She had given no interviews, and it was not known if she planned to further continue her career. Then more news came from a casual remark made in the Ritz Bar in Paris, where Sam Ueberroth had dropped the word that in a co-production deal with some Italians, Fedora would undertake the role of Nefertiti in a superspectacle, *The Blue Nile*. The most remarkable thing about the film was the way the lie was given to those who said Fedora's age had been disguised in *Santa Cristi*. Though she is talked of a good deal, Nefertiti does not appear until twenty minutes into the picture. Nor does she make an entrance; she is simply *there*. The pharaoh enters the great palace hall, demanding to see the princess. Off-camera footsteps are heard, he looks toward the doorway, but instead of cutting to the central figure, the camera remains on the actor's face, then as he speaks the camera cuts to a full shot, holding the pharaoh in the middle ground, with Nefertiti's back to the audience. Finally, in a dazzling display of cinematography, the camera slowly dollies during his speech, circling her, losing him, and slowly, slowly, gradually closing in as she listens. And there, at last, is the face.

Ageless. She was ageless. This time there could be no doubt; the camera saw it all. She hadn't grown old, hadn't suffered the mutilations of time. Who cared if the picture was terrible? One cared only to look, to see, to glory in the goddess, to hear again those inimitable drawled-out heavy accents. And though the inevitable comparisons between smiles was made—that of Nefertiti versus Mona Lisa's—it was a question which was the more enigmatic.

The French press had for many years called her *La Déesse,* the goddess. The romantic Venetians had conferred upon her the very title of their city, *La Serenissima.* The Neapolitans countered with their own *La Sublima.* But it was the Romans who now dubbed her with another title: *La Scandalosa.* Everyone knew that goddesses were impervious, and in this particular instance, quite immortal; but what now seemed apparent was that *La Déesse* was possibly immoral as well. Since she had ventured again into the public eye, Fedora's private life had once more come under careful scrutiny. Now the talk centered on reports that she had revived her old affair with Count Sobryanski, and a second gossip-ridden triangle was formed. From Hollywood both Louella and Hedda worried in print about the peculiar geometry involved. Wags said it required only two superimposed triangles to make a star. In the earlier instance it had been Fedora, the mother, and the son. Now it was Fedora, the husband, and the wife. John Sobryanski's wife was a French girl, daughter of a wealthy automobile manufacturer. Fedora was seen frequently in the couple's company, and she was known to be spending much of her time between movies at Menton, a French town close to the Italian Riviera, in their small but handsome house high in the hills. Previous to this the count had bought an old castle on the outskirts of Tangier in Morocco. An architect and a team of decorators had been brought from Paris to make it elegantly habitable, and the four principals were often in residence there, in various combinations, for the dowager countess would occasionally arrive from Crete, where she had been living since her riding accident. While she continued to avoid press interviews, Fedora worked steadily over the next twelve years. For Warners she remade *Ophelie,* which was shot in Paris, and she received another Oscar nomination, again losing, this time to Patricia Neal for *Hud.* Fedora was not available for comment. Little was seen or heard of her between pictures, though stories had begun cropping up of difficulties on her sets, of arguments and disagreeable incidents; often players were dismissed and recast, the films went over budget because of delays, and it was said that Fedora, who before had been merely tempestuous, was now temperamental. It hardly mattered. Audiences craved her. Producers vied for her name on a contract and exhausted themselves trying to dig up suitable material as vehicles. Gossip concerning her was as rampant as ever, though more outrageous. Several times she became ill and vanished as of old, usually, they said, back into Switzerland and Vando's personal care. She would hole up at the château, and though reporters established their usual watch, no eye fell upon her. There were comings and goings that even the press found impossible to keep up with, from the Montreux château, to the Riviera with Sobryanski, to the Tangier castle, where Sobryanski would be waiting, sometimes alone, sometimes with his wife. Then, when she left, Sobryanski and Fedora would be seen in Athens, boarding a boat for Crete to visit the countess, who after complications following her accident was now confined to a wheelchair. It was, the papers noted, rather like a royal progress, house to house to house, but what, they wondered, went on inside?

Certain information had not got into the papers at all, and though rumor became blatant, nothing was printed until an incident at the Nice airport, where Fedora was detained by customs, then charged with illegal possession of drugs. The scandal occurred during the filming of *Mother Russia*, which was being shot on the Dalmatian coast in Yugoslavia. She was eventually released and permitted to finish the film, but word of the incident had got around, and finally the Rome publication *Oggi* picked it up. Other incidents followed, and though many people attributed her difficulties to alcohol, insiders knew that she was taking hashish and cocaine, which she had easy access to in Tangier, and it was now whispered that she had become addicted.

She continued making pictures, each worse than the last, and by now she was considered a risk; few producers would take a chance on her. She was replaced twice, her career faltered again, then failed altogether, and *The Dying Summer* was not completed. She never made another film. She resumed her royal progresses, but gradually receded into or was absorbed by that anonymity she had sought; not that she could ever be anonymous—her face was too famous; she was still *La Déesse* or *La Scandalosa*—but she was treated like exiled royalty, to be talked of and pointed out, a little eccentric, a little bizarre, rather melancholy, continuingly baffling, and what was now saddest, passé. The high hat had become old hat.

The evening was so pleasant that Marion and Barry walked back to his apartment. He put on some records while Marion visited the bathroom, combed her hair, and freshened her make-up. When she came out he had his shoes off and was lolling in the club chair. He pointed to the sofa and she sat.

"Where now?" she asked.

Barry smiled. "To the end, I guess. It's about time, don't you think?"

Marion looked at the clock. It was after midnight; she hadn't even noticed the hour. "You're really not going to let me use it?"

"Marion, I don't think you'll want to," he replied seriously.

"Why not?"

"You said you need twenty minutes' worth. You couldn't do this story in two hours."

"All right," she said. She lit a cigarette, drew in smoke, exhaled, and waited.

"It began—and ended—with a trip I made to Europe almost two years ago. My novel had just come out in London and my British publishers asked me over to do some publicity. There I came across an old friend, Viola Ueberroth. I was in Harrods, signing copies of my book, and up she popped. She'd just flown in from Greece, she said, and insisted on having a first editon, and when I offered to autograph it she said no, thanks, and gave it to the salesgirl to be wrapped. We talked for a few minutes while she paid for the book, but when she left the store I thought she'd forgotten it, since she hadn't taken it with her. I asked the salesgirl and found out it was being mailed; not to herself, but to the Countess Maria Lislotte Sobryanski, on Crete.

"It was only an idle notion at first, but I had some free time and I conceived the idea of going to Crete to see if I could talk to the countess—beard the lioness in her den. It happened that I had another friend—also a writer—who has a small house on a nearby Greek island. I cabled him, asking if I could come and visit. He agreed, and I flew to Patmos. Peter knows the region well, but when I questioned him about the Sobryanskis, he could tell me very little. John and his wife still alternated among their several residences, and it was known that Fedora was still a not infrequent visitor both to their houses and at the countess's villa as well. I stayed three days with Peter, we said goodbye at the boat dock, and I embarked for Crete. The weather is still fine in late September in that part of the world, but the greatest blessing is that most of the tourists have gone home. I found immediately a small hotel to my liking in the port of Iraklion. My first inquiries at the hotel brought results. I learned that the Sobryanski villa was in a nearby village. I rented a car and drove over late on my first morning.

"The village climbed a mountainside, wooded and wildly overgrown and accessible only by a narrow twisting road which overlooks the Aegean, a truly spectacular view, and it was at the end of the road that I had been told I would find the villa. It was there, all right, a yellowish-pinkish stucco affair with tiled roofs and chimneys, and that was about all I could see, because there was a high stone wall, and the only entrance seemed to be a small wooden door cut into it. The few visible signs of life were a battered gray Citroën parked in the gravel turnaround, and some goats chewing on the weeds. I wasn't about to pop in on the countess, but I had written a note, introducing myself, giving my credentials, and adding that I was the friend of Viola's whose book she had recently sent, and asking if it would be convenient for me to call sometime. No one answered when I banged the knocker; I'd decided to mail the note from the hotel when suddenly I heard someone on the other side of the wall. The gate was thrown open and there was this fellow standing there. He looked like a thug. Everything about him was thick and rough, and I guessed this probably included his brain—he had a really stupid look about him, menacing, too, and I backed away several steps. When I spoke the countess's name, he only went on glowering, so I held out my letter. He took it, blinked at it, and then shut the gate in my face. I got in my car and started back down the road.

"Around the first turn there was another house, which I stopped to investigate—hardly more than a cottage, with the windows boarded up, but with a magnificent view. I went around to the back, which faced the sea, and to my right, up across a gully some six hundred yards away, I could see one side of the villa, with a terrace behind, built out onto the hillside. There was a low stone balustrade bordering the terrace, with some statues on pedestals and decorative urns at the corners, and red flowers in boxes. Part of the terrace, likewise facing the sea, was protected from the sun by a striped canopy swooping out from one blistered wall, and under the canopy sat a figure in a wheelchair. Ah ha, I thought, the countess in the flesh; I could make out her knot of white hair and a knob-headed cane, and I recalled the magazine photographs of her leaning on a cane after her accident at the Camargue ranch. Now she used it to shake it at the servant, who came out and handed her my note. She snatched it from him and he went inside again. She held the envelope in front of her, inspecting but not opening it, then rang a little bell at her elbow. It wasn't the servant who replied to her summons, but another woman. The countess handed her the envelope, from which she extracted my note and read it to her. The countess's hand came up, she snatched the paper, crumpled it, and tossed it up so the breeze carried it over the balustrade. Ah ha, I thought, so much for my interview with Countess Sobryanski. The second woman pulled up a chair and sat close to her, reading aloud from a book, and I could hear music from inside the house. Next there was a loud crash, and what sounded like an angry shout, then a third woman came through the French doors onto the terrace. She was like a character in a play, her entrance was so floridly theatrical, with volatile, dramatic gestures, and I saw at once that it was Fedora herself.

"It was totally unexpected, pure coincidence, yet somehow completely natural that my real quarry should also be in residence. No wonder the countess had tossed my note away. She'd thought I knew beforehand that Fedora was there and was trying to obtain entrée under false pretenses. Now Fedora came up to the second woman, who rose and relinquished the book, and Fedora took her chair and began reading to the countess. Was this how she was living out her years—reading to the old woman? Some time later Countess Sobryanski rang her bell, the manservant came to wheel her inside, and Fedora followed them, letting one hand trail negligently through the red flowers as she walked by the boxes.

"I decided the second woman might be her companion, Mrs. Balfour, though I couldn't be sure. I went down the hill to the village and stopped in the hotel bar. The hotelkeeper's son spoke English and I encouraged him to talk about the villa, but didn't learn much. When I asked about the smaller house, he said it originally had been the caretaker's cottage, but was now owned by one of the large olive-growing families in the village. He took me around the corner to a café, where I met the patriarch of the clan, a fellow named Vasos, with huge white brigand's mustaches and the most worn-out but the cleanest shirt I'd ever seen; it was darned and sewed and patched in every conceivable spot. I asked if I could stay in his cottage for a while, and he thought that was funny. I explained through the boy that I was a writer craving solitude, so Vasos went away and spoke with his wife. She came and looked me up and down, and after a discussion of price, the boy interpreting, we struck a bargain. Vasos would unboard the house and have it put in habitable order. I paid in advance, went back to Iraklion, stayed the night, then checked out the following day. A taxi brought me back to the village, where I was supposed to pick up someone to go with me to the house, but the hotel barman told me the person had gone on ahead. During my talk with the boy the previous evening I'd noticed a small brass telescope—a nautical spyglass, actually—in a little rack behind the bar, and I asked the bartender if he'd sell it to me. He wouldn't, but I might borrow it if I chose. He gave me a wink and said something about the girls on the beach.

"The taxi took me up the hill and dropped me at the cottage. Another, younger, Mrs. Vasos was there, cleaning; the boards had been taken down and the place put to rights. The furniture wasn't much, but enough. There were views from the windows on all four sides, one largish room and a smaller one for sleeping. The kitchen facilities were minimal, but there was a small gas stove and even a refrigerator—I had found out that the house was wired for electricity when power and telephone lines had been run up to the villa. The bathroom plumbing was even more primitive, but the whole thing suited me fine. Mrs. Vasos would come up on her bicycle late each afternoon and bring me food, which she would cook. I would lunch on bread, cheese, and fruit, and since I don't eat breakfast it was all simple enough. I'd brought up a good supply of local wine, which was un-resinated; it tasted like Frascati, not bad at all, and there was ice, so I didn't seem to need anything else.

"When Mrs. Vasos left, I did my unpacking. I put the books I had brought with me on the table, then went out and picked some asphodel, which grew all along the roadway. I put the flowers in a pitcher and set that on the table with the books, and that was about as homey as I could make the place. There were two doors, one at the front, beside the road, another at the back, where a rustic arbor had been put up. It was well covered by a grapevine—at least I thought it was a grapevine, though there weren't any grapes. Beneath this arbor was a small flagstone terrace. The view, as I said, was stupendous. To the left was a jutting headland, around whose sloping tip lay Iraklion. Directly at my feet, below the terrace, the ground fell away to the gully, with an overgrown path winding from the cottage and around the foundation of the villa terrace above. Beyond this was a sheer drop of several hundred feet, then some barren spaces, neat apple and olive orchards, and small garden plots attached to smaller houses. Way below was a narrow plateau ending in a rocky shelf that went into the water, and while Homer may have called it the wine-dark sea, this day I found the Aegean wildly blue. I waited with my spyglass for a peek at someone on the terrace, but no one came or went. When it started getting dark I saw lights go on at the windows. Sitting in the arbor, I suddenly had the feeling that not all the terrace fig-ures were inanimate, that someone human was lingering among the statues, watching. It was only a feeling, because I couldn't see anyone. I'd brought a portable cassette player, and I put on some music, I ate, read for a while, and finally went to bed. Later, I thought I heard music again, and got up and looked; but there was nothing, only the dark statues on their pedestals, picked out in moonlight.

"Next morning I rose early, went out to the arbor, pulled up a chair, and sat with my spyglass handy. Around nine o'clock I saw the second woman come onto the terrace with a basket and clippers and begin snipping the growth in the urns and the flowers in the boxes. It *was* Mrs. Balfour. She didn't look that much different from when I'd seen her at the Louvre, though her hair was considerably grayer. I wasn't being too careful and she must have noticed me observing her, because she ducked behind one of the urns, then hurried inside. I was more careful with my spyglass after that. I drank my coffee, listening to my cassette player, but remained screened behind the grapevine while I kept watch. Pretty soon I heard the sound of a broom and the servant was out, in a white jacket, sweeping the terrace. Next he had a hose and was watering the plants in the urns, then the flowers in the boxes, and when he finished he coiled up the hose and went inside. Then more music. Mine clashed with it, so I shut off the cassette and waited.

"Just at eleven, Mrs. Balfour came back on the scene, talking to someone behind her, and immediately the servant appeared, pushing the Countess Sobryanski's wheelchair. I trained the glass on her as she moved in profile; she was very old, and thin. Her white hair was done up in a tight little pug on top, giving her head a skinned look. Her coloring was not the paleness of the aged, but rather dark, as though she took the sun, though her chair was placed exactly where it had been yesterday, shaded by the canopy. She laid the cane across her lap and sat close to the balustrade, facing the sea below. Mrs. Balfour had a book; she sat and read aloud to the countess for about an hour, and at noon Fedora appeared, in a white blouse and dark-blue shorts and a straw hat. She took Mrs. Balfour's place with the book and read to the countess while Balfour went inside. Then at one o'clock I heard the bell ring. Fedora shut the book and got up, the servant came to wheel the countess, and they all went in—for lunch, I assumed.

"I had my own bread, cheese, fruit, and some wine, and ate in the arbor, still watching, and listening to Strauss's *Ein Heldenleben* on the cassette player. After lunchtime the villa was quiet and I presumed the women must be napping. I had a doze myself, and when I woke up it was after three. My cassette had stopped. I flipped it over, raised the volume, and went into the bathroom to shave. Then I heard an awful racket, a torrent of music blasting down the hill from inside the villa. I went out to the arbor again and saw Fedora at the terrace balustrade, ringing the countess's bell for all it was worth. Obviously my cassette player was disturbing her and she was turning the tables on me.

"I switched off my player and waited. She now had a pair of opera glasses, which she brazenly stuck up to her eyes. She couldn't see me, since I was hidden behind the grapevine, but she stood swiveling the glasses like a sea captain on the bridge looking for icebergs. Finally she went back inside and turned down the music, which I recognized as the Baltic Symphony. Still later, I heard the car starting up, and I went to the front window to watch it pass. It was going fast, and I saw that Fedora was driving. When Mrs. Vasos came, around four, I tried to question her. Since she had very little English, this wasn't easy and I didn't learn much more than I already knew. The villagers were fond of the Polish noblewoman because she contributed money to local charities. Though years ago she had gone to show guests the labyrinth at Knossos and the Gortyna ruins, nobody ever saw her anymore. Her son came sometimes, and sometimes the actress, *La Fedora*. Yes, Mrs. Vasos had seen her in the movies, but she never had anything to do with the villagers. Nobody did, over there. Mrs. Vasos pointed to the ceiling, saying they might as well be on the moon. Had there been any recent visitors to the villa? Yes, an American woman had lately stayed for a week; I assumed that would be Viola. I wondered about the evil-faced servant, and Mrs. Vasos made a contemptuous sound; he was an off-islander, a Macedonian, called Kritos, who saw to the shopping for the house, but never mingled with the locals.

"I asked Mrs. Vasos if I might borrow her bike for an hour or so to go down to the beach. She agreed, and I changed into trunks, took a towel, a book, my cassette player and some tapes, and rode off. At the bottom of the road, a mile this side of the village, there was a turn leading to a path running through mounds of sand and low beach growth to the water, but since the road curved just beyond, I had no way of knowing what I'd find. I was surprised to see the Citroën parked under a carob tree. I leaned the bike on its stand a good distance from the car and went along the path to the beach. It was mostly pebbles and rocks like so many European island beaches, so I stayed back in the sand. Fedora was nowhere to be seen, and I had the place to myself. I dropped my towel and bag and stepped across the stones to the water, swam for fifteen minutes, and came out, looking back up to the terrace above. I was able to make out a dark head and a touch of white shirt, and decided it must be Kritos. Mrs.

Vasos had said he was every bit as thickheaded as I suspected; his prime virtue, apparently, was that he refused to have anything to do with the villagers.

"Another dip and I went back to my towel, spread it, got out my book, and lay in the sand. I read on my stomach, chin propped on my hands, at right angles to the shoreline. My eye kept darting from the page to the horizon, where a string of freighters was working its way out beyond the headland. Then, way down the beach to my left, coming around the point, I saw Fedora. I'd brought along my spyglass which I trained on her. She was wearing the straw hat and had a wicker carryall in one hand, with a pair of espadrilles hung on the handles. Occasionally she would bend and pick something up, inspect it, throw it away or drop it in the basket. As her face focused more clearly in the glass, I saw that it looked sullen and unhappy, and her free hand absently stroked her cheeks—the strokes seemed hard ones, almost slaps, as if she were subconsciously punishing herself. When she came closer I kept low until she disappeared beyond the rise of the hollow in which I lay. She hadn't seen me—or so I thought until, a moment later, as I moved to straighten my towel, a shadow fell on it. Looking up, I was surprised to see what I had not expected to see, namely Fedora. She was standing at the top of the rise behind me, staring down at me impassively, a bit curious, but no more than one would be about a worm or some crawling insect. There was disdain there, and hauteur, and the visible aloofness that was so much a part of her legend, just as I'd noticed it that day at the Louvre, but somehow aggravated now into petulance.

" 'We are pri-i-i-vate here,' she stated before I could utter a greeting. 'No trespassing permitted.'

"I said I was not a trespasser, but the lessee of the gate-keeper's cottage.

" 'You play your music too loud,' she snapped out next.

" 'So do you,' I replied, but with a smile. Her heavy-lidded eyes pondered me ungenially for a moment, and she gave a little shrug, as if to say so what. Her boredom showed in her whole expression; her mouth sagged open, her large eyes seemed to float in an unfocused state, as if they lacked the impulse to actually see what they were looking at. She wore a lot more make-up than I'd seen on her before, and her hair was dyed, lighter than I remembered, and carelessly styled. Older, yes, lined, yes, unhealthy, yes. Still, for a woman of her years she looked remarkable.

"I'd scrambled up and given my name without mentioning

our former meeting, but since the name appeared to mean nothing to her I added that I was a friend of Viola Ueberroth's. She made a nasty face. 'She's a silly thing, isn't she?' Well, I thought, Vi's loyalty certainly had never rubbed off on her friend. 'How do you know her?' she asked idly. I briefly explained my acquaintanceship with Vi.

" 'She sent the countess a book I wrote,' I said. 'From London. Did she get it?'

"Fedora's head whipped around and she gave me a narrow, scrutinizing look, then she burst into laughter; the washerwoman's laugh I remembered from the Louvre, but somehow harsher, almost vulgar.

" 'Viola sends many books. Which was yours?'

"I supplied the title and she gave a scornful nod. 'The countess—yes, she was deli-i-i-ghted—deli-i-i-ghted.' I could hear the calculated note of sarcasm. And she had known all along which book, because in the next breath she said, 'You are not as good-looking as your picture; they touched it up, yes?' Another laugh, the ring of brass, and I wondered where the joke was, it all seemed to amuse her so. When I said I was also acquainted with Willie Marsh, she again scrutinized me carefully. I remarked that I had interviewed Willie some years back and that he had spoken affectionately of her.

" 'Ah, yes, Little Willie,' she returned with a mocking slur, 'a man of taste and discernment. And Bee—how is she, *dear* Bee?' Another, more prodigious gale of laughter; Bee, it seemed, was quite the funniest thing.

" 'Sorry; I thought they were friends of yours,' I said.

"Her look darkened and she shook her head. 'I have no friends,' she stated lugubriously, as if pandering for my sympathy, pity even. She seemed terribly weary, of everything— me, herself, the world—but I sensed that the fatigue encompassed a physical debilitation as well, spirit and body together. She had herself planted with spread feet on the rise, arms straight down and clutching the handles of the basket, but her stance seemed not so much an effect of defiance as an attempt to stabilize herself. I remembered the stories about the dope bust in Nice and wondered if she might be high on something. Or was it only wine with lunch? She momentarily lost her balance and when I reached to steady her she pushed my hand away. 'Do not touch me,' she said indignantly. Then she gave me a crafty look. 'You do not say what you are doing here.'

"I'd already concocted the fiction that I was having a leisurely holiday, I wanted to be alone and think, and that

Crete seemed a good place for it. 'I must say,' I went on offhandedly, 'I didn't expect to have you for a neighbor.'

" 'They usually don't. . . . But you lie. You came here to see me.'

" 'Actually, I came to see the countess Sobryanski.'

" 'You waste your time—she will not see you. You seek information, isn't it so? You spy on us with a glass. Don't deny it—we have seen you. Shall I tell you how to go about your snooping? We are three old women, you see, all alone. We long, we pine. You must woo us. You must write us billets-doux and send us baskets of fruit and serenade our windows, make our hearts flutter, and then we shall let down our hair to you. Rapunzel, Rapunzel, let down your hair— you remember that little fairy tale? That is what you must do. Make love to us, three old ladies, inflame our cold hearts, and we shall let down our hair and tell you all the stories you care to hear.' She wheeled and stumbled down the other side of the rise. I watched her until she reached the path and went from sight around the bend. 'Rapunzel, Rapunzel,' I heard, and shortly afterward, the Citroën engine. A moment later I heard something else as well—the sound of a sharp metallic impact—then the car drove away. I grabbed my things, rolled up the towel, and hurried along in her footsteps, already knowing what I would find.

"The bicycle was not as badly damaged as I expected, but she'd run over the front wheel and it was bent, the spokes were mangled, which made riding difficult. I walked the bike up the hill and had trouble explaining to Mrs. Vasos, who had to ride it down again, what had happened. She tapped her temple, indicating that Fedora was crazy in the head and what could you expect? I gave her money to have the wheel repaired, and she went off, the bicycle bumping and veering crazily.

"After my meal I sat in the arbor, watching the villa and thinking about my 'interview' with Fedora. It was likely to be the only one I would get, but what a disappointment. I thought that what in her had once been a witty and endearing irony had turned to bitterness, to petty meanness that was far from the exalted realm where I, to say nothing of thousands of others, had ensconced her. The goddess was a harpy. Still, the familiar famous face haunted me. I thought about the remark I'd overheard about Gloria Swanson's wrinkles: *She hasn't got them, you know.* By my calculation Fedora was at this time in her late seventies; but she looked no more than fifty or fifty-five, an incredible manifestation of age retardation. Some years earlier I had done a magazine piece on gerontology and it was inevitable that the name of Emmanuel Vando had come up. It was only in recent decades that further steps had been taken in the direction which the doctor pioneered. In the 1960s it was steroid hormones, in the seventies it's something they call prostaglandins, or PG, which while naturally derivative from animal glands, has been found to be available through chemical manufacture. These synthetic estrogens, or 'duplicate compounds,' as they are known in scientific circles, had been first announced by Vando when he read a paper to the Société de Pharmacopée in Basel shortly after the start of World War II. Rumor and fad and beauty parlor theories had done much to damage his reputation, but the truth was that Pope Pius XII owed his long good health to the injection of substances from cow's placenta into the bloodstream, while Churchill's vitality through the stress of the war was claimed to be partially the result of similar treatments. Also, whatever one might say about Vando the mountebank, the fact remained that it was he who had initiated a new phase of scientific inquiry, and if Fedora was a result of his theories, I decided she was a good one.

"In consequence of our latest meeting, though, I found myself suffering from acute dislike of her cavalier ways, and next morning I was still fuming over the bicycle business. Resuming my watch, I saw that the same daily schedule was in force up at the villa. Kritos came and swept and watered, then, precisely at eleven, the countess was wheeled out and placed under the canopy, where she sat watching the view. Mrs. Balfour came and read to her; the music played from inside. At the end of the hour Fedora appeared and they traded places. Promptly at one the reading ended and the countess was taken inside. I saw no one for the remainder of the afternoon. That evening I ate the dinner Mrs. Vasos had prepared, veal and peppers with the inevitable rice, a salad, and bread, cheese, and wine. I could get tired of Greek cooking, I thought, sitting in my arbor and watching the sunset. When darkness fell, the usual lights shone at the windows up at the villa and I felt depressed. I'd drunk not merely my usual half bottle of wine, but almost a full one, and I was feeling desolate. I wondered what the hell I was doing on that island by myself, without friends or company, all in the name of an interview with someone I'd now taken a violent dislike to, and I made up my mind to call it quits and take the boat to Athens. But then something happened that changed everything.

"It was after ten that night. I was reading in the only comfortable chair in the room, when I heard rapid footsteps in the road, then an impatient rapping on the door. I opened it and there stood Fedora. She was wearing a half-buttoned red shirt and a dark skirt, and looked disheveled. Quite out of breath, she stared at me without saying anything, then brushed by and came in, and stood pressing her crossed hands on her chest, as if trying to get control of herself. She hardly glanced at me, but gave the place the full once-over, and finally muttered, 'I wondered what this place looked like.' When she turned again I saw that her eyes were puffy, and I thought she must have been crying.

"I said, 'Would you like to sit down?' but she didn't want to. Just kept hovering, moving from the table to the window, and stopping to check the view. 'The same as ours,' she declared glumly. The spyglass was on the sill and she picked it up to inspect it, then put it down without saying anything; but she gave me a look, then took my reading chair and let her wicker basket fall beside her. 'Aren't you going to offer me something? You don't make much effort, do you?'

" 'I haven't got much, unless you'd like some wine.'

" 'What sort?' She narrowed her eyes appraisingly. I brought a bottle from the refrigerator and showed her the label. She glanced at it, then produced a comb from the basket and began combing her hair. 'It's not Vouvray, if that's what you still drink,' I told her. She stopped combing for an instant and gave me another look, but different, more speculative, penetrating. I thought she was trying to figure how I'd come by that information.

" 'Anything would be better than Greek wine. Greasy, don't you think?'

"I said I thought it was all right, and if she wanted me to open the bottle . . . She made one of those Fedora-imperial gestures, which I took for yes, then dropped the comb in the basket and made a show of settling back in the chair. She had deliberately pushed the lamp aside when she sat, as if the idea of light were repugnant to her, and it shone now not on her face, but on the red shirt. It was old and worn, shabby even; a button was missing on the placket, another on the flap; but I was sure it was the one I had brought to her in a cleaner's bag in Paris.

" 'Is something wrong?' she asked.

" 'I was just admiring your shirt.'

" 'It's very old. Very.' She sniffed at the shoulder. 'And smells.' She idly drew the buttonless threads through her fingers. 'Hardly something to admire. Admire me if you choose—here I am, *à votre service*, La Scandalosa in person. Look your fill. Do you find me ravishing? Ever young? *La Déesse?* No, say—you can be frank; one will not hold it against you.' She turned her face, offering the fabulous profile to the light. The opportunity was irresistible, and at the risk of more hostility, I asked:

" 'How do you do it?'

" 'I am a sor-r-r-ceress; it is my single greatest piece of magic. Infallible. A trick, you see. One I was taught.'

" 'Whose trick?'

"She became secretive, put on her Mona Lisa smile, hoarding her mystery. 'Somebody . . .'

" 'They say—'

" 'I know what they say. Emmanuel Vando—yes, a devilish magician. I am his handiwork, am I not? Exhibit Number One. But even a magician's tricks can fail. The rabbit does not always pop out of the hat.' She laughed hollowly. 'But presto, see how the magician is unmasked as a fake. . . . I owe nobody in the world for anything.'

"She waved away her cigarette smoke and helped herself to the bottle, but making a face to let me know the wine was not to her liking. Then she stubbed out her cigarette in the dish and wanted another. I fished out my pack and offered one. 'I don't smoke Camels anymore,' I said, striking a match. Her puzzled look indicated that my cigarette preferences were of no concern to her, and her fingers clamped around my hand, positioning it exactly where she wanted it, and I could feel tremors along the length of her arm. 'I hate those damn Greek things. Viola brought American ones, but they go fast. I have an allotment.'

" 'Who allots you—yourself?'

"She jerked her head toward the wall. 'They do. They allot everything up there. Are your eyes troubling you?'

" 'No.'

" 'Then stop with that squinting at me. One is not something to be squinted at.'

"I had in fact been doing just that, trying to get a mental purchase—not on a woman in my chair, but on the legend of all my years, the 'perfect work of art.'

"I said, 'You just said you didn't owe anybody in the world for anything. . . .'

"She lolled her head back, smoking and drinking her wine, hardly interested in what I was saying. 'I don't,' she replied airily.

" 'But you do, you see.' I bent closer with what I considered my most winning manner. 'You owe me for a pack of Camels.'

"She made a little ruffle of derision with her lips. 'I have smoked only two. They're not Camels anyway.'

" 'Not these; another pack.' When I finally refreshed her memory about the day at the Louvre, she returned my look with faint amusement. 'You expect one to remember a pack of cigarettes from—how long?—almost thirty years? You flatter yourself. One meets many people, but one does not remember them.' I recalled what Willie Marsh had told me about her use of the third person, and the way she had employed it on our former meeting; at least that remained. She sat regarding me through a haze of smoke, one of her movie poses. I kept detecting currents of nervousness, irritation, antagonism, and I wondered why she'd come. She wanted something, but I couldn't figure out what.

"Then her stern look softened somewhat, up went the eyebrows at the center, down came the heavy lids, out came the catlike tongue tip, curling smoke like a lash. Fedora, the movie vamp. 'I read the thing on your book jacket. It says you are famous; is that so?' I started to reply and she said indifferently, 'That's all right, I know many famous people. We gad about together. Bir-r-rds of a feather. Well, I'm waiting.'

" 'Waiting?'

" 'I am Rapunzel, come to let down my hair. Ask me questions.'

" 'I didn't think you liked being asked questions.'

" 'I don't. I wouldn't answer them anyway. I just want to see what you'll ask. You newspaper people ask such silly things. "What is your favorite role?" "What do you have for breakfast?" "Are you in lo-o-ove?" ' Again the sarcastic slur in the thick guttural accent. 'Foolish questions from foolish people for foolish readers. Why do you waste one's time?' She closed her eyes. The shadowed lids lowered, then raised, the long fringe fluttering slightly, and looking from her cigarette to me, she asked:

" 'Have you another kind of cigarette?'

"I didn't get it at first. I thought she meant a different brand, but her tone insinuated more, and I finally caught on.

" 'Sorry, I don't. It's not a good idea to bring grass through customs, is it? Greek jails can't be very pleasant.'

"She laughed again. 'I have done it—but not always with the happiest consequences. Undoubtedly you have read.' Then she actually pouted, the famous movie pout, which should have been followed by the ironic smile, but wasn't.

" 'You are not adven-n-turous,' she drawled. 'I like adven-n-turesome men. No hashish? No pills?'

"I made a light, open-handed gesture. Sorry, no dope for madame. She dropped her cigarette, still burning, into the dish, put down her glass, and rose.

" 'It is late. I must be going. Thank you.' She stared for the door. I could see how displeased she was, but if I thought that was all she had come for, I was wrong.

" 'Look—' I began, but her quick gesture silenced me as a light flashed through the window and we heard footsteps. She gave me a quick, worried look. 'Say nothing,' she ordered, flattening herself against the space between window and door. In a moment someone rapped.

" 'They sent me—I was to ask you—' The rap sounded again. She put her finger to her lips and nodded that I was to open the door. Mrs. Balfour stood there with a tight smile, and behind her, holding a flashlight, Kritos, with his lowering look.

" 'Good evening,' said Mrs. Balfour, oh so politely, and peered in. I kept my eyes on her, but stood blocking the doorway. She prattled on in a very Englishy way. 'Quite comfortable, are you? Got ev'rything you need? Ah, asphodel —how lovely.' She gave my flowers a nod, me another smile. 'Yes, and'—she was peeking through the crack between door and frame—'there you are, my dear,' looking at Fedora as if her hiding were the most natural thing in the world. Fedora gave me a helpless look and stepped into the beam of Kritos's light.

" 'We wondered if you were still here,' Mrs. Balfour continued, coming in a step. As she reached out her hand, Fedora backed away. 'Have you esked him? And has he said yes?' She looked back and forth between us with a bright, expectant smile.

"Fedora shook her head. 'No, Balfour, we were speaking of other things. The fact is, we hadn't got around to it.'

" 'Got around to . . . ?' I looked from one to the other.

" 'Ah, then,' said Balfour, taking another step or two. 'If I might just come in for a moment. Lovely weather, veddy mild.' She was so proper and so irritatingly nice. She smiled again at Fedora. 'Well, then, my dear, will you esk the gentleman or shall I?'

"They exchanged a look, and I detected that beneath all

the 'veddy veddy' was something else, a positiveness, even a threat.

" 'Ask me what?' I said, giving way as Mrs. Balfour ventured farther into the room.

" 'Well,' she began, with another look at Fedora, 'we were hoping—that is—'

"Fedora stepped forward and shoved the door back. 'This is ridiculous,' she said angrily, facing her companion. 'He will not do it, there is no need for him to do it, it is all ridiculous.'

" 'But surely it *won't* hurt to *esk*,' said Mrs. Balfour.

"Fedora's look darkened. 'Then you do it—not me!' She gave Mrs. Balfour a little push aside and strode through the open door, then whirled in the light.

" 'Don't do it,' she said, talking directly to me.

"Mrs. Balfour spoke up, pleasantly as always. 'But it's such a little thing.'

" 'Damn you.' Fedora spun around and moved off up the roadway. Mrs. Balfour said a few Greek words to Kritos, who followed Fedora. When he got to her he touched her arm and she pulled away angrily, then marched off. I watched them go, and when I turned again, Mrs. Balfour was all the way into the room, bending to smell the flowers in the pitcher.

" 'Ah, asphodel,' she said again, straightening with her little smile. 'Pliny says that the sad spirits of the dear departed used to cross the fields of asphodel to reach the waters of oblivion.'

"I interrupted to say I doubted I was like either the elder or the younger Pliny, and then waited to hear more.

" 'You know—oblivion—the waters of Lethe?'

" 'Sure—of course. I just didn't know which oblivion we were talking about.'

" 'Well, that's the one,' she said, looking at the chair Fedora had quitted. 'May I be seated for a moment?'

"I nodded. She sat quite comfortably, folding her hands in her lap, and all that seemed lacking was a cup and a teapot under a quilted cozy, she was that homey. 'You see, both of you being authors, you and Pliny . . .'

" 'Both authors. Yes?' I waited for her to come to the point.

" 'Yes; you see, I am not unacquainted with your name. I have, in point of fact, had a peek into your novel. It seems a most interesting story.'

"I acknowledged this and went on waiting. She hemmed and hawed, darting shy looks at me with all the timidity of a parson's wife, but I was determined not to help her out.

"Finally she got down to brass tacks. 'You are a friend of Miss Ueberroth's, we understand?' I nodded, she nodded back. 'Viola is a good friend to all of us.'

" 'I've found her to be. I don't think Fedora would agree, however.'

" 'But she gives us cause to hope.'

" 'One should always live in hope.'

" 'Ah,' she said hopefully, 'we are obliged to.'

" 'We?'

" 'Why, yes—we.'

" 'Does that mean you yourself, or is Fedora also included?'

" 'But of course.'

" 'And Countess Sobryanski?'

"Her nod was brighter, more eager. 'But that's it, to a T. You see, it's precisely why—it's precisely why madame came to you tonight: to ask a favor—for—the countess—Sobryanski.' She was rattling her words, and looking, if possible, even more nervous.

" 'Yes?'

" 'Since you are a friend of Fedora and she is a friend of'— she'd made a little cradle of her hands, with the fingertips sticking up in a row like a child's—'the countess, since in a manner of speaking we are all friends, it occurred to us that you could perform a kindness.'

" 'What sort of kindness?'

" 'You are fond of Viola?'

" 'I like her, yes. . . .'

" 'And Fedora? You have seen her in the cinema, of course.'

" 'Of course.'

" 'Then perhaps you can spare some time for her.'

" 'I would be happy to spend some time for her—anytime.'

"Mrs. Balfour positively glowed. 'Why, then, that's the nicest thing—and the simplest. You will do it?'

" 'Do what? You haven't said.'

" 'But of course I haven't—how stupid. You will read your book. To Countess Sobryanski.'

" 'Read my book?' I repeated blankly. 'To Countess Sobryanski?'

" 'Yes. You see, that is the favor, that is the matter under consideration here, it is what Madame Fedora came to quiz you about: your willingness . . .'

"I knew better about why Madame Fedora had come, but said nothing. Mrs. Balfour had risen and was still rattling.

" 'She enjoys being read to. Her one enjoyment, really. Her eyes are bad; she has trouble seeing. We take turns, you see,

Fedora and I, but since it is your book and you are, well, here—d'you see, she would like you.'

"It really knocked me out. Here I was thinking something was up, something crazy or sinister or illegal, but all they wanted was for me to read to the countess Sobryanski. I had to keep from laughing. She was sitting there, little old English lady, living in hope that I would say yes to what I precisely and exactly wanted to say yes to, since her proposition would bring me to exactly the person I had originally come to see.

" 'It seems you and Fedora do quite well reading to the countess. Why should you need me?'

" 'Because that's just it—she's so used to us, she's tired of our voices, and quite frankly, mine tires easily. I have a laryngeal complaint, so troublesome. She'd like someone quite fresh, as it were, someone new. And after all, you are the—author of the work. And,' she took pains to add conspiratorially, 'you would be well rewarded for your efforts.'

" 'You mean I am to be paid?'

" 'Not in money, not in cash, you see, but something equally negotiable. It is as good as—better than—cash.'

" 'What might that be?'

"She gave me another of those gay-old-lady smiles. 'Why, then, you'll just have to come and see, won't you?'

"I had no idea what legal tender she was proposing, or even if it was legal; I had no interest in being paid for a service I would willingly render freely, but I made a show of agreeing after some deliberation, and then only with reluctance.

"She was delighted. 'Believe me, sir, you may trust me.'

" 'But of course I trust you, for if it comes to that—why shouldn't I?' We both thought that was a good one and laughed our way to the door, which I opened, to find the ominous Kritos standing there again.

" 'When would you want to begin this—um—reading?'

" 'Why, tomorrow morning, if you're free. When the weather is fair the countess enjoys being on the terrace. She likes the smell of the sea, we make her quite comfortable there, and if you came at eleven you could read until lunch.'

" 'Fine. Shall I plan on lunch as well?'

" 'Oh, dear.' She gave me another of her worried looks, as though I might back down if lunch weren't part of the arrangement. 'Perhaps we can arrange a bite—something—yes, I'm sure. Veddy well—come along then—eleven. So nice.'

"Sprinkling these abbreviated phrases as she went, she added a good night and slipped out the door. Kritos scowled at me, then lighted her way up the road.

"I appeared at the villa the next morning a little before eleven. Mrs. Balfour admitted me at the gate, took me through the front of the house, along a hallway, and onto the terrace, where she asked me to wait, and then she disappeared. I professed to admire the exterior architecture of the house and its various details. There were matched yew trees in tubs on either side of the pairs of French doors that gave onto the terrace, and the statues whose backs I had been staring at through my spyglass were Italianate, allegorical representations with no special meaning to me. I was looking through one of the doors to see inside when I heard someone in back of me, and turned to find Fedora in the other doorway. Even behind her dark glasses she seemed the worse for wear.

" 'Good morning,' I said breezily.

"She gave me a sullen look as she advanced on me. 'So you are going to read to her.'

" 'That seems to be the . . . arrangement.'

" 'You are wasting your time,' she said dourly. 'She will tell you nawthing.'

"I smiled. 'Since I am expecting nothing, then I won't be disappointed. Okay?'

"She came closer and took hold of my arm. 'You are not to ask her questions, do you understand?' she said fiercely. 'Do not trouble her with your infernal newspaper questions about me. She will tell you nothing but lies. Do not ask—do not listen.' She clung to my arm a moment longer, then released it as the squeak of wheels was heard and Kritos appeared pushing the countess's wheelchair.

" 'Here's our visitor,' Mrs. Balfour said gaily, coming behind, my book in her hand. The countess gave me a *'Bonjour'* and a regal lift of her cane, directing Kritos to place her chair in its usual spot in front of the balustrade. Meanwhile Mrs. Balfour had exchanged glances with Fedora, who turned angrily away and went inside; perhaps I was wrong, but it seemed to me that Mrs. Balfour's look had ordered her to do this. The Englishwoman pointed out a chair to the side of the countess, handed me my book, and whispered a suggestion or two.

" 'Speak well up and enunciate clearly so she can hear, and just use a normal expression; she doesn't like a dramatic reading.' She turned to the countess. 'Here's the author himself, come to read his story to you,' taking the trouble to include my name as well.

" 'Good morning, Countess Sobryanski,' I said, with the

63

deference I felt her age and title demanded, but loud enough to bridge the interval between our chairs.

"'Pas besoin de crier, j'vous écoute,' she replied. Having assured me in her slangy French that there was no necessity to shout, she could hear, she fixed me with a look up and down with a pair of small eyes, which, while they were clouded, still offered keen penetration. Though a frail little thing, she was obviously still the mistress of her small household on Crete as she must have been of her larger one in Kraków. The years hadn't been kind to her, however: she wasn't ugly, but she had none of the loveliness that old people sometimes manage to keep. She was ravaged and blemished, yet somehow it all lent her character, just as her aristocratic air did. She seemed to take no pleasure in my being there, and her look informed me that I was of Kritos's status, come to do her bidding.

"'Commençez,' she ordered peremptorily, and turned her gaze seaward. Mrs. Balfour cued me with a nod; I opened the book and began. 'Chapter One,' I enunciated, and read the first sentence. By the time I finished the paragraph Mrs. Balfour had tiptoed away, and I moved into the story.

"I read without a break for half an hour, glancing up at her from time to time. Countess Sobryanski was practically motionless, and I wondered if she were even listening. To test her I stopped abruptly and after a moment the head turned and cocked questioningly. I went on, then stopped at the end of another half hour, announcing that I wanted to smoke. She acquiesced with a nod; I fished out a cigarette and lit it. I puffed in silence, watching her sitting in that curiously rigid and static posture, facing seaward, always seaward, beyond the balustrade. It was an especially splendid day. The water sparkled and the wind puffed the sails of numerous caïques trolling beyond the headland. Some people in bathing suits had pitched a yellow tent on the beach; their cries reached all the way up to us. Yet it seemed to me that, listening, the countess was watching none of this activity, that her gaze was directed past them, toward the horizon, as if out there across the water some strange or marvelous wonder might appear at any time.

"She wore, I noted, only three pieces of jewelry—two little red-colored buttons that might have been carnelians on her earlobes, and pinned at the front of her dress an ivory cameo, possibly the one Queen Mary had given her. Her thin white hair was done up in its usual knot, from which a few stray wisps escaped, and from time to time she would smooth them back. Now at last I was confronting the person I had come originally to see. If my interview with Fedora had failed, I was determined that the one I intended to wring, however I might, from the old woman would not. She intimidated me, though—by her proximity; by her whole demeanor, feeble as it was; and more particularly by her look, which she swung on me again, evidently tired of waiting. Her wrinkled mouth puckered, the lower lip jutted out like the famous Hapsburg lip, and she impatiently rapped the ferrule of her cane on the flagstones. When I flipped my cigarette away and resumed reading, she seemed more content. Occasionally I'd catch her nodding at the end of a passage as if marking it with her own stamp of approval, or she'd murmur something indicating surprise or interest. I stopped on the half hour for another cigarette and at the end of the second hour she rang her little brass bell and Kritos appeared instantly. Taking no notice of me, he wheeled her inside, '*Merci. À demain,*' she said as she went away. '*Comme vous voulez, madame,*' I called after her. Yes, I would come tomorrow.

"A wrought-iron table had been set for lunch between the two pairs of French doors, and I was happy to see that there were three places, which meant Fedora would be joining us. Balfour came out with a tray and began laying plates of food about. It was simple—a shrimp salad, rolls and butter, sliced cold meat, which I suspected was the inevitable Greek veal, fruit, cheese, and a bottle of wine; not Vouvray, I noted. She asked me to be seated, then called through the door. In a moment Fedora came out. Her expression was enigmatic as she took the chair I held for her, and she began to attack her plate hungrily. Mrs. Balfour picked at her food, while I ate at my normal speed, listening to her polite chatter: she understood that I was acquainted with their friend Willie Marsh, such a nice man, veddy distinguished, and Bee Marsh, tedd'bly charming, and she told several anecdotes about the filming of *The Miracle of Santa Cristi.* Since Fedora had been incarcerated in her hotel suite during most of the time on the film, I wondered how Balfour had gleaned so much information. She never touched on Willie's infatuation for Fedora during that period, while Fedora herself made no response whatever; she was too busy eating, with that unconscious greediness old people sometimes have. She'd got a smear on one lens of her sunglasses and when she took them off to wipe them with her napkin, I saw how bright her eyes were, the pupils abnormally enlarged. The sacs under them had puffed, and again I thought she'd been crying. She talked erratically and

I could see that she was high on something again, and was probably having a hunger attack. As she spoke she brandished her cutlery, and in slicing her meat, when she switched hands she dropped her knife; I bent and retrieved it, and Mrs. Balfour got up to bring another from inside. Fedora unconcernedly wiped hers on her napkin and used it to finish cutting the meat. 'One must eat a peck of dirt before one dies,' she observed, emphatically shaking her hand with the impaled veal. 'I've eaten my peck, but I don't die. Why is that, I wonder.' She was not talking to me, nor to herself, only to thin air. She half rose from her chair, looking through the balusters down to the water. 'Who are those people on our beach? We are pri-i-ivate here; why do they come with their tent, their fat, ugly bodies?' She launched into a jeremiad about the trouble people caused her. Then, seeing my eyes on her, she interrupted herself. 'You are staring again,' she said, plunking down her fork and taking up her wineglass. 'Why do you look so strange?'

"I tried to cover my amazement, but the truth was that I had suddenly been struck by something so obvious, yet so trivial, that while one aspect of my picture of her cleared, another immediately darkened and offered itself to my utter puzzlement. She pushed her chair back angrily, tipping it over as she got up, and took her glass to the balustrade. She started to shout at the bathers and wave them off the beach. I righted the chair and followed, observing her closely. Though she had stopped shouting, she kept waving in the air, though no one below seemed to pay attention; I doubted they had heard her. She sagged momentarily against the railing and drained her wine. Until now she had manifested little but that bitter, disdainful humor I had witnessed on the beach and at my cottage, but now she turned with the little-girl look that was also part of the Fedora legend, a pitiful, waiflike expression. 'Help me,' she said.

" 'Certainly,' I replied. 'Tell me how.'

" 'Help me get away from here.'

"More puzzlement. 'Surely you're free to come and go as you please . . . ?'

"She shook her head angrily, then seized my arm, and I felt that strong grip again. 'I can't. They won't let me.'

" 'Who won't?'

" 'I am not free. I am a prisoner here—you must see that. That Kritos, he is a *zloi chelovek.*' I didn't understand the phrase, but understood that the servant was possibly an impediment to her. 'He hits me,' she went on.

" 'Hits you?'

"She pushed up her sleeve and showed ugly bruises on her arm. 'He keeps me here. To read to her. That is what I do, read to her. My life is ending and I am here in this damned place reading, always reading.' She brought her face closer to mine. 'Be careful. You will end up the same—reading to her.'

" 'The countess Sobryanski is your friend, isn't she? Mrs. Balfour, also?'

" 'I told you, I have no friends, none—' She broke off suddenly and released me. Mrs. Balfour had finally reappeared in the doorway with the knife. She had been gone a long time; I thought perhaps she had looked in on the countess.

" 'Finished already? There is fruit and cheese, madame, sir.' She held up the plate of fruit, offering it as Fedora crossed back to the table, where she set down the wineglass, then started inside.

" 'I'm going for a walk,' she said, staggering slightly as she went through the French doors. Balfour bit her lip as she watched her go, then turned to me with the fruit. I took a bunch of grapes and sat again. We could hear Fedora's voice coming from behind the closed doors of what I assumed to be the countess's apartment, harsh and strident, making demands for money which she seemed to think was being withheld from her. Mrs. Balfour darted several looks at me while Fedora's tirade continued, then I glimpsed her passing through the rooms, toward the hall. She went out; the door, then the gate slammed. I was about to put a few questions to Mrs. Balfour, but she rose abruptly and said she was sorry, she must be excused, please to finish my grapes and to attempt the cheese, she would see me at the same hour next day. She went in and I heard her giving Kritos a list of things she wanted from the village.

"I sat popping grapes into my mouth and thinking, trying to puzzle the thing out, then Kritos appeared, obviously waiting for me to leave. I made as long a job of the grapes and two wedges of cheese as I could, while the Macedonian cooled his heels. Then, when he wasn't looking, I took my cigarette lighter from my pocket and slipped it behind one of the wooden tubs holding a clipped yew, stretched elaborately, got up, and walked through the doorway into the back hall. The red wool shirt hung on a hook, shapeless, and patched at the elbows. I glanced over my shoulder at Kritos, proceeded to the front door, and waited for him to open it. He followed me out and unlatched the gate, then closed it behind me with an emphatic if unnecessary bang, and I went down the road to the cottage.

"I waited in the arbor with the spyglass. Fedora appeared on the beach, as I'd expected, and advanced on the group of swimmers, gesticulating with an angry expression. I tracked her as she engineered an erratic course up toward the headland, carrying her espadrilles one in each hand, flinging her arms about, throwing her head back, and making circles as she went. Then she was walking into the water, clothes and all. I heard the Citroën and went to the front window to see Kritos passing. I estimated that if he was driving to the village it would take about fifteen minutes each way. I wanted to go back up to the villa while the countess and Balfour were taking their naps and do some reconnoitering, and figured I had at least half an hour to do it; if I was spotted I would say I had come looking for my cigarette lighter.

"I put down the spyglass and dropped over the edge of the terrace, then went across the path along the gully and up the hillside under the villa terrace. On the far side the ground was high enough to allow me to clamber over the balustrade, and I kept close to the building wall, under the windows, checking first the upstairs ones, then the various rooms behind the French doors, passing from one to the other and peering through the unwashed panes to view musty interiors, with ceilings of cracked plaster and watermarks on the walls, conventionally but sparely furnished with heavy, old-fashioned pieces. One had a large bed with hangings and a small fireplace, a few knickknacks on a table, and I guessed this was the countess's own room, for it was through these doors that she was sometimes wheeled.

"There was no time to make a closer examination, for I heard voices coming from the corner of the room, and I saw a movement and ducked out of sight. I glimpsed Balfour as she passed inside, then stopped and stood looking out the closed door. She listened to the countess, who was speaking, apparently about money, for I heard francs mentioned several times, and the Bank of Monte Carlo. It seemed to me they were discussing Fedora's finances; at least I made some connection between her name as Balfour mentioned it and the money the countess spoke of. Next I caught several other names—Mussolini, Mrs. Roosevelt, Bernard Shaw, and then my own!

"What followed was even more puzzling. Even as I stood listening I heard the Citroën rattling up the road. From where

I was I could see the turnaround outside the wall, and the car spinning on the gravel. I had to duck low not to be seen by Fedora, who was sitting in the passenger seat. Kritos came around the car, yanked open the door, and urged her to come out. I realized that instead of going to the village he had driven down to the beach to bring her back. When she refused to leave the car, he brought her struggling from it, then half dragged, half carried her to the gate, where his beefy arm held her until he had pushed it open and pulled her through. The gate slammed shut and he locked it from inside.

"Then the front door opened with a bang, and I heard the continuing sounds of Fedora's protests. A moment later she came into the countess's room and half sprawled on a love seat, strewing the pillows about, her hair awry, sobbing hysterically. When Balfour stepped toward her with an outstretched hand, Fedora batted it away. She got up and stumbled across the room, her voice rising, until she faced the countess. She bent over her, using all the four-letter words, an incoherent diatribe which stopped abruptly as the old woman leaned forward from her chair and administered a telling crack on the cheek. She motioned to Kritos, who strode across the room and took Fedora away, screaming. The others followed them out, Balfour wheeling the countess's chair, and I slipped back along the wall and dropped over the balustrade. It was only after I was back at the cottage that I realized I'd forgotten to pick up the lighter.

"I allowed myself a full bottle of wine with dinner, thinking all this over, and another half bottle afterward, sitting in the arbor and listening to the noises coming from the villa. Whatever the reason for Countess Sobryanski's violence, it certainly hadn't cowed Fedora; there were interrupted shouts and cries for a long while; the music was turned up, lowered, turned up again. Now nothing made sense to me, but I found myself giving greater credence to Fedora's talk of being kept prisoner, though what the conspiracy consisted of I had no idea. When things finally quieted down and the lights were turned out, I went to bed and slept heavily. I was awakened far past my usual time by the sound of the Citroën going by. I looked at my watch; it was half-past ten. I hurried to bathe and dress, and when I got to the villa the countess was already stationed under the terrace canopy. Balfour had admitted me, seen me seated with the countess, given me the book marked at its place, and gone away. I read for the usual period in the usual way, and nothing was any different than it had been yesterday; nothing except that Fedora was pointedly absent.

"How Countess Sobryanski could tell the time without a watch I couldn't imagine, but promptly at one she rang her little bell and gave me another *Merci* and *À demain*, as Kritos wheeled her inside again. The table had not been set for lunch, and since Mrs. Balfour showed me to the door, it was clear that no invitation would be forthcoming.

" 'It seems,' she said, with that grimly fixed smile, 'to be going veddy well, doesn't it?'

"I came back next day, read again, received another *À demain* from Countess Sobryanski, got the gate from Balfour, and at no time had I seen Fedora. The shades of her upstairs room were down, but there was no clue to her whereabouts. I now had an important piece of the mystery in my hands—or head, I should say, though my head wasn't helping much; I couldn't figure it out. I went again to read, until I finished the book. When I closed the cover I looked at the countess; she gave no hint of what she thought of my story. She rang her little bell, Kritos came, she inclined her head to me—'*Merci*'—but instead of saying goodbye, which I'd had every reason to expect, she repeated her customary *À demain*.

"Tomorrow?

"Balfour came out, doing her sweet-little-old-lady act. 'She enjoyed it *so* much,' she said. She was carrying several books, which she set on the table. 'Which do you think she would like next?'

"I stopped her short, saying I had agreed to read only my own book, and whatever reading was to follow must be done by herself or Fedora. She gave me a look of unabashed surprise.

" 'Oh, but she has left, you know.'

" 'No, I didn't know. When?'

" 'Why, two days ago. Count Sobryanski came for her. They've gone on the Athens boat.'

" 'Rather unexpected, wasn't it?'

" 'Yes—no. You see, she decided since our good weather's almost gone a change might be nice just now.'

" 'Where did the count take her?'

" 'Why, to Menton. The Sobryanskis always have a large party at the end of the season—'

" 'I thought Fedora didn't like parties.'

" 'Well, not so *tedd'bly* large, if you know what I mean, but it gives her a chance to see her friends—'

" 'She told me she has no friends.'

" 'But of *course* she does. That's just her; merely a *façon de parler*, if you see.' "

" 'No, frankly I don't. She didn't seem to me to be well enough for parties.'

" 'She is old, sir, a good deal older than she looks. She—one tires easily at her advanced years and—' Watching her face, I saw the whole parade of emotions: the urge to lie, the indecision, the groping for excuses, then finally her capitulation. 'In point of fact, she is not well,' she said flatly. 'You saw her, talked with her, you see the trouble with her. She is ill.'

" 'If she's ill, why didn't you go with her?'

" 'Alas, I am no longer of use to her, sir. The count and his wife will look after her now.'

"It was clear to me that she was lying, and I felt certain Fedora hadn't left at all, that they had her locked up in her room to keep her from making trouble, or at least out of the way.

"Balfour had taken something from the pocket of her cardigan and was holding it out to me, an envelope, from which I extracted a single page. It was the Mussolini note to Fedora; Balfour was quick to point out that it was written in his own hand, the real McCoy.

" 'It is your payment. It's worth a good deal of money.' I said I was sure it was. Then slyly, I thought, she said, 'There are others, you know.'

" 'Mrs. Roosevelt? Bernard Shaw?' She blinked at me through her glasses, mute with astonishment.

"Ignoring her surprise, I asked, 'What makes you think I won't keep this and just abscond?'

" 'You have an honest face.'

" 'Are you a good judge of honest faces, Mrs. Balfour?' I asked.

" 'Why, yes, I think so. That is—' She was getting flustered again. 'Honesty is always the best policy, isn't it?'

" 'So they say. But what's the policy here? Fedora's gone away, and you're disposing of her property? Valuable property?'

" 'It doesn't matter, I assure you. She has many letters from many famous people. She doesn't need them anymore.'

" 'Mightn't she want to leave them to someone?'

" 'To whom? She has no one, you see. Except me. I am her heir. So her correspondence will come to me.'

" 'You sound as if you expected to survive her.'

" 'That is not in my hands, sir,' she answered mildly, 'but in God's. Will you accept the note in payment?'

" 'No.' I tried to give it back to her; she wouldn't take it,

71

so I dropped it with the envelope on the table. 'But I'll read again to the countess, if you like.'

"Her worried expression changed; she became the candy-box lady again. 'Oh, you are kind,' she said, 'so veddy kind.'

"I thought so, too. But I hoped that my ingratiating myself with this one of Fedora's friends would lead her to commend me to the other one. And if things did not go well with the countess, perhaps Balfour herself could be persuaded to talk, though remembering Viola's tight-lipped loyalty, I suspected that as far as Balfour went, mum was most likely to be the word.

"The next morning I was back at my old stand. The book chosen was Wouk's *The Winds of War*. And I noted its length with apprehension. But I began, and read as was prescribed, slowly, clearly, and without emphasis. The routine never varied; the countess's arrival on the terrace and her departure were exact as clockwork. As the days passed, an unspoken intimacy seemed to grow between us, but it was that of employer and employee. She was always polite, but clearly it was a matter of noblesse oblige. The line between us, though unmarked, was precise. Occasionally she spoke to me, always in French, and I got the idea that though she could speak English perfectly well, her ease in the other tongue and my lack of it helped keep me in a subservient place. Besides her habitual *Bonjour*, there might be a commonplace on the good weather—*Il fait beau*, or if it was brisk, *Un peu froid 'jourd'hui*—and at the end of the reading always the *À demain*, until tomorrow, as if she required absolute reassurance of my return to the succeeding chapter.

"During our earlier times together I had discovered certain things about her, chief among these the fact that, like many old people, she had the habit of dozing off while I read, but unlike most, she was adroit at disguising it; her fingers on the armrest would continue their spasmodic movement, as if this would fool me into thinking she was still awake. Once or twice when I spoke her name, she would start, and raise her mottled hand, a sign that I should continue; but dozing or not, her head seldom changed its seaward gaze. The few sounds she made were light murmurs, sometimes a wheeze, or a hoarsely indrawn breath I never heard expelled. She had the querulous impatience of the aged combined with the abrupt peremptoriness of the nobility, an aristocrat of the old school used to issuing orders and seeing them obeyed. Whatever remarks I made she answered with a nod or shake of the head, or a monosyllabic response if it was necessary. Like her body, her voice was frail, but she spoke with an autocratic precision that easily carried across the distance between us.

"She stubbornly manifested that capricious defiance of the aged, as if nothing passed before her ancient eyes except that which affronted her, but in time she seemed sufficiently used to me to allow herself a direct query concerning myself, my origins, my family, and she was apparently more interested in my writing than I'd thought, for once she confessed dryly that the book had pleased her. Mention was made both of Viola and of the Marshes, Willie and Bee, all of whom she knew and obviously regarded in a better light than did Fedora. She was leading me on, but to what end I still couldn't tell; you didn't divine with Countess Sobryanski. When I mentioned the fact that she, too, used to write—the story that Fedora's picture *The Mirror* had been taken from—she sniffed and said that what had originally been a novel idea had been ruined by Hollywood, nor had she enjoyed her brief stay there. She would return me to my reading, or say she was tired from talking, ring her bell, and be whisked inside by Kritos, but unfailingly the *A demain* trailed back over her shoulder.

"One day when the reading period had ended and she should have rung her bell for Kritos, she ignored it, choosing instead to investigate me a little more. Why had I come there from so far away? I supplied the same excuse I'd given Fedora, and received the same reply.

" '*Vous êtes menteur.*' She, too, saw I was lying. 'You want information about her. Why?'

" 'She interests me,' I admitted, trying to resuscitate my French, which wasn't easy. 'There's been a lot written about her; most of it is—' I gestured with my hands: nothing of consequence, I meant. 'I didn't expect to find her here, though; it was you I wanted to talk with.'

"Balfour had meanwhile appeared in the doorway, waiting for the countess, but she was ignored.

" 'What makes you think I would talk about her to you, or to anyone?' she demanded with some asperity.

" 'I guess I really didn't expect you would. Fedora told me if I wanted to hear stories I must bring a basket of fruit and write billets-doux and serenade your windows, and then you would let down your hair.'

" 'God spare us your serenades, though I would accept

73

the fruit. As for billets-doux, Il Duce himself was not above writing one . . . as you know.' She said it with sly innuendo and waited.

" 'Yes, as I know.'

" 'One book, one letter—*c'est entendu?*'

" '*Entendu.*' Understood. 'But I would prefer having the letters from Fedora's own hand.'

" 'That is impossible. She is gone.'

" 'Will she be coming back?'

" 'Who can say with Fedora? She is a trial to those who know her. We are old friends; once we were good friends. One doesn't close the door in the face of friends. The door will be open if she returns.'

" 'She told me she has no friends.'

" 'She is right. How may one be Fedora and have friends?' She let her glance dwell on me for some moments, nodding slightly, then she drew herself up and said, 'But you and I understand one another, *hein?*'

" 'Exactly *what* do we understand, madame?'

" 'That you will read and be paid. But'—she riveted me with a look—'while you do not serenade our windows, you do listen outside them, *n'est-ce-pas?*'

"Again I lied, saying, as planned, that I'd come looking for my lighter; again she called me *menteur*, and worse, an eavesdropper, producing the lighter from the folds of her dress. Obviously she'd seen me plant it. She gave me a look of mild contempt for my clumsiness, then Kritos, despite her earlier wishes, took her away, while Balfour came and detained me at the balustrade. She seemed nervous, agitated.

" 'You must not keep her talking. It tires her, and you disrupt her schedule.' I explained that it was not I who had begun the conversation, but the countess. Balfour bit her lip, then inquired what topics of social intercourse the countess had interested herself in.

" 'Oh,' I said airily, 'we were talking about fairy tales. Did you ever read the one about Rapunzel? The one who let her hair down?' I left her standing by the balustrade, and crossing the terrace, I glanced through one of the French doors. The countess's chair was empty, while she occupied another one at a table laid for lunch. Kritos had just ladled soup into a bowl, and she was spooning it up, blowing on it to cool it. She saw me, nodded. '*À demain*,' she called through the glass. Then Balfour came up beside me and showed me out.

"I spent the afternoon in the arbor, staring up at the villa's terrace—not with the spyglass, for there was nothing to spy upon. I thought and wondered and cogitated, and found it more and more baffling. It was all very peculiar. I had been certain that the countess was somehow toying with me, drawing me out for some particular purpose, though I had no idea why. I knew I was being baited, and wondered how I could do some baiting in return. Since the morning reading session I had one more important piece to the puzzle, or thought I did, but still it made no sense to me. I decided the time had come to give the ladies a shaking up. When Mrs. Vasos came I negotiated with her to have something sent up from the village, the largest and best apricots to be had in Iraklion, and a small basket as well. If it took these to get the countess to let down her hair, I would see to it. Next morning I scribbled a note, folded it and tucked it among the apricots, which I arranged in a pyramid, and when I went up to the villa I carried along the basket by its woven handle.

"It was a brisk, bright morning, with a spanking breeze, which put white tips on the blue water below, and clouds passed intermittently over the sun. As the countess was wheeled out and placed under the canopy, I brought the basket from behind my back and presented it to her. She took it in her lap and examined the apricots, pressing several and apparently finding them to her satisfaction. But her chary look indicated that she considered the gift suspect. I knew that in itself it was not sufficient to cause her to let down her hair regarding Fedora, but I wondered how long I would have to wait until she discovered the little bomb I'd included. So far she hadn't noticed the note, but only set the basket on the table at her side and said, *'Merci.'*

"I casually asked if she'd ever read *Madame Bovary;* she said she had. I recalled to her the part in which Emma's faithless lover, Rodolphe, sends her a basket of apricots with a concealed note renouncing her as his mistress and canceling their plans to run away to Italy. She nodded, remembering the scene, but the clue went undetected, my own note unobserved. She rang her bell for Kritos and demanded a knife and a *serviette;* she intended to sample the fruit.

" 'Fedora once was to have done a film of that story,' she remarked. 'Someone made it, didn't they?'

"I said David Selznick had sold Metro a movie package, starring Jennifer Jones.

" 'Ah, yes, she won an Oscar, I believe. Fedora, no. *C'est dommage.'* I agreed that it was a disgrace that Hollywood had never honored her work. Kritos came with the knife and napkin, and when he tried to help her she pushed him impatiently away and used the knife to halve the apricot, scooping out the pit which she dropped into her napkin, and proceeded to eat.

" '*Dites-moi, m'sieu', qu'est-ce que vous y pensez?*'

"What did I think of what? I wondered; she was pointing her knife out to sea.

" 'What do you think of her, our Fedora?'

"I realized that she was indicating the direction of the Athens boat, which Balfour had particularly told me Fedora had taken with Count Sobryanski. I said I thought that she was probably the most fascinating woman of our time, and the greatest screen actress the movies had ever seen.

" 'Yes, yes, we all know this,' she said, eating the other half of her apricot, and using her napkin on her lips, "but what do you think of her, really? Do you find her beautiful still?'

" 'Certainly. She's remarkable.'

" 'And young?'

" 'Quite young. She has had a long career.'

" 'Perhaps too long, do you think?' She laid the knife and napkin on the small table at her left elbow, giving an infinitesimal nod of satisfaction. '*Délicieuse,*' she granted my gift. It was enough, she having now affirmed my carefully deduced theory.

" 'Not at all,' I replied easily. 'How old is she, would you say?'

" 'I would not say. She may tell you that, if she chooses, but not I. It would not be kind. Though kindness is hardly in her lexicon. Do you find her pleasant? Enjoyable to be with? Sociable company?' Again she was toying, her little eyes watched me closely—even as I was now watching her.

" 'I've seen her only a few times, madame. Not enough to know her, really.'

" 'A few times can be quite enough in her case, I think.' She looked out to sea again. 'If anyone can know her. She is unfortunate; she is lonely and unhappy, yet she thinks of no one but herself. She is the most selfish of creatures.'

"I observed that this was often the case with famous stars; the countess nodded thoughtfully. 'Perhaps,' she said, 'that is her trouble, being a star. She is a martyr to her fame. She was not always the way you have seen her, the world has seen her.'

"That morning I'd noticed the postman coming up from the village, a rare occurrence. When I made a point of mentioning the fact, Countess Sobryanski said yes, she'd had a letter from her son.

" 'How is Fedora?' I asked.

" 'She is in hospital. Receiving proper care and attention.' I appeared to accept her statement, though I was now certain beyond any doubt that Fedora was not in a hospital, nor was she in the hands of Count Sobryanski. I glanced up to the upper windows, where the shades were still drawn, then back to the old woman, who pointed her knife at the book and set me to reading, while she selected another apricot and sliced it in the same delicate way. I read until Mrs. Balfour interrupted us. She'd brought out Fedora's red shirt, which, because of the breeze, she insisted on draping around the countess's shoulders, then she was alarmed to see that she'd been eating the fruit; evidently a question of her digestion. Balfour took the knife and napkin, and started to remove the basket of apricots as well, which would have upset my plan, so I asked her to leave them; I might have one myself.

"I continued reading, the countess dozed. Sun streamed in several shafts through torn places in the canopy, and as her head nodded to the side a ray struck her eyes, and she came suddenly awake. She looked blankly about, as though uncertain of her surroundings, then she belched: the apricots.

" 'Ought she to make another film, do you think?' she resumed, as if there had been no interruption in our earlier discussion of Fedora. 'Would they still come to see her?'

" 'Undoubtedly they would.'

"She turned to me again. 'You are loyal, even if you are deceitful.'

" 'Deceitful, madame?' I was enjoying this. 'Perhaps, but then I am not alone in that, am I?'

" '*Qu'est-ce que vous voulez dire?*' Her voice crackled, demanding what I meant.

" 'You also have been deceitful, haven't you? Or should I really believe that I was brought here merely to read to you, and to be paid off with Fedora's memorabilia?'

" 'You have a pleasant voice,' she said grudgingly.

" 'So does Mrs. Balfour, I'm sure—nor does she really have laryngitis, I think.' She laughed, a few faint barks and said I was probably right.

" 'But such small deceptions must not be held against an old woman. When you are my age deception comes easily, and you discover that small deceits are easier than large truths.'

" 'Large truths are often painful, I know. But in my business you always look for the deceits; they make more interesting news. You enjoyed the apricots?'

" 'Quite tolerable. I hope you did not pay a lot for them— they take advantage of you, the Greeks.' She pointed her cane over toward the headland, behind which lay Iraklion. 'It is easy to be victimized, *là-bas*.' I followed the tip of her cane, not seaward, but in the opposite direction, along its length to her face. She caught me looking at her, and now jabbed the cane at the book, indicating I should go on. I did not. I closed the book and set it on my knees. She'd had her fun, played her game; now I was going to have my fun and play mine. I said:

" 'It's true, you can be easily victimized in Greece. I have been.'

" 'Is that a fact? Who has victimized you?'

" 'You.'

" 'I?' She gave me an angry snort and an affronted look. 'I fail to see how a weak old woman might go about victimizing a strong and clever man such as yourself. *Expliquez, s'il vous plaît.*'

" 'Perhaps I'm wrong. Perhaps it's not me, but Fedora who is being victimized.'

" 'Pfaugh! Fedora should be used to that; she has been victimized all her life. Say what you mean, *m'sieu'.*'

" 'I cannot say, madame. I can only suggest. Allow me to suggest, however, that there is a plot afoot here. A connivance, if you will; a conspiracy even.'

" 'Conspiracy? Of what are you speaking?' She took further umbrage as she drew the shirt closer around her shoulders.

" 'Simply this, Countess Sobryański. I've known for some time that all is not as is represented here. So allow me to suggest that Fedora has not gone away at all. I suggest that she is not in a hospital at Menton, or anywhere in your son's loving care. I suggest that she is still in this house, and that your man Kritos, he and Mrs. Balfour and yourself, keep her here against her will.'

" 'For what reason, this?'

" 'I suggest that it is a conspiracy to rob her. You say I have eavesdropped; I admit it, and I have overheard certain discussions concerning money matters. Her papers alone must be worth a good deal, yet I am being paid with them piecemeal.'

"She became more indignant, but I saw that it was only a

defense. 'You must be mad. Where do you get such ideas?' Trembling, she tried to hold on to her cane, but it slipped from her fingers and fell on the stonework. I got up and handed it to her. She clutched it, her shoulders shaking. *'Ne touchez pas!'* I moved to lean against the balustrade, looking down at her; she would not return my gaze.

" 'Or I could suggest something else—a perhaps less believable plot, but still possible. Perhaps, as you say, she has gone away. Perhaps not to Menton, but to Switzerland.'

" 'We are not at home just now in Switzerland.'

" 'Obviously, since you are here. But I suggest that perhaps she has gone to Basel, to the clinic. For more treatments.'

" *'Vous pensez de Vando?'*

"Yes, I said, I was thinking of Vando.

" 'He is dead.' She rattled her cane again, always a bad sign. 'He has been dead for many years.'

" 'I have heard so, but there has never been proof, has there?'

" 'He is dead, I promise you. And she is not there—I promise you that as well!'

"She'd become very upset; I softened my tone. 'Let me suggest something else, then. Let me suggest that what you and Mrs. Balfour claim is true: Fedora *has* gone to Menton and is being looked after by your son. Let me suggest that your man Kritos is what you say he is, a faithful retainer.'

" 'What? How's that? Speak up, stop mumbling.'

"I wasn't mumbling, but speaking quite distinctly. I think she knew what was coming, but was trying to fend off the moment with her truculence.

"I said, 'There are one or two interesting things about your friend Fedora, madame. You wouldn't know it, but this was not the first time she and I have met.'

" *'C'est vrai?'* She shrugged; the encounter I referred to seemed to afford her no interest. *'Et puis quoi?'*

" 'And what then? Well,' I returned, 'there is the matter of that shirt you are wearing. I gave it to Fedora almost thirty years ago.'

"*C'est vrai?*' she repeated, no more than glancing down at it. 'It is little more than a rag now.'

" 'True, but it has sentimental connotations for me. You can imagine my surprise, seeing that she has held on to it for all these years.'

" 'Perhaps she treasures it.'

" 'My very thought. She never thanked me for it, though.'

" 'Did you give it to her so you could be thanked? You are not only a liar and an eavesdropper; you have a petty mind.'

" 'I'm merely trying to explain to you. The shirt was sent to me by my mother, I had little money then, she wanted to be sure I would keep warm.'

" 'You have a loving mother, I am sure.' *Je suis certaine:* she snapped out the words. 'Why do you go on about the matter? Is it so important?'

" 'Only in terms of the deceits we were speaking of. In any case, my mother sent it to me, I in turn sent it to Fedora. There are certain people in the world one would always give the shirt off one's back for. I hoped she would be pleased by it.'

"She grew more impatient. 'Why, then, she was pleased, or she wouldn't have kept it. You really have a small nature.' She took me in again, shielding her eyes against a ray of bright sun that filtered through a torn place in the canopy.

" 'I suppose,' I pursued, ignoring her remark, 'that having gone to Menton and left the shirt behind, she would hardly miss it—since it does not belong to her, anyway.'

" 'Does not? What do you mean? Surely you gave it to her,' she replied caustically.

" 'No, Countess Sobryanski, I did not.'

" 'Are you an Indian giver, to make presents and then take them back?'

" 'Not at all. Where I gave it, there I meant it to be kept, even if on a hook in a back hallway. I would no more take it back than I would take, for example, these apricots.' I picked up the basket and held it before her, turning it so the tip of the note was in front of her eyes. She looked at me questioningly, then drew it out. She unfolded it, looked at it, and said irritably, 'You know I cannot see it. What does it say?'

"I took it from her and read it aloud. ' *"Rien d'ailleurs ne rassure autant qu'un masque."* '

" 'Well, then, well, then, what does it mean?'

" 'It's from Colette. And I believe you know what it means.' She was trembling more violently, and her finger pinched the red points of the shirt collar and drew it closer around her chin. She ducked her face so it was hidden from me. 'It means that I gave that shirt to Fedora—just as I gave her these apricots. I gave both to you. Because you are Fedora.'

"She struck my outstretched hand away, the fruit spilling in all directions, as she cried out, *'Vous avez tort! Vous avez tort!'* Her voice cracked with emotion as she turned to me again, tilting her face into the ray of light. *'Vous avez tort,'* she repeated, her voice gone to a dead whisper. *'J'etais Fedora.'*

" 'You are wrong. I *was* Fedora.' "

"Not possible."

Marion Walker sat immobile, staring open-mouthed at Barry, her fingers holding her cigarette, burning but unsmoked, the ash grown long. She moved; the ash fell to the carpet. She reached to brush it away, tossing her hair aside as she raised her head. *"Not possible,"* she repeated.

Barry returned her look with a smile and a slight shrug. "In this life, Marion, dear, all things are possible."

"I can't believe it."

"Of course not. Didn't I say you wouldn't? But didn't I also say that my facts were unassailable? They are, I promise you. She was Fedora."

"I see. . . . I see," Marion said, trying very hard to see. "Then the other one was—"

"An impostor."

"Which one died in Menton yesterday?"

"The impostor."

"Which one played the Virgin in *Santa Cristi?*"

"The impostor. Her first part."

"And Nefertiti?"

"Again, the impostor. She was remarkably good, good as Fedora ever was."

"Which did you meet at the Louvre?"

"The real one."

"Ahh—then I do see." She settled smugly back against the pillows and smiled at Barry.

"You're looking very Mona Lisa yourself," he told her. "What do you see?"

"I know who the impostor was."

"Do you indeed?"

"Of course." She gestured to the painting. "That's not Fedora."

"Aren't you clever. You've got it right off. It's not Fedora."

She accepted the compliment and with a confiding air asked, "Who is it, then?"

"Stanna Wilchek. Like Fedora, an actress. She was in *Mother Courage and Her Children* at the Theatre de Lys about ten years ago. Incredible resemblance, isn't it? Did you ever see her in the movies?"

"No . . ."

"You wouldn't have—she never made one. Although she was kept under contract for seven years. It's a rather sad story. Back in the thirties, some AyanBee executives saw the resemblance. They signed her without a test and put her under wraps so no other studio could have a rival Fedora. Fedora felt guilty because Stanna's career never got off the ground, and she helped her out financially for a time—until Stanna married, in fact."

"Whom did she marry?"

"Cyril Leaf."

"The designer? Ahh, then that's why she's wearing the Ophelie costume. But—" Marion was suddenly baffled again. "How could she look young enough to impersonate Fedora? She'd be about the same age, wouldn't she?"

"*I* never said she impersonated Fedora. You did."

"Oh." Her look was one of miserable frustration. "Then I *don't* see."

"Of course you don't. Nobody did; that's the beauty of it. I offer you that portrait as an illustration of how easily people can be deceived by what they think are facts, or by appearances. Appearances are deceiving, as they say. She looks like Fedora; ergo, she is Fedora. I led you to believe it, let you believe it. As I was led to believe the real Fedora was the countess Sobryanski: she looked like what I'd seen of her, behaved like what I'd heard of her, therefore she was the countess. But then she wasn't at all; not the countess—Fedora."

"Well, I'm waiting."

"The impostor? You've been a patient listener, so I'll tell you. Ophelie."

Still she didn't comprehend it. "You mean the movie?"

"I mean the daughter."

"But Fedora never had a daughter. . . ."

"She didn't?" He was looking at her, long, steadily, with smiling traces of that knowledge she'd earlier been certain he possessed. Still . . .

"How could she have? How could she have gotten away with it? You don't keep secrets like that in our business."

"It was . . . arranged."

"Who was the father?"

He rose abruptly and she grabbed at him. "Hey, don't leave me there—"

"I was just going to get us another drink." He carried the glasses to the bar and filled them partway. He brought them back and set them on the coffee table, watching her with his half-smile.

"Well?" she demanded.

"Sobryanski," he said finally.

"The count?"

"Count Jan Ivan Chernieff Sobryanski, none other."

"Ohhh, Barry . . ." Her tone clearly implied that she refused to accept his statement.

"I said you wouldn't believe it, and you don't."

"Yes, you did, and no, I don't. When were they married?"

"Never."

"Oh." She stopped her glass halfway to her mouth. "You mean . . . ?"

"I mean. She had his child, but she never married him. Refused to, as a matter of fact."

"I didn't think unwed mothers were fashionable in her day. And the child looked that much like her?"

"There evidently were certain dissimilarities, but nothing noticeable. It happens. Wait a minute." He brought a Manila envelope from the table behind the sofa and began laying photographs out before her. On each, all but the face had been masked by taped-on paper cutouts, and all looked like Fedora. "Which is which?" Barry asked. Marion studied them and then pointed. "That's Fedora in *Tsarina.*"

"Wrong. It's Ophelie in *Mother Russia.*" He lifted the cutout to reveal "Fedora" in her Catherine the Great costume.

"Then *that's* Fedora," Marion stated, pointing again.

"Wrong." It was Ophelie in *Madeleine Pomona.* "Why don't I save you the trouble?" he suggested. "They're all Ophelie."

Marion pressed her hands to her forehead and closed her eyes, trying to take it in. "You mean ever since *Santa Cristi,* none of those performances was Fedora?"

"Ever since, none."

"I assume you've checked the facts."

"Would you like to see them? Photostats of the birth certificate, the works? I have all the authenticated documents. I have also sworn statements from Mrs. Evelyn Balfour, if you need that kind of proof."

"Barry, I believe, I believe. But I don't understand. The daughter wasn't being kept prisoner, then?"

"As Balfour said, she was perfectly free to come and go as she chose. Kritos was actually a mild sort, and his main task, when Ophelie was there, was to see that she didn't hurt herself. I simply misread his actions. She was always threatening suicide, and making trouble for her mother and Balfour. They didn't want her being seen in the village when she was on drugs, and the day she went to the beach Kritos merely went down to bring her home safely. She became obstreperous as usual, and he had trouble getting her into the house, so he carried her. When she became hysterical, Fedora slapped her, not an unnatural thing to do, but one I misinterpreted. She had made up the whole plot thing; as Balfour said, it was her heightened sense of the dramatic. She was always causing scenes.

"At last the count was called, and he flew to Athens and came for her. He and his wife did look after her well; when she got out of the hospital she was moved back to Switzerland to a sanitarium. Finally they brought her back to Menton— she liked to be close to Monte Carlo for the gambling—but of course she couldn't; too ill. She evidently died at the Menton house."

"You were that close to Fedora, and you never recognized her? That face?"

"But it wasn't *that* face, you see. *That* face was gone, destroyed. The whole structure had collapsed, there wasn't a trace of resemblance to the original. That was the greatest tragedy, I think."

"How did you finally know the other one wasn't Fedora?"

"I've already told you."

"No, you didn't."

"I gave you every clue—you simply overlooked them. Like everybody else."

"Explain."

"Explain . . . yes, explain." He sat abruptly and picked up his drink. The room was silent for some moments, then he drew her back once more to Crete, to the old woman sitting on the villa terrace, but the old woman was no longer the countess Sobryanski, she was the once-great star Fedora.

She had turned her face away, and he could not tell if she was angry at him or angry at herself. For she would not speak again. She rang her bell until Kritos hurried out and wheeled her away. Mrs. Balfour had been standing in the doorway, witness to the scene.

"What does it mean?" Barry asked her.

"She has told you. She is Fedora."

The next day he did not read. Kritos appeared at the cottage with Balfour's note asking him please to wait. Two days later word arrived that he was to come again. He returned to the villa. All seemed as before; the schedule was kept punctiliously, she sat as usual in her place at the balustrade, he took up the book and read. She had not looked at him. Later he decided that it was her woman's curiosity that broke the silence between them. In the middle of a passage she raised her hand. He stopped. She said:

"M'sieu'?"

"Oui, madame? Qu'est-ce qu'il y a?"

She shook her head. "No, speak English. Your French is quite bad, and there is no need to continue such deceits now. I was afraid you might recognize my accent in English. How did you know? We fooled the world; how was it we did not fool you?"

"But you did, madame, absolutely fooled me. Until almost the last, just before—may I say Ophelie?—went away."

"And then?"

"William Marsh once told me that you never ate shellfish of any kind, yet at lunch I saw her eat a plate of shrimp salad. Then I saw her cutting her meat, and she switched her knife and fork the way right-handed people do. But, if I recalled correctly, I was told that you are left-handed. This was confirmed when I saw you, first eating your soup, then when you pitted the apricots I brought you."

"Very astute. You are correct. My eating habits were not hers, she always preferred the American style of using cutlery. It was a small thing; we thought no one would notice that." She fell silent for a moment, then: "Do you think it was clever, this impersonation?"

"Very."

"I thought so, too, but now it seems it was not. You see how matters go, the moment one blinks the eye."

"How do they go?"

"Badly, badly. They become something else, something you did not intend them to become. Still, it was never a shabby deception. She made a very good Fedora."

"Whatever she was, there is only one Fedora, madame."

She shook her cane. "Because I am her mother it is perhaps immodest of me to say so, but she is—was—remarkable. We fooled them all for a long time. It would be nice to die having fooled them forever."

"Why can't you?"

She made a scoffing sound, waved her hand at him. "You are here. You will write about it; I cannot stop you. But I should say the truth. It is why I sent for you—I *want* you to write it. It is time; there has been so much untruth. I will tell you how it was, if you will promise to write it the way it was. Can I trust you to do that?"

"You can, madame."

She nodded with evident satisfaction. "I have discussed it with Balfour; she says you are to be trusted." She thought again, then asked, "What was it, the Colette? The line about the mask?"

He quoted: *" 'Rien d'ailleurs ne rassure autant qu'un masque.' "*

She nodded again. "Yes; very reassuring. Ophelie-Fedora was my mask; she kept me hidden. I did well to stay that way. I have looked older and uglier longer than I ever looked young and beautiful."

"You had a great career."

"Ahh, car-r-r-reer. What is a career? I never wanted to be that, a movie star. I wanted only to be an actress. As a movie star one gets the best table in the restaurant, that is all. A name on the marquee. The first time I saw my name in lights, they spelled my name wrong. 'Fedroa. Fedroa in *Zizi*.' What a silly picture. How silly they all were. There are better ways to amuse oneself than by being a movie star, I tell you that."

"Such as?"

"Looking after someone. Having babies. Washing clothes." She laughed, not the old laugh, but the palest recollection of it, and it really wasn't the movie star, it was the washerwoman. Barry waited to hear the source of her amusement. "Marlene. I once talked to a steward on a plane and he told me he used to take Dietrich's grandchild's dirty diapers from Paris to New York and she would wash and iron them and send them back, all the way across the ocean. I think that was nice." She composed herself, then began, going back to her first meeting with Jan Sobryanski, the accidental encounter that had initiated their long relationship. He had been ill and was in New York; he had been bedded at Columbia-Presbyterian Hospital for three months, undergoing tests. She confessed she had never cared for Europeans as lovers, but he had struck a responsive chord in her and they saw much of each other during the Atlantic voyage. Before docking at Le Havre he had already proposed marriage. She put him off. He was charming, but too young, and she did not want to be married, to him or anyone. A summer was fine, but not a lifetime. She had only her work. They enjoyed their idyll in Europe, and she returned to Hollywood, to discover she was pregnant. She was scheduled to make *Madame Bovary*, which she would just have time to finish before she began to show, but the picture was continually postponed, and it became too late. The film was abandoned, and she went away to have the baby.

"I went to a place where no one would find me, but they did—they always did. They gathered and sat and waited until I would come out."

"Where was this?"

"In California, at Monterey. The Convent of Santa Margarita.'

Santa Margarita. Barry recalled the stories of the furor outside its doors, while Fedora sat peacefully in the garden with her secret.

"They were kind, the nuns; they told no one. But I had to go back, to earn a living. They smuggled me out under the reporters' eyes, in the back of a bakery wagon."

Her next film was to be *Ophelie*, and she liked the name, so she gave it to her child.

She had left it in the nuns' safekeeping, visiting whenever possible. When things became safe, she leased a house in Pacific Palisades, where Viola arranged for Mrs. Balfour to come and keep the house and look after the child. The three lived there from 1927 to 1938, when Ophelie was twelve. The birth certificate had been falsified, and with the exception of Viola, Balfour, and a Mexican woman who came in to do the cleaning, no one was aware of the child's existence. Her early schooling came from Mrs. Balfour, who had been at one time a teacher in England. Count Sobryanski had not married, and in 1936 Fedora informed him about his daughter. He came to Hollywood with his mother; together they tried to persuade her to wed Jan, but she remained adamant. Jan had threatened that if he could not have her he would have no one, but to ensure the family title he was obliged to marry, and this he did sixteen months later. They eventually had four children, two boys, two girls. The war threats had already begun, and afraid that she would be cut off from Vando, Fedora, too, returned to Europe.

Since a passport had been denied the doctor, and she felt it necessary to be close to him, she flew to New York, then to Halifax, where Balfour met her with Ophelie, then twelve years old. There Fedora parted with her housekeeper, and was not to see her again for nine years. She took refuge with the Sobryanskis in Switzerland, and through the war they lived together, Jan, his wife and children, the dowager countess, and in a separate wing, Fedora and Ophelie. There were other children as well, those of the servants and various Polish refugees, and at times there were as many as two dozen of them on the large estate. It was not difficult to lose Ophelie among the rest, and she had plenty of companions. She enjoyed a perfectly normal life, and in the guise of being one of the Sobryanskis, she accompanied her younger "sisters" to boarding school in Geneva. Her hair was short and parted on the side, and though she held the promise of a beautiful young woman, no one at the time could guess what a striking replica of her mother she was to become.

The war ended; people were again free to move from country to country. This Ophelie did, with the count and his wife and the other children. In the winter of 1946 they were taken to South America, while Fedora stayed with the dowager countess in Paris, and it was then that she had encountered Barry Detweiller in the Louvre. Shortly afterward, tragedy struck, one that came, ironically, at the hands of Dr. Vando. Unable to secure certain androgenic substances during the war, he had manufactured facsimiles in his laboratory. These synthetics proved effective for a time and she, now his sole patient, had undergone repeated courses of treatment. But it had not been without risk, and the compounds eventually proved disastrous. Shortly after Barry's meeting with Fedora at the Louvre, the treatments began to fail. Her androgen balance had been upset, the rejuvenation process slowed, faltered, then failed altogether, she aged more and more quickly, then her looks overtook her years altogether. Her face was ruined; although she was only in her early fifties, she looked considerably older. She fled back to Montreux, where she hid herself away, refusing to see anyone.

"I knew then that it was over for me. Not just working, but everything. I felt I had been tricked, but of course it was only the trick reversed, and finally catching up with me. I had Ophelie, I had the Sobryanskis. I did not find it very amusing, however. I felt I had just been liberated, now I was a prisoner again. Ophelie came and shared the imprisonment with me. We were close in those days, ver-r-ry close. She watched me grow uglier and uglier while I watched her grow more and more beautiful. Sometimes we would run one of my old movies, and afterward she would mimic me in a scene. It was to make me laugh. Only those who knew her in those days know how wonderful she was. Then the idea came—it was not mine, it was not hers, it was ours together.

Each of us had been thinking of it separately, and one day it just was there, the idea. It was not just the resemblance, you see, it was everything. She already had so many of my ways: of talking, of walking, of sitting; her laugh was the same; everything was the same, almost. One night she put on a dress that was like one I had worn in a film, and came down the staircase. It could have been me, so many years ago. We knew then, in that instant, what we were going to do. If we can both take the credit, we must both take the blame. I did not urge it on her, she wanted to do it. We plotted and planned, imagined, dreamed how it might be, what an enormous joke on the world. She would do a part in a picture, and later we would publish the hoax and have our laugh. So I began teaching her. Everything I knew. She learned quickly, she was so clever, so adroit. It was as if we were getting her ready for a giant masquerade party."

Fedora brought out her old scripts, which Ophelie studied and memorized. Her mother taught her the rhythm of each scene, the motivations, the line-by-line readings. The count had collected most of Fedora's films, and she ran them over and over, while Ophelie watched them until she could play each part perfectly. Time passed, Ophelie became more eager, and the work continued. She was taught Russian, and consequently could speak English with a Slavic accent. She could duplicate her mother's voice to the slightest nuance, the merest inflection. She could hold her head precisely as her mother would, her hands could make the inimitable gestures, her eyes would assume the languorous half-lidded look. Still, Fedora was fearful that if Ophelie were to play a part, the camera would expose the fraud. Somewhere they would have forgotten something, some small but telling detail. Or people would realize she was far too young. But by then Fedora had forgotten how young she used to look; it had been so long.

There were certain facial discrepancies—the nose, the pointed chin of her father—but these noticeable faults were corrected by careful plastic surgery. Her hair was grown in to a full length, and styled as Fedora had often worn hers in newspaper photographs, her eyebrows were plucked to match her mother's, test photographs were made; now it seemed impossible to tell the difference. For Fedora, seeing Ophelie was like looking in her mirror, but since she no longer dared face her mirror now she could look at her. The masquerade began. It was 1954, Ophelie was twenty-eight. They were in Tangier when Viola, who was a party to the plan, came from Rome: there was the role of the Holy Virgin, it was the perfect place to begin. Nothing taxing, no dialogue, but the face would be seen. It was a test; *the* test.

"They said she hid her age behind the radiance, a trick of light, but it was a triumph," Fedora said excitedly. "We fooled them. Ophelie was delighted, and I urged her to play Nefertiti. When she remade *Ophelie* she was better than I. I hoped they would give her the award, but they did not. Neither of us."

"Did you want the award?"

"Certainly I did," she crackled. "It never happened for me, but I thought it might for her. Who knows how long she might have gone on?"

Who indeed?

"It was a game then, a mer-r-ry game," she continued. "They could not imagine what was happening, after Jan married. How they wondered—and what did they think? Was Jan in love with Fedora, was Jan in love with his wife? Triangles, always the triangles. Oh, yes, they would say, how young she still is, how beautiful. *La Déesse, La Serenissima.* Very kind, the Venetians. But it was merry for only so long. Ophelie was beautiful, I was not."

Where it had started to go wrong she couldn't remember, but without realizing it she had become jealous. She had put her child in her place, hoping it would work; when it did she found she didn't like it. "Good," she had prayed, "be good." But not that good. She became angry that it was Ophelie on the screen, not herself. She felt that it was she who belonged there, that a matter of chemistry had denied her her rightful spot; she was displaced, passed by, forgotten. Whoever she had been, Maria Fedorovnya into Fedora, caterpillar into butterfly, she was no longer that person. The identity she had created for herself had evaporated.

And then Ophelie herself became miserable. She discovered that she resented forever playing the part of someone playing a part. She wanted to be herself, to be known as herself; she was neither Ophelie nor Fedora; she was no one. She would inscribe the name in lipstick on mirrors and walls: Ophelie, Ophelie, Ophelie. She no longer wanted to pretend Fedora, Fedora, Fedora. She was a legend, but it was not of her making.

And so they had crossed into each other's territories and both were unhappy. They grew apart, and Fedora lost her. She began drinking, then the drugs. There were long periods when her mother would not hear from her; what news there was came from the count. The uglier stories were kept from Fedora, and she learned of Ophelie's difficulties only when it began affecting her daughter's work. She had not known what to do. By that time she was living on Crete, with Countess Sobryanski, and Ophelie would come to visit. They could no longer behave like mother and daughter. Ophelie was moody, intransigent, silent; she brought narcotics from Tangier, and spent her time indulging in frenzied drug trips. Meanwhile Countess Sobryanski had died, and there was the question of burial. She had insisted on interment in her native soil, but her anti-communist activities prevented this. To circumvent the authorities, her death was concealed, and her body was smuggled from Crete and taken to Poland, to be secretly buried on the edge of a wood near her old estate. As time went on, Fedora found it convenient to let people think the countess still lived, and when people from the beach looked up and saw her in the wheelchair, they saw not one of the most famous women in the world, but merely an old, anonymous Polish noblewoman.

"So my friend Maria was gone," Fedora continued, "but there was still Ophelie. She would come back, always come back, and mock me, blame me. She said when I died I must be sure there was room for her in my coffin; we must share the same grave, the same stone. She said, please, could I die soon? It made her nervous; she wanted to be only one, not two people. The people she worked with disliked her, she hated them; she would destroy not only her Fedora, but mine, too. She went in hospital, and then out, and in again. Finally she had to stop working altogether. I couldn't look after her, so it became Jan's task. He is good, and kind; his wife is, too. They have had the worst of it, not I. She comes here, then goes away, but when she comes she is well; she goes when she is not. They always have her when she is not.

"But she is right: I am to blame. You see where one's vanity may lead one. Such foolishness at the world's expense. But more at my own." She spoke with her old, characteristic ironic amusement of the pains that had been taken, which Barry saw went beyond mere wit or intelligence; they smacked of genius, to deceive for so long on such a scale. She had conspired with herself, her daughter, a handful of others, in a stupendous masquerade. She had created man—or woman—in her own image, but it had been for her nothing more than a joke.

"How I laughed. I thought it was so funny. But it was not, not in the end. She was not *La Déesse,* only *La Scandalosa.*

It is foolish to try to be something one is not; one must always be oneself in all things. Poor Ophelie. She made only one mistake, you know."

"What was that, madame?"

"The mistake of being human. She wanted to be somebody—herself—not me."

Fedora had stood alone in her work and because of it she stood alone in her life. Her greatest suffering had come, though, not from her loss of beauty, her aging, but from Ophelie, whose existence had been such a disastrous replica of her own.

And so, little by little, day by day, she had given Barry the whole story of her life, correcting for him all the false facts that had made up the legend. The scene had changed; summer had gone, the Aegean blue turned gray, the chill wind blew the leaves onto the terrace, and though Kristos swept the flagstones each morning there were always more. She herself had the whisper of sere leaves about her; she was in a kind of mourning without the trappings, except for the hunter-red shirt which she kept around her shoulders. Then one day, when she had rung her bell, she leaned forward and slipped it off, and dangled it at him impatiently.

"Take it, take it; you'll want it back, naturally. Something Fedora wore, you can tell them. For the sake of memory."

"What was the worst of it, madame—being Fedora?"

"The worst? Having her face, I suppose. It was not an easy face to own. People always like people who have faces—as if a nose could make your fortune. They like people whose names are in electric lights, never thinking the bulbs may blow out at any time. But the worst was not to be able to go into the street like everybody else. People always looking, following, wanting to know—always to know. So I did not go out. I would not be seen. After a time I found I had forgotten what it was like to go about, to be in the streets, to watch other people, shop, visit, eat in restaurants, to do the things people do together. I would not have known where to go, what to do, how to behave.

"Still, I have ended where I always wanted to be." She pointed her cane out over the balustrade. "High up."

"How is it—high up?"

"The view is considerably different—as you see. But if you look, you see how long a fall it is to down there." She swept her cane down toward the beach, then sat nodding, thinking. Then, quite suddenly, she said, "I still owe you for a pack of cigarettes."

Barry was surprised. "I didn't think you remembered."

"Certainly I remembered," she snapped. "Nineteen forty-six, Paris, the Louvre. It was March, very cold. You were drawing the Perseus; rather badly, if I recall. You were waiting for some girl. You told me a dreadful story about wetting your pants because you were frightened by my movie. Not very gallant, to remind me how old I was, even then." Barry was amazed; her clear recollection was astonishing. But she remembered even more. She said, "Did you ever go to the man at the Crillon? Jérôme?"

"He cut my hair for the rest of the time I stayed in Paris."

"Then you must have looked somewhat better than you did when we met. I have sometimes thought of you. And here you are. It was why I had you brought to read to me—so I could see if you were the one to do the job. I am satisfied." She started coughing. She pressed her hands to her flat breast and held them there for a few moments till she gathered her strength. "And the girl," she went on after a moment. "I don't imagine she stayed around very long."

"As a matter of fact, she didn't."

"I told you you could not have it both ways. You could not have art and heart together."

"I remember. Oil and water."

"Exactly. It must be one or the other. But for me it was neither. I had no heart and I had no art. I told you that, too. Nor were we goddesses, either of us; we were only women. Foolish movies do not deify; there is no art in silly pictures."

"You had great art, madame; no critic ever said no to that."

"Cr-r-ritics?" She gave him a contemptuous look. "One does not pay attention to what critics say. It would be like feeding the hand that bites you. And between us, the two Fedoras, we did many more bad pictures than we did good. One does one's work and performs what is there to be performed. But you keep your eyes open, and if you are smart, your mouth shut. Do you know of the anthropophagi?"

"Cannibals?"

"Precisely. That is what they are; they are so hungry for success and fame and the rest, they eat one another. They are a hungry lot. Flesh and blood and bone and hair—they will eat the whole. It is a dirty business, but if the picture is good it perhaps is worth it. After all, when one eats an egg it is not wise to think of where it came from. À demain."

Kritos had come and was wheeling her away; Barry followed alongside her chair. He had the feeling that he wouldn't be seeing her much longer, that she would never see another birthday.

"But," she said, going, "when you see the Windsor duchess, tell her I stayed rich and I stayed thin."

"And the others—what shall I tell them?"

"Who?"

"The world."

"About what?"

"About Fedora."

"Tell them that she had her face on a Dixie cup cover," she returned, as the rubber wheels bumped over the threshold. "It was enough."

Silence had fallen in Barry Detweiller's living room. Marion leaned a little forward from the sofa, hands clasped between her knees, her fingertips tapping together as she looked up at the portrait.

"Well," she said finally, breaking the spell. "There certainly were a lot of Fedoras."

Barry smiled, shook his head. "Wrong again, Marion. No matter how much Ophelie looked like and sounded like her mother, she was still Ophelie. There was only one Fedora. What do you think—is it a story?"

"I'm sick that I can't use it. What are you calling the book?"

"I thought I'd called it *The Last Fedora.*"

"I like it. And I thank you."

"Anytime."

She made a move to rise, then sat again. "You haven't told me the end, though."

He shook his head. "But it was . . . the end."

"I mean how did she die? Was it long, or painful, or . . .?"

"It was long and it was painful, but not then; the pain had all come before. She just went."

"Tell me how."

"Well, it was a Friday," he recalled. "The day had begun a good one, but the weather continued changeable. You never knew what to expect concerning her health—sometimes she wouldn't come down at all—but that day, a blustery one, I went up to the villa and she was out on the terrace. I started reading. Mrs. Balfour was busy with her pruning shears, dropping cuttings into her basket, and I stopped for a cigarette. Fedora sighed, and I thought the pause was worrying her. I read again, watching her over the top of the page. Only the occasional movement of her fingers on the chair told me she was alive.

"Then, suddenly, she wasn't. I had stubbed out my cigarette and picked up reading where I left off. Balfour was standing to my right, staring at the back of the wheelchair. I read on, and when I next glanced up she had moved and she was on the far side of Fedora, looking down. I could see tears on her cheeks. I thought perhaps it was only a passing moment of sentiment, then I noticed the quiver of her mouth and when I looked at Fedora's hand I saw that it lay still. She didn't seem any more lifeless than she had many times before, but she was without life. It had gone from her, we had no idea when. She had simply died, and she sat in death as she had in life, facing the sea. That was all."

"Where is she buried?"

"Guess."

"Crete, I'd suppose."

"She was happy enough to leave Crete, I think, after so many years. She's buried in California."

"Surely not Forest Lawn?"

"Monterey. At the Convent of Santa Margarita. Strings had to be pulled, influence brought to bear to get the coffin into the country. I went with Balfour for the funeral."

"And afterward?"

"She returned to England; she's there now. She gave me all the signed statements and corroborating information, so no one could dispute me. . . . She insisted I keep the Mussolini note. She let me use what I wanted from the other letters, then destroyed them. Now she's waiting to die, just as Fedora did, only in Dover."

"Looking at the English Channel?"

"Perhaps."

"I can't get that picture out of my head—that figure in the wheelchair, always watching, watching the sea."

"Nor I," Barry said. "I told you I used to wonder why she spent so much time there, sitting just that way. So still, so silent, so unmoving. I wondered what her thoughts must be, and I thought she seemed to be waiting for something—but what? I think I know now. You probably saw *The Grim Reaper*? It was the first film she did for Improstein. I saw it last year at the Museum of Modern Art, and afterward I thought I knew what Fedora was watching for. The picture's a disappointment—only a shadow of what it originally must have been. Chopped-up scenes, obvious elisions, awkward English titles, and a badly scratched print. Fedora isn't really good in it; at first, you can't see much there that might have kindled interest in anyone. Her face looks fat, her teeth are crooked, she's wearing that silly period make-up—pale face, dark lips. The part's not sympathetic either. She's a barmaid, and half the time she's coy and arch, and the rest lugubrious and self-indulgent—all that melodramatic bathos that was in fashion then. Yet I swear to God, somehow it's all there. Unformed, hardly realized, but there. You can see what Improstein must have seen. I have a friend who was talking about someone we'd met casually, and he said, 'She has a good face but she hasn't grown into it yet.' That's what I sensed about Fedora in *The Grim Reaper*. But, at the end, there's one very moving scene. In order to save her lover, the barmaid stabs a man. She runs away. She wanders from city to city, lost and forsaken. She becomes ill, she's dying. At last she comes to the ocean and sits on the beach. As she looks out over the water there's one marvelous close-up, understated and emotionally affecting, then the camera cuts to a full shot. Fedora's still sitting, her shoulders narrowed eloquently, her arms hugging her knees. As she sits there, immobile, waiting, gradually a long darkening shape reaches out from the horizon, slowly extending and approaching her. It's a naïve conception, pure German Expressionist, and of course it's her death she's waiting for. But what a tremendously powerful scene! And it seemed to me that the old woman sitting on the terrace—that's what she was doing all that time. She was waiting for her private vision of death to reach out across the sea and take her. She was tired. She'd lived a long time."

Lorna

The hotel is not widely known outside the tourist trade, but those who enjoy really "getting away from it all" have heard through friends who have visited there that if one wants only to sun and swim and fish and read and drink and make love, Boca de Oro and Las Cinco Palmas is "just what the doctor ordered." Less a cut-rate resort than an undiscovered paradise, it lies on the western coast of Mexico several hundred miles southeast of the tip of Baja California.

Since the government has not seen fit to build a road or airstrip, Boca is inaccessible except by water, and an excursion boat comes and goes daily from the nearest large town, Mirabella, an hour or so away. There are no telephones or direct mail service; electricity is limited.

Life is slow, easy, even boring at Boca de Oro. The *playa*, or beach, is crescent-shaped, the "mouth of gold" from which the place derives its name. The hotel is built on the north point of the curve, which is situated at the mouth of the Río de Oro, where the river spills out of the jungle onto the golden sickle of sand. Half a mile away, on the opposite point of the crescent, are some houses belonging to foreigners, one with a handicraft shop attached, which is run by an unmarried American couple, and a ramshackle dock, bar, and restaurant combined into what is called, but hardly passes for, a "yacht club." Beyond these, over a quaint wooden bridge, lies the village: a score of adobe dwellings, a store, a cantina, and a church. The villagers live mainly by fishing and by the practice of native crafts which are sold in the Americans' shop, or they are employed as menials at the hotel.

Las Cinco Palmas (since there are considerably more than five palms, one wonders at the name) is owned by a Mexican consortium in the capital and is managed by Esteban "Steve" Alvarez, from Guatemala City, and his Swiss-born wife, Cupie. The hotel compound consists of a large, rambling open-air bar and dining room with a thatched roof, the structure fronting the view and surrounded by individual native-fashioned cabañas of stone and clay foundations, timbers, bamboo, rattan meshwork, and more thatched roofs. Scorpions live in this hard-packed brush and are a nuisance, or worse; more than eighteen thousand people in Mexico have died of scorpion bites in the last ten years. The cabañas are set attractively among winding paths colorful with flowers and shaded by palm trees; a parrot—red, blue, orange—lives in one of these, and it whistles rudely like a drugstore cowboy appraising the girls on a Saturday evening outside a pool hall. Each cabaña has its private patio—many of which overlook the bay—with a table and two rainbow-painted chairs and a native-woven hemp hammock strung between the porch posts.

Though Boca de Oro undoubtedly manifests the exotic allure of all such tropical places, the atmosphere is generally peaceful. There is nothing spectacular about the bay, which is warm and clear and placid. In the morning, with the change of tide, it rouses itself from slumber, seems to turn over with an audible flop, makes itself comfortable, and returns to drowse again. Even before the mangy dogs start to bark, the motors of the fishing boats setting out from the village can be heard moving around the points of the horseshoe. Their catch will be a source of interest to the curious tourist: orangey-green fish with unfamiliar Spanish names, *róbalo,* and *bacalao,* and *merluza,* hooked together in wet, shiny clusters. Most of the fish will go to the hotel to feed the guests, local seafood being the one dish the chef seems unable to ruin.

Every day is alike. When the boats have put out, usually around six, the hotel begins to stir. The kitchen fires are lighted, and then can be heard the clink of china and silverware as the checkered cloths are set at long communal tables where guests share in the informal atmosphere characterizing Boca de Oro. Soon the beachboys come forth and rake the sand, and the canvas chairs, stacked the previous night, are set out in rows within a roped-off enclosure.

While the beachboys are attending to these duties, the

maids have appeared, gathering from the village or from quarters behind the kitchen, and the gently percussive whisper of their straw brooms is heard, as they sweep from the curving walkways fallen bougainvillaea petals, hibiscus blossoms, spiders' webs spun in the night. One girl goes to plump up the cushions in the open-air pavilion that houses a collection of dog-eared paperback books left by former guests; this is called the "library," a pleasant, shady spot in which to relax in a hammock and read or watch the sea. Another girl goes to the cement and rock basin near the kitchen to feed the giant sea turtles, and to wet them with buckets of sea water. A gardener comes with a hose and swishes the walks and plantain leaves when the maids have finished sweeping. With their brooms they also rout the pigs that have snorted their way out of the brush behind the hotel to scrabble for leftovers where the garbage is dumped.

Meanwhile, from farther up the mouth of the river, a string of horses is being led to be tethered on a rail under a *palapa*, the traditional palm-thatched umbrella common to the beaches of Mexico. Horses may be rented for riding excursions up in the hills; the gentler burros as well.

The first guests appear from their cabañas, shading their eyes at the bay, then wander into the dining room, where coffee has been set out on the bar. After breakfast they go onto the beach, each taking the chair and umbrella in the place allotted to him. By then, speedboats will have put out from the yacht club, towing water-skiers—jaunty and nearly off balance—to the mouth of the bay, where they crisscross each other's blue-white wakes.

At noon the excursion boat appears from around the point, and the lilting Latin rhythms of marimba and accordion and maracas are heard. Day-trippers wave from the rail, while the boat anchors out from the hotel and smaller craft bring them ashore. Their complacently inquisitive looks change to ones of startled apprehension as they are borne beachward on a sweep of waves, until they can clamber onto the sand, trying not to wet their ground-gripper shoes.

For three hours they swarm across the beach, take over the bar and dining patios for lunch, ride the burros up to see the view, or snap their Instamatic Kodaks at local color: women squatting at the edge of the river, using wooden paddles on their cotton clothes the way their ancestors did in the days of the *conquistadores*. The river does not flow immediately into the bay, but is checked in a brackish lagoon by a tidal sandbar until the lagoon floods and runs over the top of the bar, the current devouring the sand and cutting a channel which eventually widens to empty the dammed-up water into the bay, fresh water meeting salt. The tourists gather to watch the sides of the bar cave in, when the river exerts its final pressure, and a good deal of Kodachrome film is exposed to record the phenomenon. That is what one does at Boca de Oro, watch the river flow into the bay.

Around a quarter to three they will load up again and be returned to the excursion boat, the marimba will play, maracas shake, the whistle sound, the boat will weigh anchor and be gone. Ten minutes later the *playa* will be peaceful again, back in the possession of the hotel guests. By five it will be deserted as they all disperse for their naps and to get ready for dinner.

Between six and eight they gather in the bar, drinking. From eight to ten they dine. Days are short at Boca de Oro, and few are not abed, singly or otherwise, by 1 A.M. Tomorrow will be no different from today, the fishing boats putting out at six, the beachboys raking, the maids sweeping, the gardener watering, breakfast, beach, the excursion boat, marimbas, maracas, burros, the rest. The only thing that changes is the guest list. As the brochure says, Las Cinco Palmas is perfect for "getting away from it all." At ten the Delco generator is shut down, and illumination is provided in each cabaña by candles or by kerosene lanterns, which are difficult to read by, but cast romantic shadows. Later, those still awake are in the bar, drinking again, and applauding the young and handsome couple who perform the flamenco as it is done in Madrid; the rest are making love or sleeping.

One morning in the autumn of 1975, however, the almost invariable and inviolable tranquillity of Boca de Oro was shattered by a piercing scream, so loud that it seemed to rush from the *Número Uno* cabaña, where it originated, all the way across the bay to the village, where the church bell was tolling. It first awoke, then froze, the tenants of the other cabañas, while dogs roused themselves and barked, and the help came running in alarm, first the maids, then the waiters, then the manager, followed by his wife. Scream sounded on scream, while guests tumbled from their beds and grouped themselves outside the cabaña from which the cries issued. Both Alvarezes were inside, discovering what the trouble was, and finally the dread word was heard:

"Scorpion!"

At last the screams ceased, and a measure of calm was restored. Steve, followed by Cupie, backed through the door and shook his head at the assembled group.

Scorpion, no. *Cucaracha,* yes.

So concluded the brief drama over a cockroach. My, didn't she holler some, they said on their way to breakfast. "She" had arrived the previous evening from Mirabella, not on the excursion boat, but by privately chartered craft. The hotel register gave the name in a not altogether precise hand as Ms. Norah Dunn, though this was not her true identity, which was far better known. But her fellow guests, unaware of who she really was, were nevertheless interested, since she did not appear in the dining room at dinnertime, but asked that a tray be sent to her cabaña. This request had made her the object of immediate speculation, meals never being served in the rooms, but Cupie Alvarez reported that Ms. Dunn was not feeling well after the boat crossing.

After the *cucaracha* episode, she appeared for breakfast only when the dining room had emptied, eating by herself at a corner table. She came onto the beach at midmorning. The beachboy had given her a chair prominently situated in the midst of everything, but Ms. Dunn preferred that it be placed far to one side, close to the library, where nobody sat. She wore a bikini, a Hermès scarf covered by a chic straw hat, and dark glasses. One of the regular guests, a Mrs. Atwater, whose husband owned a chain of lube and transmission-repair stations in Arizona, said that this Miss or Mrs. Dunn must have tender skin because she stayed completely under her umbrella. She had that pale, milky flesh that many brunettes have, though Mrs. Atwater was not sure that Ms. Dunn was a perfectly natural brunette; she thought she detected the tone of Clairol, or Preference by L'Oréal at best. (Mrs. Atwater was not wrong.) She obviously had money, because her bikini was a Gernreich original and her beach tote came from Gucci. Evidently a reader, she had brought out of the tote a number of hard-back books, one of which, *A Guide to Inner Peace* by Dr. Bert Fleischer, she was already halfway through. The dark glasses she wore were large, with narrow gold frames. They looked expensive, too, and hid a good deal of her face. She made frequent applications of sun lotion, rubbing the cream in well and wiping her fingertips with a violet-colored tissue so sand wouldn't stick. Her fingernails and toenails were immaculately lacquered a frosted lilac shade. She was "busty" and rather large through the hips. She didn't smoke, but occasionally would pop a Tic Tac mint into her mouth. She obviously took good care of herself; Mrs. Atwater judged that she owed her figure to massage and diet, and was probably fifty if a day.

Ms. Dunn lunched by herself, under a *palapa*, and after lunch she walked up the beach to see the lagoon filling, then was observed entering the American couple's handicraft shop. She returned after the excursion boat left and retired to her cabaña. She was not seen at cocktail time, but Mrs. Atwater was quick to note that one of the single window tables had been set and there were flowers on it; she surmised (correctly) that arrangements had been made with the management for the new guest to take her meals independent of the family style of the rest. Rather hoity-toity, Mrs. Atwater said. Ms. Dunn did not appear until everyone was seated and forks were already clattering, when she slipped into her place and was greeted by Cupie, who served her herself.

Her history was a curious one. She was not Norah Dunn, but, in fact, Lorna Doone, of the movies. And she had come as a quasi criminal, in flight not only from the law, but from her own problems, fancied or otherwise. Several months before, she had walked out of Robinson's department store in Beverly Hills, to be apprehended on Wilshire Boulevard by two plainclothesmen who requested that she return to the store, where it was discovered she was wearing, under her own clothes, garments from the ladies' department, all unpaid for. The ensuing legalities had caused her such acute mental distress that she again began consulting a well-known Beverly Hills psychiatrist—he had treated her on numerous earlier occasions, with no noticeable results. Seven weeks after the embarrassing Robinson's contretemps she set fire to the shot-silk bedroom curtains of her Brentwood house, which resulted in considerable damage. When the insurance investigators responded to her claim, she said it must have been the fault of the wiring where the lamp plugged in. They could find nothing wrong with the wiring, and because the claim was a large one, including coverage of a full closet of clothes and two fur coats, and since it was the third claim registered by the policyholder in as many years, an investigation more thorough than might have been normal was instituted. Unable to face such fastidious inquiry, and with legal difficulties erupting in the shoplifting matter, she had abruptly decided that she must "get away for her health."

There was a particular reason she had chosen Boca de Oro, which had nothing to do with its obvious physical attractions. It had been her hope that she would be invited to race with her friends the Sandlers on their yacht, the *MorryEll,* from La Jolla to Cabo San Lucas at the tip of Baja California, and from there to Acapulco. Not that Lorna especially enjoyed sailing, but one of the members of the group was a man in whom she had for some time been interested. The hoped-for invitation not materializing, she had decided to arrive well in advance and surprise the sailing party when they put in at Boca.

She had plenty of time to get herself in hand. The doctor was correct, her nervous crisis had been coming on again for some time, but with the sun, the sea, and some quiet, she would condition herself, and when her friends arrived she would be in the pink. All that was required was that nature should do its work, that she eat and sleep and relax. No one knew where she was, not even her son or daughter, her doctor or her attorney; only her best friend, Nan Pringle. She found it an agreeable condition, knowing there were no telephones to bother her; no lunch engagements to keep; no psychiatrists' appointments to remember; no letters arriving with disturbing news. The weather was practically guaranteed, and by the time the *MorryEll* put in she would have a very nice tan, thank you. Just getting on the plane had given her a sudden surge of relief, as if when the rubber wheels lifted from the runway she had become a disembodied spirit and that spirit were racing away, somewhere ahead of her, leaving behind those multitudinous heaps of problems, irksome, annoying things. She couldn't imagine what had made her do such a silly thing, setting fire to the curtains, and she had herself one last good cry—she was certain it was the end of those lachrymose fits that burst on her at the most inconvenient times—and felt buoyant and forward-looking. The past was the past, and once the Sandlers et al arrived, she hoped they would bear her away again under white sails to who knew what, but surely not inconsiderable, joys. All she had to do was get hold of herself.

She really must.

She hated the name. Lorna Doone. When her teachers called on her she had shrunk with embarrassment. In grammar school the other children had called her Lorna Dumb or Lorna Doom. Then one day in the A&P she passed a pyramid display of Lorna Doone cookies, on sale. She stole a box. On the wrapper was a picture of a pretty girl, and the cookies were buttery and sweet. She brought them home and asked her mother if she was named after the cookie. No, from a book, her mother told her. Lorna found the book at the library; it was by Blackmore, the Victorian tale of an English country girl who survives a clan feud, inherits land and titles, and marries the man she loves. In time the real Lorna identified herself with the original heroine, and thought it was all very romantic. Then, on another day, in a stationery store where they sold French records and periodicals, the saleswoman, having learned her name, asked if she was related to the star. What star? *Eeraynee Doone.* Lorna had never heard of Eeraynee Doone. Turned out it was Irene Dunne; Miss Dunne became her idol. From there on, given the book and the movie star and the cookies, her name didn't sound so dumb to her. She took boxes of the cookies to school and displayed them prominently on her desk, and found the boys stopping by to be offered one. Soon they were all calling her "Cookie," but she knew it wasn't the cookies they were after when they whistled "Lookie, lookie, lookie, HERE COMES COOKIE. Walkin' down the street." She knew what they were after, and she knew she had it.

Since babyhood her hair had always been blond; since childhood she had always been told she was pretty. Pretty enough to be in the movies? Certainly. It had not been difficult. The distance from Santa Monica, where she was born and brought up, to Burbank, where she was first put under contract, was less than twenty miles. At fourteen she was a baton twirler with the band at Santa Monica High; she wore a white helmet decorated with gold feathers, a short, flirty costume, and white kid boots. She had the best legs of any of the girls, and all the boys said they were sensational. Her marks were not good. She did the lindy hop to "And the Angels Sing" and "Elmer's Tune." At UCLA, after the war, she was still twirling a baton for the Saturday afternoon games. She wore a Ginger Rogers pageboy with her hair parted on the side and held with a silver barrette, and cashmeres, and plaid skirts and imitation pearls. All the boys were still after her, and they listened to "Racing with the Moon" by Vaughn Monroe; but her marks were still not good. Then her picture was on the cover of *Look*, heading a feature called "Vets Go Back to School . . . with Girls." She and nine other beautiful coeds had been picked by the editors to illustrate the article. The agent Viola Ueberroth brought the picture to the attention of a studio executive, a test was arranged, and she was signed at Warners. She had no training and got little help, but they put her in a picture with Dolly the Talking Cow. Her mother, Selma, had told her she was just a dumb bunny and to keep her mouth shut or people would find out how stupid she really was. She did what they told her to. In the studio commissary she would see Alexis Smith, who was working with Cary Grant; and Lauren Bacall, who was working with Humphrey Bogart; and Bette Davis, who was working with Glenn Ford. Lorna was working with a cow.

After that she did a small part in *Nora Prentiss,* with Ann Sheridan, a small part in *Flaxy Martin,* with Virginia Mayo, a small part in *The Adventures of Don Juan,* with Errol Flynn. Her mother worried about her working with Flynn; there'd been the statutory rape scandal, and Selma didn't want him "in like Flynn" with *her* daughter. Lorna said oh, no, Mr. Flynn was a very nice man, a gentleman. Shortly after that, Warners dropped her. She went to RKO. Went to Columbia. Went to Fox. She did twenty-seven pictures between 1948 and 1953, all B's. She was always terrified of the camera, never knew what she was doing, she moved where the director told her, said the lines the way the director told her, and if she was required to cry, they blew glycerin in her eyes.

Ann Sheridan was the "Oomph Girl"; the studio flacks decided to push Lorna as the "all-American Cookie" and couldn't you just eat her all up, mmmmm. Privately she thought of herself as Lorna Dumb. The image of the "all-American Cookie" somehow eluded her. But through trial and error she had concocted a screen persona out of fragments of other personalities, actresses she had watched and who seemed to have something. She always thought of people as "types": there was the "sexy type," the "outdoor type," the "lady type." She wondered what type she was. The cute type, they told her, the adorable type. You know—"all-American Cookie"? Oh, I get it. But she wasn't sure. She pieced herself together the way a film cutter puts together a picture, from snippets—a gesture here, a hairdo there, a way of wearing a flower, a penchant for mantel leaning, a manner of sweeping into a room as if she weren't terrified, and what didn't work for her she quickly scrapped: Joan Crawford's ankle-strap shoes, Marie Windsor's pompadour or Jane Wyman's bangs, Stanwyck's walk, Paulette Goddard's eyebrow arch. The year she'd been named one of the Deb Stars by the make-up artists and hairdressers at the Palladium, she didn't bother with tiaras or a crown that lighted up by means of concealed batteries hidden under a peplum, the way Lori Nelson had, but simply asked the hairdresser to give her a Grace Kelly French twist and had Wardrobe lend her elbow-length white kid gloves, and she maintained an enviable decorum while the rest gushed like the starlets they were. If Hitchcock needed a new Grace Kelly, here she was, Martha Hyer notwithstanding. She had a little sewing lady on Cynthia Street who could copy anything and run it up on her Singer, and you could be sure the darts would be in the proper places. Publicity was all right, but she had never gone in for gimmicks. Let Debra Paget stick her T-bird all over with plastic jewels, let Vicki Dugan wear a dress cut down to the cleft in her buttocks, let Jayne Mansfield cavort in her pink shag-rugged bedroom, let Debbie Reynolds sell Girl Scout cookies. She maintained an expression that was cool, aloof, even a trifle prissy, but it spoke volumes to the right observer.

She married to get away from her mother. He was a cameraman, Harvey Lacks (Lorna Lacks was a *very* bad name). Harvey was the type person who wanted to adore you, and he thought she was the most beautiful creature he'd ever photographed. He lusted after her at breakfast, would come home from the studio at lunch to have her, would be waiting for her downstairs before they went to a party. They were living in the San Fernando Valley then, in a really sweet ranch-style home, and when she came down he would look at her on the landing, and she was so beautiful he couldn't take his eyes off her. He would get her on the couch, then the floor, literally tearing her clothes off, and they would never get to the party at all; when he was through with her, her make-up was a mess and her hair, too, to say nothing of the clothes. It was legal rape, she thought.

After Harvey came "Brownie" Brown (a little better, Lorna Brown), a packager of frozen foods. They had two children, Jeffrey and Carrie; eventually broke up, reconciled, took a "second honeymoon" cruise to the South Seas and Far East, broke up again, divorced. By that time she'd worked her way back from Van Nuys to the other side of the hill; from ranch style to English Tudor. Then there was Cape Cod, followed by Southern Plantation. There were plenty of men: Jerry the jockey, who used to hit her; Wes the stunt man, who hit her harder; and Stan the baseball player, who didn't hit her but would have liked to. In between, an assortment of musicians, small-time directors, actors. She hadn't really known any of them, any more than they'd known her. Why was it always so difficult for someone really to get to know her? Somehow it didn't matter in the end; she was a rolling stone, and what moss she gathered was mostly accidental. She did, however, learn to do centerpieces out of vegetables—flowerettes of broccoli and cauliflower, and little cherry tomatoes for accent. Pillar to post, man to man, and she kept looking for the one she could really love, really respect, really worship, but somehow it never panned out. She was a man's woman and she needed a man to tell her what to appreciate; she never dared laugh at the theater until he laughed first and then she knew it was all right. One of them—Brownie, she thought it was—said she'd invented herself, which was probably as close to the truth as she could get. Eventually she was hidden away in the hills behind a wall, where she was maintained in style by a famous industrialist–movie producer notorious for his eccentricities and the women he kept hidden behind walls in the hills; Lorna knew of at least three others in similar situations. She didn't care; the checks came, the bills were paid; she saw him seldom, and she had a Georgian silver tea set on the sideboard and original oil paintings.

Through Viola she met Sam Ueberroth. He was an important man, up by his bootstraps and his sister Viola's help, but people said he was a cold fish. He told her he liked her class, would put her in a picture, an A. She moved out of the industrialist's house to an apartment, where Sam could visit her when his wife wasn't looking. One night at Ciro's she was overheard from a partially open telephone booth: "Listen, Sam Ueberroth, if you don't give me that part, the fuck's off!" She was very angry. The part was that of the girl in *The Miracle of Santa Cristi*. She got the part; afterward she got Sam.

She had done nothing but B's—oaters, cops and robbers, and programmers—and now she had done her first A. The picture was religious, but hardly faithful to the book. Fedora's presence in her comeback role as the Virgin caused a sensation. The premiere was at Hollywood's famous Carthay Circle and she had swept under the long canopy in a Jean Louis strapless and a white fox, and Steve Allen interviewed her on TV. She was "very excited," she "knew it was going to be a wonderful evening," and afterward the audience had risen en masse and applauded the actors. Irene Dunne, who was a good Catholic, said she had been greatly moved, and Louella Parsons, who was gooder because she was converted, wept positive buckets. Later, at the post-premiere party, Louella poked her face between Willie and Bee Marsh's heads for the photographers: The Three Converts. Lorna envied them their faith.

She intended to retire and become a Brentwood matron.

Sam had bought a large house, she wore Chanel suits and good jewelry, drove a Mercedes and carried status pocketbooks. She involved herself in Good Works.

Acting had never been an end with her, but a means to an end. She was never good at equations, but one she knew: Work + Bed = Success. Success = Fame = Happiness. For men she had filled as many beds as there were to be filled. She hopped in and out and in again without chagrin; remorse she never knew. With her fine, supple body, and her voluptuous breasts that tipped provocatively upward, and her legs that seemed to go all the way up to her armpits, she had done all right. Still, she wasn't terribly happy. And then, somehow, Stan the baseball player had come back into her life, and Sam threw her out. After that she had her first nervous breakdown.

Selma had already had hers, six or seven of them. Lorna's poor mother was halfway between Culver City and Beverly Hills, the same distance between sanity and madness, in a "home" on Motor Avenue, behind a wire grille. She couldn't remember anything that had happened since Eisenhower was president and Perry Como was on TV. When the astronauts went to the moon and she watched it on television, she maintained that it was a fake and had been staged in a New York studio; anybody knew that men couldn't go to the moon.

Lorna did not permit herself the luxury of feeling sorry for herself, about either her family or her own lack of success with husbands and men in general. She never thought the world owed her a living. She assumed this task herself, but because she lived for the future (believing she had not lived in the past), she did not realize she was not living in the present. In the thirties she had dreams, in the forties she worked hard and faithfully, in the fifties she got her big chance, in the sixties it somehow all went sour, in the seventies—a big question mark. She asked herself those questions any thinking person asks:

Who am I?
What am I doing here?
Where am I going?
Is there more?

She asked, but found no answers. She thought it all rather funny; had been good at laughing at herself, until her breakdown. Then she had become frightened and had skulked away to Menninger's, where they tucked her into bed and a doctor came and talked to her.

She had already begun manifesting "odd" behavior patterns. She had been swiping things from stores since grammar school; once she'd been caught, and it had terrified her that Selma should find out. Still, it was a thrill. Only her friend Nan Pringle had known of this aberration, and had cautioned her: what kind of headlines would it make? She would go into Bullock's gift department with a shopping bag, and start loading things into it. If a salesperson asked if she wished to be helped, she replied airily, "No, thank you; just looking." The swag was monumentally stupid, things she didn't want or need. Once she stole a bottle of expensive perfume from a countertop and when she got it home she discovered it was a display item, filled with colored water. She was furious, wanted to return it and demand her money back.

Then, one day, she had noticed one of her gowns hanging on a closet door. The skirt was tulle, and for no reason she touched a match to the hem to see what would happen. It went up like a shot, singeing the front of her hair so she had to cut bangs again. But she liked the sensation of fire, and she would toss lighted matches into the paper-towel containers in ladies' rooms, and leave the place in smoke. Or she would drive through the alleys that ran behind the streets in Beverly Hills, touching off trash cans with lighter fluid, then wait to hear the sirens.

She went back into analysis, and a nice new doctor dredged up enough of her childhood to determine that she had a condition of hyperkinesis, which meant simply that she was the victim of senseless and uncontrollable urges. The cure: love and understanding. Lorna could not resist the impulse to laugh in his face. He was good, that doctor, but not so good that he could resist her body; she invited him to her place, he succumbed, it became a futile relationship, she left analysis again.

When money ran short she got into the habit of kiting checks and it provided problems for her business managers. The checks were usually for small amounts, so she was never prosecuted, but it was embarrassing. The time came when the money Sam had settled on her ran out; she called Vi and said she wanted to go back to work. Vi was kind, said she'd look around, came back with the answer that things were difficult just now. Lorna saw what that meant: nobody wanted her. Naturally, the problem was Stan. Though they only saw one another privately, word had got about in certain quarters. Still, they wanted her on *Hollywood Squares,* for scale. Then, almost apologetically, Vi came up with an offer to do a series of commercials for Perkies, the pop-up breakfast tarts. She became known as the "Perkies girl," friendly and ladylike, with just the touch of class to push the fake blueberries that were inside the "mouth-watering" tarts. Then she made that oh-so-foolish scene at the Biltmore Hotel, in front of the whole baseball team, and when the scandal hit the papers she was finished with her sponsor. "Tart's tarts" they called Perkies; and then the fire. Nan Pringle had told her about Boca de Oro, and though there was no money in her account, she kited one more sizable check, devil take the hindmost, and flew away. Behind her was one burned bridge after another; ahead, the abyss. She did not know why she did the things she did, or neglected the things she did. She did not know why she suffered anguish, felt afflicted, sensed hopelessness. All she knew was that things had a way of not panning out, and that she was becoming terribly afraid.

Peace, she thought, peace. Peace had not come readily to her, she was so used to turmoil in her life; but peace was coming, was just around the corner. Nan was right: Boca was both restful and gay. There was a mariachi band consisting of young men from the village who played familiar melodies like "The Mexican Hat Dance" or "La Paloma," which Lorna knew meant "The Dove." And "South of the Border" and "Maria Elena," which was one of her old Glenn Miller favorites. She adored that parrot up in the tree; the whistle, too fresh. She loved the wash of the waves that lulled you, the sprinkling hoses, the brush of the brooms, the children's cries, the profusion of flowers. The hotel help were polite and clean-looking. The maid who did her cabaña—her name was Rosalia—was considerate and friendly. Rosalia had a narrow waist, flat hips, and breasts like apples, and at fifty-two, Lorna could well envy her.

The manager, Mr. Alvarez, was both too casual and too condescending to suit Lorna's tastes. He was small, lean, dark, and slightly seedy with a Clark Gable mustache and bland brown eyes, one of which seemed to be covering the guests while the other stayed riveted to the cash register behind the bar. He maintained a proper, businesslike attitude toward everyone, leaving Cupie to deal with the social amenities. And no friendlier creature than Cupie had Lorna ever discovered. She was enormous, and never cared what she looked like, but was happy and merry the day long. Her face, for all its poundage, was really very sweet; she must have been a pretty girl at one time. Everyone loved her. Even with all that weight she moved gracefully, on light feet, but how she could have let herself get so large was a mystery Lorna wasn't prepared to plumb. Each morning she would bring her child, Sashia, and the baby, Heidi, out for their morning swim. You couldn't help adoring Sashie either, only four years old but already a coquette. She had a plastic mirror-and-comb set which she carried everywhere, her ears were pierced with gold hoops, and her mother let her use lipstick. She owned "a whole buncha" dresses, and wore a doll-size bikini. How daintily, how balletically she would point her foot into the water, how she would laugh, squeal, flirt with the world. Lorna's daughter, Carrie, had certainly been no Sashia, or Heidi either. . . .

When Lorna arrived at Boca de Oro she had initiated a strict regimen which she observed religiously, a kind of back-to-health-and-sanity program, and adhering to this self-imposed discipline gave her a sense of worthiness. She had not had a cigarette since boarding the plane in Los Angeles. She did not drink, but permitted herself one glass of wine with lunch, another with dinner. She avoided starches and desserts. She performed her exercises unfailingly, both physical and mental. She spent two half-hour periods meditating, and she did her gymnastics twice a day, and swam three times, once in the morning, twice in the afternoon. When she came out of the water she was always careful to cream her elbows.

When her skin had adjusted to the climate she began working on her tan, step by careful step. Meanwhile she kept to herself behind her glasses, under the hat, and improved herself with Dr. Fleischer's *A Guide to Inner Peace*. Still, complete concentration was impossible, for her eyes, behind their plastic lenses, wandered continually, following the steps of the boy named Emiliano. She had been watching him since the very first day.

The awful business of the *cucaracha* hadn't got her off to a particularly good start at Boca. It had been in her bathroom, crawling around the shower pan—imagine mistaking a cockroach for a scorpion! When she finally composed herself, she had to sit on the patio and meditate until the other guests left the dining room; she couldn't face them after such a scene. It was while sitting, admiring the view, that she had a second shock, but of a different kind altogether—a shock of joy, of recognition, yes, even of mystery. She had had in her mind for some time pictures or images of two particular types of men; one was a solid, down-to-earth pipe-and-tweeds sort, stable and intelligent, who would act as her anchor, her rock, who would tell her what to do, and when and how to do it. He represented Security. Richard, who was on the *MorryEll*, was this type. Then there was a second type, a man whose sheer

113

physical impact caused her heart to beat faster when she just looked at him, made her juices gush, made her feel all hot and cold—a man who might carry her off without a thought of what had gone before, of what was left behind, into some bright, silver-shining future where there would be only love and passion through every day and every night. Naturally this man represented Romance. For her, he would be a god she could worship, and how strange it was, how incredible, how miraculous, that on this very first morning at Boca de Oro the god should have appeared to her.

She had completed her meditation period and was looking out past the point of rocks extending from the walk below her patio, where the water lay calm and blue in the early sunlight. Suddenly she saw a shape under the limpid surface of the water. She thought at first it was a large fish of some kind, until the shape came closer to shore, and closer, and then with a sudden, wet, dazzling rush, emerged from out of the depths, walking through the shallows. This god. A type of merman, with fishfeet, and carrying a kind of trident, which had a fish impaled on it. Like a sea god. His face was masked, so she couldn't see it, but she knew how beautiful he must be. His skin was brown and shining, he had a perfect body, a torso like a piece of Roman armor. She thought she could span his waist with her two hands, it was so slim. On he came, drops of water like jewels flinging about as he shook his arms, his hair, that dark, glossy blue-black hair.

"Emiliano!" one of the beachboys called, and the god waved. He pushed his snorkeling mask onto his forehead, slipped his feet out of his swim fins, and carrying his spear gun and catch, he went loping along the sand toward the hotel. Emiliano? She hadn't heard of any gods named Emiliano, but in her private pantheon, he would do. She rushed through breakfast, and put on her brightest bikini and went onto the beach. She had the beachboy put up the umbrella where she could observe this wonder, Emiliano, without being noticed. He was around all day, in his white trunks, being friendly with everyone, a flashing white smile, so lithe, so graceful, so . . . godlike. Tall, dark, and handsome, every coed's dream. At lunchtime she inveigled Cupie into sitting a moment at her table, and information was subtly elicited concerning Emiliano's true self. The god, it seemed, was employed for the season as a flamenco dancer; he and his partner performed every night in the bar. And his partner, it turned out, was Rosalia, the maid.

Well, Lorna said, she had traveled all through Spain, and adored flamenco; she certainly would enjoy seeing the team perform. In addition to dancing, Emiliano sometimes tended bar, or oversaw the beachboys, or helped Steve manage the hotel. Behind her dark glasses, Lorna watched him carefully that afternoon; he seemed to enjoy everyone's respect and admiration, he had presence and authority and the grace of a *caballero* of old Mexico. In short, a most special man.

Starting at sundown and continuing through the evening and into the night, everyone gathered at the bar. It opened out onto the beach patio, and the guests all congregated to drink banana daiquiris or coco locos, a deadly concoction of four rums, brandy, cream, and other exotic ingredients—no one was ever specific as to the recipe—served in a coconut shell and made pretty with a flower. Coco locos cost four dollars and were meant to last a long time. Lorna wouldn't touch them; she had an orangeade or a Coke with lemon. Nor did she go into the crowded bar itself, preferring instead one of the patio tables, well away in a corner. There was candlelight and music and it was really very lovely. Over the bar was a mural, a curved panel behind the cash register, framed in bamboo. The scene depicted an Aztec temple, with renderings of Montezuma on one side and Cortés on the other. Between them was an eagle, and below this a serpent, crowned by a bird. The serpent was intricately decorated with reticulated designs on its scaled back, and a forked tongue protruded from the mouth; the bird was brightly feathered. Lorna had no idea what these figures represented. From her conversation with Cupie she knew about some of the people in the bar: the honeymooners, always hand-in-hand—he was plain, she plainer; they nudged and touched and whispered and laughed; their skins were unattractively red and Lorna didn't know why people didn't take more care in the sun; she speculated as to what the newlyweds had in common and how they would make a go of things. There was the couple from Duluth —she'd heard "Duluth" several times—God knew what people did in Duluth. There were the people called Atwater; she knew those types: he was hearty and full of jokes, she was gushy; both were to be avoided. Mr. Atwater ankled over, introduced himself as Walt, and asked if they mightn't buy her a drink; she thanked him politely, but no. She had nothing in common with them, they would only talk about themselves and would ask how *she* was in order that they could tell her how *they* were; wasn't that always the way? There was Joan

Taylor, who ran the handicraft shop—she was tall and cool and stylish, though hardly what you'd call beautiful—and the man she lived with, Bob something—craggily handsome, with one of those healthy year-round tans and bright eyes; an innocence about him, the innocence of age, Lorna decided. Though they nodded and smiled pleasantly, they didn't trouble her, but continued talking with an elderly couple named Tashkent, who lived in a house up on the hill and came down in the evenings to socialize. They seemed sweet enough. Later the group was joined by the young local doctor, Patrick O'Connor, who ordered a coco loco and tried to smile at her. She avoided him. There was also a smart New York couple; he a fashion photographer, she a writer of children's books. Cupie said they had a town house that had been featured in a magazine and were often mentioned in Suzy Knickerbocker and even Earl Wilson. Cupie came and asked if Lorna would like to sit at the communal table; Lorna appeared to give it thoughtful consideration, it honestly sounded so tempting, then with a rueful laugh said perhaps she'd better just take one by herself in the corner, if that would be all right. Be our guest, Cupie said.

After the meal she resumed her place on the patio, half hidden in the shadows, but her face attractively illuminated by a candle, to watch the dancing. The couple appeared in a spotlight in ruffled costumes, snapping castanets, and they were really quite good. They put on that scowling gypsy look flamenco dancers always have, and stamped their feet and cried out Spanish words no one understood, and arched their backs and profiled their heads and clapped their hands, Rosalia throwing her long shining hair across her face and swirling her ruffled train, Emiliano flashing his dark eyes, grimacing passionately so his teeth shone white, his black wet hair falling over his eyes, the material of his shiny mohair trousers cut so tightly it showed the bulges of his thighs and the incredible curve behind. When the dancing was over she hoped they would come past her table so she could tell them how much she enjoyed them, but instead they sat with Joan and Bob and the doctor, who, at last catching her eye, indicated an empty chair. But she shook her head and left.

She went along the walkway, where the dried bougainvillaea petals fell like confetti; she stood looking out on the beach. Couples were huddled in the dark and she supposed some were making love. She went to her cabaña, and when the Delco went off she lit her lantern and read herself to sleep: *Centennial* by James Michener. She'd been meaning to get to it.

She found herself getting up earlier than she had for years; she liked the quiet morning, the little boats going out with their long rods and nets, the busy beachboys, the barking dogs, the sweeping maids; she thought of her cleaning woman's vacuum on the wall-to-wall carpeting; none of that at Boca de Oro. She sat on her patio and did her meditation exercises, and when she would again open her eyes, bringing her from that inner peaceful world she sought, there would be Emiliano out on the point of rocks. She would wave and call *¿Qué tal?* which her Spanish phrase book said was "How are you?" She liked watching his lithe brown body in the water, to see his powerful legs kicking the blue rubber fins, like a dark brown fish down there. She simply had to bring her camera and take some shots of him and his catch and have him tell her the names of the fish in Spanish. Oh, *trucha?* and Oh, *bacalao?* She was glad she could appreciate his remarkable qualities without falling all over him, as the other women were inclined to do, thinking up little extras for him to bother with, showing him snapshots of their daughters, suggesting he give them snorkeling lessons, asking to be shown his spear gun. Though his *Buen' días, señorita,* was no more friendly to her than to them, though his smile for her was exactly as it was for the others, she liked to think he harbored the secret knowledge that they were fellow entertainers, and thus kindred spirits. And after all, when you came right down to it, he was just a beachboy; but *muy simpático.*

It had occurred to her that in the matter of Emiliano she had perhaps made a mistake darkening her hair, she had heard that Latins liked blondes, but there was nothing to be done about that now. She wondered what impact it might produce on him to learn who she really was, so she dropped hints to the maid, Rosalia, but evidently Rosalia hadn't seen her movies. Then she removed her glasses right in public; still nobody recognized her. Finally, one noon when the excursion boat had come in and she was having lunch, a little girl came and poked a camera in her face. Click! Don't do that, she told her. My mother says you're a movie star, the child said; are you? Lorna smiled, wouldn't say, and then the mother came over. I'm terribly sorry to bother you, she began, but we've been wondering just who you are. So have I, thought

117

Lorna, and smiled. The woman seemed to recognize the smile. Why, you're Lorna Doone—the Perkies girl! Lorna's smile faded. Nearly forty movies and she was remembered for pop-up tarts. Word got around the beach fast after that; the dreadful woman Mrs. Atwater hurried over and said, Well, Miss Doone, we *tried*. Tried? Lorna repeated. Tried to keep your secret. We knew who you were and we want you to know you can just go on being any way you want to. She said her name was Celia and just to call her "Ceel," and if Lorna wanted to play cards or join them for drinks, her daughter was crazy for her on *Hollywood Squares* and who would have thought that Lorna Doone would be a brunette and what was that lovely nail polish? Oh, Revlon's Misty Lilac?

The loss of her incognito seemed to do nothing to alter her effect on Emiliano. He was as friendly and smiling with her as he was with everybody; but no more. She would wave, he would wave back. She tired of waving, and beckoned instead; he came. Her beach mat had oil on it; might she have another? *Cierto, señorita.* At least he didn't say *señora.* When the exchange of mats had been seen to she initiated a little conversation. She was edified to learn that he was named after Emiliano Zapata, savior of Mexico; Emiliano's brother, Benito, was named for another savior, Benito Juárez. Oh, *Juárez!* Very interesting. She thought it was nice, rather like colored people—no, *blacks*—naming their babies George Washington or Abraham Lincoln. She watched him lope away, those long brown legs, the pale soles of his feet.

At lunchtime she told Cupie that Emiliano ought to be in the movies. Cupie laughed her rich laugh and said, oh, that was just what Emiliano would like.

Ah ha.

Cupie must have mentioned this, because he was more attentive after that. He nodded pleasantly when she asked him the next day if she might be served lunch in the library, it was so restful and shady there. He would check to see. He ran off, she watched him go. He returned, she watched him come. *Sí,* he said, if the *señorita* wished it; the *señorita* did. She handed him a bottle of lotion and asked him to put some on her back. She had on another of her bikinis, aqua and yellow; she lay on her mat while he dropped the oil on her shoulders and she watched the round shapes of his brown knees as he knelt by her to perform this task, and when he was done she offered him a violet tissue to wipe his hands on. Then he went away.

Yes, she thought; a very good type; definitely in the movies. She sunned on her stomach for half an hour, then half an hour on her back, then went into the water. Afterward she called Emiliano again and asked him to put more oil on her shoulders. Following lunch, carried by a smiling Rosalia to the library, she took some more sun, first on her back, then on her front. The glass of wine must have made her drowsy, for she fell asleep. When she awoke she touched her abdomen: her finger made a white spot which immediately became red. She hurried to her cabaña and tore open her cosmetic case, looking for sunburn lotion.

Oh, she said, oh. It was going to hurt and it was going to peel. It was stinging badly by the time she got out of the shower and at dinnertime she felt sick to her stomach. She sent for Rosalia, who sent for Cupie, who got Steve Alvarez, who sent a boy up the hill for the doctor. Dr. O'Connor came and gave her a sedative and a painkiller and a salve. She stayed indoors all next morning, hurting, and gingerly applying the ointment. Returning at cocktail time to see how she was, the doctor brought his drink from the bar, and sat by her bed and made small talk. Call him Pat, he said; Doctor was too formal. He was boyishly affable, red-faced, puffy and bibulous. He cracked jokes while his eyes roved the lines of her body under the light nightdress. His risibilities escaped her; she knew what he wanted. He held her hand in a professional manner, but his hand was as hot as hers. After he left she lay burning on the sheets, and when they brought her a tray she only picked. Emiliano didn't come, as she had hoped he might, to see how she was. She took more painkillers and a Tuinal to make her sleep.

By the following day the burn had stopped hurting but the red remained, sore-looking and ugly, and she fretted about the extent of the peeling. She shrank from the thought of anyone seeing her this way, so she sat under her straw hat and behind her glasses on the patio, first meditating, then reading or doing needlepoint, a therapy she had taken up after Menninger's.

Rosalia was sympathetic, and they had many conversations. The girl seemed intelligent and spoke good English. Lorna professed an interest in her and—what was his name? Oh, yes, Emiliano. Rosalia's face glowed, her eyes shone as she talked of him. He spent six months of the year in "México," which was what they called Mexico City, dancing in a club. There he had another partner, but one day Rosalia hoped to work with him as a team in the capital or in Rio de Janeiro. Had he made love to her? Lorna asked. Rosalia smiled; Emiliano was the best lover in the world.

Lorna nodded; she was sure he was.

When she felt better, she thought she must get away from the cabaña, and since she was still unable to go to the beach she planned a trip to the village, which she had not visited yet. She put on her white Jax slacks and the red bandanna blouse and the pale-blue sneakers, she tied her hair Apache fashion with a scarf, and walked down the beach.

The lagoon had halfway filled and a trio of burros stood knee-deep in the teal-green water, staring vacantly at her. They looked like such amusing, friendly creatures; once she'd had her picture taken astride one in Tijuana, when she and Jerry the jockey went down for the bullfights. She passed the yacht club, and Joan Taylor's shop, went over the bridge, and along a dusty path into the village. She was disappointed. It was dirty and dusty, the houses were ramshackle adobe-and-stick affairs with roofs of broken terra-cotta tiles, and chickens and goats in the yards. Children played there, thin and dirty, and she wondered how people could live like that.

There were some men outside the cantina, and they eyed her as she went past. One of them, tall and gaunt, his face shadowed by a wide-sombrero, nudged his companion and said something. He picked his teeth with a match, his nails were dirty, and the teeth were mostly gold. He wore soiled dungarees which hung in worn, droopy folds about his thin shanks, and a cowboy shirt with a lanyard at the collar. She hurried past and went into the church.

It was the most impoverished church imaginable, adobe walls, thatched roof, and sorry benches for pews. There were plaster figures of saints, garishly decorated with gimcrack ornaments, with the painted faces of cheap dolls. Some women were kneeling before the altar, praying. They were dressed in black and their leather huaraches squeaked as they rose wearily; one of them massaged her knees as she stared at Lorna, who wondered what there was about such a poor, unlooked-after place that made them believe God's Presence was actually there. In the corner was a bottle with bent plastic straws, 7-Up, *hecho en México*.

She had brought her camera and she took several pictures of the most interesting local color she could find, and headed back toward the bridge. The man in the sombrero left his companions in front of the cantina and moved along the shadow of the building. He stood under an awning, picking his gold teeth, watching her go. She hurried across the bridge; when she looked back he was following.

She went quickly up the steps of the handicraft shop and

entered. Bells on the door tinkled, and a voice called from the patio. Joan Taylor was weaving at a loom under a *palapa*. She rose to greet Lorna warmly and invited her to sit down. The patio overlooked the bay on one side and the village on the other. Who is that man? Lorna asked; she could see him at the far end of the bridge, leaning on the railing and looking down into the water. Joan said the man was called Ávila; he was a local character, *El Loco*. The crazy one. He trapped birds up in the hills, and sold them at Mirabella for zoos or bird fanciers. And snakes as well. Why snakes? Lorna asked. Joan explained: they were sold for their venom, their skins, their flesh; in Mexico snake meat was considered a delicacy,

She left her weaving and took Lorna into the shop, adjoining the house that Bob—Somers was his last name, an ex-professor from Oregon State—had built himself. They had been in Mexico for twelve years, and they loved it. There were bolts of fabric, Hong Kong silks and Egyptian cottons in beautiful colors; Joan traveled to pick them out. There were Mexican handicrafts, Oaxaca blackware, silver from Taxco, bright woven belts with tassels from Cuernavaca. Lorna remembered that Rosalia's sister Eusabia, who worked at the hotel, had just had a baby, and she thought a little christening gift might be nice; she picked out a sweet blouse—it wasn't expensive—and had Joan wrap it. Then she found a lovely pair of real tortoise-shell barrettes she wanted, and some soap, and a candle in the shape of a pineapple. Afterward Joan made tea and they went back to the patio and watched the fishing boats come in. It was very peaceful and relaxing—a good life, Joan said. Oh, said Lorna, she could see that; it must be fabulous. Privately she wondered how they could waste their time in such a place, letting the rest of the world go by. They certainly weren't getting any younger: Joan must be all of forty and had crepy elbows; Bob's hair was silver-gray.

Joan confessed that she'd had three husbands, and wasn't taking any more chances on marriage; Lorna said she knew what she meant.

She had the habit of taking off her glasses when speaking personally to someone, and also, at times, of removing them to listen. She put them on and took them off constantly as the conversation went on. She found Joan *muy simpática,* and talked at length about herself. She liked Joan, she really did. She was the sort of person you'd like to have as a friend, and Lorna mentioned her breakdowns and some of the problems

121

she'd experienced. She said that when she got home again, she thought she might take up cooking, a gourmet class, and perhaps some extension courses at UCLA, possibly in psychology or social sciences, *eck cetera.* Joan thought that was a wonderful idea. Lorna said she had friends who donated time to Mount Sinai and Saint John's hospitals; she thought she might do something like that. Joan nodded agreement. Lorna said she meant to spend less time on the telephone or visiting at coffeeklatsches around the neighborhood, waste less time on trivial things like that. Joan thought that was a good idea. Or travel was broadening; perhaps a trip to New York—shopping, theater, Fun City; Joan agreed. Lorna talked about her children. Like Joan, Carrie had also managed three husbands, but in seven years, and she was only in her twenties. Presently she was living with a professional skydiver in Malibu canyon, but who knew when she would show up on Lorna's doorstep with her three-year-old twins; as mother and daughter, when apart they naturally missed one another, but together they were impossible. Jeffrey was another problem, a perpetual adolescent, incapable of settling down at any job. Successively he'd been an assistant director, an apprentice film cutter, an agent at William Morris, a producer who had produced nothing, a quick-sketch artist at the Renaissance Fair, and a rodeo rider, *eck cetera,* and he brought home the most dreadful girls. But, Lorna said, she was determined to look on the bright side, she was taking a positive view, she was working with good attitudes. That was wonderful, Joan said.

Maybe, Lorna said, she might open up a gift shop, like Joan's; was it difficult? A lot of hard work, she supposed; Joan said that it was. Well, Lorna said, conversation becoming confidences, confidences confessions, she really had no idea what she wanted to do; one day it was one thing, one day another. Her doctor never pressed her into decisions, and since her last collapse she had felt disinclined toward any decisions. Truth to tell, in order to pay hospital expenses and medical bills—hers, her mother's, Carrie's—she had mortgaged the property and a balloon payment loomed, threatening foreclosure. The indiscretion of these generously offered confidences did not extend to the more distressing matters of the theft or the fire, but there were other topics: she just loved that Cupie Alvarez, though how she could let herself get so fat, don't say it was mental, it was gluttony, and how between them she and Steve had made such an adorable child, except Lorna didn't think children's ears should be pierced so young; she could remember back to when Carrie was that age, *the* age, for after that they were only problems, but it wasn't easy raising a child in Hollywood in that kind of environment—how did people from Duluth know what Hollywood was really like—and when Lorna had suggested dieting to Cupie, Cupie had only laughed and said Steve liked her that way, so why bother?

Why indeed, Joan said.

Lorna sensed that she was rattling and forced herself to stop, then Joan suggested a small dinner party in the near future, and asked how long Lorna's stay would be. Without alluding to Richard by name, Lorna spoke of the Sandler's boat, the *MorryEll*—his name was Morrie, hers Ellen—and that they were in the regatta and should be arriving soon at Cabo San Lucas; meanwhile she would love to come to dinner. She left feeling that she had made a friend, and sensed a lightening of her spirits.

She walked back along the shore, telling herself it was the children that mattered. She would Keep On for their sakes, but knowing that "their sakes" didn't enter into it. They didn't care; they had their own lives. Let them go, Nan had said over and over; she had already let Selma go, in her mind anyway, but not her babies. After the awful business with Stan she'd come home and swallowed pills, but had taken the precaution to see that Nan's lights were on down the street. She came, took care of her. Hospital again, stomach pump, Carrie crying beside the bed, Mummie, haven't you learned anything? Jeffrey sullen and embarrassed; she couldn't get either of them to laugh, though the whole episode was just that: funny.

The lagoon had broken through the bar and lay flat and nearly empty. She looked up to where the sun hung low over the highest peak of the mountain, which they called the Sleeping Maiden. It was like a tall green conical hat, and at the very top, wheeling spokes of light rayed out as if a jewel were buried in back of it. Then, as her eye returned to the level again, she saw the man called Ávila, *El Loco*. He was standing by a palm tree, watching her. As she passed he touched his two fingers to the brim of his sombrero. She did not acknowledge him. She looked away, out to the bay, and hurried back to the hotel.

When she had taken her purchases to her cabaña, she returned to the beach for a sunset walk. The man was nowhere to be seen. The beach was deserted, the bay was bright gold, the sand, where it was wet, a silvery purple and blue, all the pale colors of the caftan she'd put on. It was her blue time of day; she was often subject to fits of melancholy during this twilit hour, while people gathered at the bar and the music played and Cupie went around lighting the candles. It was the time of day she most disliked being alone. She asked herself why she didn't join the others; answer: she just didn't feel like it. She saw Emiliano at the bar, setting up his glasses and peeling lemon rind. She had put a hibiscus blossom in her hair, and the feel of the sand on her bare feet made her think she was a girl again, in the good old days of "Elmer's Tune," and she began to run along the shore, her shadow flying before her across the sand. The girlish shadow of an older woman reaching out for something that lay just ahead, a blue shadow rippling over the wet sand, and her heart felt suddenly certain that things were going to pan out after all.

Several of the familiar faces had disappeared from the dining room during her sunburn—the chic New York couple, the people from Duluth—but there were new ones. Among them, a trio of secretaries from Minneapolis, Cupie informed Lorna. They looked her over carefully but didn't invade her privacy. None was really what you would call pretty, though they all seemed sweet enough. The most attractive one was a Jewish girl, Miriam Seltzer, who had a marvelous figure and a crushed-fruit look, and wore heavy make-up—scarlet lips, dark eyes. It wasn't difficult to tell what type of personality Miriam Seltzer had: she was vivacious, she flirted with every man, and by way of flaunting her charms, she wore evening things that were cut down to *there*. On the very first night, Pat O'Connor had made a big play for her, and she ate it up. Lorna thought Miriam Seltzer was very foolish: she should be able to see that Pat was only interested in one thing. All that sitting and talking seriously over the candle, as if what he was saying were important or profound, when all he wanted was to get her into bed. He did. Miriam made no bones about leaving the bar after the flamenco dancing and going up the hill. When she came down next morning nobody said anything, no one even paid attention. She lay on a mat getting sun and oiling her sleek tan and looking very rested.

Lorna wondered how Pat was in bed.

That evening they were together again, and oh, the looks that passed between them at dinner. Didn't she realize it was only a one- or two-night stand, that she was just one of any number who came and went, that Pat would have them all if he could? A woman on her own in a vacation spot: Lorna had seen it all before. It was stupid of Miriam to give it away like that, and when she got home she'd look back on it and regret it.

Later, after the Delco had gone off, Lorna watched from her patio. Miriam went to her cabaña, and moments later, carrying a tray of drinks, Pat came. She could hear them in there, talking, then after a while they weren't talking. Lorna went inside and read *Centennial*. The book was heavy, she doubted she'd ever get through it. She lay alone by lantern light, sometimes reading, sometimes thinking. The night sea sounds made her remember other places, other beaches, in other times when she had felt other than she did now. Other beaches, other times, and always with the sea and a man beside her, a man's shoes akilter on the floor, the after-smell of a man's shaving in the bathroom. In the dark, in the unfamiliar silence, with only the sound of the lapping waves and the cries of birds in the jungle, she was easily unnerved. She always took pains, as she had been told to, to shake out her shoes, a precaution against lurking scorpions; but sometimes she thought she heard things crawling in the thatch, could imagine their segmented bodies working their way through from the outside, or breeding in there, could envision their dreadful sting-tails driving into human flesh and secreting their deadly venom. It didn't help to tell herself it was only the night breeze in the straw; just the thought, or threat, of scorpions kept her awake. Occasionally she would hear something drop on the terrazzo flooring, a hard, lumpy, metallic sound. She would light the lantern, get up and shake out her bedclothes, and then kneel on the bed, bending to inspect the floor as far as she could see beyond the circle of light into the darkness. She would leave the lamp lighted on the table, and when the last of the barflies came along the walkway, she could hear their voices; sometimes they were talking about her, not in denigrating terms but only wondering at the lateness of her light, and she had to fight down the impulse to jump up and invite them to stop at the patio for a nightcap. She hated being alone with the thought of scorpions.

Often, having got to sleep at last, she would awake again, her sheets damp from perspiration, and her pillow—but this was from tears, cried unconsciously in the dark. She would lie awake, hearing nothing but the ocean, but hoping for the sound of a voice. Whosoever it might be, she would call or go to it, talk, be friendly, the way other people were. Or she would construct elaborate dialogues in her head: what she

125

would say to Carrie on her return to Los Angeles, or to Jeffrey, how she would confront the insurance people, long involved scenes which gave her every opportunity to spill her guts, using all the clever turns of phrase, all the right words that she couldn't ever think of when she was actually talking to—fighting with—people. And as she lay there, slowly, as though it weren't a part of her at all, her thumb would creep into her mouth, her teeth would scrape nervously, thoughtlessly against it, peeling away the carefully applied polish, and in the morning before she went to breakfast she would have to take the color off and do a new coat.

After breakfast she would not go to the beach, but would sit on her patio, staring at the water, fighting tears whose sudden appearance again dismayed her. When she felt like it, she would get into the hammock and loll, staring impersonally out at the bay, feeling strangely detached from what Nan's travel brochure had described as the "hidden jewel of the Mexican coast," and wondering why she was so unmoved by it. It was like another form of waiting; but for what, other than the *MorryEll* and Richard, it would have been difficult to say.

She saw Emiliano coming out of the water, brownly glistening, in his white trunks. She went onto the beach then, and sat under her umbrella. When he went by with his spear gun she said she'd never seen one, could she have a look? While he obliged her, pointing out and explaining its various mechanisms, she kept noticing little details about him, that his fingernails were trimmed and polished and that his hands were like a sculptor's, or a pianist's. She had friends who talked at lunch about checking a man's thumbs as a clue to the size of more intimate parts, but she'd never believed it. She particularly liked his feet. She thought it remarkable how the foot was overlooked as a beautiful part of a man's anatomy. She would have to get the word for "foot" in Spanish from her phrase book and surprise him with it. That afternoon she asked Emiliano if she might borrow his fins and goggles "just to see what it was like." It was an unfortunate experience, and caused her such a shock that she talked of it for days. There were few bathers other than Cupie and little Sashie in the water at the time. Lorna had waded out to her chest, with her head down, peering through the oval glass, with the plastic snorkel in her mouth, when she saw going past her range of vision a long dark undulating line, like a length of telephone wire. What was attached to the other end of this wire was the most enormous and horrifying creature imaginable, the size of a grand piano, a great batlike creature whose tail the "wire" was, slowly skimming along the bottom. The awful wings as they rose and lowered were black on top and palely spotted underneath, and the thing had a hideous bat's face. She thrust her head from the water and screamed. She splashed her way to shore, crying to Cupie to get Sashie out. Thank God for Emiliano, who came running, and when she told him what she'd seen, he said it was a stingray. He ran for his spear gun, took his fins and snorkel, and his goggled head disappeared in the water. Half an hour later he had shot the ray, and they dragged the ghastly thing up on the beach. They showed her the sharp spear near the base of the tail, which was its poisoned weapon, then some of the villagers came and took the ray with them and cut it up for stew.

She didn't go in the water anymore.

To recover, she spent the remainder of the morning in the library, reading. She had given up *Centennial* in favor of *Atlas Shrugged,* a dog-eared paperback someone had left behind, its pages stained with suntan oil, but she had read *The Fountainhead* and thought she might like it.

Later she saw Rosalia in a hammock near the office, under the tree where the parrot lived. Cradled one in each arm were Sashie and a Mexican child, looking happy as Rosalia sang a song and they sang along with her. From inside the office Lorna could hear the plock plock of Steve Alvarez's typewriter. When Rosalia went back to work Lorna left the library and walked over. She gave each child a hug, then had the little Mexican get out of the hammock until she got in, the way Rosalia had been, and then coaxed the Mexican child back in and put an arm around each of them, telling Sashie she mustn't be afraid of the stingray. Oh, Sashie said, she wasn't afraid; but Lorna was. Well, Lorna said with a nervous laugh, it was such a big thing, and so unexpected. She gave them hugs again, but the children wriggled and the hammock swung uncomfortably. She tried singing to them as Rosalia had, but they didn't like that and they scrambled out, leaving her alone in the hammock. Steve Alvarez was standing in the office doorway, watching. One of the dogs came ambling by and she called it to her and made a great show of petting it; then the dog went away, too.

The excursion boat had brought some new guests: four young men from Los Angeles, tennis players en route to an important match in Mexico City. Lorna thought they couldn't be much older than Jeffrey, but she wished Jeffrey were more like them. They were all very good-looking, with healthy, lean bodies and exuberant spirits. Miriam Seltzer evidently thought they were good-looking, too, for when Lorna came out on the beach next morning, she saw the young men playing volleyball, and Miriam had stationed herself by one of the net posts, applauding the game. She sat with her knees up but spread, showing the crotch of her bikini, and she kept one hand dangling in front of her, which rather than obscuring the area only called attention to it. She was the most vulgar type.

Lorna talked with one of the boys later that afternoon. She stayed under her umbrella with a towel covering her knees, reading. The tallest of them came over and introduced himself. Very polite. His name was Bud, and he asked if they could all have her autograph for their girlfriends back home; she said she would be happy to oblige.

She was waiting at the bar, wearing her shocking-pink Pucci and her white sandals and the pearl earrings Brownie had bought her in Japan during their reconciliation trip. They all came in with Bud in the lead, wearing shorts and alligator shirts, and they reminded her about the autographs. She was prepared, had brought her own pen and four eight-by-ten glossies, which she signed individually, pretending not to notice the other guests watching. There were lots of jokes and good-natured fun, and she accepted the boys' invitation to sit at their end of the family table. After dinner, when the other three, Gil, Dick, and Barry, went to the bar, she and Bud stayed at the table having coffee and watching the moonrise. Emiliano was tending bar, so she laughed a lot and was animated, bending forward over the candle so it caught her features, and sometimes touching Bud's hand to emphasize a point. Then she grew serious, leaning her cheek on her hand and looking out toward the bay with a faraway expression. Why so pensive? Bud asked. She shook her head. Oh, she replied, I was just thinking. She talked about meditation and how very much it was helping her, and he listened with interest. Then she allowed herself to be persuaded to join the others in the bar, and she watched Emiliano making drinks; he seemed not to notice at all how much the center of attraction she was. She allowed Bud to put his arm around the back of her chair, and she turned several times and spoke in his ear— the music was quite loud—her lips brushing against him, and then she let Emiliano see that several times Bud had taken her hand.

She thought she would make herself conspicuous by her absence during the flamenco, and asked to be excused. She stood at the edge of the patio, looking out across the beach and the bay, with the flames of the tiki torches leaping around her, the breeze lifting the corners of her Hermès scarf, and thought she made a pretty picture. Naturally Bud came after her and begged her to stay. No, she laughed, she had to get her beauty sleep. Aw, he said, you're too beautiful, you don't need sleep. But she prevailed, and he walked her back to her cabaña. It was then that he mentioned that he knew Stan Wyckoff. Lorna felt a sharp chill at the mention of the name, but passed it off lightly. Ah, she said, how *is* Stan? She didn't care at all for the way Bud laughed; obviously he'd heard something. On the cabaña patio he tried to kiss her, but she pulled away from his arms and said a firm good night.

Later she could hear the flamenco music and the clatter of Emiliano's heels on the floor and the staccato clap of his hands and his Spanish cries. The passion of the dance. She creamed her elbows and performed her other nightly beauty rituals, put on her nightdress and got into bed. She read by the kerosene lantern, absently rubbing the "frownie" paste-on between her eyebrows. Finally she went to sleep. She was awakened by footsteps along the walkway, then a light rapping at her door. It opened and she saw a dark shape. Hi, Bud said. She could tell he was drunk. He came to the bed and looked down at her. She had cream on her face and curlers in her hair; she told him to leave, but he sat on the edge of the bed. She drew away and when he leaned down to her she struck him. Aw, come on, he said, he knew Stan, didn't she get it? She didn't have to be so careful—he wouldn't tell. He left only when she threatened him with Steve Alvarez. Okay, he said, laughing; he'd be around if she changed her mind.

Next morning they were over near the horse *palapa*, where the three secretaries sat, and they all played volleyball. Miriam Seltzer was with them, and they lunched together, and went to the village in the afternoon. They laughed a lot, and made a very cozy group. That evening they were at the bar, drinking coco locos. Lorna put on her blue caftan and went for a solitary walk along the beach, stopping now and then to examine something the water had washed up. She ate alone that night, resuming her solitary window table, and bringing her book with her. She thought Bud might have apologized for his behavior, but he didn't, and Miriam was dancing with him after dinner. Lorna returned to her cabaña, and whenever she went out onto her patio she could see them, over on the beach on blankets, smoking pot in the moonlight. Very romantic, she *didn't* think.

The next morning she awoke feeling irritable and with a headache. She didn't go to breakfast, but sat on her patio, needlepointing. She knew she ought to meditate, but somehow she couldn't concentrate. There were some plantain leaves hanging down, partially obscuring her view, and she had asked the gardener several times to cut them, but in *mañana* style he had neglected to do it. She tore them away, and when the gardener came by he saw the leaves on the walkway. He looked at them, then picked them up and carried them away. Later, Steve Alvarez spoke to her about breaking down the plantain trees. She didn't care for his tone and told him as much. She decided that despite Cupie, she definitely didn't like Steve. She knew the type—sharp and opportunistic—and she didn't like the elaborate pains he took in referring to "L.A.," saying what a wild place it was and that he knew a "lot of people" there. The implication was clear: Bud had said something to him about the Stan Wyckoff business. She had noticed that Steve's hands often trembled; he drank a lot, and she'd heard about how northerners went to seed in the tropics; all those coco locos. She didn't like him at all.

Next day at lunch she heard talk among the tennis players and the secretaries of taking a ride up the mountain. She hurried to Pedro, the horse man, to reserve a mount, since she had never seen the view, but found that all the horses were taken; she would have to settle for a burro. The party was already starting by the time she had changed into her jeans, and she clambered awkwardly onto the beast's back, with no way of showing what a good horsewoman she could be. Miriam had a horse, but jogged in the saddle like a sack of potatoes, and made the mistake of wearing shorts, which only revealed how fat her thighs really were. They were all up ahead, while the burro plodded patiently behind with some day-trippers off the excursion boat, and she had to listen to their talk all the way up the hill.

The view was most spectacular at Pat O'Connor's house, or across the way at the Tashkents'. When they got there, Lorna stayed aloof from the others, preferring to absorb the splendors of the vista alone, until Bud came over. How ya doing? he asked, trying to be friendly. She adopted a cool attitude. When he asked what the matter was, she demanded to know what he had said to Steve Alvarez about her. He denied having said anything, but she didn't believe him. She moved away, trying to hear what Pedro was explaining to the group in his bad English about the high peak, the Sleeping Maiden—something about the *conquistadores* arriving, and a legend about a temple which they had plundered, and how in bringing the gold down, some greedy Spaniards had drowned in the river, which was why it came to be called the River of Gold. Lorna was more interested in the view—you could see the lagoon filling, and the thatched roofs of the hotel, and she could pick out individual figures. One she had already recognized, Emiliano in his white trunks. He had been talking with some people on the beach; now she saw him come around behind the kitchen and enter the cinder-block cubicle he shared with his brother, Benito. He did not come out again, but then Lorna saw someone who was unmistakably Rosalia going in where Emiliano had already gone, and not coming out either.

The party was already mounting for the descent when Lorna turned away. The sun was hot, her legs were sore, and she regretted having wasted her time on the trip. She regretted the burro more. As slow as it had been coming up, the creature was maddeningly balky going down. He jolted her over the rocks, causing her to sway and lurch, and she was glad she was last in line so no one could see her. Up ahead was Miriam, riding beside Bud, and of course they were laughing. She was more certain than ever that Bud was talking about her.

She had dropped well behind when, from around a bend in the trail farther back, she heard the nicker of a horse. Turning, she saw the man called Ávila, coming down the path; she urged her burro to the side, to let him pass. The great brim of his sombrero was tilted downward over his brow, shadowing his eyes, but he tipped it as he went by, and drew his lips back from his teeth, showing the gold. He said nothing, but went on, a donkey following, and on its flanks hung two softly jogging cloth sacks, under which were curving shields of leather. Not birds, she thought; snakes. Her burro shied as Ávila went by. Then, when he had gone, the burro trembled all over and refused to move, but only stood in the path, twitching his ears. The others were going on; shouting for Pedro, she got off and tried to tug the burro into motion. She found a stick and shook it in the animal's face, but it wouldn't look at her. She was close to crying, and then she did cry, and hit the burro on the rump with the stick. It moved, but not much. She went on hitting it and crying until Pedro rode back and grabbed the stick out of her hands. He ordered her into the saddle, and took the reins, and the burro followed along docilely behind the horse. She didn't look at the others when they caught up to the party, and she tried to explain about the snakes, and the man called Ávila.

By the time they got back to the hotel she knew everybody had heard how she had hit the burro with the stick. She sat on her patio and tried to meditate, but she was in an agitated state. At the cocktail hour, Bud and the other tennis players came out of their cabaña and went along the walkway, none of them looking at her. She sat, burning with shame and hot resentment. She hadn't meant to hit the little beast, only it wouldn't go, what was she to have done?

She was surer than ever that Bud had leaked information about the Stan Wyckoff scandal. Of course it was all true, so what could she do? They had been deeply involved, she and the baseball player, and when the Perkies people had got wind of the affair they had made it known that they didn't want their spokeswoman linked with a black man, a prominent and married one to boot. She was crazy for him, but even if he'd been free, he'd made it clear that he wouldn't marry her. People said it was her mother who objected, but it had been his; her son was not going to marry a white woman no matter how famous. The scandal erupted at a public function. Stan was being honored as Player of the Year at a banquet at the Ambassador Hotel, and it was during the after-dinner speeches, when the jokes had become broader and the talk rougher, that Lorna Doone made her appearance. She was got up like a kootch dancer, in spangled bra and tights, she wore a black Afro wig, and her body was covered with brown make-up. She sauntered casually up to the dais, where the honored guest, her lover, sat, and stood before him, one hand on her hip, the other toying with the curly wig. Well, Stan, she said, am I black enough for you now? She took a drink from the table and dashed it in his face, then turned and just as casually sauntered from the room.

Effective, but it scotched the Perkies contract. People talked about it for weeks.

She never understood why she did the things she did. She was not proud of her past, merely grateful that she had got away with it for so long. Nor was she particularly ashamed; it was the way she was, that was all. The front she had put up for so many years hid many secrets, ones even *Confidential* had never managed to expose. What if they had printed the true story? She had had her first sexual experience at thirteen—not so early, as it turned out when she had compared notes with other women. There was never any notion of love from his side; he had taken, she had given. Once, then many times. After him others, older, more grown up, sophisticated; they took, she gave. Lorna Dumb.

In high school, since she twirled a baton in the band, she came in contact with a lot of athletes; she became a sort of "sports enthusiast," and obliged each of the teams through the seasons, football in the autumn, hockey and basketball in winter, baseball in the spring, and for extra measure there were counselors at a camp up in Malibu; she "saw" to them all. Lorna Doone, the all-American cookie. Later she spent a lot of time in Errol Flynn's trailer; he'd told her that he wanted to see how the cookie crumbled. But what went on in the trailer didn't hit the papers, never got beyond gossip on the set, and her mother never knew.

She had been with the industrialist for four years before Sam, and no one would have believed what went on behind the wall, beyond the manicured lawn and neat flower beds. If Hedda or Louella knew, they never printed it. But she was used to gossip. The scandal over Stan hadn't fazed her; she planted herself firmly at prominent tables in the Polo Lounge or at the Brown Derby, daring anyone to laugh at her. They hadn't; only behind her back, but she was used to that, too; who cared what people were saying over their Cobb salad at the Derby?

Still, somewhere along the line it had dawned on her what a fraud she was. Lorna Doom.

She sat watching the fishing boats come in, hand pressed against her breast, feeling the flutter. Peace, she thought; peace. But where was it? Day by day she could sense it departing, like a bird within grasp suddenly eluding her. When she went to have her shower the water was cold, and she had to shout for the boy to come and light the fire under the boiler. He came, eventually. Fortunately she didn't have to face anyone in the dining room over the burro incident, for she was to dine at Joan Taylor's. She put on some of her prettiest things and walked up the beach. There was the usual crowd at the yacht club, sitting out on the deck, and bobbing at their moorings the usual boats, the *Molly g*, the *Alrae*, the *Paradiso* from San Francisco, the *I Dream of Jennie*. She saw, leaning on the rail, the club's owner, an American called Jack. She stopped and asked him about the regatta. He told her there had been a series of bad storms in the California Gulf, and that the boats in the race had been forced to shelter at Cabo San Lucas until fairer weather. When would that be? she asked. Jack didn't know; who could tell when storms might blow themselves out? She said she was expecting friends, the Sandlers from La Jolla. Yes, Jack knew the *MorryEll*, but he had no idea when they might be arriving.

Jack smoked French cigarettes, which he had flown in from Martinique; she suddenly found herself engulfed by their aroma. She still had not smoked since leaving Los Angeles, but she stopped at the cash register and bought a pack of the same brand.

She was surprised to find the Tashkents at Joan's house, and she thought, Oh, God, one of those evenings. But Bob proved a good host, warm and friendly, and no one made any bones about the fact that there was a movie star in their midst. The Tashkents—her name was Ethel, his Irving—were diffident, and careful not to look at Lorna for too long at a time. She was glad she'd worn her jade necklace, and let the older woman admire it. Ethel had one of those comical Yiddish accents, and it turned out that the Tashkents came from Santa Monica, too. Before retiring, they had owned Tashkent's Select Kosher Deli at the beach, close to where the young Lorna Doone had gone to school at Santa Monica High. Tashkent, Tashkent; Lorna tried to remember. No, sorry, she couldn't recall Tashkent's Select Kosher Deli.

Joan was interested in knowing what Fedora was really like; Lorna disappointed her by saying they'd never met, none of their scenes were together and Fedora had remained hidden in her hotel room during most of the filming of *The Miracle of Santa Cristi*. Inevitably the name of William Marsh came up; she didn't like talking about Willie, but since they asked . . . He had been one of the most prominent figures in Hollywood for many years, and since his success in the Bobbitt films, one of the most popular and beloved. It was perhaps a blessing that Bee Marsh had died last year, and hadn't lived to see the tragedy; or perhaps if she had lived, it never would have happened. The others, of course, were well acquainted with the details of that ghastly night last summer; the papers had been full of them for months.

Upon arriving, Lorna had accepted only her usual pre-dinner glass of wine, which she drank right down, and then, because it was, she said, a "special occasion," she allowed herself to be persuaded to have one of the frozen margaritas the others were having, and which Bob Somers made so well. She interested herself in Bob, taking his arm and drawing him across the room away from the others, admiring the work he had done on the house. And all with his own hands? Remarkable. She was in awe, she said, of a man who could do things. Why, he ought to have been an architect. Bob said he preferred fishing.

On one wall was a series of framed prints, featuring a

serpent similar to that in the bar mural at the hotel, with the feathered bird over it. He told her that in Mexico the snake had been a prevalent symbol in native art when Hernando Cortés had come to the New World, only a few years after Columbus. Believing he was the incarnation of their god, Quetzalcoatl, they welcomed the Spaniard, little knowing that he was to destroy them. After the great Montezuma was slain, when Cortés was further exploring the country, legend had it that he had come to the village of Ixcal, afterward christened Boca de Oro, the mouth of gold. The legend told that high up on the Sleeping Maiden was a temple to Quetzalcoatl, a great gateway with stairs and a sacrificial altar in the shape of a jaguar, whose eyes were jade. Quetzalcoatl was called the Plumed Serpent, and was represented by the snake, whose crown of plumes was the feathers of a bird, and whose robes were the leaves of the jungle itself. Though she had already heard Pedro telling most of this to the tourists, Lorna nodded solemnly, listening in rapt attention. No one had really seen the temple, Bob said, but old villagers still spoke of it, a few claiming ancestors who had accidentally stumbled across some ruins, and there were tales of the flight of stairs leading upward, where Quetzalcoatl had ascended to heaven. The stairs were called *Las Escaleras de Oro Que No Conducen a Ninguna Parte*—The Golden Stairs That Lead Nowhere.

Pat O'Connor, the doctor, arrived late; he'd been treating a patient for snakebite. The Plumed Serpent? Lorna asked; no, just *culebra de cascabel*—rattlesnake. At dinner, Pat, who came from West Virginia, described the outlawed snake-handling cults in Appalachia congregations, who fondled poisonous reptile, believing so devoutly in their ability through God that their faith overcame any danger. Handling, caressing, even kissing the venomous snakes proved the domination of Godly power over the Devil, virtue over sexual desire. Didn't the snakes bite? Lorna asked. Frequently, Pat said. Lorna shivered; it was a devotion she couldn't contemplate. Still, she said, if you truly believed, you could possibly overcome the reptile's natural instinct to bite by controlling its natural fear. It was probably something conveyed from the human to the reptile, like the music Indian snake charmers played to make a cobra rise from a basket and dance; she'd seen one in New Delhi on her second honeymoon cruise. She went on to say that such faith was not unlike what had happened that day in Italy when they were shooting *The Miracle of Santa Cristi* and Willie Marsh had that old woman die in his arms. The woman, a peasant, had believed that

135

Willie, in his clerical robes, was a priest and had asked his blessing; Willie had been so moved that he had converted to Catholicism and become a very religious type of person. It really was a moving story and—Oh, dear, she was rattling again. She leaned across and asked Mrs. Tashkent how Santa Monica was these days.

Pat was seated on Lorna's left and she realized that Joan had invited him on her behalf, so she would have a man. She wasn't sure she appreciated the favor. Still, he *was* a man. She'd had several margaritas and felt suffused by a warm lethargy she hadn't experienced in some time. She'd been careful not to have more than any of the others, but with the wine, she felt a little giddy. Then there were after-dinner liqueurs, and she took just a *touch* of Kahlúa with her coffee. Pat's face was quite red by that time, and he had taken over the conversation, in an obvious attempt to impress her. She remained unimpressed. She urged him to help Joan with the dishes while she talked to Bob Somers again—being "early to bed," the Tashkents had said their good nights—but Pat wanted to go over to the cantina for the dancing. For some time they had been hearing the sounds of the mariachis across the bridge, the cries and shouts, while the locals got drunk on beer or *ricea*, the native brew, which Joan said tasted like kerosene. Well, Lorna said, she would go if Joan and Bob did, so when the dishes were done they all went together.

It was the mariachi band from the hotel, playing near the long wooden bar, and around the wall the tourists were watching the natives dance. The girls wore pretty if modest dresses and pretty if modest expressions; the boys were mostly in white, white pants and long white shirts that hung out and were embroidered white on white around the yokes. The first thing Lorna saw was Emiliano dancing with Rosalia. She let Pat buy her a beer, Dos Ekkies, and asked him to light her cigarette. She refused his invitation to dance, but swayed with the music to indicate that she had the rhythm, her attention divided between watching Emiliano and listening to Joan, who was on her left. Behind her was Bob Somers; he seemed subdued. Lorna decided that Joan must have said something to him about spending so much time with Lorna before dinner. There were other guests from the hotel, and she nodded graciously to them, deciding that this was perhaps the best way to confront them after the burro incident; she wanted them to see the type person she really was. Then she saw Bud and the rest of the tennis players; they were with the secretaries, and Miriam Seltzer's dress was bright with native flowers and kitchen rickrack everywhere: obviously she was going native. After a while Pat excused himself and went and asked her to dance; they were out on the floor making absolute fools of themselves, trying to do those intricate steps. Emiliano and Rosalia were another story; they moved with such agility, hands behind their backs, feet crossing in front of them, their eyes locked with those secret lovers' smiles on their lips. Lorna felt a tightening, a physical gathering in her stomach. How young they were; Emiliano was not much older than Jeffrey, but still she had to look at him and think the things she was thinking.

These private thoughts were intruded upon by Bud, who had appeared at her elbow. Joan and Bob had gone to talk with someone in the orchestra, and she was alone. Hey, come on, Bud said, don't be mad at me. She wasn't mad, she said formally, merely disappointed; she had taken him for a different type altogether. No, thank you, she didn't care to dance. She hoped that Pat would come back to her, but he was engrossed with Miriam now. She regretted not having accepted his invitation to dance. She smiled over at Bob, but he only smiled back and returned his attention to Joan and the rest of the group.

Well, she said finally to Bud, if he'd be a little nicer to her she *might* dance with him. Oh, he said, he'd be nice. They danced.

She really enjoyed herself then, and told herself everything was all right again. Bud held her close and she liked the feel of someone's arms around her; it had been so long. Nothing was mentioned about Stan Wyckoff, and for a while she felt herself being calmed and lifted out of her depression. Perhaps it was just the *ricea*, which Bud insisted she try; it tasted not like kerosene, but a little like Japanese sake. She asked the bartender to cut it with grapefruit juice. He punctured the can and poured her a glass, and Bud added the *ricea*. Not too much, she told him; she didn't drink. They danced again, and she was feeling warmer and more relaxed, and she hadn't had this good a time in she didn't know how long. Joan and Bob had left, and she reminded herself to write a little thank-you note for the nice dinner. Then she dragged Bud over to the musicians to see if they could play "Elmer's Tune"; they didn't know it, but they knew "One O'clock Jump," and she was out on the floor jitterbugging the way they used to in college. Then she saw Emiliano and got him out on the floor and tried to make him jitterbug with her, and she could tell that Rosalia didn't like that. The others did; they were all laughing, she could see them. Then the band played a slow number and she held on to Emiliano and insisted he dance again with her, clutching him tightly and pressing her body against his, until Rosalia went out the door and Emiliano, embarrassed, followed her. Why were Latins always so jealous? Lorna wondered vaguely.

She looked again for Bud, who was waiting for her at the bar, filling the half-emptied grapefruit juice can from the bottle of *ricea*. He took her arm and propelled her through the back door, where some of the others had gone, then across the yard of the cantina to the rear of the next building, where people had grouped themselves as an audience around a series of wire pens housed under a ramshackle roof set on posts. Lanterns hung from the posts, and in their flickering light she saw the face of the man called Ávila. He was standing behind one of the pens, in which was a large *culebra de cascabel*. Bud put his arm around Lorna's waist and drew her to a position where they could watch as the man took up a chicken whose leg had been tied to one of the posts. Holding its wings against its body, he extended the chicken toward the wire screen. The snake coiled, and its rattles sounded a warning. The chicken struggled frantically, and made muted sounds in its throat. Lorna wanted to look away, but couldn't, she watched with the others in fascination. The snake's rattles sounded like the dried gourd seeds in a maraca. On its back were the same bright diamond designs that bordered the rattan around the windows and doors of Lorna's cabaña; the same as in Bob Somers's wall prints. Ah, they said, the *culebra de cascabel*, the snake of the rattles. The man lifted the top of the pen and thrust the chicken inside; it flew to the corner opposite the snake and stood trembling. The rattling ceased and the snake struck. Lorna stared as, fangs bared, it uncoiled and flew across the pen to bite the chicken. It drew back, then struck again. The chicken moved, wobbled, toppled. People applauded. Bud was drinking from the grapefruit juice can, then handed it to Lorna; she felt it burn as it went down. When she looked again, the chicken's wings were flapping, and occasionally it kicked, while the snake waited, watched. Then whatever movement the chicken made was only motor reflex, and it was dead. Thinking it was all over, Lorna started to move away, but Bud gripped her arm. The snake was sliding along the bottom of the pen, and curling up around the dead chicken. It unhinged its enormous jaw and slid the chicken's neck in under the fangs and began ingesting the bird. Lorna could not stop watching with the others. It was a disgusting process, and when the entire body of the chicken had disappeared, inflating the snake's neck to the size of a small football, she finally yanked away from Bud and ran back across the yard. The cantina was practically empty—even the mariachis had gone to see the show—and she hurried out through the front. She passed the church and went across the bridge. The lights were off at Joan's; they must have gone to bed. Were they making love? She was at the yacht club when she heard the mariachis start up again in the cantina; the dancing would probably go on all night. She walked along the sand, thinking first of Emiliano, then of Richard, then of Bob Somers, then of Emiliano again, and hearing the lilt of the marimbas, the rise of the muted trumpet, and she was crying. Whatever happened to the good old days and "Elmer's Tune"? Someone was running along the sand behind her. He came upon her with a rush and a low chuckle; it was Bud, with his grapefruit juice can and *ricea*. He wanted her to come back and dance, but she would not, so he walked along with her. She said the chicken and the snake was a horrible sight, but he only laughed and said it was something she could write home about.

Home, she thought, engulfed in a wave of emotion she could only faintly understand. Sobbing, she threw herself against Bud and felt his arms go around her. She laid her face against his chest until her tears subsided, and she let him walk her along the wet sand, his arm encircling her back. When they got to the hotel she didn't want to go to the bar, so they went instead to her patio, and sat in the moonlight, and poured from the grapefruit juice can into her drinking glass, which they shared until the can was empty. Then Bud suggested smoking a joint, so they shared it between them. Then he came and put his arms around her again and held her, and said he wanted to take her inside. No, she said, he'd tell everyone. No, he said, he wouldn't. *Eck cetera.*

She told herself next morning, with her awful hangover, that she remembered little of what had happened, but she couldn't convince herself of this, for even with its fuzzy edges, she could vividly recall most of the rest of the night. He made love to her—Bud, who, like Emiliano, was young enough to be her son; but that didn't matter. When it was over, though, she had felt—she didn't know exactly how, but she was sad, and she'd thought that if they made love again she would be able to find joy. But he had said he was tired, and that the bed was too narrow, so he had left her. And then someone else had come in, this was Gil, and she'd let Gil make love to her, and she had her eyes closed, and when she opened them she saw that they were not alone: Bud had returned and the two others with him, and they were watching and after Gil both Barry and Dick wanted to make love to her, and they kept telling her she was really fabulous, really great, Lorna, sensational, and she wanted to show them how great, how fabulous she could be, and then, suddenly, they were all gone, and she heard them talking as they went along the walk, laughing about Stan Wyckoff and saying she wasn't really so great after all, there was this girl in Cincinnati, and she had stumbled from the bed, out onto the patio, where she hung over the railing, shouting at them, telling them what she thought of types like they were, not caring how loud her voice was or who heard her screaming. . . .

By the time breakfast was over there wasn't anybody who didn't know about it. She took her coffee and rolls at the corner table, with *Atlas Shrugged* propped up in front of her, and paid assiduous attention, then smiled brightly at Rosalia, who served her. Rosalia wasn't smiling back, though.

Later, under her umbrella, in a bikini she hadn't worn before, Lorna sat waiting for her depression to pass. She always felt guilty after such foolishness, nothing more, nothing really to get upset about. Her book was on her knees, but she was not reading. She was watching Emiliano, over by the turtle basin. He was wearing cut-off Levi's with frayed edges, the denim bleached nearly white against his bare brown legs. She thought a picture with the turtles would be nice, and she had her camera with her in her raffia bag, so she brought it over to where Emiliano was squatting. Along the protruding knobs of his spine she could see golden blond fuzz, and there were gold hairs mixed in with the darker ones on his forearms. She said how gay the dancing had been last night; he said *sí, señorita*, that was all. She asked him to tell her about the turtles, and he said they were sea tortoises, their meat was in the stew she'd had two nights ago. Oof, she said, making a face; *tur*tle. She snapped several pictures of the turtles, including Emiliano generously in the shots, and then called to Cupie to snap the two of them, never mind the turtles. Emiliano seemed reluctant and stood rigidly beside her when she put her arm through his and smiled for the camera. She could see Rosalia going by, carrying a load of bedding out back. As she went into the laundry room she stopped and gave Lorna a little jealous look, but Lorna tilted her chin defiantly and placed her leg next to Emiliano's.

Los pies, she told him, *muy bonitos.* Very pretty feet. He ran off onto the beach, his brown legs working against the bright sand, the muscles in the backs of his thighs tensing and elongating, the calves bunching. She did not know the Spanish for legs.

When he had gone she insisted Cupie come over to the horse *palapa* with the camera and take another picture. There were a lot of people on the beach, and she hoped they were watching as she hugged the littlest burro to her, putting her cheek right next to its head and telling Cupie to hurry, catch this one, and she hugged and smiled while the rest of the roll was exposed, and everyone could see that she would never hurt the little creature.

That afternoon the tennis players left. Secluded in the library, she watched them go out in the small boats to the larger one. They were wearing their alligator shirts and had their tennis rackets in matching green covers, and they held up their drinks at the rail, toasting Miriam and the other secretaries, who waved fluttering scarves at them and shouted that they would see them in Mexico City. Lorna wished them the joy of that; she was not unhappy to see Bud and the others leaving, but she told herself, whatever blame you could put on the *ricea,* they were not very nice boys.

She watched the boat out of sight, and heard the music die away, saw the beach grow calm again. She wondered how long she had been at Boca, but had no precise idea. One day had melted into another in succession, and she could only mark one from the other by the bad things that had happened to her. This day she had got sunburned, that day she had seen the stingray, that other day she had struck the burro, last night she had got drunk. Today she was back on the wagon, where she would stay. She ate only a little dinner, but all her dessert—chocolate cream pie—and tried to read. She heard the dancing from the bar. She went and lingered on the edge of the patio, hoping to catch Emiliano's eye, but he did not throw it. When everyone had left she sat at the bar and had an orangeade. Steve asked when she'd started smoking again. She didn't really, she said, she'd just picked these up—they were the French kind, like Jack smoked. Oh ho, watch out for Jack, Steve said. He mentioned her bill, which had remained unpaid that week; she said money was being wired. No problem, he told her, be our guest. She mentioned the possibility of a trip to New York; shopping, theaters, Fun City. He came around the bar and sat on the next stool and put his knee against hers. Have a drink, he said. No, she was on the wagon. Sure, have one, he said. Well, maybe just one.

After he closed the bar he brought his flashlight and showed her to her cabaña. He wanted to come in; she wouldn't let him. Come on, we all know about you, he said. She slapped him and heard his laugh as he went back down the walk.

It was dark and quiet. She sat smoking and staring at the terrazzo floor. She admitted to herself that she was bored, and that somehow things weren't panning out again. She tried to read; the lantern light danced; her eyes felt itchy. She took her raffia bag and went out along the pathway to where they stored the housekeeping supplies; she put bars of soap with *Los Cinco Palmas* on the wrappers, and boxes of tissues, and other things in the bag and took them to her cabaña and hid them. She slept badly and next morning brought *Atlas Shrugged* back to the library, chucked it on the shelf, and began a Mickey Spillane.

She kept wondering how Emiliano was in bed.

She was having dreams, and the dreams were about the snake. She wasn't stupid, she knew perfectly well what that was supposed to mean, and she imagined the doctor's dry amusement if she told him the dream. It was purely phallic. The dream snake was long and large and thick, dark, without designs, without scales. They said snakes were cold-blooded, but this was warm and she circled it with her hand, measuring its circumference, staring at the eyes that stared at her. She did not know what she was to do with the snake, or what she wanted to do, but it was not a part of the dream that the snake should bite her. She could not tell if it was supposed to be an abstract representation of something or a person, but it seemed that she knew the snake and it knew her. A mutual recognition; but who was he, this snake? In the dream she wasn't frightened; it was only afterward, when she woke up before daylight, that she was frightened.

She smoked and thought and thought and smoked. Faces swam before her unconscious vision, close and then far away. She reached out to none of them; they were familiar but uninteresting, the faces of men she had known, who had not been able to give her what she sought. She tried to see past the faces into something else, some part of herself that remained hidden, both to her and to the doctors. She tried to see past herself into the vague, unaccountable void that lay all around her. It was not unfamiliar territory; she had viewed it many times before. She had struggled for more years than she could count, trying to see somewhere beyond herself, past anything to do with family, children, career, friendship, dreams of success, even love, and she thought of some nice man with a kind face, a silver-haired uncorrupt gentle placating intelligent generous man whose hand she loved the touch of, not in any overt sexual way, for this was no profane fantasy, but rather a grandfatherly person, not unlike, perhaps, Bernard Baruch, with his rimless glasses and hearing aid and briefcase on a Washington park bench, and the touch of his hand doming the top of her head would be like a benediction. He would know what was right and proper, what was wrong and ignoble. He would tell her. Or sometimes she thought he might even be a priest, a good Catholic priest (she had discussed this with Bee Marsh after her and Willie's conversion), and she had avidly watched Bishop Sheen, that hypnotic Irish prelate with the fascinating eyes, on television, and the way his long ascetic hand made the sign of the cross or, fingertips touching, formed devout peaked church roofs, or, holiest of all, toyed with his pectoral cross as he spoke, and she thought how a man like that could make her feel cleansed and purified. For there was a God. She knew it, believed it. But where she came from, in those Protestant churches she had been forced to attend, He had not shown His face nor had His countenance ever shone upon her. There was a time, long ago, when she had thought the world was good; it was something like Columbus believing the world was round when everybody said it was flat. She had this feeling in her, and this need. Everyone had needs, of course, but to her, hers seemed special—and unfulfilled. There had to be a way that all things could be made comprehensible to her. She had gone from one possibility to another, looking, sampling, testing, examining. She had read Dale Carnegie and Norman Vincent Peale and watched Billy Graham's revivals for Christ on TV. She did not feel like a better person. She had investigated something called Biofeedback. She had listened to people talking about Transcendental Meditation. She had attended lectures. Nothing much had happened. She had heard about Scientology and had gone to the meetings and had read some material; it seemed easy at first, then became difficult. She hadn't gone to another meeting. She had heard of something called Mind Control lectures. Nothing. Intermittently she had taken courses in self-hypnosis, in speed reading, and had participated in ladies' yoga breakfasts.

She had attended classes at the Actors Studio's West Coast branch, but she was terrified of getting up and doing a scene in front of the others and would make up any excuse to postpone the moment. While Alexis Smith and Betty Bacall and Angela Lansbury all were Broadway stars, she was playing Uta Hagen's part in a scene from *The Country Girl* with a boy who didn't shave and wore a tank top; she could smell the sweat from his armpits, and wanted to tell him about Ban roll-on. Her instructor said she was making progress in Moment-to-Moment Realization, but she didn't believe him. She quit the class after five sessions.

Her trouble was that she had no faith. She saw nothing to believe in. Her dead father, yes; but he was dead. Her mother was a vegetable. Son, daughter—aliens in her house. Behind her a string of males who had used her, and who one by one had shown themselves as weak and lost or weaker and more lost than she. She told herself that what she needed was some tremendously moving religious experience such as Willie Marsh had had. She wanted to be struck as Saul of Tarsus had been struck on the road to Damascus. She wanted to know God-by-miracle, to have water turned to wine, fishes and loaves to feed the multitudes. But she did not think of religions, or of nations, or of any of the complex manifestations that rule groups of men. Government, civil compacts, a unionized America, Black Power—these were only abstracts and as distant from her historically as the industrial revolution. She scanned the headlines, then turned to the movie page. Politics never interested her. She was aware of welfare problems, of orphaned children, of charitable agencies, CARE, WAIF, UNESCO; she sent checks when she remembered to, but thought there was little she could do about such problems. She believed in women's liberation, but she didn't see what she could do except read Nora Ephron. Love. Love was her universal panacea. If she was in love, everything was hunky-dory. If she wasn't, depressions of the worst imaginable sort beset her, preyed on her, held her in thrall. It was not in her nature to be manless, one of those bachelor girls, successful but alone. She didn't enjoy lunching with the girls, even as she lunched with them. Given a choice between men and her career, she would always take the man. She had some knowledge of loneliness, and she did not like it. She could not cope without a man, some man. Sometimes she would invite the milk-man in for her need; the postman was too old.

One morning she awoke earlier than usual. She had a funny feeling, a kind of premonition. She washed her face, combed her hair, dressed, and went out on the beach. Emiliano was spearfishing off the rocks, and Benito was raking the sand. She walked down to the water's edge, staring out at the horizon. The sun was just coming around the left-hand side of the bay. Opposite, from the direction of Mirabella, she saw a dark speck. It grew larger, became a speedboat, rip-ping over the waves. It came closer and closer and somehow she had a feeling that it was her the boat had come for. It spun into the bay with a roar, shot toward shore, the motor stopped, the Mexican in the boat pulled up the outboard and called to Benito. She heard her name. Benito pointed silently. The boatman pulled nearer with an oar. He called in Spanish: she didn't understand. Benito, come, please? He came and translated. The man was from the hotel in Mirabella and someone had telephoned; she was to call back. She hurried to her cabaña, changed her clothes, shoved things out of sight as quickly as she could, put on a full make-up, and left with the boatman before breakfast.

Arriving in Mirabella, she went immediately to the hotel. The operator said the call had come late last night, not from Cabo San Lucas, as Lorna hoped, but from Los Angeles. A Mrs. Pringle. Lorna felt a stab of worry as she went into the booth and waited for the call to be put through.

Nan's voice was bright and noncommittal, they exchanged remarks about how was the weather down there and how was it up there? and yes, she was having a marvelous rest, but why the call? Nan's tone became serious and she said that Lorna's lawyer had called regarding the fire: the insur-ance company was instituting proceedings against her. The lawyer wanted her to give a deposition about her side of the story. It could be messy, Nan said. How messy? Very. There was even the threat of prison. Lorna said she would think it over and call her back. Tell the lawyer to wire money. She might go to Fun City, ha ha. Thanks and love.

She walked along the streets of Mirabella and visited some of the shops. Unnoticed, she took from one half a dozen colored Bic Banana pens and a spiral notebook, from an-other some plastic earrings. In a third she tried on a belt, and walked out with it before the man noticed. She never took

145

anything expensive, so it wasn't really stealing, but she felt an excitement she thought she'd lost. She had lunch in a patio restaurant and bumped into Bob Somers, who was there on business overnight. She let him pick up the check, then they had several drinks in the bar of his hotel, and when he suggested dinner she accepted. They went to La Madreña, which was lovely, and there was outdoor dancing. Bob held her close and talked in her ear. She laughed and asked, What would Joan say? She called to cancel her return boat and stayed with him that night in his room. He was drunk and not a very good lover. She wondered again what Joan saw in him. Coming out of the hotel next morning, who should they stumble across but the doctor, Pat O'Connor. He was all sly smiles and innuendo, and when they met again on the noon boat she said, I know what you're thinking. You're right, Pat said. She asked him not to say anything to Joan or anyone and he said he wouldn't. She didn't believe him, though.

She didn't call Nan back.

Rosalia had become impossible. She didn't like Lorna and it showed in her work. Corners were unswept; the bed was carelessly made; often she neglected to hang up the clothes that Lorna had not hung up herself; the glass in the kerosene lantern was sooty; fresh soap was lacking in the bathroom. For some time Lorna had suspected her, though of what she wasn't quite sure. It could be that she thought she might be stealing. She had grown distrustful, and to catch the girl prying where she had no business Lorna had gone to elaborate lengths, sticking matches in just so, to indicate if drawers had been opened in her absence, or putting out an enticing number of pesos, but counting them carefully and arranging them in seemingly casual piles, so she would know if any had been taken. Certain that the girl was trying on her dresses, she would lay a thread across the hangers in her closet.

It was when she came back from Mirabella that she discovered she'd been robbed. Her pearl earrings were missing. She knew exactly where they were always kept, in the bottom tray of her cosmetic case. Though it was locked and stowed under the bed, she sometimes forgot and left the key lying around. Rosalia had found it. Lorna did not immediately raise the matter with Steve Alvarez or Cupie, but bided her time. That very night, while Rosalia was serving dinner, Lorna saw the pearls on the brazen girl's ears. When she passed with a tray Lorna stood and blocked her way, tapping her foot and holding her hand out, but Rosalia pretended not to understand. She tried to pass and Lorna demanded the return of the earrings. Diners stopped eating and watched, but she didn't care; thieves deserved exposure. Emiliano looked over from the bar and Steve Alvarez came out of the kitchen to see what the trouble was. Lorna trembled with indignation, but spoke in a carefully modulated voice. She said she didn't want to make trouble, but Rosalia must return the pearls; they were expensive, in addition to their sentimental value. An exchange in Spanish followed between Steve Alvarez and the girl. Understanding what she was being accused of, she reddened and dropped the tray. Talk died in the room, heads turned, all eyes were on them. Without thinking, Lorna reached and tugged at one of the earrings. Rosalia cried out. Lorna was horrified, realizing her mistake; none of her earrings fitted pierced ears. Translating, Steve identified Rosalia's pearls as a present from Emiliano. They weren't worth ten dollars. Emiliano had come from the bar and was standing beside Rosalia, his face dark with anger, while Lorna stammered that she was terribly sorry. She was shaken with hot waves of shame, she was unable to look at anyone; she would have liked to run from the room and hide. She followed Rosalia into the kitchen and apologized, but the girl impassively refused to acknowledge her. Lorna went back to the bar, to Emiliano; he wouldn't listen either.

The mystery of the missing pearls was solved next morning. Another maid—Rosalia refused to go into Lorna's cabaña—cleaned and dusted the room, and in rearranging the shoes she discovered certain items in the toe of one, things Lorna had hurriedly put away before leaving for Mirabella. Among them, wrapped in Kleenex, were the earrings. Steve Alvarez had them in his pudgy hand as he approached Lorna at lunchtime, and she tried to look anywhere but at his face, and saw only other faces watching. She accepted the pearls in confusion and later again tried to apologize. Crying, she flung her arms around Rosalia, saying over and over *Mi dispiace*, which was Italian, but the languages were very similar, weren't they? Rosalia still wouldn't look at her and when Lorna released her she walked away. Incredible how proud those natives could be over a little thing like that.

She had taken the spiral notebook and pens for a purpose. She had thought for a long time that she had a flair for words and she wanted to begin her autobiography. She chose the violet-colored pen and took the notebook under the umbrella and started writing. She saw that people were watching her. She wrote with a very serious expression, and when she had filled six pages she read them over. They told of a doll she remembered—it was called Lola—and then she had described a visit they had had from a relative, and how she helped her mother bake a cake one Saturday. She intended these opening passages as a revelation of the child that had been, but it seemed that cakemaking was much easier than bookmaking. She scribbled some notes, then made some doodles, then used the other colored pens to fill in the violet outlines. They were very pretty. Then she began a letter. It read: *"Dearest Carrie, you can't imagine . . ."* She stopped there and closed the notebook.

She wanted to describe the scenery, but it was too much trouble. She had been to Tahiti with Brownie on the South Seas cruise and had seen the colors there, which Gauguin saw and painted—the vital, primary, uninhibited blues, greens, yellows, the ochers and umbers of the earth tones, with purple in the shadows and gold in the lights. Boca was a little like that, with a wild, primitive, unspoiled beauty. She had seen it, noted it in its many details, and though it was a "nice place to visit," she "wouldn't want to live there." But for the past three or four days the sun had not felt good to her. It was sun, but it wasn't healthy sun, if the distinction could be made. It was not just hot, but half obscured by a fine haze that made the rays seem greasy, melting over her in a film. The haze was like a pestilence, the breeze had stopped, the heat became oppressively humid. It made her logy and irritable, and she found much to complain about. Carla, the new maid, was even sloppier and more careless than Rosalia, and when Lorna confronted Steve Alvarez with several instances of her laxity he listened, but did nothing. She sought out Cupie, who said she would take care of matters, which meant that Cupie went and cleaned the cabaña herself, until Steve put a stop to it.

A few days later, she tried to finish the letter to Carrie, adding to the sentence she had begun: *"can't imagine how beautiful it is here. It's so quiet and peaceful. I'm having a ball, and a good rest, you wouldn't know me, the way I've calmed down. Went to a place called Mirobello close by, they have a wonderful little flee market, all sorts of things to buy. You would love the snorkiling its like a tropical garden. Tomorrow"*

She didn't know how to continue the sentence, so she stopped again. She would wait until she had done something interesting tomorrow and put it in then. Regarding the auto-biography, she thought that kind of writing was beyond her; what she ought to do was get a tape recorder, and someone could listen to the tapes, then write it up. People were always doing that sort of thing: "By Lorna Doone as told to."

For a time following the departure of the tennis players, Lorna had effected a campaign of fence-mending with the other guests. She went about putting herself out for them, going over to talk with "Ceel" Atwater, who for once did not seem talkative, or coming early for dinner so she could have a good place at the communal table, where she told them long, involved stories which somehow ended without a point, the joke lost. She would hide her embarrassment at the flat ending and ask for the butter, putting an "and" at the end so she could continue on, but not knowing how to. She sensed that she was rattling and she had to eat her soup with her bread because her hand shook. She gave the honeymooners a present. It was the pineapple candle from Joan's shop, and it had a very nice scent, and she hoped they liked it. They said they did. When cards were being played after dinner she would take a barstool and sit at the corner of the table, kibitzing, but no one paid attention to her. She had never enjoyed cards, so she wasn't familiar with the game, but she could play gin; when she suggested it, nobody else seemed to know how to play.

It hurt her that no one seemed to like her. They tolerated her, but no one liked her. They sat in groups and whispered. They laughed. Bitterly she thought to herself how nice that she could provide them a measure of amusement. It was ridiculous. She was likable; they ought to like her. How often do you spend a vacation with a movie star?

Emiliano remained angry with her. She wanted to make it up, but didn't know how to go about it. If she called him he would send Benito or one of the other boys. If she sat at the bar when he was on duty, he was busy making drinks or slicing limes or measuring simple syrup. Once when he looked up she gazed at him with a bewildered expression and said again a heartfelt "I'm sorry." *"No importa, señorita,"* he replied, with a shrug that was eloquent. When he went back to work she watched not his face but his feet and the way the leather thongs of his sandals separated his big toe from the others. The nails were plum dark like his fingernails and had white edges where they needed cutting.

Then several unpleasantnesses occurred, one after another, sufficient to make her wonder why she had ever come to Boca in the first place.

Cupie was taking Heidi, the baby, to the doctor in Mirabella. She would be gone overnight. Having decided to revert to her original blond color, Lorna asked her to be a darling and bring her back a suitable hair product, and described the shade she wanted. Cupie said she ought to come to Mirabella and have it done there, but Lorna didn't want to go back again, the boat made her seasick. Cupie said she would try. Lorna spent the afternoon finishing the Mickey Spillane, and when it came time for her shower, again the water was cold. She called in vain for the boy; no one answered. She took her wastebasket and went out to find some kindling to start the fire. There was plenty of it along the back walks, but she was furious that she had to do it herself. It was as she passed one of the outbuildings that she heard Emiliano singing. There was a small window to his cubicle propped open with a stick, and by turning the wastebasket upside down she found that she could stand on it and look in. What she saw, she suddenly realized, was what she had wanted to see for a long time. The window looked onto a small ell of the room, across which was the bathroom; the door was open, and in the metal stall Emiliano was showering. Surely Lorna Doone could not be doing what she was doing, standing on the turned-over wastebasket and watching, but she was; she could not be experiencing the rush of emotions she felt, but she was; she could not be thinking the things she thought, but she was. Somehow all of it was happening—not to her, of course, but watching, she thought of how she would describe the scene to Nan, who would certainly get a kick out of it, soapsuds and that brown flesh, the most sensual thing imaginable, that blue-black hair flat and straight over his eyes, water running from it in a sheet, down his body, and she thought you could really tell a lot about a person's type from the way they bathed, it was such a personal thing, and the way he touched himself, so intimate, so . . .

Again she told herself she had no business doing what she was doing, but she could not help herself. She watched as he soaped himself, and his head came back, a smile playing on his lips, his eyes closed in the water, as he performed an act which caused her knees to go weak, and when he was done he opened his eyes and saw her watching. He did not try to hide himself, but stood looking up at her, his smile slowly fading, the water gurgling down the drain, and she thought she read an invitation in his look. She moved to get down, her head struck the window, the stick fell out, the frame dropped. She tumbled backward from the basket, barely managing to keep from falling. She saw Steve Alvarez standing at the end of the walk under a bougainvillaea. He'd been watching her while she had watched Emiliano; there was no way she could be sure of this, still she knew it. She clutched her wrapper around her and went toward him, angrily demanding why her fire had not been lighted. He took the basket from her—but with such a sly look—and loudly bawled for the boy to see to hot water for *Número Uno*.

She went back to the cabaña and waited for the water to come up. While she waited she undid her wrapper and dropped it on the terrazzo, facing the door, on which there was a long mirror. She scrutinized herself carefully, turning one way, then the other, looking back over her shoulder, touching her body in various places. There was no doubt of it, she was putting on weight. Her belly bulge was more prominent and the pockets of fat had returned around her waist and hips. It was the desserts. When the *MorryEll* came and they got to Acapulco the first thing she must do is find a masseur. She must begin her diet all over again; but not now, dear God, not now. She touched, lifted, caressed, assayed her breasts. Still firm, up, not sagging. She had those, anyway. She held them as though in offering, and closed her eyes. It was the beautiful Emiliano to whom she gave them.

That night she watched him dance, her eye following every line of his body, tightly encased in the black shiny costume, and smiled to herself, knowing at last what lay under that fabric. When the dancing was done she hurried away to her cabaña. She undressed completely, then put on her white negligee. She lifted the ruffles at her wrists, and felt them lightly touch the backs of her hands. She combed her hair and touched up her make-up and put perfume behind her earlobes. Then she went out onto the patio, breathing deep gulps of air, and her heart was beating fast. She went down the steps and slipped along the walk, like a romantic heroine on her way to an assignation.

She had decided that what she must do is go to him, offer herself; he could not refuse her. How could he? Yet something inside her despised this plan, denounced it as foolishness beyond foolishness. A Mexican boy, young as her son, who had indicated no interest in her whatever, committed to another, who if she were in other circumstances she would not look twice at; except yes, she told herself, she would look, she would, he was so beautiful, she loved the lines of his body, she must touch and caress them, he had appeared to her as a god and she would go to him as a worshiper. She approached

151

haltingly, one hand extended before her as a blind person moves or a sleepwalker, and truly she might have been asleep, so little of the reality of what she was actually doing occurred to her. Then she turned the corner under the bougainvillaea and she was there. Lantern light shone through the open door, and she could hear soft music playing. She used her still-extended hand to scratch on the screen, softly saying his name. *Emiliano . . . Emiliano . . .* There was movement from inside, and he appeared, loomed, out of the darkness, and was standing behind the screen. Please, she said, allow her to come in; he only stood there, looking out at her, half his face caught in the lantern light. And now as if in the same dream she came closer to the screen and talked to him through it, as a prisoner might—and she was his prisoner—and she said things to him. They came out in a long rush of breathy passion, the offer she was making to him, and he stood there making no reply. She grew impatient, standing outside, whispering these things, her breast rising and falling and the ruffles at her sleeve fluttering in the light as she moved her hand against the screen, pleading now, knowing the foolish thing she was doing but unable to stop herself. Another figure appeared behind him. A hand came out, pushing Emiliano from the space behind the screen, and Rosalia's angry features took form in the light. *Vaya, vieja.* Go away, old woman. She swept backward and wheeled, her gown fluttering; go away, old woman. That was a wicked, wicked girl, that Rosalia. Yet it was not her laugh she heard, as she went, but his.

She trembled, whether with passion or shame she could not be sure. She stayed in the dark under the bougainvillaea, listening to the sounds of her breathing, biting her lips till they hurt. As she had hoped *he* would hurt them. She had thought everyone was asleep, but in her haste to reach her rendezvous she had missed the clack of the typewriter; now she heard it, coming from the office. Steve was hunched over the desk, his bony fingers hitting the keys. His chair squeaked as he leaned back, looking up to see her standing outside in her white gown. He turned down the lantern wick and came outside. He put his arms around her and pulled her to him, so hard that her breath came out of her throat with a rush. No, she thought, not this one, the other, the beautiful one; still, she was kissing him. His rib cage protruded against her, and his mustache felt damp, and softer than she'd imagined. There was oil in his hair, a flowered fragrance she found unsuitable on a man. His body was softly moist and heated, and she tried to keep his hands from fumbling crudely over her as he kissed her. He was

152

not, she thought, romantic. He leaned, still with an arm about her, and swung the office door shut, and brought her along the walkway toward his house.

He put on a record, playing it softly, and they sat in the dark, smoking. He gave her a drink, then began removing his clothes. He looked over at her and said, Well, what are you waiting for? He came and undid the cord of her gown and urgently hurried it off her shoulders and down her arms. The white melted onto the dark floor and she worried about the ruffles.

Afterward she took one of his cigarettes and lay against the hot pillow, smoking, thinking not of him, or of Cupie, but of Emiliano and Rosalia in the other house. He was not very nice, to have laughed. Steve lay curled away from her, his lips burbling, his nose humming as he snored. Then a flashlight shone in the hall. Sashie came to the door and stood looking at her in the bed. She thought she had never seen such a fiercely angry expression. She drew the sheet over her exposed breasts and put out her cigarette. Sashie said, You leave my father alone. She watched, small and defiant, while Lorna rose and picked up the fallen negligee. Steve Alvarez hadn't moved. You don't understand these things, Sashie, she whispered, you're too young. No, I'm not, Sashie said. I heard about you. Everybody heard about you. She pressed back against the cinder-block wall, making room as Lorna passed. I'm sorry, she whispered, going out. No, you're not, Sashie said.

Next day Cupie returned on the noon boat and Sashie ran to meet her. Cupie's merry face grew grave as the child walked along beside her—Lorna watched through her dark glasses from under her hat, scarf, and umbrella, and pretended to be engrossed in her manicure. Cupie glanced over, then went to the office.

At lunch Cupie was not to be seen, and Steve Alvarez worked the bar, keeping busy with customers. Emiliano had pointedly remained at a distance, while Rosalia refused to serve Lorna's table. That evening, when she came into the dining room before dinner, Cupie was lighting the candles, bending her great weight over the netted glass holders and reaching in with a match. When she looked up Lorna was relieved to see that her face was the same as always, fat and merry. Lorna sat down at her solitary table, thinking she'd had a narrow escape. It was incredible how a woman like that could be forgiving.

But Sashie wasn't. She did the most outrageous thing. The

following morning she came onto the beach in an oversized pair of high heels, swinging an adult pocketbook and sashaying with a hand on a hip. She had a lot of make-up on, and gold hoops and bangles. She did a vamp's wiggle-walk along the sand and everyone laughed, saying Tatum O'Neal. When she came up to Lorna's umbrella she put on the most embarrassing act, it was almost obscene, saying, Don't cook your breakfast, pop it, with Perkies pop-ups, the one with the berries. Not knowing what else to do, Lorna fled.

Next time she saw Cupie she went up to her and touched her and said, I've got to talk to you. No, you don't, Cupie said wearily. But you don't understand. Cupie said, I understand. She didn't seem angry, only sad. She turned her head away, and Lorna's heart turned over. Cupie was hurt, she'd been crying; but Cupie was one of those marvelous philosophical fat people who never got hurt. They were always merry and happy. Look, Lorna said, in a rush of dismayed laughter, I don't want your husband. When Cupie turned to her, the merry look was no longer there and her voice was bitter. Yah, I know you don't, she said.

Downhill. She was in the tropics, but she was skiing and it was all downhill. She stayed in her cabaña, coming out only to swing in the hammock. She swore out loud, cursing the stifling weather and the slow passage of the *MorryEll*. It was never going to get there. Richard, she said aloud, Richard, swapping Romance for Security, swim fins and a white bathing suit for a pipe and tweeds. Would he come; *would* he? Would he understand, be sympathetic? She wanted to go home, she wanted Selma, Carrie, Jeffrey, Nan, coffeeklatsches, lunch at the Derby, familiar things. God, how she hated the tropics. When money was sent, she thought she might fly to Mexico City, then, not home at all, but to New York, then to . . . ? She had gone through her book of traveler's checks; she had only a little cash left. The money hadn't come from her lawyer. She knew why; she owed him too much. She read *Andy Capp* comics in paperback.

She sat staring at her hair in the mirror, not believing what she saw. The dark color had been bad enough, she had realized it now; it wasn't her at all. Richard would have been shocked to see her. But this, this was an awful mess. Cupie had not got what she had asked for, it was another preparation entirely, with directions in Spanish. She had interpreted them as best she could with her *diccionario,* but it had come out all wrong. The stripping required the entire morning, and the bleaching and coloring the better part of the afternoon. Now she looked like a waitress; or worse, a hooker. The color was blatant, brazen as a brass bell. It had an ugly, metallic sheen, none of the soft baby-blond tints that were her natural heritage. She had been careless getting the stripping down into the parted roots, and there were dark places. She wore a scarf at dinner, sitting alone with her book propped up on the water glass. She smoked between every course.

After dinner she hurried from the dining room. She changed her clothes and walked up the beach in the dark. The haze that hid the sun also hid the moon. She went to the yacht club and talked to Jack, trying to get news about the *Morry-Ell.* She had three banana daiquiris, then asked if they had the recipe for coco locos.

She didn't make it back to the hotel that night. She sat at the yacht club bar, talking with people from the boats, her hair hidden under her scarf, seeking information about the regatta. The yachts were on the way again, they told her, the storm had broken, and she tried to find relief in that knowledge. White sails carrying a trim hull through the mouth of the bay. Then everybody was gone and she was alone with Jack. She talked at length, and seriously, about meditation and how much it could change your life, and he listened and snapped his fingers for the waiter to bring more drinks. Later he said no, he wouldn't walk her home; it was too far. If she wanted to stay the night, okay. It seemed the easiest thing; his rooms over the club were very pleasant and the bed was a Hollywood type, very large. He was rough with her but she didn't mind. Next day her head hurt again and she looked awful, but she could make the usual repairs, so that was all right.

Because she hated going back to the hotel in the same clothes, she went over to Joan's. She didn't mention having stayed at Jack's, but Joan was a big girl, she knew. Somehow she wasn't as *simpática* as she had been. Lorna decided that Pat must have talked about the night spent in Mirabella with Bob Somers. She passed it off, asking if she couldn't borrow something to put on, and Joan loaned her shorts and a shirt; they both had her own label.

There was only one way to get to the cabaña without being seen, and Lorna worked her way around the back of the lagoon, under the trees. Fruit, there was fallen fruit all along the ground, rich, soft, opulent fruit, with something decadent about it in its unused, wasted condition. Ripe, yellow, split open, leaking with seeds. Then she saw the man called Ávila. He was standing back in the shade, his sombrero tilted away from his face, which was pushed into half a mango he held in his hand. Eating, he looked at her, and when he took the mango away she saw the glint of his gold teeth. His free hand moved slightly, and she stopped, stared at him as he undid the buttons of his jeans and exposed himself. Then she ran, not looking back but wondering how he dared, did he do that to other women, or was it only her, and what had she heard about her? *El Loco.*

She got back to her cabaña, where the maid was pushing a wet mop over the terrazzo. She ordered her to leave, then threw herself on the bed, panting, wanting to throw up, telling herself the *MorryEll* would soon be coming. Jack had not given her much rest, so she slept, and when she awoke it was late afternoon. She longed for one of those beautiful Mexican sunsets, but the sun went down in a murky haze, leaving the clouds an ugly red color, like blood. She called for Benito and told him to bring her a coco loco; no, two.

She drank them, one after the other, sometimes in the hammock, sometimes in the painted chair, but her eye directed along the point of rocks. Emiliano was out there, with his fins and goggles. No more a god, but a Mexican dancer, flamenco, *olé.* She watched him steadily while she sipped through the twin colored plastic straws, putting her hands together as if in supplication, looking up at the sky, praying to God with a mute and, she hoped, beseeching expression.

Emiliano came out of the water, dripping, brown, a fish flapping on the end of his spear. She watched him go. He did not see her.

Inside, on a hanger on a hook, was the white negligee. She sat staring at the white ruffles around the neck, the sleeves, the skirt; she watched them, thinking they needed pressing. She had an unlit cigarette in her lips, and a box of wax matches; the cover of the box said *Las Cinco Palmas.* When she had lighted her cigarette she watched the flame of the match, the small wavering flame, until her fingers grew hot. She blew it out and dropped the burnt match, then she went inside.

Five minutes later a shout went up. Someone had seen the smoke; it was pouring out the windows of Number One. The bartender rang the ship's bell, while Lorna Doone came falling through the door onto the patio, coughing. The waiters and kitchen crew were running, then they went back for buckets and from the point they dipped up water and passed the buckets hand over hand. They came with the garden hose and turned the nozzle on the flames. The fire was put out, but the cabaña was uninhabitable. They moved her to another, in the back. She said she had no idea how the fire had started. Most of her clothes had been ruined by either flame, smoke, or water, and she had salvaged only a few things, including several bikinis and her cosmetic case. Also her copy of *A Guide to Inner Peace*.

When they had got her moved they found secreted away among her possessions all kinds of strange things—bars of hotel soap, rolls of toilet paper, dozens of matchbooks, knives and forks, several maids' uniforms, an entire china service for two with the *Las Cinco Palmas* emblem—cups, saucers, dinner and salad plates. Also office supplies, Sashia's plastic mirror and comb, and a pair of Emiliano's white bathing trunks.

Steve Alvarez issued orders that the bar was to be shut off to her and the waiters were not permitted to bring her any more drinks. She went down the beach in a scorched caftan to the yacht club, where she made a disturbance, and Jack had her forcibly removed from the premises. She went to the village, and when she returned she carried a paper sack: grapefruit juice and two quart bottles of *ricea*. She called to the boy to bring her a can opener.

It rained, and she stayed inside. They could hear her all the way down the walkway to the dining room, crashing around and talking and shouting and crying, sometimes breaking things. These outbursts would be followed by long periods of silence. When it grew dark she would sit on her patio under the dripping thatch, in her caftan, a towel stamped *Las Cinco Palmas* draped burnoose style over her head, keening into the night. They watched her from the bar, orange faces hung like jack o' lanterns over the candles. Later, naked, she stood in the shadows, arms upraised like Astarte, Venus, the nipples of her breasts brilliant with red, her face a painted mask, howls coming from her mouth. Whatever happened to the good old days and "Elmer's Tune"? she cried. *Silencio!* someone shouted, and she was silent.

She complained of illness, fever, and Cupie said they ought to get Pat O'Connor down to look at her; he came, but she wouldn't let him in, she screamed at him and rushed through the door onto the patio, trying to strike him. He waited around the bar, undecided, then went back up the hill.

She wouldn't eat. Cupie went with soup and buttered

bread. She lit the stove heater with kindling and newspapers and sat while Lorna lay on the bed, holding her head and crying. Cupie took and cradled her in her great arms against her rolling bosom. When she got up she brought her into the bathroom and then into the shower. She held her there and helped her wash—there had been vomiting—and shampooed her yellow hair and rinsed it, and got her out and dried her. She left her sitting in the chair while she stripped the bed. She brought clean sheets and cases and made them up, then got her back into bed and sat with her. When the Delco went off Cupie had to leave her in the dark, because Steve said she couldn't have matches for a candle or lantern. She wanted cigarettes and Cupie had been lighting them for her, one after the other, and putting them out for her. Don't leave me, Lorna whispered, I'm afraid. Cupie stayed and sat with her in the dark, talking.

It remained overcast for several more days. Cupie went to the yacht club to learn news of the end of the regatta. There was no word. She returned and brought Lorna out onto the patio, and sat her in a broken rocker from the storeroom. She sat there, they said, like an old grandmother, rocking, and you would hardly know her. The hair; the make-up. Someone went and secretly snapped pictures of her through the bougainvillaea. They said they bet that those papers they sell in the supermarkets would pay to put them on their front page.

What's happening to me? she asked no one, sitting on the patio in the rocking chair. She could hardly remember. They had moved her from the front, that she remembered. There had been a fire, that she remembered. She had been drinking, that she remembered. She was waiting for something, that she remembered.

The *MorryEll*. She longed for one familiar friendly face. *Richard,* she thought; *oh, Richard.* She knew she looked terrible, her mirror had told her that. But she would put it all together as soon as her hands stopped shaking and her heart stopped booming and her eyes stopped crying. It was what the doctor had warned her against: too much external stress, which produced internal stress. That's what he had said, and it had happened, way down here in Mexico, South of the Border. That was strange and a little funny; you came to "get away from it all" and it was all right here waiting for you.

People certainly weren't being very sympathetic. Cupie

was, but it was a sympathy Lorna couldn't understand. That sort of forgiveness only embarrassed her; she thought Cupie was really silly, stupid even. She herself could never forgive a thing like that.

She had been thinking of suicide again. She realized that she'd been considering it as far back as when the tennis players were there—how long ago was that? Walking on the beach, she had wanted to walk into the water and swim away, as far as she could swim, until she was tired, and then she would just drown; it would be easier, she had thought. Now she didn't know. She didn't want to cut her wrists again; she hated the sight of blood. She didn't have enough pills.

Perhaps the doctor was right, perhaps she did have this urge to destroy. Not others, surely not others—she never wanted to do that. Herself, her own body, her own soul, she could hurt them as much as she wanted to; they were hers. But hurt somebody else? Never. She couldn't bear to see others suffer, or to be the cause of their suffering.

She didn't know what she was going to do. Cupie said sit and rest, just rock. Sit. Rest. But what would she do when she had rested? Rocked? Would she stay here forever, resting, rocking?

Where was Richard?

What was happening?

How was the weather in New York?

What will I do? she asked no one.

No one replied.

It rained again. The sun came out. The place steamed. It rained again. She could not say which she disliked more; both were oppressive, both inimical. Both seemed fatal. Back there, behind the bougainvillaea, it was like a swamp. She sweated interminably, dabbing with Kleenex and sighing. What should she do?

Cupie came with news. Jack had gone to Mirabella for the weekend, had been on someone's boat, had talked on the ship-to-shore telephone. The *MorryEll* with three other boats had left Cabo San Lucas two days before. She waited, dying of excitement, but no boats arrived. She sat on the beach, not caring what she looked like, gazing out at the mouth of the bay, praying. To hold back her cries she bit the back of her hand and tasted the salt deposits secreted through her pores. They didn't taste any different from her tears.

She watched, waited, yearned. She whimpered like a dog waiting to be released, to be taken for a walk on a leash. She begged silently. God. God . . .

She made another survey of herself. Her fingernails were bitten so far back she hardly recognized them as her own. Or her hair, yellow, lank, horrible. And her face. She applied more make-up, foundation, eye shadow, liner, lipstick, rouge, powder, anything, everything. She ransacked her case, trying to find something else to add. Eyelashes, plenty of those. She chose the longest. Glue. Trembling hand. Sticky mess. Faulty vision. What did it matter, it was a face, wasn't it?

But whose?

Oh, God.

Rain.

Sun again. Someone had left behind a green plastic eye-shade, and she appropriated it. On the beach in her scorched caftan, sitting, staring, waiting. She was so tired. People kept looking at her, but no one asked for an autograph; except one. A woman who came up from out of the blur of faces that had got off the noon boat, holding out a Wrigley's spearmint gum wrapper. Would she sign it? It was for her niece. She said, I'm so happy to have met you, Miss Doone, and good luck with your career.

Didn't she *know*?

This was how the cookie crumbled.

Cupie would come and talk with her, about anything, talking but receiving no replies. Don't you think you ought to go home? she would suggest gently. Go home and get well? Lorna would shake her head. Can't. Can't. Any day now, any moment, just a little longer, look, see the sun, good weather, white sails, just a little longer, see the birds, what kind of birds are those?

She felt more feverish. Pat O'Connor sent some pills. She didn't know what they were; she flushed them down the john. She went to the village for more *ricea*, hiding the larger bottle and using a small plastic one from her cosmetic case, keeping this in her raffia bag so it was with her at all times. *La Loca,* they called her.

Steve came with her overdue bill. She said she hadn't the money to pay it. He said she must make other arrangements, they would be needing the cabaña. She asked how she could leave; he must wait until money was wired or her friends arrived. She called the boy to bring her grapefruit juice and spiked it from her plastic bottle.

It was a curious thing that she sometimes thought she saw

things quite clearly when she was drunk. Perhaps it was a property of the *ricea;* she didn't know. But she saw how foolish she had been about Emiliano. She had traded Security for Romance, and she should have learned from past mistakes that this was folly. The fatal error. He had lured her; this Mexican, with his winning smiles and *caballero* ways, had come on with her, and she knew about that type of person, on the make for rich American divorcees. That fatal type. She did not find it difficult to hate him now, that dark Emiliano and his wretched Rosalia. She told herself not to think about either of them anymore. She told herself to cream her elbows too, but didn't. . . .

The sky cleared and the sun came out again, for once and for all, it seemed. It was very hot. Of the clothes she had salvaged from the fire there were few that fit her, she had put on so much weight. She struggled into a pair of sharkskin shorts and tied on her bandanna halter, and a pair of kick mules whose heels balanced her precariously. She did her face, then tied her hair back with the Hermès scarf, and screwed her pearls onto her ears. She put on her wrist watch; it had stopped, but she wound it and reminded herself to check the time and set it.

She went to the dining room and ate her breakfast, chattering across the room to anyone who would listen to her. Wasn't it nice to see a blue sky? Wasn't it hot, though? Had anybody heard what the weather was like in New York?

She spiked her *jugo de naranja* with *ricea* from her plastic bottle, and had her usual coffee and rolls, with lots of butter. Her hand trembled as she drank and ate. She thought she ought to do something about her nails, and after breakfast she went clicking along the walkway in her heels, going to *Número Uno*, to look through the burned cabaña for her good nail file, which had been lost. She found it under a piece of rattan that had peeled from the plaster wall. The file was black and bent from the heat; she threw it away.

She stood on the patio, supporting herself by hanging on to a post. It was charred, and the soot came off on her hands and her shorts. Through her dark glasses she looked out to the bay, where people were water-skiing. There was no sign of a boat from Mirabella.

Then she saw Emiliano.

He came along the beach, carrying his equipment. He did not look at her, but went out on the rocks, where he sat putting on his fins and goggles. He slipped into the water and disappeared. The god returned to the deeps. *Muy bonitos, los pies,* she thought, very pretty feet—but of clay. She watched the path of the snorkel projecting along the surface, and the bobbing cork that kept water from getting in the tube. She could see Emiliano's dark form under the water, his powerful legs scissoring, then idling as he swam down there. She went along the walkway until she got to the sand. She took off her mules and placed them side by side, then went out on the first rock. She looked over to the beach, which was filled with sunbathers and swimmers. When she had crossed several more rocks she was out of sight. She went rock by rock until she was where Emiliano swam. His head came to the surface and he looked up at her. She had sat down and she smiled at him. *Buenos dias,* she said. He nodded. My watch stopped, she told him, *¿qué hora es?* She pointed to the marine watch on his brown wrist. He told her the time, then submerged again. *Gracias,* she said aloud, and set her watch. Very nice of him to give her the time of day. His spear gun was lying on the rocks. She bent over it, looking at the thick black rubber band that stretched over the spring mechanism. She could see Emiliano's brown body under the blue water, and his white trunks. Her hand trembled as she picked up the gun and pointed it. She couldn't control the tremors, but she saw how to lift the safety catch and pull the trigger. The shining steel spear hit him through the back of the thigh, exactly where she had aimed. The blood that rose around him was dark, and he thrashed, the blue fins breaking the surface of the water, and the foam was red. She dropped the gun and clambered to the highest rock where she could see the beach, and started screaming. Hurry, she cried, there's been an accident.

When she turned back, Emiliano was holding on to a rock, his leg stretched immobile behind him. There was a lot of blood, brighter now. He bit his lip in pain. I'm sorry, she told him with a little shrug; it just went off.

They carried him to the sand and laid him down. Someone got a horse and rode to Pat O'Connor's house. Lorna stood at the back of the crowd, trying to explain how the accident had happened: it was the safety catch; it hadn't been set. Emiliano's eyes were closed and he was suffering. She couldn't bear to look at him or at Rosalia either. Rosalia was crying. When Pat came, he needed a hacksaw to cut the metal spear in order to slide it out of the flesh, then they brought a speedboat from the yacht club and when the wound was dressed they took Emiliano to Mirabella.

Lorna picked up her shoes and went to her cabaña. She drank *ricea* and sat on the edge of the bed, holding her stomach. The sight of blood had made her sick. Pat O'Connor came in and said it was a rotten thing, what she had done. The spear had severed the knee tendon, hamstringing Emiliano like a horse; he would never be able to dance again, would probably spend his life on crutches. She said she was very sorry, honestly, but it had been an accident.

When Pat had gone she sat waiting for something to happen, someone to come. Nothing, no one, did. She ventured out of doors, coming along the walkway, and when she passed the office she heard Steve Alvarez talking with Pat O'Connor; Steve was saying he'd sent for the police. She would be taken to Mirabella and held. She did not go past the office, but went behind it. She passed through the mango grove, across the fallen, rotting yellow fruit, to the horse *palapa*. No one was there, and she untied a horse and led it away. She tightened the girth and got into the saddle in her sharkskin shorts and high-heel shoes. Her raffia bag hanging on her free arm, she urged the horse around the lagoon, toward the village. She looked behind her; no one seemed to have seen her leave.

She went first to the cantina, where she bought a pint bottle of *ricea*. She bought Mexican cigarettes and asked for matches; these were American, and on the cover they read "ENJOY!" and below that "HAVE A GOOD DAY!" She went to the store and bought a box of emery boards. She had tied the horse in some shade, and when she came out of the store she went into the church and sat on a bench. It was hot in there, but somehow she was shivering. Two women with black handkerchiefs tied over their heads came in and prayed. One noticed her and nudged the other. *La Loca.* They spoke with their flat, brown faces close together, then went out. A little Mexican child stood in the doorway. She was the most beautiful thing; she ought to be in the movies. Lorna held her arms out to her; the child looked, then ran away. Lorna sat filing her nails with one of the emery boards, and tried to pray. She thought of herself as some tragic heroine who had taken sanctuary in a church; she had seen such situations in the movies. Maureen O'Hara in *The Hunchback of Notre Dame.* Sanctuary! Sanctuary! Then Charles Laughton had poured caldrons of hot liquid down on her tormentors. Lucky Maureen. Scratch scratch scratch with the emery board.

She stayed in the church until she heard the whistle, then went to the window and saw the excursion boat coming into the bay. The plink plonk of the marimba floated melodiously over the water, and she tried to decide which of the figures at the rail had come for her. She could imagine what Mexican jails were like. She reached into her bag and took out the package of matches. ENJOY. She lit one, and stared at the flame in her shaking hand. HAVE A HAPPY DAY · · ·

Later she stood looking down at the beach from Pat O'Connor's terrace, watching the burning thatch of the church. There was a lot of activity. People were streaming across the beach from the hotel, boats were maneuvering in the bay. Horns and whistles blew. The Tashkents were out on their terrace watching, too, as the small figures tried to save the church, and the smoke rose upward in a straight black pillar as if it were holding up the blue sky. Tashkent, Tashkent, Lorna thought, filing her nails and watching the flames; no, she couldn't honestly recall Tashkent's Select Kosher Deli in Santa Monica. Scratch scratch scratch · · ·

She shivered again, and used the little tin cup at the faucet for water, into which she poured some *ricea*. She screwed the cap back on the bottle, returned it to her raffia bag, put the cup on its hook, and mounted the horse, heading it for the trail. Neither of the Tashkents noticed her. On the adobe wall a little spotted lizard moved, darted, sunlight into shade. She started up.

Like most of the beach horses, this one was only hoofbeats away from the glue factory. Even with the saddle and pad she felt its raw boniness, the thews, the flanks tight and dry as beef jerky. It panted and heaved loose-jointed over rocks and stones, its head circled with a nimbus of flies, nodding rhythmically at the end of the taut, sinewy neck, the dusty mane coarse and bristly, the short ears flat against the skull. She could feel the saddle slipping and she yanked on the reins. The horse came to a grateful halt and she got off. She tightened the cinch, got back on, and kicked the ribbed belly until the pathetic creature moved again, bearing her up the hillside.

Jungles she did not find amusing. Nor glamorous, mysterious, or exotic. This one was merely a green forest, green above, around, below, and though there was nothing in it she particularly dreaded, no unseen animal she thought of as waiting to pounce on her, it was the jungle itself she feared. But she feared more being put aboard the boat by the police before the *MorryEll* arrived, and so she lived with her fear

164

and went up. Hot, dank, stifling, a moist steam bath, condensed vapor and humidity that clogged the nostrils and made her breath rattle as the motion of the horse joggled it out of her.

Her back ached, bent from keeping her head ducked against low-hanging foliage. Even with the moisture her eyes felt dry, scratchy; even with the heat she felt a chill, and her forehead where she touched it was cold, and her neck and breast. Her sweat felt cold and she undid her scarf and used it to blot herself. The path grew narrower as the horse, obeying the constant urging of her nervous swinging feet in the stirrups, plodded upward.

For a time she followed the reverse course of the river, and near the water the air seemed fresher, easier to breathe. From time to time she lost sight of the stream as the trail veered away, but she could still hear its sound. She let the reins hang loose, but the horse paid no attention to the absence of command; it went on at its own dogged pace, making its own way.

The water flow grew louder, and she recognized the sound of rapids. No, not rapids, a waterfall, spilling between some mound-shaped rocks into a clear pool where brown fish hugged a sandy bottom. Was this where the greedy Spaniards with their looted gold had drowned? She got off the horse and pulled it under a tree, weighting the reins with a rock. The horse yanked free and ambled loose-hocked to the water and drank noisily. It threw up its head and nickered once, twice. There was a pause, then something, another beast entirely, answered from the green depths beyond. The horse's ears pricked up and she snatched the reins, led the horse to a berry bush, and tethered it. She pulled up a tuft of grass and held it out. Horsie, horsie, she said mildly; horsie didn't want any. It ate at the bush instead.

She went toward the pool, undoing her halter. She kicked off her shoes, pulled off her shorts, then undid her wrist watch and unfastened her earrings. She folded her clothes and placed them on a rock, and keeping on her bra and panties, she stepped out into the icy pool. She could not suppress a shivery cry, then she was in all over and it felt actually good, revivifying. She didn't swim, but floated, arms and legs making an X outward from her body. She looked up at the sky, past the lacy green edges of the forest canopy, and it occurred to her that no one, not a single person in the world, knew where she was at that moment.

She thought it was the horse, and at first she paid no attention. Then she realized it wasn't and she lifted her head out of the water to see what was making the sound. A donkey. A pair of them, with cages hung on their backs. The sun was behind the two men leading them, so she saw them only in silhouette, their faces darkly obscure, staring placidly down at her in the clear water, idly curious, one with a hand angled on a hip, the other chewing on a piece of grass, just watching her. Looking up at them, she felt not only embarrassment, but unaccountable fear. She made her way awkwardly under the rocky overhang where she could touch bottom, then submerged to her chin, arms crossed over her breasts. One of the men laughed and said something in Spanish to the other one. That one laughed and replied. They both stood looking down and not saying anything.

Go away, she said, gesticulating and swirling the water about her. *Vaya, vaya.* She tried to sound angry, but her voice trembled.

Okay, lady, the first man said placatingly. He tugged at his donkey and moved on. The second remained for a last look, then started off behind the first. As he turned into the light she recognized him. It was the man called Ávila.

She waited, crouched under the rocky outcropping, and when her ears told her they had gone she came out. She wrung out her hair and combed it back with her fingers, then tied the folded scarf around it. Her nylon panties were still damp as she slipped into the shorts, and the halter clung to her wet bra. She put on her high heels, untied the horse, and led it to the trail; it made an *Oof* sound as she slung into the saddle, dangling feet groping their way into the stirrups. They moved forward and up, through the steaming jungle. Why up? she asked herself. Because she could not go down, she answered.

She wondered how far it was to the top. She had no idea, and looked to the river to see if its course had narrowed at all, since she had been told it was fed by a spring somewhere high upon the peak they called the Sleeping Maiden.

There was a grove of large-trunked trees with peeling bark, with half-broken branches that had gone dead, and beyond them, past the rough trunks, she saw something move. A flash only, but she remembered the men with the donkeys. She had thought they were going down the mountain, but now it occurred to her that perhaps they were going up instead. They were there ahead, waiting for her. Under her, the horse heaved dreadfully, its belly expanding and contracting like a leathery bellows, head dog-hung from the neck, patiently waiting with her. She listened, indecisive, fearful; heard nothing; went on.

She became increasingly afraid, not only of the men, but of the horse. It seemed to her it might give out at any moment, and she got off and led it; the reins drooping back over her shoulder. She could feel its hot jolting breath on her back, could smell it. Turning, she saw a greenish foam forming around the steel bit. She remembered there were little berries on the bush it had been chewing. She turned to feel the horse's forehead. A silly thing to do; there was no flesh there, only a layer of hide with matted hair. She remained undecided for some moments, hearing the rattle of breath in her chest, then tugged the horse after her, walking this way until, fatigued, she had to get back on. She felt the rough, chafed spots where the stirrups rubbed her ankles. She looked for a place where the jungle cleared, with a view to the sea, but there was none, only the ceiling and the floor and the walls, all green; it was like being in a great green room. It grew less stifling as they went up. A breeze riffled the green leaves, not a warm, but a cold one, and she felt herself shivering again. The horse as well. It was wet under the edges of the saddle and where the bridle went around the head, and its movements grew more and more pronounced, more jerkily annoying. From ahead she heard a noise of rocks or stones being dislodged, a trickle of pebbles, then silence. She made a low, quavering sound in her throat, and undid the Hermès scarf and tied it around her neck. The trail had left the river some time ago, but now rejoined it. Finding a shallow place, she let the horse wade out and drink. It dropped its head against the slack reins and sucked greedily, then, head still down, it shook all over. Each of its limbs trembled with shock, until she felt the shuddering beast collapse under her. She cried out as it fell heavily into the water, and she pitched sideways and out of the saddle, one leg pinned under the horse's back. She sat in horrified surprise, pushing at the withers, trying to get the animal to move, but it remained lodged against her.

It was dead. It had stopped breathing almost immediately, and she felt annoyed that it should have done such a thing, there in the jungle, under such circumstances. She hadn't been hurt, she would be all right if she could only free her leg, and she dug at the sand and rocks, trying to release herself. When she lifted her head again she was looking at Ávila.

He was in half-light at the bank, staring down at her. He signaled over his shoulder and the other one appeared and they waded out and both tugged at the horse until she could extricate her leg. She got up and staggered to the bank, feeling her wet clothes pressing against her, revealing her body. The two men continued heaving at the horse until they had dragged it out of the water. Flies were already circling, large green buzzing ones. She looked at the men and said, What should I do?

Ávila shrugged and smiled. His gold teeth shone as he thoughtfully scraped the palm of his hand along his unshaven chin. He watched her, his smile fading, and she heard the other one moving behind her. Before she could turn he had her around the waist; her shoes flew off as she kicked, and he lifted her from the ground and held her. Ávila came up to her and began undoing her halter.

There are only two kinds of women, she had often told herself, those who fight and those who submit. She had wondered which category she fitted, thinking of course that she would fight, that she would somehow hurt them as they hurt her. She did not fight. She went limp in the other one's arms while Ávila continued working at her clothes. They had lowered her onto the grass in the shade, and Ávila got her out of the halter and skinned her shorts down and off, and she heard his harsh breath as he knelt over her, and his anticipatory sounds of wonder and appreciation. The second one grasped her hands while she lost first her nylon panties, then her bra, Ávila clumsily fingering under her back to undo the hook and eye and then snapping the bra away and staring at her breasts.

The second one waited until he saw she was offering no resistance, then she heard him walking away. Ávila was standing over her, undoing his belt buckle. She turned her head to the side, staring at the cadaver, the head angled grotesquely, the eyeballs staring from their sockets, the large flies all over it, shining green-gold in the sunlight. She closed her lids, flung her bent arms across them as she heard the sound of buttons being worked, urgent, determined, then his steel buckle being unfastened, and the rustle of his jeans as they dropped. She winced but did not cry out when he touched her. She opened her eyes again.

He had a small medal around his neck and it hung down on a chain, swinging before her, and she could see the stamped form of the madonna moving as he moved. She kept her eyes on it, the swinging disk in front of her; it was, she supposed, a form of hypnotism, which produced a certain mental state, and she told herself it was this that got her through the act without screaming or fighting.

It was worse with the second one. He wore no medal and she doubted he even went to church. He hurt her badly. It was in no way a religious experience, nor one of knowledge or enlightenment, merely of endurance. She couldn't have borne it if he had tried to kiss her, those lips on her mouth. He didn't try.

She had lived through worse things, she told herself afterward. She lay back in the shade, feeling cold instead of warm, and reached for her clothes. They had taken her wrist watch and pearls, and were now a short distance away, hunkered down like cowboys, smoking and watching her. She got up and went to the river and squatted and washed herself. She wondered if anything inside had been damaged. She blessed her hysterectomy and the doctor who had done it. She moved behind a tree, into the sun, drying off. The horse lay frozen in ghastly death, fly-covered, its belly grossly swollen. She paid no attention to the men as she dressed, slowly and methodically. She wanted to bind her hair back again with the scarf, but it was tightly knotted around her neck. Ávila had hung on to it, gripping it in his hands and pulling her up to him, and now she had trouble undoing the wet knot. When she was dressed she moved from behind the tree. She found her sunglasses; one lens was shattered, but she put them on. Overhead she saw birds circling, large, dark ones.

The men had come to standing positions beside the donkeys, blocking the trail. As she moved, Ávila laughed; his hands fumbled at his fly and he stood exposed again. She cried out then, turned and ran. She stopped a short way up the trail, clutching at her stomach, sobbing. She heard them talking, then heard the chink of the donkeys' harness and gear as they moved. They went down the trail and the green room was silent except for her whimpering. She waited until she heard another noise, the rush and flapping of wings, and turning back she saw three vultures drop onto the carcass of the horse, their beaks stabbing into the hard flesh. One of them swiveled to gaze at her, bald, crowned with a ring of dirty fuzz, the beak dripping red. She turned away and her scream seemed to shake the very leaves of the trees. From below, through the green, came the sound of laughter. She couldn't tell if it was Ávila or the other one. She screamed again, and felt that she might never stop.

Still she went up instead of down. The trail continued clear and open, and the only difficulty was her fatigue. The last time she had looked at her watch, before Ávila had pocketed it, it had said four o'clock. It must be five by now. Would they miss her at the hotel? Certainly not before dinner, and by then it would be dark. The Tashkents hadn't seen her leave. She had been a fool not to tell anyone of her plan. Or to leave a note. Well, she had been a fool before and had survived. She would survive this. The cigarettes in her bag were wet, but the matches had dried. When she got to the top she would make a fire and pray they saw the smoke before nightfall.

She went on, making her feet move, her arms swinging at her sides as if disconnected, moving with her shoulders, but somehow unnaturally, as if they didn't wish to be a part of her. She wanted to stop crying, but couldn't. Every part of her hurt, her head ached, and she had pulled muscles in the backs of her legs; whether from the horse or the men she couldn't tell. When she thought, really thought, about what could happen, was going to happen, to her, she felt the greatest terror of her life. She tried to think of Carrie, of Jeffrey, of Richard, but their names, faces, beings, only frustrated her and made her more afraid. She realized she might be close to never seeing another human being again, ever. She would turn and go down. Then she thought of Ávila and the other one, on the trail below, she thought of the dead horse and the vultures, and she continued climbing.

The way was narrower, the river lost to view. She saw that other trails branched off, small tunnels into the green darkness. She became confused, not at all sure that she hadn't left the main trail for one of the side ones. She stopped, wondered what to do, cried again, continued on. Most of the other trails sloped away downward, and she thought that if she stayed with the one that went up she would be all right. But the trail appeared no less confused than she; it couldn't seem to make up its mind which way to go. Overhead the foliage grew lower and lower and she often had to stoop to pass. Long vines hung down and she pushed through their tangling loops and twinings, urgent and more terrified than ever.

Then, inexplicably, she could go no farther. The jungle had closed in around her, the passage narrowing until she was confronted on every side by moving, waving green. The trail had ended, she had no idea when. She cried out again, loudly, and the sound hurt her to make it, hurt her to hear it, her own spoken terror. She turned and started back down. Everything looked different from the way it had been coming up and she had no idea which trail to take. There was some grass and, her knees giving way, she collapsed on it, falling in a slow graceful movement. She lay panting, then rolled over with a quick motion as something moved under her; what it was she couldn't tell, but something alive. Her head struck something and the green became black.

There was blood all across her eyes when she came to again, she could feel it, wet and sticky. She put her hand up and took it away red. She felt gingerly with her fingertips, trying to ascertain the extent of the wound. It was on her temple, a gash which she bandaged with the scarf. She stared at the blood on her fingers, then put them in her mouth and licked them. She was talking, to whom she had no idea, or even what she was saying. How could she feel so cold, so chilled, when she was in the jungle? She looked around. It was all unfamiliar, but she was certain it was not the place where she had fallen. Had she come to it before without knowing it, had she walked there without being aware? Had she gone up, or down, or to the side? She couldn't tell. She started out again, turning to her right because the ground there seemed to slope down. She let herself be drawn by the pull of gravity, slipping and sliding, touching her bandaged head, pushing the yellow hair from her eyes. She ducked low again under some branches and passed through a green tunnel and came out into sunlight.

On the other side, she collapsed again. It was like having walked through a wall of green and come into another room altogether. She felt dizzy and light, the same feeling she had in airplanes, up there above the world, disconnected, cut off. Perhaps it was that feeling alone that produced the sight, like a mirage in the desert, for what she now saw appeared to be a stone gateway rising out of the jungle growth, surrounded by green and covered with vines. There were wide steps leading to a low platform, on it crude square pillars, with carvings. Beyond and through the apertures they formed was more green. The sun shone on the stones; they stood out in the light like giant blocks of gold, brilliant against the green. She stayed where she had dropped, leaning on one arm, holding her head with the other, staring at the sight. She wasn't sure she was really seeing it at all, it seemed so unreal, so movie-like, such a figment of her mind, yet it surely was there. Turning her head slightly, she saw, through the glaze that clouded her vision, a flight of stairs on the right-hand side of the platform, between two of the columns, rising upward to the top, where they broke off, leading into space. She sat staring at them for a long time, still holding her head, then she got to her knees and rose unsteadily. She walked across the clearing until she came to the first long step at ground level. She reached down with her hand, felt the sun-warmed stone. When she lifted her head she felt dizzy and the pain was terrible. She sat and rested for a moment, then got up again and continued to the platform. It, too, was made of stone blocks, pitted and cracked like ancient buildings she had seen in Europe, like the statues in the Tivoli gardens, like a deserted movie set. She stepped among the green vines half covering it and went to the next stairway. She started up, feeling dizzier and trying to keep her balance. When she came close to the top she crouched and moved upward step by step by sitting on each one. Then, as her head came level with the top one, she looked down.

The view past the trees was that of the small end of the telescope, so far away was the beach and the hotel. Yet she could see them, the infinitesimally tiny thatched roofs, the spread of the lagoon, which even now was cutting its way through the sandbank, and as usual people had gathered to see it break into the bay. She could see the burned church and the *palapa* where the horses were tethered, and smoke came from the kitchen chimney. She could see the roof of Bob and Joan's house, and the end of the yacht club, built out on pilings, and the boats bobbing at their moorings. There were the usual ones, the *Molly g* and the *Paradiso* and the *Alrae,* and there was another. A large sailboat, with a tall mast and a reefed sail. She recognized it: the *MorryEll.* She even thought she could make out figures sitting on the fantail. One, one of them must be Richard. She drew farther up on the last step but one, and sat staring down, holding her head with one hand, the other flattened against the pain in her breast. It was funny, so she laughed. It didn't sound like her laugh, but she recognized it as someone's laugh. She tottered up and waved her arms over her head. She called and cried and laughed; surely they must see her if she could see them. She screamed as loudly as she could, but the sound seemed to go no farther than her own ears. Then, having strained on tiptoe, she was falling, and the green all around her seemed to catch and swallow her up.

When she came to again, she was not herself; she did not know who she was or where she was or why she was there. Her head hurt, and other parts of her body; she was thirsty. She had come here with some vague desire or purpose in mind; she did not know what this was. She was lying halfway down the stone steps, on her back, staring up at the blue sky. She lay still, in pain, sucking hot air through her open mouth. Somehow she got herself around to a sitting position, and looking up, she saw the steps leading nowhere, only into the sky. Shade; she wanted shade. She moved downward, to where a pillar cast a long shadow, and sat against it. Something bound her head tightly and she felt the fabric of a bandage; no, a scarf; but whose she had no idea, or how she had injured herself. She undid the scarf and spread it on her lap. There was dried blood all over the blue flowers; she knew their name but couldn't remember. Anemone? She sang snatches of a song—"The Dove," was it that?—thinking she really had a pretty voice. She held the scarf up and watched the chill breeze ripple the silk from the corners, then she let it go altogether, and it flew across the stones and caught on the corner of the opposite column. She tried to think, feeling she must come to some resolution regarding something, some problem, but she couldn't. The shade felt nicer than the sun. She was thirsty and wondered when they would bring her something to drink; water would do. Inner sounds seemed to catch in her chest and throat, refusing to issue through her dry lips. Then she saw the bag.

Someone had left a raffia bag by the lower steps, and she inched her way toward it. When she could reach the cord she dragged it back with her into the shade. She opened it and took out the things. There was a package of wet cigarettes, matches, a bottle of suntan oil, emery boards, and another bottle, a pint of *ricea*. She unscrewed the tin cap and tilted it to her mouth. She struck her head on the stone behind and felt a blinding jab. The liquor was hot going down her throat, but it was wet and she drank, drank again. She was panting as she took away the bottle and held it in her lap. On the printed label was a picture of a bird clutching a snake in its talons; where had she seen it before? She drank again, trying to remember. The *ricea* tasted both hot and cold, and she shivered in spite of the sun all around her. She sat staring at the wall of green, watching as the wind hypnotically shook the leaves, green, unequivocally green. The wind died and the leaves fell still, then moved again, slowly, sinuously, agitated by the unseen currents.

It was like a garden, for all through the green were bright flowers, and above them flew a little bird, bright with colors. It hung in the air with the green behind it, the way a hummingbird hangs, supporting itself by nearly invisible wings. There was a cluster of insects and the bird darted among them, pecking, picking, snatching. She laughed, holding out the bottle to it; the bird paid no attention. She drank again, and felt the liquor flowing through her, the sharp pain slowly ebbing to dullness, and she was overcome with lassitude, and it seemed that in this green and gold and flowered garden nothing mattered that she could think of. While she drank she undid her halter, and when she could get to her feet she took off the rest of her clothes. Why, she did not know, but she felt she wanted to be naked, and she put down the bottle and uncapped the suntan oil and began dribbling it along her arms and thighs and massaging it in. Her skin was a deep, golden brown, almost like a Mexican's. She let the oil run sensuously over her shoulders and down her spine, and put her head back and let the oil drop there, rubbing it in on her forehead and cheeks. She ran the oil between her thighs, sliding her hand between them, trying to comfort the soreness.

The snake drew in along the platform from her left, from behind the base of a broken column. She was not frightened, nor even surprised, but watched it with interest. The snake was large, about four feet, perhaps even longer, and it moved with a curious sideways motion. It slid along the stone blocks, perhaps a foot at a time, then would laze itself into a wiggly pattern and lie still for a few moments, then come farther on, idly, provocatively. She thought it was coming toward her, but no, it paid no attention. It had glittering patterns along its thick back, a kind of artistic geometry, like the pieces of mosaic you saw in old Italian churches, and along its softly rounded sides were shiny metallic scales, and hollow pits beside the nostrils, and the little forked tongue rippled wetly from the blunt snout. The snake paused, in that slack half-wiggled shape, its head lifting half a foot from the stone, the head swaying one way and the other, and she could see its pale underbelly, segmented with broader, larger scales, like plates of bone-white armor, and the head swung to and fro, and the eyes shone. It stayed that way for some moments, then the head lowered and it came farther on.

Now, she told herself, it would come toward her, but it didn't; it moved past her to the far pillar, where it stopped again. It lay without moving in that sloppy, loosely formed S shape and for all she knew might have gone to sleep. She remembered something Pat O'Connor had told her about the snake handlers, the Appalachian people who believed so devoutly in their God-given ability to control the snake's movements, and how their faith could inhibit the reptile's natural instinct to bite. It was an act of faith; if you believed, if you truly believed . . . She went on staring at the snake, which lay motionless in the sun. The wind played with the green leaves behind, softly rushing, lifting and turning them, rustling the green wall, and again the little bright bird flew out of it, hovering above, where the insects massed in a dusky cloud. The movement caused the snake first to stir, then to slide back across the platform until it was under the bird. It waited there, coiled, its brilliance suddenly muted, brown like the stones it lay on, then the head lifted slowly, so slowly, the long body tensing as it rose higher and higher, the little bird swooping brightly over its head, like a bright-colored crown of feathers, and then with sudden knowledge she realized who the snake was, Quetzalcoatl, the Plumed Serpent, and this was his temple, with the golden steps that led to nowhere. Divine snake, divine crown, snake and bird together, symbolizing that ancient deity, whose ruined house this was.

A holy place; she had come to a holy place, and this bright scaled and feathered creature was its spirit, master, guardian. It had dwelt here all the years of that lost civilization Cortés had destroyed. Here among the billowy green it had remained hidden, and through some miracle it had been made known to her. A revelation. The god-miracle she had sought. She would tell of it one day, tell how the Plumed Serpent had come from the green plumed jungle and had held its private ceremonies, and that where it now strained upward to achieve its feathered crown there had been an altar, an altar to the sun, and these steps beside her were the golden steps to the sun and those others were the next flight, upward, upward, for surely there was a God in heaven; it had been promised to her, and with a rush of sudden insight she beheld the epiphany, saw a bright clear picture of what the god had been, what it was and would forever be.

The god Quetzalcoatl lived in the green, where he hid in the shadows, and came forth to behold the sun, and the bird came to make his feathered crown, and through some mysterious accident of fate it had been allowed to her to discover the place and to witness this rarest of happenings. She had never seen a god before, and few crowns, but here were both before her. She inched away from the column and came nearer. The snake paid her no attention, stretching its long neck upward, rising on strained muscles from the stone floor, while the bird danced overhead, amid the black life it fed on. Then, like a scaled lance, the soft, limpid coils tensed, became stick-straight as in a blur the snake shot upward and tore the bird down out of the air. The bright feathers beat wildly as they hung from the clamped jaws, the upper overthrusting the lower where the fangs pierced. Then the jaws jacked open and the bird fell to the floor, hopping around, mutilated, dazed from the attack, while the venom eased through it until it toppled, a small mass of crushed colored feathers. The snake had gone soft again, and lowered itself, watching the bird's feeble movements, curving itself along the stone.

She crawled nearer and reached to take up the bird. She held it in her hands and felt it throb against her shaking palm. Her movement had caused the snake to coil again, with a warning buzz from its tail. It reared up, the god Quetzalcoatl, and she offered the bird to it, sacrificially. She stretched her nude oiled body along the rough stones, reaching out her hand with the bird in it, holding it to the head of the god, inching forward, longingly, toward the scaled god, presenting it with the feathered crown.

The snake struck. It drew deep into its coil, the triangular head sharply angled, the neck engorged, the body thickened like a flexed muscle, then it erected itself with sudden swiftness and struck, sinking its curved fangs into the soft flesh of her forearm. *Eat,* she said, *eat me.* Partake. Have me. She hardly felt the pain, so enraptured, so enamored was she of what was happening to her. She caught up its full length in her other hand, gripping with her fingers that hard taut body, entwining it about her head, brought it nearer, while it struck her again. Near and nearer, strike followed by strike, flash upon bright flash, until she could touch with her lips the plated scales, the brilliant designs along the back, and the ivory fangs drove again and again, paired punctures into her skin, her hands, arms, shoulders, breasts. It bit methodically without hurry, decisively yet with indolence, the rippling muscles contracting, then elongating as the jeweled head drove at her, the jaws hinged wide, and she could see into the pale wet tunnel of the throat, the fangs suppurating as the venom poured from the sac behind the jaws, those godly juices. He struck at her cheek, kissing her, once, twice, and she returned the embrace, kiss for kiss, her lips pressing against the warm, scaled flesh, crooning and sighing, not feeling the pain at all as she thrust its rigid form down, down to her abdomen and along her thighs, and at last to the place where she wanted him most. There she felt his kiss again, and she was crying with joy: she had captured the god, in her hands, with her flesh, and with a wave of intolerable ecstasy she sensed that her female body was dominating that powerful thing, that thing she had worshiped all her life; that now, finally, she was mastering both herself and the god together, the feathered serpent. It was something she would remember always. A passionate engagement, the man and the woman, the god and the mortal, for he was not merely one god to her but all men, and whatever it was that Willie Marsh had known on the church steps in Italy at the moment of his spiritual illumination was now revealed to her on *these* steps, the golden ones that led to nowhere. And when she had loved the god and in turn had been loved by it, time after stinging time, she flung it away with one sharp triumphant cry and watched it grow weak and soft again, watched it crawl in its S shape back to where it had come from, out of the cool shadows behind the pillar where the green leaves rushed and billowed.

She lay back against the steps, relaxed, exhausted, feeling release and an incredible rush of warmth, smelling the heavy scent of flowers and the dimly remembered aroma of suntan oil, and her eyelids drooped languidly as she watched the bird, still palpitating in its feathered splendor—so bright, so terribly bright—and she wondered why the serpent god had not taken with him his crown.

For two days they had searched the green mountain, men and boys on horseback and burro, with sticks beating on pans and calling, spreading along the trails like beaters on safari. *La Loca*, quite mad to have gone up there alone; and they found signs—a broken necklace, then the horse, gutted— then, almost at the top, her body out on the covered-over trail where she had somehow made her way. A blessing, they said, that she had fallen where she did, for surely if the vultures had found her they would have left little of her. Even so, she was not a pretty sight. Her flesh was mottled dark red and green, the colors of sinister jewels, with double holes everywhere. They had never heard of a *culebra de cascabel* striking so many times, an orgy of bites, her face, breasts, thighs, even the more intimate place. They took blankets and made a crude package of her, stiff and bloated, and slung her between two burros, and that was how they brought her down. Flies followed in swarms. The people from the boat called *MorryEll* came ashore and identified the body. One, a man called Richard, arranged for the remains to be sent first by boat to Mirabella, where it would be flown to Los Angeles; she had children there. He was, he said, surprised to find her in this place; in any case, he scarcely knew her. He used to see her in the movies, though. Then they went back to the boat and weighed anchor just before sunset, while the mariachis were playing on the beach, marimba, accordion, and maracas, and the last of the fishermen came in with their catch, while the beach was turning blue and the hotel guests gathered in the bar, drinking their coco locos.

Bobbitt

Everyone must have a name, but since he said he did not, he was called Mr. Thingamabob. Sometimes they called him Mr. Thingamajig or Thingamacallit, but these names sounded more or less the same, so it didn't much matter. For variety's sake he might be Mr. Spritzsinger, or Lord Calliope the Fifth, or J. Farquewell Harboomsteen. "What's the 'J' for?" they would ask him. "Jack? Joe? John?" "Joke," he would say. Of all the many street entertainers in the park that spring, he was the best. Every day through the fine May weather, when the children were still scratching themselves out of their winter woolens, while under their yellow and blue umbrellas the Sabrett hot-dog vendors were selling Italian ices, and the balloon men were blowing up balloons, and leggy adolescent girls floundered on roller skates or chalked out hopscotch squares or jumped rope, and their younger brothers sailed toy vessels in the boat basin just north of Seventy-second Street, on almost any day through that spring-time would come Mr. Thingamabob (or Mr Thingamajig or Thingamacallit), rattling his tambourine with the colored ribbons on it, or tootling his whistle, or squeezing the black rubber bulb of his curly brass horn that went *hwonk! hwonk!* —not like a duck but like the horn of something rare and grand, say of a big Rolls-Royce. And when the children heard him coming, his nonsense pack bouncing on his back, they would troop along after him, he nodding and winking and urging them to follow, so it became a sort of parade, and he would go dancing on ahead, bowing and strutting or doing

181

a funny jig, leading them around the curve of the boat basin, until they arrived at the little park-within-a-park north of the Conservatory Water. Here were the Alice in Wonderland statues, a group of sculpted bronze figures including the White Rabbit checking his large watch, the Mad Hatter, and between them, seated atop the broad cap of a bronze mushroom, Alice herself. This was where Mr. Thingamabob would set up shop and entertain the children. He always wore funny clothes: sometimes cut-off baggy trousers with gingham patches and a polka-dot shirt and clog shoes and a flower behind his ear and a crazy hat on his head, and a clown's nose made from a red sponge ball and held over his own by an elastic band, and a big orange wig; or sometimes he would be dressed as a gypsy; or sometimes in white tie and tails with a tall top hat which would flip open and a bird would pop up on a spring and twitter. Out of his nonsense pack he would bring oranges or hoops to juggle, or put puppet figures on his hands and make them talk to one another or to the children, or do a clog dance—he could leap straight up in the air and knock his feet together, side to side, before they ever touched the ground again. When the children—the grownups, too—were gathered in a circle around the statues, then Mr. Thingamabob would suddenly jump up onto the mushroom in front of Alice, where he would sit cross-legged, with the children watching and waiting below, and when everyone had quieted down—there was always a good deal of laughing and talking—he would waggle his big bushy eyebrows once or twice over his enormous glasses, twitch his nose from side to side, until the laughter had finally died away, and he would begin.

That was when Mr. Thingamabob became the Storyteller, and for an hour, perhaps even two, he would keep his young audience spellbound while he sat on Alice's mushroom telling stories to them. The grownups would have taken places along nearby benches and the children clustered around the mushroom while Mr. Thingamabob spun his tales, seemingly out of the air, for that was part of the magic of Mr. Thingamabob: everything seemed to come out of thin air, from nowhere.

There was one thing about him: he would tell his tale, but always he would stop just at the best part; he would peer as though to check the time from the White Rabbit's watch, and then he would utter some foolishness like "Ohmigoo'ness, it's late—" and he would stop, as if he had to hurry away right then and there; the children would jump up and shout and plead with him to stay and finish the story, and cry More! More! but no, that was all for today. Tomorrow, he would say, come back tomorrow for the end. But would *he* come tomorrow? they would clamor. And oh, yes, he would come tomorrow, or if not, the day after. Then he would pass his funny hat around to the grownups, who would put money in it, and off would go Mr. Thingamabob, tootling his whistle and rattling his tambourine with the colored ribbons, his pack on his back, the children tumbling along behind him, skipping and running and shouting and laughing.

But nobody ever knew where he came from, nobody ever knew where he went, nobody knew who he was.

Now, one afternoon late in May, two elderly ladies came walking in the park. It was one of those perfect days New Yorkers see all too rarely, when everybody seemed to be out in the park watching everybody else out in the park, when everything seems clear and clean and lovely, as if a giant broom had suddenly swept out all the corners of the city, swept all the ugliness under the rug, so that the eye could view the world as it should be seen, a lovely place to live in.

At least this was what Nellie Bannister was thinking as she and her best friend, Hilda, came into the park on that fine fair afternoon. They often liked to take a stroll together, or to sit on a bench, chatting and feeding the pigeons, and though they seldom ventured farther than the south end of the park, around the Sheep Meadow or along the Mall as far as the band shell, today they walked longer and farther, all the way to the boat basin. It was a gay scene, with the white-sailed toy boats cutting across the water in the breeze, with dogs running free of leashes, and people playing their radios as they sat sunning on the benches. Nellie gave Hilda's hand a little squeeze; it was just so good to be alive, wasn't it? They walked on until they arrived at the Alice in Wonderland park, where they found places on a bench, sharing it with three nursemaids in a row, their shiny blue perambulators close by so they could keep an eye on their charges. Then, faintly in the distance, above the sounds of traffic from Fifth Avenue, were heard the sounds of a tootling whistle and the rattle of brass bangles on a tambourine, and down from the crest of the hill came the strangest sight.

"My stars," said Nellie, "look at that."

"Mr. Thingamabob," one of the nursemaids was heard to say, and along the fellow came, around the boat basin, collecting children every step of the way. He was dressed outlandishly in a long embroidered robe of red, like a wizard's gown, and a blue Arabian turban with a feather curling up at the front and held with a jeweled pin. More and more children came trooping after him, as with comic pomp he proceeded to the bronze mushroom. On one earlobe was hung a gold hoop, and he wore a long hooked nose with a wart on the end and bristly mustaches that swept out left and right like two shoe brushes, a pair of bushy black eyebrows that moved up and down, and large round tinted glasses, the color changing as he moved his head, sometimes pink, sometimes blue, sometimes yellow. He put his whistle and tambourine inside his nonsense pack, and after some shenanigans which kept the children giddy with laughter, he clapped his hands until they were settled quietly all around him, then took up the thread of his story.

"Now," he began, "you remember yesterday there was a fearful battle at the very gates of Ferdival Castle, and no one knew how many lay dead on the field. The brave knight, Sir Forticoeur, had waited till he saw that all was lost, and after rescuing the fair Princess Gwinnathred from unthought-of horrors, they retreated to the Grimly Wood. There, against a hummock, weary after so many hours of wielding his mighty sword, he slept, with his golden helmet with the scarlet plume hung on the branch of the tree where Olduff, the owl, roosted, and beside the knight sat the Princess Gwinnathred, careworn but watchful. Evening was nigh and the gloomy wood was fearful quiet, and yonder some four hundred leagues lay the castle, and who knew when the king would arrive with help?"

Until now (though the nursemaids all were lending an ear to the tale) the two ladies on the bench had gone on talking to each other, but as Mr. Thingamabob continued, Nellie turned her head and listened more carefully.

"Now, as everyone knows, there was no stronger, no nobler, no more wise nor valiant knight in the whole kingdom than Sir Forticoeur, but on this day, after such evil tidings and fell deeds, his strong heart was near to breaking, and who was there to mend it, since the king himself had not come? Who was to help him from this worst of predicaments? Surely not the sad and mournful maid, the Princess Gwinnathred."

"Princess Gwinnathred?" echoed Nellie aloud to her friend. "Why, I believe he's telling one of the Bobbitt stories." Matters became clearer with Mr. Thingamabob's next sentence.

"Then, having mistaken their way, who should come into the gloomy wood but Bobbitt and Missy Priss—"

"Why, that's you," said Nellie's companion, Hilda.

"Hush," said Nellie.

"And who should Bobbitt and Missy Priss come across but Sir Forticoeur and the Princess, who cried softly, 'Whatever shall we do?' while the gallant knight slept. 'Well, this is a pretty kettle of fish, I'm sure,' said Missy Priss in her starchy fashion, eying the sleeping knight and the mournful maid, who, glad to see her friends again, repeated, 'Whatever shall we do?' 'Yes, Missy Priss,' asked Bobbitt, 'what indeed shall we do?' 'Why,' returned Missy Priss without a moment's hesitation, 'we must put pluck in our hearts and mind our manners; that is what we must do!' Here she took up Sir Forticoeur's sword, which was not easy for her, since it was very heavy, and used it to make a fearful bang on his buckler, so that Olduff the owl flew away as the sound rang throughout the wood. When Sir Forticoeur awoke with a start, Missy Priss gave him a good shake. 'No nonsense, sir. On your feet; this is no time for sleeping. Dark things are afoot and it is for us to trip them up.' So saying, she handed him the golden helmet with the scarlet plume, and telling the Princess to take heart, and with Bobbitt safely by the hand—for who knew where he might run off to next?—she led them farther into the wood until they came to the cave of the Evening Witch, and here they prepared their strategy. . . ."

Meanwhile a baby in one of the prams had become fretful, and Nellie nodded to the nursemaid to quiet it down so that she might hear the rest of the story. It was all so familiar to her, and yet how strange, hearing it thus, in Central Park, from this very odd-looking creature in his weird raiment atop the bronze mushroom. He told it, she thought, very well, and there was not a murmur from the children. The next part, of course, was the retaking of Ferdival Castle after the meeting with the king, then the famous tourney between Sir Forticoeur, the Golden Knight, and Sir Mordant, the Dark Knight, on the field of valor.

Happily, in short order Mordant was toppled from his horse by Sir Forticoeur, who stood above him, ready to part his head from his shoulders, and then mercifully offered him his life. Mordant is sternly ordered to leave the kingdom under pain of death, and afterward there is a great celebration, the fair Princess Gwinnathred is given in troth to her knight, Sir Forticoeur. Alfie, late as usual, arrives on the scene in time to toast the betrothed lovers, Bobbitt and Missy Priss receive the thanks of the king and court, and then the three are magically whisked away from Ferdival Castle and back to the Wickham house for a jubilant retelling of their adventures.

"More! More!" the children clamored, but as usual, Mr. Thingamabob shook his head, clapped his hands, and sprang down from the mushroom. "Tomorrow," he told them, "or perhaps the day after—who can say?" And he began an antic little dance, tootling his whistle and shaking his tambourine. Then suddenly he stopped, shielding his eyes against the sun, and looked over at the nursemaids and the two ladies seated on the bench. He took up his pack, put away his whistle and tambourine, and walked over to them.

"Hello, Nellie," he said. She gave him a puzzled but proper nod. "Hello," she replied as Mr. Thingamabob removed his turban, then the nose, glasses, mustaches, and eyebrows, all of which came off in one piece, and stood before her with his real face.

"Don't you recognize me?" he asked, laughing. " 'Tis me. Bobbitt."

Nellie stared at him, unable to believe her eyes. "Bobbitt?" she said, while *BobbittBobbittBobbitt,* the nursemaids repeated down the line on the bench. Then Nellie was laughing and crying all at once, and she got up, throwing her arms about him and kissing him, and saying to her friend, "Hilda—this is *Bobbitt!* My *Bobbitt!*"

Hilda had been hearing about Nellie's Bobbitt for years. Bobby Ransome had been the most famous child actor of the fifties; his star had shone for less than a decade, a bright comet blazing across the Hollywood heavens, and many people had held their hands up, trying to catch some of the falling stardust. Nellie said it was a miracle, finding him this way. She held him off at arms' length and exclaimed, as if this were a very strange fact of life, "Why, Bobbitt, you grew up!"

As it had been fifteen years since they'd last seen one another, this was a perfectly natural thing, and when he sat down beside her, holding her hand, all she could do was drink him in, still unable to believe it all. Fifteen years had wrought their changes in that adored face. Gone was the little pug nose, the cherubic mouth, gone were the peach-blown cheeks, the golden curls of "the Gainsborough Boy." His face was lean and tanned. But the eyes were as bright as Nellie remembered, and he had lost neither his ingratiating smile ("Bobbitt's smile is a yard wide," people used to say) nor that winning way of cocking his head when making a point: "See what I mean?" His hair was neatly trimmed and made attractive ringlets over the back of his collar, and was only slightly darker than it had been when he was a child. His voice was low and pleasant, with an eager, humorous timbre, and that trace of bantering Irish brogue that had endeared him to millions.

"Bobbitt," she repeated, pressing his hand against her cheek, while he discreetly mentioned the fact that perhaps she might call him Robin, which was the name he was known by now.

"Robin," she repeated, and *RobinRobinRobin* was passed along the line.

Don't tell her, Nellie said, that he was living here in New York and she hadn't known it! He laughed and gave a droll wag to his handsome head. No, he'd only recently arrived from Europe; but he was here for an indefinite stay. Mr. Thingamabob, he explained, was merely a diversion, something to keep him occupied and to amuse the children while he was waiting for an important piece of news, which was to say that he was having discussions with some Broadway producers about a show.

A show! Bobbitt was going to do a Broadway show? No, no, he put in quickly, he wasn't going to be in it; he had written the music and lyrics. They were hoping Gwen Verdon would do it, and Joel Grey. Robert Preston was also interested. *GwenVerdonJoelGreyRobertPreston*, went the names down the line of nursemaids. They sat in subdued astonishment as the famous names reached their ears. Robin had seen Deborah Kerr only the other night—*DeborahKerrDeborahKerrDeborahKerr*—and he had recently bumped into Van Johnson on the street—*VanJohnsonVanJohnsonVanJohnson*. He'd dined in Paris with Olivia—One of the babies had begun to cry and the nursemaid gave the pram a shake to quiet it; she wanted to hear. Olivia who? Oh, de Havilland, yes—and?—and Olivia had asked Robin to call her sister—*Joan FontaineJoanFontaineJoanFontaine*—and this weekend he was going to Southampton to visit Carol Channing and audition his songs.

The conclusion of this brief, pleasant, and unlooked-for reunion was that Bobby (she must remember to call him Robin) wrote Nellie's number down, saying that when he got back to town he would call so they would get together for a longer visit, "For old times' sake," they said, exchanging a secret, private smile.

They parted, he going along one side of the boat basin,

Nellie and Hilda along the other, still waving until they lost sight of Robin as he went over the rise, and then they continued on to Central Park West and down to Sixtieth Street, where they lived. Two other friends of theirs, Naomi and Phyllis, also had apartments in the building. They had known each other for years, and back in the days of vaudeville they were known as "The Four Belles." They still called themselves the Belles, they were all widowed, wealthily or otherwise, and though they were no longer in show business they spent a large part of their time together. Every day they gathered to exchange their news at what they referred to as "The Belle Telephone Hour," which was cocktail time, getting together at each other's apartments on a rotation basis. They lunched, or dined, watched the soap operas, occasionally took in an early movie or theater matinee, and held poker sessions on an informal but more or less regular basis.

Though the Belles had, as people will, grown a good deal alike in their attitudes and behavior, they were easily distinguishable one from another. Hilda had become fat; she was big and horsy, with a long face, and because her step was heavy you always knew when she was about to arrive; Nellie said it was heavy because she had a heart of gold, and you know how much gold weighs. Phyllis was a "petite seven," if people went by dress sizes, pert and pretty, and fun to be with, though no one in the world was more naïve. She often joked that after having buried two husbands, she still had never learned about the birds and the bees. Naomi was the one to watch or listen to: she had a dry, acerbic wit. "Did you hear what Naomi said?" was the common phrase among them, and usually she found plenty to say. She had a sharp eye and a sharp nose, and a tongue sharper than either. The most that Nellie's gentle nature would allow was that Naomi was satiric, and perhaps this word fitted her as well as any other. Still, they were warm friends, accustomed to one another's foibles and idiosyncrasies; and at their ages, with no males about, it gave them a feeling of safety and comfort to have each other so handy.

Though Nellie Bannister had been an actress for more than fifty years, now, in her early seventies, she was almost retired, except for an occasional TV commercial; but she lived comfortably on her carefully planned annuities. She was sometimes inclined to go off the deep end in the matter of gifts—and was famous among her friends for an impulsive generosity. She always liked to look on the bright side of things, she never wanted to hear bad of people, and her loyalty was an oft-cited example of virtue among those who knew her. In her youth she had been considered a beauty; what traces remained she was not prepared to fuss over, not even for the sake of a TV commercial. Yet even with age her looks remained warm, inviting, grandmotherly, pleasing to behold.

When Nellie and Hilda got home it was Naomi's turn for The Belle Telephone Hour. Naturally, both Phyllis and Naomi were excited to hear of the unexpected meeting with Bobbitt —excuse it—Robin Ransome. Where had he been hiding all these years? they wanted to know. Was he just another has-been? What did he look like? Hadn't he been one of those spoiled movie brats you were always reading about? Sipping her martini while Naomi passed the Ritz crackers and Liederkranz, Nellie said nothing could be farther from the truth. Generally it took a mother to spoil a child, but Robin's mother, Lady Ransome, had never even come to Hollywood. As for the has-been business, like most child stars, Bobbitt had merely grown up and gone on to other things. He harbored no yearning for movies, he wasn't one of those who, once having got out of the business, was always hanging around the fringes, trying to get back in. Bobbitt wasn't interested in being rediscovered; he had other fish to fry.

Between them the girls recalled all the movies: *Bobbitt, Bobbitt and Alfie, Bobbitt's Flying Carpet, Bobbitt and the Magic Castle, Bobbitt and Missy Priss, Bobbitt Royal, Bobbitt in the Enchanted Forest, Bobbitt Over the Moon, Bobbitt's Lucky Day,* and *Bobbitt Forever.* Ten in all. Oh, said Naomi, aren't we forgetting *Bobbitt in Love?* Such a bomb; and there went Bobbitt's career down the drain. Nellie passed the Ritz crackers, conceding that the picture had not been good, but then it was not taken from the Bobbitt books, they'd made the story up in an effort to bolster Bobby's career, but by that time his Adam's apple had dropped and besides, everybody knew how fickle audiences could be.

And what, continued Naomi, sucking the pimento from her olive, about that dreadful Aunt Moira; a woman like that was bound to influence a child's psyche, and not for the better. And nightmares . . . Naomi remembered Hedda Hopper or was it Louella Parsons saying—

Oh, bother what Louella or Hedda had said, Nellie protested mildly. It was true that as a child Bobby had been prone to nightmares; he had been put into the hands of a Beverly Hills psychiatrist, who determined that his troubled dreams were caused by the purely imaginative flights of

189

fancy engendered by the world he lived in. The doctor had deemed them no cause for alarm, but it became essential that the books he read and the movies and television he watched be carefully monitored. But after all, Bobby Ransome had not grown up as Mrs. Jones's boy or Mrs. Smith's; he had lived the celebrated life of a miniaturized adult in the fantasy land that money and fame had provided him with.

God had somehow endowed him with those qualities adults look for in their children: looks, graceful manners, a bright, inquiring mind, plus the supreme talent merely to be himself before the camera. Even Louella had pointed out that the reason he made such a marvelous Bobbitt was that he was able to lose himself in that purely imaginative world Bobbitt inhabited, for it was not to see him in the real world that audiences packed the theaters, but in the fantasy one that lay beyond the real.

It was true, Hilda spoke up; people had wanted to forget their troubles just as much in the fifties as they had in the thirties or forties, and the notion of Bobbitt lying around on a living room rug was not as juvenile as it might have appeared; everyone wanted to go somewhere, if only to Baghdad in a movie.

The whole thing had been an accident anyway, Nellie said. Master Bobby Ransome's career had begun at the tender age of ten, when Viola Ueberroth accidentally came across him in a Dublin tea shop. Here was this little Irish lad sitting with his aunt, whom he was visiting from Galway, where he lived. It was a chilly afternoon and together they were having a "cuppa" the national beverage. The boy was bundled up so only his face peeked out from under his cap and muffler, but it was a remarkable face, or so thought a chance visitor to the tea shop, she having a "cuppa" herself. Viola, having noted the boy, had been suddenly inspired by an idea—her sudden "ideas" having made her the important person she was. In his expression, his demeanor, his bright, cheery looks, and more particularly his angelic expression, in all this was something that struck Miss Ueberroth so strongly that she was compelled to make herself known to the boy and his aunt, and to inquire if there might be any possibility that he could play a little part in a movie.

That was how it began. Removing the cap and muffler from around the boy's face, Viola was delighted to discover that he was even more beautiful; he had the enchanting looks one finds in some of Gainsborough's work, and it was with this impression that she hurried to London, where she was to meet her brother, Samuel, then engaged in casting a film. Bobby Ransome was brought to London, Samuel concurred in his sister's opinion, and the boy was given a screen test, then whisked away to Rome, where he was handed some pages with lines to learn and quickly put in front of a camera in a movie that, as it happened, starred the eminent actor William Marsh, and Sam Ueberroth's girlfriend Lorna Doone, and in a cameo role, the once-great Fedora. Bobby proved himself an adorably natural performer, easily able to hold his own in scenes with the older, more professional actors, and when *The Miracle of Santa Cristi* was released, Master Ransome came in for a large share of attention and critical acclaim.

His appearance in the movie, however, had been managed only with difficulty and through the persuasive powers of both Ueberroths. Studio publicity provided the information that Lady Ransome, of the old Irish peerage, whose antecedents went far back into the pages of Irish history, did not want her child being a "picture player." The mother herself not being present on the set, the task of looking after Bobby fell to the father's sister, Aunt Moira, and through all the havoc of the celebrity that was to follow, Aunt Moira kept strict watch over her charge. She had been the object of considerable speculation during the shooting of the film, a thin, obscurely driven spinster who stood beside the camera, watching Bobby's every move and gesture, nodding or shaking her head, depending on the quality of his performance.

Nobody knew exactly why his aunt rather than his mother was looking after the child, except that Lady Ransome had to see to the running of a large estate—the father was in banking, and one day Bobby himself would succeed to the pererage. Both Louella and Hedda twanged away at this fact as if it were the only string to their harps, while Walter Winchell's column noted a barrage of dukes, earls, and viscounts, all friends of the Ransomes, who were well connected in London court circles.

His career might have ended after one film, except that Viola Ueberroth had another "idea." This was that Bobby should play Bobbitt, and she went and told Papa Baer just that. Emil Baer—or "Papa," as he was called—had been persuaded by his wife, Heidi—his "Mama" Baer—to invest what little capital they had saved in buying the rights to the Bobbitt books, which, though they were not known in America, were extremely popular in England. Until Viola approached him, Emil Baer had been turning out cartoon musical shorts featuring puppets animated in stop action. Baer Comix was located in small quarters near the old Monogram lot in Hollywood, and Papa Baer was far from successful. His dream was one day to make a full-length puppet feature with one of the Bobbitt stories, but it was Viola's notion that instead of puppets he use live actors, and to this end she brought Bobby Ransome to Mr. Baer's attention. Since brother Sam had, at Viola's suggestion, put the boy under personal contract, and could also lend a hand with the financing, it was proposed that the movie could at last be made.

The Bobbitt books told of a London wartime waif discovered in a bombed-out ruin by a warden during an air raid. It became a famous introduction: the child stumbling from the blitzed ruins after the Luftwaffe has flown over, innocently asking, " 'Oo put out th' lights?" He strikes a match, and in its glow, surrounded by a total wartime blackout, is Bobbitt's face, the winsome, heart-tugging face that was to become known to millions. His parents having been killed in the raid, the child is taken in by the kindly and rich Lord Wickham and his family, and brought up under the tutelage of the butler, Alfie, and the nanny, Missy Priss—Willie Marsh and Nellie Bannister respectively. "Popping up out of thin air," and accompanied by his friends, Bobbitt experiences all sorts of magical adventures—flying on an Oriental carpet to Baghdad, discovering a treasure in an enchanted forest, jousting with a knight at Camelot—after which adventures all three are restored safely to the Wickham manor in East Devon. The rest of the casting was seen to perfectly: Cathleen Nesbitt played the grandmother, Mary Astor Lady Wickham, Reggie Gardiner Lord Wickham, Angela Lansbury the upstairs maid, Gladys Cooper the aunt, and Richard Haydn the eccentric uncle who invents the contraptions that whirl Bobbitt from place to place. Since it was discovered that Bobby Ransome had musical talents as well, each picture featured several numbers, many of which made history—"Lotsa Pluck," "Gonna Dance Off Both My Feet," "Ditto," "Hokum and Bunkum and Bluff," "Really Truly True," and "For Old Times' Sake."

The first, modestly budgeted picture earned back its cost in the first week of play dates, and theater owners began clamoring for the "little tyke" to make personal appearances. The box-office child-star tradition had already been established: Jackie Coogan in *The Kid,* Jackie Cooper in *The Champ,* then Shirley Temple, Judy Garland, Deanna Durbin,

Freddie Bartholomew, Mickey Rooney, and now the country had a new star, Bobby Ransome.

While plans were rushed for the second Bobbitt story, the flesh-and-blood version was sent on a whirlwind cross-country tour, making stage appearances. Nothing like him had been seen, it was said, since the child prodigy Mozart played at Versailles. In blue serge shorts and an Eton collar, with his dimpled knees and mop of blond curly hair, with his great big Bobbitt smile, he ran out on stage and proved a phenomenon, wrestling with the too tall microphone, joking with the audience, and in no time he had them all in his hip pocket. He played piano and accordion, he sang the songs and did the dance routines from the picture, he walked on his hands, did imitations of William Marsh as Alfie, of Clark Gable as Rhett Butler, of Fess Parker as Davy Crockett, of Eddie Fisher and Johnny Ray, and when he finished with an impression of Charles Laughton reading the Twenty-third Psalm there wasn't a dry eye in the house.

And that, more or less, was how Bobby Ransome, the little lad from Ireland, became a prince of Hollywood; known as "America's Fantasy Child," he was the most angelic, best behaved, most loving child imaginable. In the glare of enormous publicity he became the hero of children all over the world. Now he was "The World's Fantasy Child." People seldom called him "Bobby," for always he was "Bobbitt," or sometimes "The Gainsborough Boy," as Viola had dubbed him after their first meeting in the tea shop. A craze began that swept Davy Crockett from popularity, replacing his coonskin hats on youngsters' heads with the little Bobbitt cricketer hats, while their elders sported Alfie's striped butler vests on campus. Two new catch phrases entered the language. In the midst of his wonderful adventures Bobbitt was always asking, "But is it really truly true?" and was assured that it was. The line caught on; everyone imitated Bobby's engaging speech defect, and at cocktail parties they said, "But is it weelly twooly twoo?" In *Bobbitt and Missy Priss*, the nanny scooped him up for a hug and said, "Bobbitt, I love you." Said he, gazing out of those saucerlike eyes, "Ditto." They wrote a song, "Ditto," which Bobbitt and Missy Priss sang together; it climbed the Lucky Strike *Hit Parade* in weeks and remained there so long that Dorothy Collins and Snooky Lanson were hard pressed to find new ways of presenting it. With the release of the third film, *Bobbitt's Flying Carpet*, Bobbitt had become Big Business. Gone was Baer Comix, and Baer Productions was now flourishing in a more elite location in Panorama City, with the happy cognomen of Shady Lane Studios. It was a new, CinemaScoped, stereophonicked Bobbitt, and Bobby Ransome's smile grew as wide as the screen itself. Everything, in fact, grew. Papa Baer, always sizable, grew fatter and richer. Louella and Hedda grew more saccharine, the public grew more eager, Bobby's fans more fanatical, Samuel Ueberroth more important, William Marsh more famous, Bee Marsh more ecstatic, and, most terrifying, little Bobby just grew.

What, Papa Baer was heard to wonder, would happen when his voice changed? No one dared answer, no one dared think. "Please don't let Bobbitt grow up" was a plea that became a prayer. Bobbitt was not an adolescent, he was a child, with a child's heart and mind and imagination, and everything possible was done, every sort of chicanery practiced, to keep him that child. His hair was left long and boyishly curly, he was made to wear the Eton collar he had made famous, the little velvet suits and patent leather shoes that were his trademark, and he lived in the fantasy land he had been catapulted into, in a castlelike house that was every child's dream palace.

Pictures of Bobbitt were everywhere. His face was on all the movie-magazine covers, his image on everything from balloons to T-shirts. There were Bobbitt dolls, with Bobbitt costumes—fireman, policeman, cowboy, marine, knight in armor, regimental guard—there were Bobbitt plates and mugs, Bobbitt planes, Bobbitt trains, and "Bobbittmobiles." There were Bobbitt flying carpets, Bobbitt tops, Bobbitt phonographs. There was a Bobbitt dollhouse. There were Bobbitt comic books, sweatshirts, blue jeans, sneakers. There were Bobbitt camping outfits, Bobbitt sailing outfits, Bobbitt race car outfits, all with the "official seal" of Shady Lane Studios.

The final accolade came when Norman Rockwell painted him in the same costume and pose as Gainsborough's famous "Blue Boy" for the *Saturday Evening Post*. *Life* and *Time* followed with cover stories. Total wordage of his interviews mounted into the millions. And what did Bobbitt say? "I'm so happy." For the millions, he lived out all their hopes, dreams, and ambitions. He had been down in an atomic submarine, had been up in the Goodyear blimp. He had put his foot and hand prints in the forecourt of Grauman's Chinese Theatre, between Joan Crawford's and Betty Grable's. He had been invited to Eisenhower's second inauguration, where he was presented with cuff links bearing the presidential seal, and photographed in the rose garden with Ike and Mamie. He was made a tribal member of the Sioux Nation, and a Kentucky colonel. He was guest of honor at the Seattle World's Fair. He had been on Jack Benny and Perry Como and Bob Hope, had made eight guest appearances on *The Ed Sullivan Show*. He headlined the Christmas pageant at Radio City Music Hall. He was invited to the Command Performance Gala at London's Palladium, where he sang and danced with Britain's most celebrated actors, Olivier, Gielgud, Coward, and Richardson.

Then he got his Oscar, a special statuette awarded to him for the best juvenile performance of the year in Papa Baer's production of *Peter Pan*, in which he made a greater success than ever playing the fantasy boy who lured the Darling children to Never Land and meets Captain Hook, played by William Marsh in one of his best-loved roles. But while Peter Pan might remain a boy forever, not so Bobby Ransome. "America's Fantasy Child" was ten when he made *Bobbitt*, fourteen when he did *Bobbitt Forever*, the last in the series of books. The fact was undeniable that Bobbitt had reached the "awkward age." In desperation, Papa Baer ordered a new character to be created, "Flying Rodger," who, as some wag put it, never got off the ground. Bobby was temporarily "retired," while scriptwriters were put to work fashioning a suitable vehicle. It was eventually called *Bobbitt in Love*, and Viola had found a lovely young Irish girl to play the love interest. She was called Pretty Kitty Kelly, but the movie proved only one thing: audiences weren't interested in Bobbitt's First Screen Kiss; they wanted more magic carpets. Bobbitt sat out a second period of "retirement" while another vehicle was found. Again Viola waved her magic wand. Since her tag of "the Gainsborough Boy" had enjoyed such wide usage, a script was turned out by a top team of screen writers, and an expensive production called *The Blue Boy* was mounted. Announcements followed this initial display of enthusiasm stating that the cost of the film had become suddenly prohibitive, then the project was abandoned.

Thereafter Bobby Ransome and Aunt Moira departed for Europe, where an English production, *Bonnie Prince Charlie*, was marked for filming, with Bobby Ransome as the young Scottish prince. It, too, never saw a foot of film exposed.

And there it was. The End. Time alone had put the quietus to the career of the lovable tyke whose face had appeared above a single match flame in the darkness of an air raid; the flame had burned out and in no time he was forgotten. "Ditto" passed out of the popular slang, and "But is it really truly true?" was considered pure corn. Kids were now wearing astronauts' helmets, Bobbitt caps being as passé as hula hoops. As far as Bobby Ransome was concerned, it seemed it wasn't really truly true at all.

Since he had mentioned that he was spending the weekend at Southampton, Nellie Bannister was surprised when her telephone rang that Saturday afternoon and she recognized the voice of Bobby Ransome.

" 'Tis me, Nellie—Robin," he said. His plans had changed, he was staying in town. Was she free for dinner and could they just talk? Of course she could. Her friends were dropping by for The Belle Telephone Hour; why didn't he come and meet them and afterward they could slip away quietly by themselves.

He arrived casually dressed, in blue jeans and a flowered shirt and sneakers, and proceeded to charm and captivate the Belles. Nellie had told them what a sweet, gentle child he had been; the amazing thing being that he still was. Nothing seemed to have touched him, he wasn't at all conceited about either his past or his present. As Nellie had pointed out to Naomi, it was never required of him to act endearing; he simply was.

The Belles watched him carefully as Nellie showed him the apartment, the two budgerigars in the cage over the spinet piano, her collection of porcelain figurines, and the pictures of her family: her son and daughter, who both lived in Tucson; her grandson, Roger, who was close by in Garden City, where he operated a flying school; his wife, Nancy, and Nellie's three great grandchildren, Karen, three, Linda, four, and Roger, Jr., who was six. Ah, said Robin, just Bobbitt's age. She didn't immediately understand him, but he brought out his wallet and gave her some snapshots to look at. Who is it? she wanted to know. Surely you . . . Robin nodded. My stars, said Nellie, think of that! She could scarcely believe her ears when he told her he had married his movie sweetheart, Kitty Kelly. It was like a storybook romance.

Nellie felt the tears start in her eyes as she saw the dear little face: Bobby's own son. What should be more natural than that Kitty should call him "Bobbitt," though his real name, like his father's, was Bobby. Nellie couldn't decide which of them little Bobbitt looked more like: surely he had his father's eyes, certainly his mother's mouth. But was it true, she asked, that Robin and Kitty had really fallen in love? Robin nodded; they had been married in London, and spent much of their time at Castle Baughclammain, the Ransomes' ancestral home at Galway. The house looked out on the bay, and Bobbitt had his own horses to ride, just as Robin had had ponies when he was a child in Hollywood.

Robin brought out his wallet again to show pictures of Rose, as he called his mother, a beautiful, sophisticated woman, handsomely coiffed and dressed. Around her neck was a diamond chain, at the end of which was suspended the Ballymore emerald, a gem almost as famous as the Hope diamond. Nellie found Lady Ransome a trifle lacquered for her own taste, but she could see why Robin was proud of her. A light seemed to spring into his eyes as he spoke of her, almost a kind of worship, but with an edge. Rose was radiant, she was dazzling, but Nellie felt Robin's disapproval of her and his resentment that she had given him so little time when he was growing up, something he was determined not to do with his own child.

As for the Broadway show, though he was hopeful of getting it on, he could do nothing but wait for word from the producers, who were trying to raise the capital. Meanwhile he was just "in town," with plenty of time on his hands. Could he see more of Nellie? She held her hands out to him, turning them palms up and down. See, she said, nothing but time on hers, too.

The following night, the Sunday, they went out to the Sheep Meadow to see "Broadway Stars for Children," a huge open-air benefit for the Orthopedic Hospital, sponsored by a local television station. Nellie had fixed a picnic, and they sat on blankets in the enormous crowd, watching and listening to the host of stars who were entertaining. Afterward Nellie asked Robin if he'd had any desire to be up there; he laughed. No, he said, you'd never catch him on a stage again.

They were together a lot during the next few weeks. He would pop by the apartment on his way to and from the park, or she would meet him there while he played Mr. Thingama-bob for the children, and she would sit on a bench and listen to the stories. Later he would walk her back to her apartment, and often stay for The Belle Telephone Hour with Hilda, Naomi, and Phyllis. Nellie found him like a new breath of life around the apartment. She loved his casual dropping in at odd hours and shaking her out of her summer doldrums. She felt guilty that she was taking up his time; he should be off enjoying his friends. But no, he said, he wanted to be with her. She realized it was because she had once been part of another life. That life had ended, but she was there again and between them existed an accumulation of shared memories. In those days she'd been almost a mother to him; now she saw that beneath his gay and charming exterior, he was vulnerable and needed looking after. She discussed it at length with the Belles; they couldn't imagine what it must be like, having been one of the most famous children in the world. People had fought to be near and touch him then; now, it appeared, nobody even recognized him. But that seemed the way Robin wanted it. "Bobbitt" was a thing of the past, and he even objected to Kitty's calling their son Bobbitt; Robin himself always called him Bob or Bobby.

For a person who had been so famous, there was nothing jaded or bored about him. Everything interested him, most everything struck him as funny. He was seldom out of sorts, and his gay good spirits, his easy amiability, his diverting talk—never banal, always *au courant*—never palled. The girls were charmed by his expressive eyes with their look of candor, his beguiling humor and persiflage. He was boyishly eager, yet there was a healthy, mature outlook about him.

Nellie admitted she'd got into a rut, but he kidded and cajoled and charmed her, and she never would have thought anyone could have wooed her away from *As the World Turns* the way he did. If you lived in New York, he said, you ought to take advantage of what it offered, so East Side, West Side, all around the town they went. She'd always hated shopping, but with Robin it became an event. Saks, Bonwit's, Henri Bendel; so many new things in the stores, she had no idea. He took her to Halston's, where she would never dream of going—and the *prices*—and found things he said were made for her, less fuddy-duddy, more youthful. She learned she could rely utterly on his taste; he planned a visit to Mr. Kenneth, and though Robin and the hairdresser suggested the white hair be tinted gold, she thought it too daring, and meekly submitted to a blue rinse, quite enough change for one day. When Robin mentioned the new Lehman wing at the Metropolitan Museum, a trip was immediately planned. Afterward they went downstairs to see the exhibition of movie costumes mounted by Diana Vreeland. There was Vivien Leigh's dress from *Gone With the Wind*, Garbo's from *Queen Christina*, Dietrich's from *Blonde Venus*, and Fedora's from *The Player Queen*, for which Cyril Leaf had received an Oscar. The costume was magnificent, with its wonderfully exaggerated farthingale, the high collar of starched lace, the velvet and satin brocade encrusted with pearls and *diamantés*. Nellie said she had never realized Fedora was so small.

It was lunchtime, so they took cafeteria trays to a table by the pool and talked. Because there were just the two of them, Robin was not averse to recalling the old days; inevitably Viola Ueberroth's name came up, since it was she who'd been mainly responsible for all their successes in the Bobbitt series—Robin's, Willie Marsh's, and even Nellie's—and the clever stunts she had pulled with Papa Baer to get them cast.

One evening Vi had arranged to bring the Baers to the Biltmore Theater in downtown Los Angeles, where Willie Marsh was playing a supporting part in a revival of *The Red Mill*. Warned ahead of time, when Papa and Mama Baer came into his dressing room, Willie put on his best British accent, he and Bee Marsh charmed the Baers, and he was signed for the important role of Alfie, the butler. His career rejuvenated, he went on to become "The Grand Old Man of Hollywood."

Similar nimble machinations on Viola's part saw to the casting of the equally important role of Missy Priss. There was, Viola informed Papa Baer, a certain actress about to sign for a major New York play; contracts still hadn't been finalized, however, and if one was fast and if the money was sufficient . . . Papa Baer was immediately intrigued. How much? Vi named a figure considerably higher than what they could have had Beulah Bondi for; nonetheless Papa jumped at the chance. Soon after, Viola and the two Baers drove to the airport and greeted the plane that had borne Nellie Bannister west. Papa pinned an orchid corsage to her dress and off they went to sign the contracts.

It was part of Viola's fairy-godmother technique that this flight was the second transcontinental trip Nellie had made in a two-day period, for the actual fact was that she had been living in Los Angeles all the time. Vi had known her since her days as a secretary at the old AyanBee studio, when Nell had left "The Four Belles" and become a struggling young actress. Now, years later, she was a resident of a run-down Hollywood hotel, where she had been living in near penury, unable to find work at any of the studios. Remembering her old friend, Viola had decided that Nell and Nell alone would play Missy Priss, and to this end she had looked her up, loaned her money to fly to New York, where she turned around again and arrived back in Hollywood, presumably as the star of a Broadway show, but in reality a down-and-out and nearly forgotten woman.

Like his alter ego, Mr. Thingamabob, Robin came and went like quicksilver, Nellie said. He came like a Greek, bearing gifts: a bunch of flowers, a box of Godiva chocolates, which Hilda doted on, a book. If Nellie was out, he would pop down to Phyllis's or up to Naomi's, then he was gone again, to meet friends. He knew all the famous people in New York, what *Women's Wear Daily* called the BP's and the QP's (the Beautiful People and the Quality People), and the names came rolling from his lips as unconcernedly as if he were speaking of the corner butcher: Babe Paley, Chessy Rayner, Nan Kempner, Mica Ertegun, those ladies who oiled the machinery of New York's social set. Visiting Nellie, while she was cooking in the kitchen, he sat with his feet up in the chintz-covered chair, doodling on the memo pad, and she couldn't help hearing as he laughed and joked with the president of Henri Bendel, a Miss Strutz—"Hello, Gerry, 'tis me, Robin"—and when he'd hung up, he'd immediately dial Nancy Martin and they'd have a chat, or Shirley Clurman or Marti Stevens. Other calls followed; when Nellie tore off his doodles she'd glance at his list: Hal Prince, Milton Goldman, David Merrick, Arnold Weissberger.

To her he was always the same, her Bobbitt, but then again he was always different; or to her eyes he seemed different. He would come like a troubadour, in embroidered jeans and a loose-sleeved shirt of Greek cotton, with a guitar slung on his back, and when the girls were gathered he would sit on the rug and play gypsy songs or Irish ballads. He was an artist with words, the way he could create a scene. None of them had been to Europe, but he took them there, most especially to Ireland. Ah, Ireland, he would begin with his hint of lilting brogue, describing the castle Baughclammain, in which he and Kitty and little Bobby lived. It sat amid the rolling green Galway downs, such a green in springtime no eye had ever seen, with the old stone ramparts built by the last king of Ireland still facing the sea, where you could walk on the turrets and feel the salt air in your face. It was horsy country, and everyone in the county rode, and he painted pictures of those fox hunts with the men in their red coats, the women in top hats, the drinking of the traditional stirrup cup, then the flying hoofs, the barking pack, while the huntsman wound his horn and the fox tried to save his brush.

Then, every summer, there was the Galway Race, one of

the most famous horse races in the world. Lady Ransome's stables had won the trophy six times, and hoped this year to earn a seventh; she was running Caliph, a thoroughbred of great promise, and named after a character in *Bobbi's Flying Carpet*. The race week was one gala after another, culminating in the famous Galway Ball, given each year by Lady Farquahar, whose guest list was the most exclusive imaginable: people were known to have come from as far away as Africa and South America. All the great houses were opened, the inns of the countryside filled to the rafters with guests, the men in white tie and tails, the women in their finest gowns, and they had to hire special guards to watch after the jewelry that would be worn.

Robin now was often on the telephone to Lady Keith, an American and a great friend of both Robin's mother and Lady Farquahar; plans were already being laid for the gathering of the BP's at this year's Galway Ball. Meanwhile, betwixt and between, Robin still was quicksilver. One week he was at the Plaza, then the St. Regis, then the Pierre. But he hated hotel life, and at one point announced that he had temporarily moved in with an old friend, Madame Potekka.

Madame Potekka was a painter, and it was to her *vernissage* that Robin invited Nellie to go with him one evening; Nellie said she would love to, but didn't know what a *vernissage* was, how should she dress? He laughed, saying *vernissage* was only a fancy word in art gallery circles; Madame Potekka was having an exhibition and this was the opening.

The gallery was in SoHo, and there were crowds of people there, nobody paying much attention to what hung on the walls, but rather drinking champagne from plastic cups and talking to each other. The artist herself was gay and vivacious, flitting from group to group in a gown the shape and colors of a butterfly, and chattering so much that Nellie had no more chance than to say How d'you do before Madame, who seemed particularly fond of Robin, whisked him away to meet some friends. Madame's pictures were all of flowers, and there was one, a small bunch of violets tied with a ribbon, that Nellie liked, though the price was far beyond her modest means.

When they came back uptown Robin suggested the Russian Tea Room for dinner. Nellie mentioned the violets, but Robin hadn't seen the picture; he'd been too busy—there were a number of people there who he was hopeful might serve as backers for his production. Was Madame Potekka one of them? Nellie asked. Robin's expression became grave. Ah, no, he said. His friend, though no one knew it, was a tragic case. She had cancer and had exhausted herself putting the show together, trying to make some money to cover the expenses of cobalt treatments; though you'd never know it to look at her, it was probably terminal. He was helping her out financially, but the treatments were draining his bank account, and since he had moved in with her to help look after her, it was also taking up a lot of his time. If he could just get the musical going he was certain things would work out.

As Nellie had learned, the production was called *Sweepstake*, and the plot centered on the Galway Race itself. It was set in nineteenth-century Ireland, and Robin's music had several beautiful Irish ballads in it, including her favorite, "Ah, Fair Love of Tara's Hall," which Robin had played for her on his guitar. Usually, in discussing the project, he was happy and optimistic; tonight, however, he seemed depressed. Drawing him out, she discovered that things at home were not all that he had indicated they were. He and Kitty were not getting along, which was one reason he was happy to be in New York. He wanted her to come and join him with little Bobby, but she insisted on remaining in Ireland. She was willful and had a fearful temper and was used to getting her own way. Lately they'd been having lots of arguments, mainly over Bobby, whom she spoiled outrageously, and Robin was afraid the child was going to grow up to be a brat.

"You never did," Nellie told him with a smile. He understood what she meant. As a child he had had everything, and he'd turned out all right. Together they recalled the "castle" he had lived in when he was a star. Papa Baer's studio designers and decorators had transformed the house he lived in with Aunt Moira into a child's wonderland. His bed had been a pirate galleon with sails and rigging and a gangplank. The dining room was a reproduction of the Cave of the East from *Bobbitt in the Enchanted Forest*. The living room was draped like a circus tent, another room was like a Persian potentate's. His bathroom was a Napoleonic camp pavilion with military drums and banners. The rumpus room had a real soda fountain, a jukebox, and a stage with lights and a curtain and real theater seats.

Robin agreed that that had all been wonderful, but still, it was only fantasy. Here was little Bobby, living in a real castle, and while that was wonderful too, Robin wanted him to grow up normally, like other boys, which was why he never liked hashing over his days as a child star. Since Kitty was so busy with other things, while Robin was away the boy was in the charge of Pat, a wonderful old character from Cork, who'd worked for the family for years; he spoke with a heavy brogue and was a local institution.

Kitty, however, was still so entranced by the idea of what had once been that she talked of nothing else. She was passionate, she was beautiful, he adored her, but she had notions of romance that were plain silly. Robin was afraid of the child's being torn between them, so he let her have her way; still, from his own experience, a fairy-tale world was hardly the best world for a child to be living in. He was hopeful, he said, that later in the summer, if Kitty wouldn't come herself, she would at least let Bobby visit New York; there were so many things Robin wanted to show him.

Against his protests Nellie insisted on picking up the dinner check—she knew he was short of cash—and afterward, because the night was pleasant, he asked her is she would like to walk or would prefer a taxi; she agreed that a walk would be nice, and they joined the people in the street, idly drifting in that somnambulistic way New Yorkers have on summer nights. At Columbus Circle some people were just getting down from a hansom carriage; taking Nellie's hand, Robin announced he was taking her for a ride. "Where to?" the cabby asked, and Robin, the incurable romantic, threw up his arms with a happy cry and said, "Drive away, my man, away into the night." They went up Central Park West, past the Majestic, the Dakota, and the San Remo, and then into the park and back down the curving drive, which was still brightly lighted. People were walking hand in hand, there were the sounds of music; somewhere along the way a man was playing a hurdy-gurdy. Nellie looked suddenly at Robin: they were both thinking the same thing—the hurdy-gurdy man in *Bobbitt Royal*, before Bobbitt rides off in the coach with Queen Victoria, when Arthur Treacher, as the hurdy-gurdy man, stepped up, raised his derby, and said, " 'Ats off ter Bobbitt." The song that followed had been one of Willie Marsh's greatest hits in the series.

As the carriage stopped for a light, and while the hurdy-gurdy continued the tune, Robin leaped out and began dancing along the drive in front of the hansom, singing the song. He had appropriated the cabby's top hat, and he broke into the famous "Gonna Dance Off Both My Feet" number. Out of nowhere a crowd collected, and when Robin realized he had become the center of attraction he stopped and jumped back in the carriage, obviously embarrassed to have people watching him. Nellie tried to imagine what they would have thought if they'd recognized him, if they'd known it was one of the most famous stars in the world performing for them, and for free; but of course they hadn't.

"You're mad," she said as he gave the cabby back his top hat, and he laughed. "It's me Peter Pan shadow," he told her. "I can't help it." He drew her arm through his and gave her a pat. "Aw, Nell, it's such a wonderful world, isn't it? Just the way it is? That Peter Pan, he crept inside, right here"— he placed her hand over his heart and she could feel it beating from his exertions—"and I don't want to grow up. I don't care if I never do."

"Darling," she told him, "you're a father now."

He laughed again. "Don't I know it. And if I have my way, Sir Bobby'll never have to grow up either, never have to go to war, never know sorrow."

"Like his pa?"

"Sure. Like his pa." His face grew thoughtful as the hansom moved along. The horse's hoofs went pleasantly and rhythmically clip-clop, the hurdy-gurdy music fading, and with her head back, looking past the festoons of plastic flowers that overhung the carriage, and the branches of the green trees, Nellie must have dozed or dreamed off, and under the spell of the moment, or the spell that only Bobbitt could create, she had for an instant thought she was back again on the lot at Shady Lane Studios. But no, she was here in New York City, it was a summer night, and they were merely having a lovely drive in the park.

When they got back to the apartment, he said he was tired and wouldn't come up; she told him she'd been thinking about Madame Potekka's problem, she had a little money tucked away, and she wanted him to have it to help her. "Ah, Missy Priss," he said, "you're too foine, by far."

"It's for you, Robin, because I love you."

"Ditto," he said, and of course, the next time he came he brought her another present. He had called several days later from Madame Potekka's, after depositing Nellie's check; he had news, some good, some bad, all important, could he drop by? Oh, dear; she would love it, but Willie Marsh and Fedora were on *Classic Movies* tonight, and the girls were coming up to watch the picture. Would he join them? Yes, he would. He arrived in a state of high excitement, bringing a small paper-wrapped parcel, which he presented to Nellie. Undoing the string, she found the little painting of the violets that she had loved. Oh, she told him, he shouldn't have. He shrugged and laughed; what people wanted they should get. Besides, it was nothing; Potekka had given him a rake-off on it. Other news: lunch that day with his producers indicated that the necessary money would be forthcoming, and a February rehearsal date had been tentatively set, with *Sweepstake* to open in the spring. Then he was at the piano, playing what he hoped would be the hit song, "Ah, Fair Love of Tara's Hall," and he got the Belles to singing the words and doing some of their old vaudeville routines. Then, while Hilda played the spinet, he performed some of the Bobbitt numbers he used to do with Willie Marsh. He kept them in stitches while sitting around before the broadcast, and then was having chatty confidences with Phyllis in the kitchen. No, she told the others when they emerged, it was between her and Robin, nobody else's business, and gave him a kiss. Meanwhile Robin had a call to make, and waving his plastic credit card at Nellie to indicate that the charges would go on his account, he proceeded to telephone Galway. Right from Nellie's living room to Castle Baughclammain.

Then the picture came on; it was *The Player Queen*. Robin had never seen it, and the girls agreed it was one of Fedora's best, though often neglected by critics. Her role was that of an Elizabethan Cheapside hoyden who wants to be an actress. Since in the time of the Tudors the stage appearance of women was taboo, and the famous female Shakespearean roles were essayed by males, Fedora masquerades as a man and takes the stage in the role of the Player Queen in *Hamlet*. There is a romantic triangle consisting of herself, the playwright, played by Adolphe Menjou, and Burbage, the actor, played by Willie Marsh. Their romantic escapades arouse the jealousy of the Virgin Queen, who in a flight of screenwriting fancy arrives at the Globe Theatre in midperformance to stride onstage and unmask the Player Queen's identity. All ends happily if preposterously, and at the fade-out Fedora reprises her role in a command performance. When the movie was over everyone agreed that Willie Marsh was dashing and handsome in his doublet and ruff, Fedora was fascinating as always, and they all loved the scene in which Menjou's wife, Verree Teasdale, playing Elizabeth, confronts Fedora, while she, all velvet and lace, laughs daringly and tosses an apple at her.

Afterward Nell had Robin describe for the girls the party Willie and Bee Marsh had given for him at their house. Though he was only twelve at the time, he remembered it well, a kind of real-life version of the scene from *Bobbitt Royal*, when he had been presented at court. He had worn a velvet suit with short pants and a ruffled shirt, and he had been taken from room to room to meet all the famous people. Humphrey Bogart and Lauren Bacall, Audrey Hepburn, Frank Sinatra, Judy Garland, Rosalind Russell, Noël Coward, Ginger Rogers, Lana Turner; the list was endless. The Marshes had been famous for their parties; everyone went, and this one was special. There was a particular room he remembered; it was all glass and mirrors, with a huge crystal chandelier. The room looked out on the pool, where candles had been set floating among flowers. There was an orchestra in a pavilion, and each of the dinner courses was named Bobbitt something-or-other. In the center of the buffet, which took up practically the whole dining room, was an enormous ice sculpture, a copy of the crown he'd worn in *Bobbitt Royal*, and there were candles all around it.

Later everyone entertained—Sinatra, Garland, Coward, then Willie, who insisted on Robin's joining him in their duet of "For Old Times' Sake."

Nellie sat down at the spinet, Robin beside her on the bench, and they sang the number for the girls, a sentimental song, but one that had enjoyed enormous popularity at the time.

> *"Let's take a little cuppa tea, just you and me,*
> *   For old times' sake.*
> *Or maybe yet a glass of wine, yours and mine,*
> *   For old times' sake.*
> *Rememb'rin' all the things that went before,*
> *Memories, we'll have a score or more,*
> *When my hair's gone gray and I can't dance*
> *And you're so big you need long pants,*
> *It'll still be you and me, a cuppa tea, yours and mine,*
> *   a glass of wine . . .*
> *For old times' sake."*

"Schmaltzy," Nellie said when they were done, and they smiled at each other: it was Willie's line, "Give 'em the old schmaltz." He'd been saying it for years, and often claimed it was the secret of his success. Robin had wandered to the window, where he stood staring out, then he suddenly turned.

"Let's call him!"

"Call him?" Nellie asked.

"Call Willie. Let's call him up. I've just had the most marvelous idea. There's a part in the show—he could do it perfectly. Sort of a 'Pat' type, you know—local character, a bit o' the ould sod? Willie does an English accent, he could just as easily do Irish. Let's."

He went to the phone, then suddenly realized he didn't have the number. Nellie found it in her address book, Robin gave the operator his credit card number, and placed the call. It rang and rang, but no one answered. Twelve-thirty New York time made it nine-thirty in Los Angeles.

"Maybe he's out," Phyllis suggested.

Nellie shook her head. "He never goes out Monday nights. Besides, wouldn't he want to be home watching himself on TV?"

They tried again; still there was no reply.

Robin would call again tomorrow. He concluded the evening by relating what had happened to the crown of ice on the buffet. Someone had wanted to take Bobbitt's picture there, and when they went back to the dining room the candles had melted it, it was nothing but a giant circle of ice, and water had run all over the expensive damask tablecloth; Bee Marsh had been furious with the caterers.

The following morning, when Nellie was in the kitchen making breakfast, Hilda called and said to turn on the TV, the most dreadful thing had happened. Willie Marsh had been murdered. Nellie sat in shocked silence in front of the set as the ghastly details were reported. The housekeeper-cook had returned and discovered the body. The details were unthinkable. Willie had been an old and cherished friend, and Nellie had always received a card each Christmas from the Marshes before Bee died. Now Willie was gone. All she could think of was Robin, and how he would take the news. She waited, wondering if he would come by, but he did not appear. Later she heard the buzzer, and thought it must be he, but found instead Naomi, who rushed in with the newspaper. "LITTLE WILLIE MARSH KILLED," shouted the headline; "MURDER OF THE CENTURY." Had Nellie heard? asked the excited Naomi. Wasn't it too awful? It just gave her the shivers, knowing there were monsters like that running around in the world.

Something told Nellie to go to the park, and when she got out of the taxi at Seventy-second Street and went down the incline toward the boat basin she could see Mr. Thingamabob sitting on the mushroom, with the children gathered around him. Her usual bench was occupied, so she found another spot, and waited.

When the storytelling hour came to an end and Robin had shooed the children away, he and Nellie met and walked along by the boat basin. She chattered on about anything she could think of, trying to decide how to go about the dreadful business of telling him the news. She failed to notice as he stopped behind her, and when she finally looked back at him he was standing stock-still, staring at a man on a bench. The man was holding the paper Naomi had come in with; there was the same enormous black headline. As Robin stepped up and snatched the paper from the hands of the startled man and read, Nellie got the paper back, returned it to the man with an apology, and tried to lead Robin away. He yanked his arm free and began to run. "Robin! Robin! Wait."

He didn't stop; wildly he ran along the walk, careening into people. He leaped up on the coping of the pond and ran along it, then jumped into the water, and went splashing knee-deep through it, dragging his robe after him. People stopped and stared, the children laughed, thinking it was part of Mr. Thingamabob's act, and a policeman blew his whistle at him, but Robin paid no attention. Nellie sank down on a bench, watching as he made his way to the far end of the pond, where he clambered out and ran up the hill like a madman, people watching all the way.

Nellie went back to where he had dropped his pack and brought it home with her. She waited the rest of the afternoon for him to call. When the phone didn't ring she became worried. The girls had gathered in her living room to discuss the tragedy in all its gory details, then cocktail time had come and gone, and still no Robin.

She failed to hear from him the next day, or the next. By then the papers reported the Los Angeles police as having booked three suspects, two men and a woman; they had been tracked down because of a long-distance call made from the Marsh house to Nashville. Nobody could talk of anything but the murder except Nellie and the Belles, who had the additional worry of what had become of Robin.

She went every day to the park and sat on the bench, hoping he would appear, but it was time wasted. There was no Mr. Thingamabob. The weekend went by, and Monday. Then on Tuesday, when the mail came, she found a long blue envelope, with an embossed crest on the back: Castle Baughclammain.

Dearest Nellie,

By now you surely must think I've slipped over the edge of the world (or maybe just over the edge?). In any case, you see where I am—way across the ocean—and there you are in the Big Apple; As the World Turns. (Joke.) Just couldn't think about anything after Willie—what a terrible thing, that poor, dear fellow. I suddenly felt the decks going awash around me and decided to hop a plane, and here I am at Baughclammain. Sorry not to have called before leaving but it was a hasty decision. The right one, I think; it is so beautiful here. I am in the tower room, the dogs are on the floor beside me, Bobby is off with Pat somewhere, Kitty has gone into town for a spot of shopping, the house is quiet. View incredible; I wish you could see it one day. The window just beyond my writing table looks out on the Arans, where the fishermen still speak Gaelic (I can see them putting out their lobster pots from here). We've had our first theft since I can't remember when—someone stole Bobby's bicycle from the lane where he had gone blackberrying, but Father Flynne raised such holy Ned during his Sunday sermon that the bike suddenly and mysteriously reappeared. So much for crime in these precincts. Incidentally, the lane, called "Maureen's path" (for what reason?), is full of rabbits, they seem to haunt it, and when I walk down it I'm always reminded of Missy Priss's line: "surely not to chase rabbits." Perhaps Kitty is right, perhaps it's better for Bobby to be here—God knows it's difficult for a boy to get in trouble. He loves it and seems happy, and I guess that's the main thing. I don't imagine it can be very easy for any child growing up in these times, so maybe being tucked away in this small corner is the proper thing.

I didn't know whom to write about Willie, or what to do. With Bee dead, I guess he didn't have anyone. I read in the London *Times* that there was a memorial service, and in lieu of flowers people were sending contributions to the Actors' Home, so I have done the same. He truly was "The Grand Old Man of Hollywood," wasn't he?

Am still waiting out news of the show; the producer (and yourself) are practically the only people who know where I am. Rose is actually down in the kitchen making blackberry preserves with the cook, if you can get that picture of Lady Ransome in your mind. She and I speak of you often, she says she owes you so much for being so kind to me during all the H'wood years and wants to write you, which I'm sure she'll do as soon as "presarvin'" is done.

Will see you before you know it, so if you have a notion to write, don't trouble, the letter and I will only cross one another. Much love to "The Belles" and more for yourself. Am enclosing some snaps of Bobby—he seems to shoot up the minute I blink my eyes.

Fondly,
Your Robin

Relieved to have discovered Robin's whereabouts, Nellie brought the letter along to The Belle Telephone Hour that evening. Yet without Robin there, the spice had somehow gone out of their get-togethers, and Nellie made excuses to leave early. She wanted terribly to write him, but decided to take his advice and wait. Meanwhile, at the end of the week her grandson, Roger, was bringing Karen, Linda, and Roger, Jr., into the city for a visit to "Nana," as they called Nellie, and she had many plans to make.

They arrived on Friday, to stay through the weekend. Roger and Nancy were continuing on to Philadelphia to visit Nancy's mother, so Nellie had the children by herself. The girls were to sleep in the spare room, kept for this purpose, and Roger, Jr., on the living room couch. Oh, dear, she wondered, what am I to do with them for three days? She looked in the paper to see what suitable family movies might be playing. "They don't make Bobbitt pictures anymore," she muttered, scanning the pages.

Then who magically reappeared that same evening but Robin himself. Her buzzer rang and there he was at the door, looking fresh as a daisy. "Fell out o' the blue, mum," he said, kissing her. After that she didn't have to worry about the children; Robin took them over in the wink of an eye. Usually shy with strangers, they fell to laughing with him immediately, and began making a list of things they wanted to do in the next several days. Robin, he told Nellie, would arrange all.

There were New York excursions everywhere, to the Bronx Zoo, to the Battery and Staten Island, to the Statue of Liberty and the top of the Empire State Building, lunch at the Autopub, where they could see the racing cars hung from the ceiling, then the Museum of Natural History. Halfway through the second day Nellie found she couldn't keep up with the pace and left Robin in full charge.

That night, after the children were put to bed, she and Robin slipped just down the hall to Hilda's apartment to catch up on his news; with the children there he hadn't had time to talk.

He seemed in good spirits, Nellie thought, and no mention was made of Willie Marsh; it was as if Robin had put the terrible episode completely out of his head, which was just as well, Nellie decided. When he asked if she'd had his mother's letter, she said no, nothing had come. He seemed surprised, then laughed. "Oh, Nellie, 'tis such a lovely letter you'll be gettin', such a lovely thing to do. You, too, Hildabraun"—his pet name for Hilda—"all o' yez, in fact."

In fact—what? They couldn't imagine what Lady Ransome's letter would contain. Well, he said, they'd just have to wait and see—" 'twill be a grand surprise and you'll have to get yourselves long dresses, y'know." He smiled cryptically and Nellie and Hilda were left wondering what long dresses would be required for.

But there was one surprise he could tell them about: *Sweepstake*. Was it set, then? Hilda asked. No, he said, but practically. Only ten more backers' shares remained to be sold. But that wasn't it. There were some important parts to be cast, not leads, but four funny American tourists who come to Galway for the races, and who could do the parts better than The Four Belles? Nellie looked at Hilda, Hilda looked at Robin, Robin smiled at both. Yes, The Four Belles, back on Broadway. They would have their own number; he hadn't finished it yet, but he was working on it. It was a comedy number called "Erin Go Blah," and would bring down the house. With this piece of news Robin left them, and Nellie and Hilda called Naomi and Phyllis, and an emergency meeting of The Belle Telephone Hour was called in the wee hours. The only concrete result, however, was the decision to begin diets immediately.

But how were they to sleep, thinking about it all? In addition to *Sweepstake*, there was the mysterious matter of the communication from Ireland. The following day, the Sunday, brought no mail at all, and the suspense became unbearable. Meanwhile Robin had come dressed as Mr. Thingamabob and had taken the children with him to the park, where he was going to hold a storytelling hour for the first time in quite a while. Later the girls walked over to the park themselves, and there was Mr. Thingamabob up on the mushroom with Alice, in the middle of a story.

" 'Garumph,' said the bear, and 'Harumph,' said Missy Priss, giving the bear's nose a tweak. 'Oh, my goo'ness,' said Bobbitt as they ran down the path together. 'Bears don't bother me,' said Missy Priss, 'they're just very large, but nothing to be frightened of. We must put pluck in our hearts, else why did the good Lord put us here? Surely not to chase rabbits!' "

Nellie listened as her great-granddaughter interrupted. Said Linda, "But what's a Bobbitt?"

Robin stopped his tale. "A Bobbitt?" he replied, and gave it some thought. "A Bobbitt's a make-believe fellow and a very silly one at that." He continued the story, and today told it right up to the end, because he knew Nellie's charges wouldn't be back for "tomorrow."

When it was done, Linda said, "I want to see a Bobbitt."

Robin winked at Nellie. "You have, sweetheart, you just don't know it."

"Where does he live?" Linda pursued.

"He lives where all children in books live," Robin explained, touching her head and her heart. "Here, and here."

"I think he's very nice, Bobbitt," Karen said.

He and Nellie exchanged an amused look; explaining to children was so hard sometimes, wasn't it? They walked past the boat basin and up the incline to Seventy-second Street, then down through the park, and finally to the toy farm next to the zoo, where Robin showed them the chickens and ducks and geese, and the swans on the miniature ponds. Then they went to see the seals, and then it was time to go home: Roger and Nancy would be coming at four. Nana would see them again next month, when she came to Garden City for her birthday. But no, that wasn't enough. They didn't want to go; they begged to stay, to be with Mr. Thingamabob, but there was no help for it. They said goodbye and Robin watched Nellie and the Belles leading them back to the apartment. They were passing the Sheep Meadow when they heard a call, and there came Mr. Thingamabob chasing after them with his nonsense pack on his back. Out there in the meadow, putting on a performance for them, with his crazy leaps and clogs and nip-ups, arriving breathless to say goodbye to the children once more, lots of goodbyes, but not to worry, he would be seeing them soon—and, what was best, they would get to meet a Bobbitt after all, because the littlest Bobbitt in the world was arriving from—"Guess where?" he asked, turning to Nellie with a yard-wide smile.

"Not—Ireland?" Robin nodded. Kitty had relented, and was allowing Bobby to pay his first visit to America, and the children would have a "foine toime" with him. Nellie and the girls were delighted; and there was the solution to the question of Lady Ransome's letter: Bobby was coming.

"But don't think *that's* the *surprise*," he called, which left them as mystified as ever.

Nellie waited the next morning for the mail to be sent up, but when it came there was no letter from Lady Ransome, or indeed any letters at all. Since Robin was busy, she and the girls were kept in continuing suspense, until he dropped by for The Belle Telephone Hour. Ah, he said, what a wonderful brood of kids; he had loved being with them. Nellie marveled at his way with them, so easy and natural, and he began making plans for what they would do when little Bobby arrived. Then an inadvertent remark from Robin caused the girls more surprise than ever.

"Everything, of course," he'd said, "will have to be seen to and done quickly, for soon we'll be leavin'."

Leaving? Who would be leaving? Aw, he said, there it was, he'd gone and spoiled it all. Spoiled what? The surprise. It all came out in such a rush of excitement that the girls could only sit there, stunned and staring at one another. Long dresses—for the Galway Ball! Lady Ransome was inviting them all to fly over for race week, they would be guests at Castle Baughclammain and stay for the gala.

That is—if they cared to come, Robin added shyly. Cared to *come*? They sat up practically all night talking about it. He left them in a dither and in a dither they stayed. Lady Ransome's letter arrived, with the embossed crest and the family coat of arms, penned in a neat script, formally extending the invitation to Nellie and the girls. Its arrival was followed by a flurry of activity. They had to see about their passports and pictures were taken for this purpose, arrangements had to be made regarding the farming out or boarding of pets. Clothes had to be seen to; the ones they had were sent to the cleaners, and new ones bought. They spent all their time shopping, and the choice of the long dresses was a difficult one. It became a whirl of excitement and planning, of telephone calls and letters. Robin, too, was writing letters. He'd brought over a box of his personally engraved stationery and a leather writing case, from which he dispatched notes, seemingly to all parts of the world. Everybody, simply everybody, was coming. When he wasn't writing letters he was back on the phone, not that the calls went any less distance than the correspondence; his telephone bill must be enormous, Nellie realized.

Among the girls there was much discussion as to the proper way to compose the acceptances and when these were finished Nellie collected them—nobody had any stamps—and she and Robin took them to the post office, where he waited in line to buy postage, then mailed them off. He popped in and out of all their apartments, checking various details with them, from Hilda to Phyllis to Naomi and back to Nellie again, and the excitement mounted—Nellie found she was having difficulty sleeping—until suddenly it was time for Bobbitt's visit.

Nellie had seen little of Robin during the preceding week. He was having meetings with the producers, lunches with his lawyer, Arnold Weissberger, who was seeing to the contract details, and in between times he was making last-minute plans for young Bobbitt's arrival the following Monday. That was fine with Nellie, for she was making some plans herself. During their usual poker session, the girls hatched a plot, which they hoped would meet with Robin's approval: a surprise welcoming party. Robin was not to know of it until the last minute. The girls worked the menu out in minute detail, then shared in its execution, each one cooking part of the dinner, while it fell to Nellie herself to take care of the cake and decorations. She made numerous trips about town assembling the necessary items—balloons and streamers and special place cards and little paper baskets to hold jelly beans. At F. A. O. Schwarz she bought the biggest teddy bear she could find, a reminder of Bobbitt's own bear, with a blue bow around its neck, and the girls each went in turn and bought their own welcome presents. The cake was enormous, decorated with a structure somewhat resembling the 747 plane Bobbitt would be arriving on. "Welcome Bobbitt," read pink frosted letters, and below, "Really Truly True." There were yellow rosettes and scallops around the edge, the candles would be white, and Nellie was going to put on the entire two dozen in the package; they would make a lovely light.

The day before Bobbitt's arrival, when Robin called, as a way of ensuring that the surprise would come off she suggested they all go to the airport and meet the plane; no, he said, he didn't want her to go to that trouble. Then she suggested that as soon as they got in and settled, Robin must bring Bobbitt straight to her house. Well, he said, the child would be tired after his trip, and he didn't want him overtaxed. Nellie saw what he meant; there was no help for it, she had to confess the welcome party they had planned. Robin said that was a kind thing for her to want to do, but wasn't really necessary. Oh, she said, everything was arranged; the food was cooked, the cake baked, the presents were bought—what was to be done?

"You're a darlin' dear, Nell," Robin said, after consideration, and of course they would come. The Aer Lingus flight from Shannon would arrive at Kennedy Airport at five-thirty, and allowing for traffic, he and Bobbitt ought to be at Nellie's apartment by seven. Dinner would be promptly at eight, and right afterward Robin could take the child home and put him to bed.

This was how matters were arranged, and the next day Nellie went to Mr. Kenneth's. Under the dryer, she had an odd feeling. Was everything all right? Had she forgotten something? When she got home, the girls were already at work blowing up balloons and hanging them in clusters, and twisting and draping the paper streamers, then setting the presents out on the sideboard, while the cake was kept hidden in the kitchen. When all was in readiness, they dispersed to dress, while Nellie saw to the finishing touches. Robin called from the airport, saying the flight would be delayed half an hour, and not to worry. She thanked him, then rechecked everything, wondering what she might have forgotten. Then it struck her: champagne. She called the liquor store and ordered six bottles of the Taittinger that Robin liked; after all, it was to be a celebration. Then the girls arrived, and they waited, chatting as the time drew nearer. Then the time for the arrival had passed, and the missing guests were late; Nellie glanced more frequently at the clock as Robin grew tardier and tardier. Then she became worried. It wasn't like him to be late, or not to have called back. She was certain now that her feelings at the beauty parlor were not merely whimsical or capricious; something had happened. She called the airline, and was told that the flight had arrived, but they were unable to give her any information regarding its passengers. Finally it was well past nine, and deciding she must feed her guests, Nellie went into the kitchen and put on her apron. They were halfway through the soup course when the downstairs buzzer rang; the doorman announced Mr. Ransome. Nellie waited anxiously for the elevator, holding the apartment door ajar, alternately peering nervously down the hall and over her shoulder to the others at the table. At last the elevator door opened and Robin came out alone. He halted briefly when he saw her, then approached.

Nellie hurried to meet him. "What's happened?" she asked. "Where's Bobby?"

He shook his head in bewilderment. "I don't know. He didn't come." He entered, said hello to the girls, and flung himself into a chair. "I don't understand it. He just wasn't on the plane. I called Galway, but there's no answer at the house. None of the servants—nobody. They showed me the passenger list; he was supposed to be on the flight. It came in, but he wasn't there." He rose and began striding rapidly about the room. "Something's happened; I know it. Something's happened." He sat down again at the desk in the corner by the birdcage.

It had. Nellie knew it, too; the funny feeling she'd had at the beauty parlor. The girls remained at the table, watching but saying nothing. Nellie brought a cup of coffee and set it at Robin's elbow on the desk, while he dialed Long Distance, gave his credit card number, and placed the call. Nellie withdrew to the dining room and sat with the girls; they sent a chain of worried expressions around the table.

"Hello . . . hello . . .?" Robin had got through, but the connection appeared to be a bad one. "Pat . . . is that you? Where is everybody?"

Nellie waited while Pat talked on the other end of the line. She watched Robin, half turned away, looking out across the window ledge to Lincoln Center. Some fearful thing was stalking him, waiting to clutch, to pull him down. She leaned her elbows on the cloth, clasping her fingers till her rings hurt her fingers.

"How did it happen, Pat?" Robin was asking quietly. He listened for the answer. Then, "All right, I'm leaving right away. I'll cable the flight." He hung up, put his card away, and sat at the desk chair, leaning toward the window. "No," he was saying. "It must be some mistake." He turned, looked across the room to the table, tried to speak, couldn't, then managed a hoarse "I'm sorry." He was seized by a paroxysm of trembling, his shoulders heaved and shuddered; he sat bent forward in the chair, holding his head in his hands.

"Oh, my dear." Nellie went and knelt beside him and put her arms around him. "What is it? What's happened?"

He took his hands away and looked at her. The tears coursed down his cheeks and he wiped them away at his chin. He shook his head, looking wildly at her, then at the others, who sat frozen in their places.

"Oh, dearest, tell me," Nellie pleaded, putting her hand to his cheek. He pressed it there with his own and murmured into it.

"It's Bobby—and Kitty. . . ." His voice broke again, and he fumbled for his handkerchief; she gave him one of her own.

She waited until he had blown his nose, then asked again. "Robin, what's happened?"

"Bobby's dead."

He pushed past her and rose quickly, striding rapidly about the room, his head held back, and clenching the handkerchief in his fingers. He whirled, stared at her with a disbelieving expression, and repeated the words. "He's dead." She had risen also and he came quickly to her and threw himself against her, burrowing his head against her shoulder while the others stared in shock. She drew him onto the sofa and held him until he could tell the rest of it. Kitty and Bobby had been driven by limousine from Galway to Shannon Airport. En route they stopped for something to eat, then continued on. Evidently mistaken for a diplomat's vehicle, the car had had a bomb planted in it. It exploded just as they arrived at Shannon. Bobby was killed, Kitty and the chauffeur were in the hospital.

"My dear," was all that Nellie could murmur, "my dear, I'm so sorry."

"It's my Bobbitt, Nell, my little boy. He was coming to me. And now he's dead." Robin shook his head in disbelief. He blew his nose again and asked for a glass of water, which Hilda hurried to fetch, while Naomi whispered to Phyllis that they should go. Robin stared around at the decorations and their funny paper hats, and the tears came to his eyes again.

Nellie sat holding Robin's hand; Hilda began quietly clearing the table. Naomi and Phyllis got their things and slipped tactfully away, then Hilda left, too. Nellie and Robin stayed together in the quiet room, while currents from the air conditioner wafted the streamers and balloons, and the teddy bear sat with button eyes and blue bow on the sideboard. She asked him if he wanted her to make a plane reservation for him; he shook his head. It would have to wait until morning. She went into the kitchen for more coffee. When she came out again, she glanced around; his jacket was there, but not Robin. She looked in the bathroom, and in each of the bedrooms. She became frightened, wondering what had happened to him, then was more frightened when she found him. He was beyond the raised window, sitting on the outside ledge, staring down at the sidewalk. Though she forced herself to pretend there was nothing unusual in this, she felt rushes of terror, that he might at any moment just let himself go, or even jump from the ledge. She approached the window and spoke casually, and he replied in a seemingly normal tone, but wouldn't come in. When she brought him a cold drink, he sat out there gulping from the glass and swirling the ice cubes; still he would not come in. She could feel her hands trembling and a choking sensation.

"What are you thinking, Robin?" she asked.

When he spoke, it was quietly and quite rationally. "I was thinking about your family. Linda and Karen and Roger. Bobby really would have had fun with them, don't you think?" Yes, she said, just as quietly, she thought he would have.

He went on, talking about children, but still he would not come in. She sat waiting, listening, growing more apprehensive, until at last she spoke sharply to him, as she might to a recalcitrant child. He came in then, drank his coffee, and asked if instead of going to Madame Potekka's he might spend the night. He couldn't face talking to her about it just yet. In the morning . . .

She put him to bed in the spare room; he lay with the pillow pulled over his face, muffling his sobs. His shoulder felt pitifully thin when she put her hand against it. She got him quieted, and when he had finally sunk into exhausted sleep, she went out and closed the door. The next morning she woke him early, as he had asked her to. He showered and dressed, ate little of the breakfast she'd made, gave her a hurried kiss, saying he would be in touch, and left.

He called the following night, having arrived at Shannon. He was going directly to the hospital to see Kitty, then to the funeral home. His mother and father were with him; he would write. Please no flowers. Three days later a letter came:

Dearest Nellie,

It is done. I have only just returned from the cemetery, and am sitting in Rose's room, writing at her desk, looking out on the bay. Very bright, sunny. I thought it always rained for funerals and people had umbrellas. I had wanted the grave to be on the house grounds, but there is some medieval statute which prohibits this; consequently the burial was at the church of Kilaraty (a small village close by), fitting, I suppose—much greenery and

218

flowers, but so lonely. I cannot bear to think of him under that cold, cold Irish turf. The trams run by the cemetery and there is a good deal of offstage noise, so I wonder how the little fellow may have any rest, but there is a school nearby and the children come and play among the gravestones, so I suppose he will have company, if Eternity ever needs company. From the corner of the churchyard you can see across the vale to Baughclammain. I had forgotten to order any flowers myself, so I had nothing to leave, except I was carrying the handkerchief you loaned me and I put that on the grave, so you will know you protect him with some of your love. Kitty is still in hospital at Shannon, and I must hurry off to her. Rose is a wreck and is experiencing some problems which seem to have nothing to do with Bobby's death.

More anon. Thinking of you,

Love,

Your Robin

Three days later there was a brief note from the Dorchester Hotel in London, explaining that Robin was there with Lady Ransome, looking after her affairs. There followed another note, this time from the Prince de Galles Hotel in Paris, where he and Rose had gone for a brief stay to meet with the Rothschilds, and though Nellie was not good at reading between the few lines, she thought they indicated that some sort of financial transactions were taking place.

At the beginning of the following week another letter arrived, postmarked Galway, with the family crest. It read:

Darling Missy Priss,

Here I am back home again, and will be glad of the rest. London, Paris most hectic. Kitty is out of hospital and has gone to stay with her family in Cork, where she says she wants to remain until the fall. Meanwhile, I've been trying to deal with Father and Rose. I told you there were financial problems, but they now appear far worse than I'd imagined. Rose is talking of turning the castle into a guest inn (really!) and renting out rooms to weekenders. I told her we weren't three-in-a-bed Irish yet, and obviously the thing to do was to sell the Ballymore, hence our trip to Paris. One of the Rothschilds has coveted it for a long time, so I think it will end up in their hands, rather than going on the block, which was

Father's suggestion. Never mind, Rose has plenty of other necklaces; though I must admit we shall all miss the Ballymore—in the family for over three hundred years. Please don't worry about me, I'm all right, will be popping up on your doorstep to surprise you one of these days.

Lovingly,
Your Bobbitt

P.S. Reading that, I just saw how funny it sounds. Your Bobbitt. Alas, there is only one again, isn't there?
Loving you, thinking of you. B.

Nellie reread the letter and cried a little, and when the girls gathered at Phyllis's she brought it along to share with them. Sad, it was just sad, that's all. Partway through the reading, Phyllis, who had her drink in her hand, spilled some of it on the rug; something seemed to have taken her aback. She rose hurriedly and made herself another drink, and later, when Nellie asked her what was wrong, she patted her shoulder and said nothing, nothing. . . .

Then, as she was seeing the girls out, she took Nellie aside and asked plaintively, "Nell, do you really think we're going? To the race?"

Nellie couldn't tell, they must wait and see. But: "Why?" she asked Phyllis, who only smiled and kissed her cheek. "Nothing," she said. "I was just wondering."

Nellie rested uneasily that night, lying awake and thinking about Robin, then about the letter, then about Phyllis. In her mind she went over the letter paragraph by paragraph. Finally she went to sleep. It wasn't until the next morning, reading the *Times* at the breakfast table, that the thought struck her. There were pictures of the jewelry collection in the Victoria and Albert Museum. She had seen them many times, and suddenly—quite impossible not to have realized it, but she had not—a light went on. She put the paper down, still staring at the pictures, but her mind was elsewhere. She let her coffee get cold, thinking, then she went into the living room, pacing and thinking. From time to time her mind flitted back to the jewels, but that was only absurd and served to irritate her. Her irritation turned to distress, her distress to agitation, and finally her agitation to fear. She tried to think it out, piece by piece, wishing there were somebody she could talk to about it, but there seemed no one. She went back to the kitchen and there were the pictures. She poured more coffee, and while she was stirring in her cream the answer—or part of it—came to her. She went to the telephone and called the New York Public Library information service, feeling a creeping dread as she posed her question and waited for the answer, which, coming, caused her infinitely greater distress. She sat and thought some more, and when Hilda telephoned she said she couldn't talk and hung up quickly. She got out her telephone directory and looked up a name. When she found it she made another call and asked for an appointment, which was given her for later that afternoon. She took a good deal of trouble getting ready, and spent the remaining time pacing the room, waiting for four o'clock. At a quarter to, she called down to the doorman and asked for a taxi, and then she set out to visit Madame Potekka.

Robin's friend was waiting for her and quickly invited Nellie to be seated. She appeared warm and friendly, though obviously she didn't remember having met Nellie before. Her living quarters were small, hardly the grandeur Robin had described, and her easel was crammed in a corner by the window. "As you see," she said, sweeping a bangled arm to a half-finished canvas, "I am working."

Nellie apologized for taking up her time, mentioning that she owned one of the artist's works. The artist's brows shot up.

"Ah, which is that?" The violets, Nellie explained. Madame's look of surprise was adroitly covered as she seemed to arrive at some private understanding concerning the painting. "Ah, yes," she said, "the little violets. Very pretty. Bobby . . . gave it to you?"

"Yes. A most generous present. He is so kind-hearted, isn't he. And generous. You are quite . . . recovered?"

"Recovered?" Madame was surprised, as Nellie had feared she might be. "Have I been ill, then?"

"Haven't you?"

"I had a cold last winter, nothing more."

"Yes. I see. Colds are to be guarded against."

"Surely it is not my state of health that brings you here. Something about Bobby, is it?" she asked, lighting a long cigarette, which she inserted into a longer holder. "How can I help you?"

Nellie took a breath and plunged in. "Madame, are you acquainted with the Ballymore emerald?"

"I have heard of it, naturally." She blew smoke in the air, but discreetly, in the direction of the electric fan that cooled the room. "It is very famous."

"Yes. Bobby—Robin—tells me it is an old family heirloom, and that his mother has been reduced by circumstances to selling it."

"Oh?" Again a look of surprise which was quickly disguised by a smile. "And . . . ?"

"I wondered, since you are so closely connected with Robin, if you could tell me if you believe this to be true."

"Offhand, I should say that I doubted it," Madame returned easily.

"So should I," said Nellie, "considering that the Ballymore emerald is in the British Museum, and has been since thirty-five years ago, when it was given by the Farquahar family. Yet I have been led to believe that it belonged to Lady Ransome and that she has sold it to the Rothschilds, and that she may have to turn the Castle Baughclammain into a sort of weekend hostelry."

Madame Potekka could no longer control her surprised expression. Her mouth dropped open, then she covered her face with her hands. In a moment she spread her fingers and peered through them, her little black eyes wide with either mirth or astonishment. "Oh, my dear," she said, shaking her head, "you don't mean it."

"Mean what?"

"Bobby is doing it again, yes?"

"Doing what?"

"Telling little stories."

"Little . . . stories? Yes, so it appears. I called the library and they assured me that that is where the emerald is."

Madame Potekka had plucked up a painted Japanese fan from the table and was stirring the air around her with gusto. "A charming boy, Robin, is he not? Charming. Such a love. Who is more enchanting than Robin?—though I call him Bobby."

"Have you recently seen or heard from him?" Nellie asked.

"Let me think." She struck a thoughtful pose, then sprang out with, "Yes, to be sure, I heard from him just two weeks ago. A small financial matter . . ."

"Financial?"

Madame employed her hands in a European gesture of *laissez faire*. "With Bobby things are always financial, are they not? You know. . . ." She gave Nellie a broad wink. "I was only helping him out of a jam, anyways."

Nellie cleaved to the word. "A jam?"

"It is nothing new. Bobby is always in some sort of jam. . . . But why do you look so worried, if I may ask? If it is that you have not heard from him, oh, my dear, let me assure you there is nothing to fear, nothing whatever. He often disappears—*pfft*." She made him disappear again. "That is his way, Bobby's. A part of his charm, I think, for who is there one wants to see constantly? Fish and guests, you know, they all stink after three days."

"Madame, I beg you, it is no joking matter. Do you know of the tragedy that has happened to him? . . ."

Madame, it appeared, did not. Nellie related as quickly as she could the details: the planned arrival of the child, the surprise party, Robin's return from the airport, the fatal call to Galway. . . .

"The child was killed in a bomb explosion, you see."

"Ah, this is surely a tragedy," Madame Potekka agreed dolorously, though she seemed bewildered by the account. "But what child is this?"

"Little Bobby. Bobbitt, they call him. Robin's son."

Madame's eyes widened over the rim of her fan. "Oh, dear, oh, dear . . . I see." She fanned herself rapidly and blew out her cheeks. "I agree, this is no joking matter. You must tell me all, then."

"You have met him, little Bobbitt?"

"I have . . . heard of him from time to time." She waited while Nellie brought out the facts she had discovered during Robin's tempestuous scene after the phone call, and the terrifying period he had spent out on the ledge. Madame listened without interrupting while Nellie elaborated on Kitty's injury and the funeral arrangements. Then she pressed Nellie's hand with a reassuring gesture. "My dear, my dear Miss Nellie," she began quietly, "I must tell you something. You will not believe me when I say it, you will think me cruel and heartless, but if Bobby has told you the little boy is dead, then it is better so."

"Better?" Nellie snatched her hand away as if it had been burned, and straightened herself against the chair back. "How can you talk that way? How could he be better off dead?"

Potekka heaved a sigh and resumed fanning. "I can only repeat what I said: the child is better off dead. That is to say, *Bobby* is better off having him dead."

"Was he some sort of monster?"

Potekka nodded slowly. "In a way. In any case, it is no problem for the child, you see."

Nellie was aghast. "Do you understand that he was blown up in an explosion? The IRA . . . ?"

"Yes, yes, the IRA. Of course it would be the IRA, or the Mafia, or an abduction by Turkish Janissaries."

"What *are* you talking about?" Nellie cried in alarm.

Madame Potekka held a quick, silent consultation with herself, tapping the fan against her lips, then, with a helpless shrug, said, "My dear Miss Nellie, I hope you will not mistake what I am going to say to you, but I say it for our friend, Robin. We are agreed between us, I think, that we both love him. Then I say to you that we must go on loving him, no matter what. I say to you that if he admits the child is dead, then he is better off, by far. *He* is better off, *I* am better off, even *you* are better off. Anyone who knows him is better off." She peered across her fan to see what effect her words were having. "I tell you also this," she added, "the child was not killed."

"Not?" Nellie drew back in surprise. "You mean he's alive?"

"I mean he never existed." She tapped her temple. "Have you not found in your experience with Bobby that he is an imaginative young man? Full of fancies, dreams, enchantments? The child is merely one of them."

"You mean there isn't any Bobbitt?"

"I did not say that."

"You said—"

"I said Bobby had no son. As for Bobbitt, yes, there is one of those. You know him as Robin. He is the only Bobbitt there is. The child is something he made up. A fiction. And if he now tells you the child—this Bobbitt—is dead, why, then, I say to you our Robin is better off. And therefore, it you are truly his friend, so you will be also. As we are agreed, our Bobby is a charming fellow. He is nice to have around, he is gay and witty, and fun. He sings, he tells amusing stories, he dances, does tricks; but a trained monkey can do some of those things. I know no one I enjoy being with more, but I say to myself I must always have some salt with me, and I must take him with a grain of it. You see, he is—" Again she tapped her temple.

"Please stop doing that." Already distraught, Nellie was becoming angry. "Is he crazy?"

"How shall I say what I mean? What is crazy? Perhaps I am crazy, perhaps you are crazy, perhaps we all are crazy— and he is sane. He is not crazy; he certainly is not dangerous, not even to himself, I think. But it is his imagination, you see. That is what happened to him out there, in Hollywood.

Anyone can remember what it is like to be a child, but how many people remember or ever knew what it is like to have been Bobby Ransome? It is not easy, I should think, to be that famous, and to be a child as well. You are way up there" —pointing her cigarette at the ceiling—"then suddenly one day, *pfft*, you are not, you are down there"—pointing at the floor. "He was a very big somebody, then one day he was a nobody again. That is the way it happens out there. It is enough to break the heart or turn you bitter. But not Bobby; he has no bitterness. He is kind and loving and generous. But I will tell you what happens to him. They tried to keep him a child, so he has stayed a child, here"—touching her head again—"and here"—touching her breast. "Sometimes that is not such a bad thing, but in Bobby's case I am not so sure. He lived in a make-believe world for so long, and he has clung to that make-believe. He will not give it up. For everybody he was Bobbitt, then for nobody was he Bobbitt any longer, if you see what I mean. So he made up another Bobbitt, for himself. You are not a stupid person, Miss Nellie, obviously, yet he has fooled you. He has fooled so many, for so long. He has dragged those borrowed snapshots with him to every cocktail and dinner party from here to the North Pole. He dines out on the little fellow, and his great romance with this Kitty Kelly. He has not seen her in years but in his mind they are the world's greatest tragic lovers since Romeo and Juliet. The little fellow, he is a source of amusement, of wonder, and of income. 'I'm a little short,' Bobby will say, 'and it's the little tyke's birthday. Can you lend me fifty till next week?' You lend him, next week comes, he has forgotten the money. He has borrowed from you, has he not? Yes, I see he has. Me, too. You are sick, I loaned him money for your recovery."

"I, Madame, am not sick. I have not even had a cold."

"So much more your good fortune, I'm sure. But you see how it works: a little concern, a little sorrow, a little tear, a lot of dollars. He is a borrowing institution, our Bobby. So. And your grandchildren—"

"They are my great-grandchildren."

"Excuse it, please, great-grandchildren—they come to visit, and you all have a good time, he told me so, but in consequence he pretends that Bobbitt—his made-up Bobbitt—should pay such a visit. Then he finds you are really truly believing, he is frightened, he can go no further without producing the child, so he kills it off. And you may believe me, when he did that he believed it, absolutely; that death

225

was as real to him as if he had seen it happen before his eyes. This make-believe world he creates for himself, it is not an unhappy one, because then he could not live there, but in it there is always tragedy, just as in a real world, our world. He is very clever, our Bobby; he gives himself both—it is the artist in him."

She stopped to light a second cigarette, then wafted the smoke away with her fan and made another helpless gesture. "But I do not think it will last. He will resurrect the child, somewhere, sometime, at another dinner party. He cannot resist it. Of course you have heard the stories about the mother, the father?"

"I have heard a good deal of Lady Ransome and Lord Ransome. I do not think they can be a healthy influence on him."

"My dear, my dear." She gave a piercing shriek of laughter. "Do you also believe that pigs fly or that the moon is made from green cheese? There is no Lady Ransome, nor no Lord Ransome. There is no castle in Galway, none of it. Oh, I know, he talks of nothing else: Lady Farquahar, the Earl of Kerry, and all those fancy New York names—Chessy and Mica and Gerry Stutz. He knows none of them. He reads about them, sees their pictures in the papers, that is all. I will tell you who Lady Ransome is. Her name is Ethel, and she lives where she has always lived; in Galway, true, but in a little house. Her husband was a hatter. Yes, a maker of hats. *He* truly is"—again she tapped her temple—"not all there. The mother looks after him, since he cannot do it himself. Something in the acids they dip the felt in affected his brain. A long time ago."

"But the pictures; Robin has so many photographs. . . ."

"The Lady Ransome he shows you is a French woman, the Vicomtesse de Choiseul; he liked her looks and style, and he made her his—how shall I call it?—his surrogate mother. He collects stationery from hotel lobbies. He even had some printed up, engraved, very expensive; he writes many letters to many people on it. He mails them to friends in Europe and has them returned, postmarked, in a second envelope. A hobby, do you see? Has he invited you to the Galway Ball? Yes, I thought he would. Great fun, if it were possible. All I can tell you, though, is that you will not be there."

"And"—Nellie hardly dared ask it—"his show, *Sweepstake*: what of that?"

Sweepstake also got wafted away by Madame's fan. "It is another . . . fiction. A little something he has concocted, a little dream, perhaps. He has written a song or two, that is all. Lovely songs, but nothing more. He *could* do it, you see, if he wanted, but he does not. He merely pretends he is doing it. All those calls and lunches with producers, the money people. He likes to imagine he is in the heart of all that Broadway hustle and bustle. To tell you the truth, he would be terrified. It is not for him."

"What is for him?"

"Who can say? His way is not our way, but who is to say which is better? Perhaps I am wrong. Perhaps he *is*—" Again she touched her head, but Nellie missed the gesture. Eyes lowered to her lap, she tugged nervously at the corners of her handkerchief.

"Where is he now?" Nellie asked in a low voice.

"I cannot tell you," said Madame Potekka.

Nellie looked up suddenly. "Cannot—or will not? Are you protecting him?"

"Bobby needs a good deal of protection, for as I have said, he is still a child. But I cannot tell you, for I do not know where he is. He is a will-o'-the-wisp. I have never known where he stays. He told me once the only place to live was New York, it is the capital of the world. He laughed and said he was the worm in the Big Apple. Who knows—perhaps he has finally found the apple rotten and has gone back to Europe."

"Would his friends know?"

"Perhaps. Except he has few friends. And I think I can see from your look that he may no longer count you among them."

Nellie drew herself up primly. "He has done bad things, wicked things."

"Bad? Wicked? What sort?"

"He has upset people's lives, he has let them make plans he had no intention of seeing through, he has borrowed money under false pretenses, and as you say, with no intention of paying it back. I and my friends are not as well fixed as you—"

"*I? I?*" Madame Potekka was shocked. "You think I can afford it? You see how I live here. But when you love someone you do not think of yourself, you think of them. Of course, with Bobby a dollar bill always has wings on it, so quickly it flies away." She gave Nellie a swift, shrewd look. "But does he spend this money on himself or on you, heh? Ah, yes, I can see, a little present here, one there, a little trifle to surprise you, to bring you pleasure. The violets, for

227

example. He told me he must have it, I thought he wanted it for himself, so I 'sold' it to him, knowing of course I would never see a penny of the money."

"You must let me pay you for the painting," Nellie insisted. "Tell me how much; I will send you a check."

"Not a bit of it, dear Miss Nellie. It is my pleasure, since it is Bobby's. He gives it to you because it pleased you. I am glad, he is glad, you are glad. That is Bobby. He makes everyone glad, even though"—she burst into a mounting roulade of laughter—"he goes about it as a nimble-fingered fellow opens a safe. But he does not crack it or blow it open; he does it oh, so gently."

Nellie shook her head with indignation. "Something must be done. It is too much."

Madame made a helpless gesture. "What must be done? And why, my dear?"

"He cannot be allowed to go on, he must make amends, he must pay back what he owes. Cheating people is not right."

"Well, I am glad finally in my long life to meet someone who knows what is right." Madame Potekka rose abruptly. "I have spent my time trying to find out what is wrong; now I see it was wasted time. How kind of you to point out the error of my ways."

Perfunctory if not angry goodbyes were said. Going down in the elevator, Nellie told herself: She is wrong. He is wrong. He must be made to see the truth, what is real, what is actual; he cannot go on living in this dream world. Wrong, everything was irretrievably wrong. By the time she reached the street she had shredded her handkerchief, her face working with indignation. The tatters she used to wipe her tears.

Robin, oh, Robin.

She was dying with shame and humiliation. Something in her cried out, the shouting voice of betrayal, but she stifled it. *Liar*, it said. *Cheat. Monster.* And after each of these, an echo: *Bobbitt.*

Out in the air again, she walked as if in a dream, past shopwindows whose contents she never saw, past faces she never noticed. She walked until her feet were tired and then she walked some more. She did not want to go home. She felt defenseless and in need of armor, so she seized on what came most readily to hand, the armor of anger. In her mind's eye she saw a tall, thin youth, with blond curly hair, who loved sitting on a mushroom, telling stories to children.

Why, Bobbitt, you grew up!

He hadn't, of course, merely older and taller.

She went back over it all, step by step, day by day, realizing how she had been duped. The child, she kept repeating to herself, Bobby, *Bobbitt*, whom she'd believed in so completely, was only a fiction, didn't exist. None of it existed; Robin was a sham, a fake, a hoaxer. Nothing was "really truly true." She thought of the deceitful lengths he had gone to, making up stories to borrow money from her for Madame Potekka, and from Potekka for her. He was no better than a con artist, and a clever one at that. Then, with a dreadful pang, she remembered the Belles. He'd borrowed from them, too, she was sure of it, each in turn, and Heaven knew on what pretext.

She pleaded fatigue that evening and did not appear at Naomi's for The Belle Telephone Hour, nor did she on the next. She couldn't bear facing them; what was she to tell them, how could she explain? The passports, the plans, the clothes, the money spent; they were practically on their way to Ireland. She felt so ashamed to have been taken in, for them all to have been taken in. Oh, she thought, if she could just get her hands on Robin.

The opportunity presented itself next morning. The buzzer rang, she went to the door, and there he was. Out of the blue, thin air—Bobbitt style—looking just the same, fit as a fiddle, his smile a yard wide. He kissed her and came in and sat. "Well," she said, "how've you been?"

Well, he said, he was all right. When had he got back from Ireland? she asked. "Oh," he answered, "only last night. Sad, it was all very sad." "Yes," she said. "Sad; terribly sad." "Are you all right?" he asked. "Oh, yes," she said, "quite all right." Had she missed him? Well, she told him, he *had* been *very* much on her mind. He was glad, he said. "And Kitty?" Kitty was coming along fine; the chauffeur as well. She supposed he must miss Bobbitt dreadfully. "Oh, yes," he said, "dreadfully." But he had talked with his mother— "Lady Ransome, you mean?" she broke in. Yes—he nodded —Lady Ransome, and they had decided that in spite of the tragedy they wanted to go ahead with the plans they had made. "Oh," said Nellie, "do you think that would be quite right, with the poor child scarcely cold in his grave?" "Life must go on," he said. "Yes," she agreed. "And so?" And so they must all come to Galway for the races. Rose wanted it so. Well, Nellie said, perhaps it was best. Certainly the Galway Race was not to be sniffed at. And the gala, of course; they'd got their long dresses. "Then all will be going forward as

planned?" she asked. "Yes," he said, "exactly to the letter."
Ah, yes, she said, of course; always to the letter. Or ought she
to say letters; he'd written her so many. "Well"—he laughed—
"the gift o' gab in longhand." Oh, she said, that was a good
one; he was a caution. Terribly sorry about the selling of the
Ballymore; family heirloom and all that. Yes, sad. "What's
wrong?" he asked, having noticed, probably, how pale she
was, how she had to grip the arms of her chair to keep her
hands from trembling.

"How is it possible," she asked finally, "that the Ballymore
emerald was just sold to the Rothschilds when it has been in
the British Museum for thirty-five years?"

He stared, stammered, began a faltering explanation. She
impatiently waved away his attempt, and began speaking,
and once having begun, found she could not stop. She had
never spoken so angrily to anyone in her life; but then she
had never been so angry. To see him sitting there, smiling a
yard wide, in his Bobbitt innocence . . . Bobbitt indeed; she
would Bobbitt him. She had been Missy Priss in too many
pictures not to know how to act like Missy Priss with her
starch, and starch was what he got from her. She had no
trouble at all finding words to tell him what she thought of
young men who went about preying on helpless women; who
were cold and heartless and selfish, liars, cheats, pusillanimous
good-for-nothings, and there was one thing more, she added,
showing him to the door, she never never never wanted to see
him again, that was what he could rest assured of, and as,
wordless and defenseless, he went out, she gave the door a
good slam. Then she opened it again and called after him,
"That for you, Mr. Bobbitt!" and slammed it again.

That afternoon she telephoned Hilda, then Naomi, then
Phyllis, and told each one individually—she couldn't face
them in a group—that Robin was forced to stay in Europe on
business, that the money people had backed out of the show,
and that it was all off, incidentally dropping the news that the
trip to Galway was off as well. The girls accepted this news
without the furor or disappointment Nellie had anticipated;
it was almost as if they'd suspected something. She announced
to each of them that she herself was going to visit Roger and
Nancy for her birthday, and made a hasty retreat, leaving
Hilda to feed the budgies.

She packed her bag, bought presents for the children, got
on the Long Island Rail Road, and went to Garden City.
Nothing new, nothing unusual, the same old thing, just one
more of Nana's visits, but as much as she loved them all,

she found she did not enjoy her stay; she had too many other things to think about. Mainly Bobbitt—Robin—Bobby —Mr. Thingamabob. She dreaded her birthday party, though she put as good a face on it as she could, kissing the children as they each presented her with a little gift, and wincing when the cake was brought out with one tactful candle: she remembered the boxful she had planned for "Bobbitt"'s cake. She was relieved when it was all over. She was one year older, but certainly not one year wiser. Later Nancy and the children drove her to Roger's air school for a special "surprise," as they called it, and again she cringed; she had had the last surprise she ever needed in her life. They heard the sound of a plane, and Nellie watched with the others while it made loop-the-loops and barrel rolls in the sky, then zoomed low over their heads. The pilot held up a thumb, threw the stick, and the plane shot upward, banked, and as it turned and slowed, several puffs of smoke issued from its tail. The plane banked again, and more puffs came out, then again, and gradually the puffs blended together, forming a large white "H." Oh, dear, thought Nellie, her hand at her breast; she knew what the surprise was to be. The plane looped and turned, dove and rose, with puff after puff exploding into the blue, forming letters, until they spelled out "HAPPY BIRTH-DAY NANA." Well, she told them, that certainly was a nice surprise, relieved that it was over. No one who was as big a fool as she needed that sort of advertising.

Then the plane landed and the pilot was getting out, and of course it was Roger, all smiles, but all she could think of as she kissed him was "Flying Rodger," Papa Baer's failed attempt to continue the career of young Master Ransome. She let them think her tears were ones of gratitude and drove home chattering about how wonderful that planes could write in the sky, but she'd read somewhere that if you put twelve chimpanzees in a room with twelve typewriters they eventually would write *Hamlet*.

Everyone laughed at Nana's joke, though no one quite understood it. She stayed through the week, spending time with the children, and glad that they at least seemed to be leading normal, happy lives, and even if their smiles were not a yard wide, they were genuine. Then she packed her bag again and got on the Long Island Rail Road and went back to the city.

No sooner back than she was sorry she had returned. Every-where she looked, there was something that reminded her of Robin, some trifling whimsy he had brought by as a gift. She collected them all and pushed them to the back of a drawer, including the box of engraved stationery he had used to write his notes on.

One morning's mail brought just such a one, not, however, on monogrammed stationery. A plain dime-store piece of paper in a matching envelope, it read:

> Dearest Nellie,
> You can imagine how foolish I feel. I told you I'd never grow up, and I haven't. I just wanted to make things interesting and fun for you, then it all got too much and I didn't know where to stop it. Please try not to think too badly of me. I only wanted you to love your Bobbitt.
>
> P.S. I guess they'll put me back in my rubber room again. Meanwhile I'll send you something to add to the enclosed until our account is squared.

The "enclosed" was a certified money order, payable to her, part of the sum he had borrowed. She started to crumple the note, then returned it to its envelope and stuck it with the other things in the back of the drawer. Then she sat down and wrote a check to Madame Potekka for the painting of the violets, and put the picture away; she couldn't bear to look at it.

The rest of the summer seemed particularly long; she thought the cool weather would never come. People began arriving back in the city after their holidays, ready for autumn, and she thought over and over again how she had spent these last months, being victimized. It would not do, it simply would not do, and she choked with rage every time she thought of Robin. What made it worse, the Belles wanted to talk of nothing else, were always asking if she'd had a letter, had he telephoned, when was he coming back? She made up one excuse after another, until she ran out of excuses. She was bad company, more satiric than Naomi had ever been during The Belle Telephone Hour, which she gave up for good, then showing her irritation at poker, which caused her to be the continual loser, and she finally said she didn't want to play anymore, they would have to get someone else. Finally Hilda came to her and asked point-blank what the trouble was. Oh, nothing, she said, she was just out of sorts. They'd seen so much of each other for so long, perhaps it was better to see less of one another for a while. Hilda went away miffed, Nellie felt guilty, and became even angrier at Robin.

The weeks went by and she found herself bored to tears. She seldom went anywhere, never to the opera or the theater. There were no intimate lunches, no impromptu suppers. No music on the phonograph, the spinet piano—certainly no guitar music—nobody in the empty apartment but the budgies. Oh, she thought, what has happened, how did I get into this, what will get me out?

Nothing, it seemed. She went to the YWCA and took up a course in yoga, thinking it would calm her, but it wasn't Eastern mysticism that was going to turn the trick for her. What she had to do was forget. The Galway Ball had been reported at length in the magazines and papers. Nellie looked at her dress hanging in the closet and cried.

Late in September she ventured by herself into the park again. She had not been there because it held such unpleasant memories, but almost of their own accord her feet bore her to the Alice in Wonderland statues. The nursemaids were on the bench, just as they had been last spring and summer, and the first thing they wanted to know was where was Bobbitt? He was such a nice young man, one observed. "Oh," Nellie replied airily, "over the moon, I expect." They didn't understand that, and she gave them short shrift. There were children playing around the bronze mushroom, where Mr. Thingamabob used to sit, and Nellie overheard the delightful, inconsequential, often wise things they said from time to time. She thought with a terrible sadness of how they must grow up and face the hard realities of life. All too short, it was, and not a moment to be wasted. *Oh, Nellie*, Robin had said, *I don't think I'll ever grow up*. What he had meant was *Oh, Nellie, I don't ever want to grow up*. Foolish boy, foolish man. Everyone had to; it was the way things were. He had lived in a storybook world, had lived the fairy tale children dream of, then one day the fairy tale ended, but he did not live happily ever after. He had grown up in his body and his mind, and if he had been unable to face life's realities, it was his sorrow, none of hers. Hers were the lies and the cheating and being led down the garden path. Fantasies, she thought, must be very difficult to live with, they take so much imagination; such an effort.

Then, sitting there on the bench, watching the children, she suddenly realized what her trouble really was. She missed him. She had denied it to herself over and over, but she missed him. When she drove him from her door, all the fun

233

had gone with him. Up in thin air, with Bobbitt. The nurse-maid was right: he was such a nice young man. She felt a quick, cold chill. What had she done? Something terrible. She hadn't understood him at all, hadn't even tried. She cried a little then, slipping her handkerchief from her bag, lifting her glasses to dab at her eyes and staring at the spots her tears had left. She realized that what he had done wasn't as bad as she'd thought. After all, what was a thousand dollars? She had it, he needed it, she would have given it to him under any circumstances. She pictured him again in her mind's eye, that beautiful, dear child, her Bobbitt. *"Oh," said Miss Priss, sweeping him up in a great armful and giving him hugs and kisses, "I love you, Bobbitt." "Ditto," said the boy, giving her kisses back.*

She started home again, thinking her way along, step by step, block by block. Where could he be? What was he doing? How was he surviving? This was the important thing, his survival. She had already begun worrying about him, and when she passed through the door she had slammed—not once, but twice—on him, she felt the greatest regret of her life. Oh, she thought, he must come back. He must.

But he did not. And something, somewhere, deep down inside her, told her that he wouldn't. He was gone, irre-trievably lost. She listened to the budgies chirp, and wondered what to do. First things first, she thought, and called the girls, each in turn, and invited them up for The Belle Tele-phone Hour. Before they came she rehung the picture of the violets, and put out all the little things that Robin had bought her. Then she got from the drawer the box of engraved stationery she had hidden away, and got out the typewriter, and sat down and wrote a letter. It began, "Dearest Missy Priss, You can't imagine how beautiful the autumn is here in Ireland. . . ." She called forth all her powers of description, and when these were not sufficient she got out an old issue of the *National Geographic* with an article "Splendors of Ireland," and copied some phrases from it, and when the letter was completed to her satisfaction she found one of Robin's old envelopes, folded the letter, and slipped it inside. When the Belles arrived, the first thing she told them was that she had had a letter from Robin only that morning, and would they enjoy hearing it?

It was as chock-full of news as she had been able to con-coct, with frequent references to Lady Farquahar and the stables and the shepherds, and when she was done reading the girls sat rapt in silent marvel; my, Naomi said, he certainly can write a letter.

Well, thought Nellie, pleased with her cleverness, if he can, so can I. Enclosed was a money order he hoped would cover the loan he had gotten from the girls—"sorry to have been so neglectful, but I have been frightfully busy"—and when she cashed "Robin" 's check and paid the girls back she felt a little better. The letters continued—she found she enjoyed making them up—a constant stream of communications from across the Atlantic (she had to use the same envelopes over and over), each filled with all sorts of news and happenings designed to interest, titillate, or otherwise divert during The Belle Telphone Hour, to which she had returned in a natural fashion.

It was no good, of course; the more she wrote letters from Robin, the more she missed him. She was both sender and recipient, and somehow it didn't seem fair. Worse, she worried continually. She remembered what Madame Potekka had said, that he was probably in the city, but how to find him was another proposition altogether.

Then an idea occurred: she would take an advertisement in the personal column; perhaps he would see it. She called *The New York Times* and inquired about rates, settling for two lines specifying that *"RR call NB all forgiven love."* The notice ran a week, without results. She realized that while many people read the *Times,* it was quite possible that Robin did not. Then she remembered that on several occasions he had been carrying a copy of *The Village Voice,* and she took out a similar ad, with similar results. Namely, none. It was the same with the *Daily News,* and when that ad expired, so had her patience, nearly.

She and Hilda having resumed their companionable walks in the park, they were sitting one day on the bench by the Alice in Wonderland statues enjoying the fine fall weather, which reminded her so of last spring that it pained her. She had gone to considerable lengths to be friendly to the nursemaids whom she had been so rude to that one day, and they were all sitting there talking when Nellie, glancing south across the trees, saw a plane going over, its wings flashing silver in the sun. She watched it out of sight. "Why, you foolish thing," she said aloud: Hilda and the nursemaids gave her a look. She told Hilda she must get home right away, and they hurried off together, Nellie rebuffing all of Hilda's questions, but saying it was terribly important. When she arrived home she telephoned Garden City. She talked with Nancy, then the children, but it was Roger she most particularly wanted to speak with.

The next day the weather was as fair as it had been the day before, and Nellie was out in the park again, just before twelve. She took her place on the bench and waited. Roger was on the dot. At precisely twelve o'clock his little plane could be seen high up over the city and in a moment three puffs of smoke burst from its tail. The puffs formed a single line, and then two loops were added, making it a "B." Then Roger made a full circle, the smoke coming out in one long curl as the plane turned; the ends of the curl met and formed an "O." There came another "B" and another, an "I" and then a "T." Oh, dear, Nellie thought as the plane maneuvered eastward, he's forgotten the other "T"; but no, the plane zipped back, drew another line, then crossed it. "BOBBITT," the blue sky read in big puffy letters. People around the boat basin were already pointing upward, and the children were letting their sailboats go. By this time Roger had added below "Bobbitt" another large "O," and then another "Bobbitt;" and then, below that, the words "I LOVE YOU." The top line was already melting away as the plane dipped once more and added a neat "N" underneath, with a curl at the end, just the way Nellie made her initial. Then the plane flew away. Nellie hurried home, watching the letters disappear as she went. By the time she reached the apartment they were gone altogether, but she hurried to the elevator, let herself into her vestibule, and went and sat by the phone.

She sat all that afternoon; it did not ring, except once, at six o'clock, when Roger called. "No," she told him, "there was no answer." He must skywrite another message tomorrow.

Roger did as his grandmother asked, and at noon sharp his plane appeared high over the Empire State Building and began writing again. People in the streets looked up and pointed as the letters were formed: "BOBBITT CALL NELL." There is nothing Manhattanites love so much as a general confusion or mystery, and they stopped in groups as they came out of the subway entrances or got off at their bus stops, wondering. Bobbitt? Nell? What a novel way of communicating. People out in the park lay on the grass, awakening from a nap or looking up from their books, and in their boats on the lake rowers stopped their oars to watch as the letters hung in the sky. Bobbitt? They nudged their collective memories. Wasn't that that movie star kid, back—when? Some publicity stunt, they decided, as the puffy white letters dissolved in the sky, and they returned to their naps or their books or their oars. Next day the plane appeared again at the precise hour; the message this time read: "BOBBITT FOREVER." There was an offshore wind and the letters didn't last long, but still people were talking. *BobbittBobbittBobbitt*. Sure, they remembered, some of them, the kid in the London blitz with the match: " 'Oo put out th' lights?" Publicity stunt, they said again. But why? The editor of the *Daily News*, who had been watching from his office window, remembered Bobbitt, and sent a reporter out to see what he could discover; the paper was always looking for human-interest items for column fillers. No information was forthcoming, however, and the following day there was another, more perplexing message. The plane appeared and spelled out: "BOBBITT TRULY TRUE." It was signed: "MISSY PRISS." Next day the same message was repeated, but the plane flew under the message, putting in a little proofreader's caret, which meant a word had been omitted, and above it Roger wrote between "BOBBITT" and "TRULY" the word "REALLY." Then the plane zipped back again and let out one long stream underlining the word; the message read:

REALLY
BOBBITT ⋀ TRULY TRUE

That evening the girls met for The Belle Telephone Hour. Of course they'd all been watching the messages, too; Phyllis had seen one from her window and had called Naomi, who called Hilda. The cat was out of the bag, and Nellie confessed to her friends the truth about her deception. Robin had disappeared, she didn't know where. He wasn't in Ireland, nor was he writing letters from Ireland; Nellie had written them herself. It all came out then: Robin wasn't rich, his father wasn't a lord, he had made up all those stories.

Oh, they said, they knew it all the time. Well, not all the time, but Phyllis had smelled a rat; the Ballymore emerald was in the British Museum, certainly.

"Why did you let me go on, then?" Nellie asked them.

They loved her, they said. If she wanted to pretend, why, that was all right with them. Everybody pretended something, sometime. Nobody was ever really what he seemed.

Phyllis had tears in her eyes as she kissed Nellie. "Oh, we hope you find him."

But she did not. The messages went on, and public interest in them continued, and the *Daily News* featured a picture on its fourth page. Every day Nellie Bannister would go out to the park and look up while the message was being written, and then hurry home to wait by her telephone. Bobbitt never called. Then it occurred to her that he might have lost her unlisted telephone number, so she arranged another message with Roger: "BOBBITT CALL 649-2283." When she got home the phone was ringing off the hook. First it was a reporter: "Say, lady, what's the story here?" There was no story, she informed him; it was a purely private matter. Then others called—well-wishers, nosy-pokes, cranks. Nellie began wishing she hadn't written her number out for all New York to see. It didn't seem to matter anyway; there was no word from Robin. Another idea struck her and she again telephoned Roger. The next day, a beauty and not a hint of breeze, she went to the park and watched as his plane made two graceful opposing curves, and when the ends joined they formed a perfect heart. And in the center Roger spelled out: "PLUCK." The design hung there for perhaps a quarter of an hour, while the entire city looked up wondering what it meant, a heart with "PLUCK" in the middle of it. Each evening, after waiting for the call that never came, Nellie would think out a new message: Once it said, "Bobbitt, Come Home"; another time it said, "Prissy Loves Bobbitt"; a third time it said, "Key Under Mat." By now pictures of the messages had hit the front page of the *News,* for the editor realized he had a great story and that people were following it. Suzy Knickerbocker carried an item, also Earl Wilson. *Time* magazine picked it up, followed by *Newsweek* and *People.* Finally even *The New York Times* took notice of these messages, and printed a story. Finally a reporter from the Long Island paper *Newsday* tracked down the source of the skywriting, Roger himself at his flying school, and he admitted that he was the one making the messages, and that they were for his grandmother, who was trying to locate an old friend. The other papers copied, and the story grew accordingly. "HEARTBROKEN ACTRESS SEEKS MISSING FORMER CHILD STAR," read the headlines, and "BOY ACTOR MISSING; ACTRESS GRIEVES."

Still no word from Bobbitt, and in her heart Nellie truly was grieving. She waited and waited, but there was no reply to her skywriting appeal. Then a curious thing happened. One of the local TV station managers ran the first movie of the series, *Bobbitt,* for the station personnel. It had, they thought, a pleasant, old-fashioned appeal, so they put it on the air at five o'clock, just at the time when the kids were all home from school, waiting for supper. The reaction was instantaneous and overwhelming, a singular repetition of precisely what had happened almost twenty years before. Out of the darkness of the London blitz a small voice quavered: " 'Oo put out th' lights?" A match flared, and the same wondering face took shape on the small television screen just as it had in the great movie palaces. And people fell in love with Bobbitt all over again. *Bobbitt* was followed by *Bobbitt in the Enchanted Forest*, and the station discovered that its local rating jumped measurably; the whole series was bought as a package and then began regular weekly runs. Soon it was not only the children who were watching, but the grownups as well. In twenty years they had forgotten the charm of Bobbitt, but now, seeing the pictures again, they found they were reliving parts of their own childhood. A wave of nostalgia swept over everyone, and people rushed home from work to catch the latest on what had become known as "The Bobbitt Hour," *Bobbitt and the Magic Castle* or *Bobbitt Royal*. They started saying, "But is it really truly true" again, and it had the same antiquated sound as if they'd said, "Twenty-three skidoo" or "Hotcha." To get a laugh, all one had to do was say "Ditto"; everyone knew that everyone else was watching Bobbitt.

The question was, and remained, what had become of Bobbitt? Where was the little tyke? Sorry—where was the man? Reporters delved, but came up with no answers. As for Nellie, she had not heard from him, and she felt surer than ever that he had left the city and had seen none of her messages. The next thing that happened was that she received a call from the talent coordinator of *Good Morning USA*, inviting her on the program. The notion of appearing live on early-morning TV made her nervous, but she thought that Bobbitt might see the show, so she went to be interviewed by Marion Walker, the hostess. Naturally Nellie couldn't tell the truth of the matter, but she was quite adept at fielding Miss Walker's questions and they spent a pleasant twenty-minute segment talking about the old days at Shady Lane Studios, when she was Missy Priss. The inevitable question was put by Marion Walker: Why was Nellie trying to reach Bobbitt and where was he now? The only things she could think of to say were some of the things Robin had told her about Ireland and the castle and the Galway Ball, so she used these, finding herself not even blushing as she told about Lady Farquahar and Castle Baughclammain and the Galway Race. Oh, she thought, she was such a liar—as bad as Bobbitt. Then she laughed out loud. She was in a taxi, and the driver, looking at her in the mirror, said, "Hiyuh, Missy Priss." She was quite surprised as she listened to him tell her how his kids never missed a showing of a Bobbitt movie. Then she noticed people looking at her as she went about her daily errands, and it slowly dawned on her: she was becoming a celebrity. *Missy Priss Missy Priss,* she would hear people saying as she went by. Some of them would stop and talk to her, asking how she was, and so on, and she found these moments strangely satisfying.

It seemed the city now had one thing it shared in common, Bobbitt. Matters had not stopped with the television program. A manufacturer of printed T-shirts put out one with Bobbitt's face on it ("Bobbitt's smile is a yard wide") and kids began buying them, then it became a fad and finally even the adults were wearing Bobbitt shirts. By now everybody knew about Missy Priss's famous line "We must put pluck in our hearts," and the emblem appeared on shirts and the backs of jackets.

Next a paperback publisher picked up the reprint rights and released the series in paperback, and you couldn't go to a drugstore or a tobacco stand without seeing Bobbitt's face smiling out at you from row after row of Bobbitt books. Someone else put out a comic magazine, *The Adventures of Bobbitt,* then there were *The Further Adventures of Bobbitt,* and *Bobbitt and Missy Priss,* and *Bobbitt and Alfie.* "America's Fantasy Child" lived again.

Nellie's new-found fame grew—along with Bobbitt's—and she was asked to ride in the Macy's Thanksgiving Day Parade. There she was on a float, in a rocking chair, with a big Bobbitt book on her lap, surrounded by children. Her costume from the films had been copied; she wore her bombazine dress and apron, and the enormous bonnet, tied under the chin with a great black bow. They'd even found a reticule rather like the original, and lace mittens, and she wore screw curls down the sides of her face, which bobbed almost as much as the bonnet.

Then it was Christmas. Nellie was famous as Missy Priss, she was enjoying her new popularity, and her bank account was swelling, but still there was no Bobbitt to share this success with. On Christmas day she had Roger fly over the park and write: "MERRY CHRISTMAS BOBBITT FROM MISSY PRISS," and a cheer went up from among the skaters at the Wollman rink; and at Rockefeller Center, when the carolers came to sing under the giant tree in the plaza, they sang the "Bobbitt Christmas Song."

She spent an unhappy holiday that season. Of course she went to Garden City to visit the family, and she did her best to play Nana for the children, but in her heart she would rather have been playing Missy Priss for Bobbitt. She saw the bumper stickers Roger had put on his Ford Maverick: one side read: "Why did the good Lord put us here?" the other: "Surely not to chase rabbits." Good advice from Missy Priss, but there was little she could do to take it. All the fame, all the money, all the love, were not enough to make up for the loss of Robin, and when she was alone she would try to tell herself that one day he would reappear, magically, out of nowhere. But the nowhere in which he existed was beyond her ken, and she realized that the tide of publicity could not possibly have passed him by; he must surely know, wherever he was, what had happened, but was rejecting it all and wanted no part of it or her. Occasionally Roger would fly over on a clear day and make the heart and put "PLUCK" in it, or write "BOBBITT *REALLY* TRULY TRUE," but Bobbitt remained hidden and made no attempt to contact her.

It went on that way all winter. Spring came again and she returned to the bench in the park and watched the children playing around the mushroom, and she thought of Mr. Thingamabob. One of the children she recognized from the year before, and she asked, "Whatever happened to that—what was his name?" The child gave her a stare, didn't know what she was talking about. "Mr. Thingamabob?" The child shrugged; how quickly they forget, she thought. She was resolved in her heart that she would never see Robin again. He had disappeared forever.

The school term was ending—it was now June—and the television station was planning its annual benefit, "Broadway Stars for Children," a mammoth program in which famous performers appeared on an outdoor stage in the park's Sheep Meadow, then donated their fees to the Children's Orthopedic Hospital. Already the papers were full of publicity regarding the event, and one day Nellie's telephone rang. It was the head of the program committee, asking her if she had any idea of the whereabouts of Bobby Ransome. It was hoped that since he was the performer most popular with the children, he might be persuaded to appear at the benefit in the next-to-closing spot. Nellie said she was sorry; no idea where he was. If she heard from him, would she let them know?

they asked. They would be holding the spot for a long time, she wanted to tell them; Bobbitt's act had closed years ago. But yes, she said, if she heard anything she would let them know.

Then one day she happened to be passing a shop in whose window something caught her eye and made her stop. The painted sign on the glass read FASCINATTO'S MEMORY MARVEL SHOP, and in the window were various advertisements for old photographs, sheet music, movie posters, books, and magazines. What had attracted her glance was a row of six green-and-gold plates, each with a small crown in the center. She could scarcely believe her eyes. She went in and spoke to the proprietor, whose name was Sam Fascinatto. Yes, he informed her, the six plates were originals, from *Bobbitt Royal,* and she was shocked to learn what he was asking for them. But she paid his price and had them wrapped. She took them home and hung them in two rows on the wall near the budgie cage. Several days later, passing the shop again, she noticed that in the window was a Bobbittmobile, one of the really old ones, but in good condition. It, too, was expensive, but she bought it. She asked Mr. Fascinatto by what chance he had come by these items. Oh, he told her, everybody was Bobbitt-crazy these days. Yes, she agreed, but these were original pieces. Had they come from someone's attic? Mr. Fascinatto was too smart for that one; he wasn't about to reveal his sources, not when original Bobbittiana was at such a premium. All he knew, he said, was that someone came in every week or so and gave him items to be sold on commission. He seemed in need of money.

Nellie asked Mr. Fascinatto to telephone her if anything else should turn up, she wanted first call on it, and a week later he rang her up, saying he'd come by an extraordinary piece, an original Bobbitt dollhouse, in remarkably good condition. Would she be interested? Certainly she would, and she told Mr. Fascinatto to have the man wait; she wanted to talk with him. But by the time she arrived at the store he was gone. She almost cried when she saw the dollhouse—it was perfect in every detail—and she paid for it and asked that it be delivered, since it was much too large for her to carry. The boy who worked for Mr. Fascinatto brought it to the apartment and set it on the table she had prepared for it by the window. As he was leaving, she thanked him and gave him a dollar tip. Then she flashed a ten-dollar bill under his eyes, suggesting there was a small favor he could oblige her with. He stared eagerly at the bill. All he had to do, she explained, was, the next time the man came in with something to sell, follow him and find out where he lived. She gave him the ten dollars. If he could do this, she would give him ten more. The boy pocketed the money, along with her telephone number, said, "You bet, lady," and left.

Nellie's heart skipped a little beat. From lying to hoaxing to bribing; it was so easy, once you got started, wasn't it? She called the girls up for The Belle Telephone Hour and showed them the dollhouse; Naomi said she'd paid too much for it.

After they left she took all the furniture out, and the dolls, and gave the interior a good washing, shined the windows, and waxed the floors. She polished all the tables and chairs, shook out the rugs, and cleaned the dolls—Cathleen Nesbitt, Willie Marsh, Mary Astor, Dickie Haydn, etc., including herself as Missy Priss—then she arranged the figures in the various rooms and plugged in the lights so she could fully admire her new acquisition.

Robin, she thought, where are you?

It was not long before the bribe produced the desired results. The doorman called from downstairs, saying someone was there to see her, a Joseph Karmachino. She had no idea who that was, there was a consultation on the other end of the line, and the doorman informed her that Joseph Karmachino had a personal message for her. She suddenly remembered: the delivery boy. He came up, she gave him the promised ten dollars, and he left her with a matchbook cover; on the inside was scribbled a name and an address. "J. F. Harboomsteen, 451 W. 47th Street." She got her things and hurried out, meeting Hilda going to the elevator. They rode down together. "Nellie," Hilda asked, "what's happened? You look like the cat that swallowed the canary."

"No," she replied, "I'm just going chasing rabbits." Arming herself for this venture with nothing but a balloon, a Bobbitt promotional gimmick from the TV station, she took a taxi to the address. She was faced with a dingy brownstone building in a badly run-down neighborhood between Ninth and Tenth avenues. Holding tightly to her bag with one hand, the balloon with the other, she climbed the stairs and entered the vestibule. She read down the list of names alongside the buzzers, looking for J. F. Harboomsteen. There was none. Darn that boy, she thought, he's had me and my twenty dollars. She rechecked the list, then went out. At the bottom of the stairs, lounging against the railing post, was a Puerto Rican. He smiled at her balloon, but it was her bag that she clutched more tightly.

"Are you looking for someone?" he asked in very good English. Nellie was so surprised it took her a moment to reply. "I'm looking for Mr. Harboomsteen," she said. "I am told he lives in this building."

The man pointed behind the staircase. "Down there," he said. As she hurried toward the gate beside the ashcans, he called after her. "But be careful."

"Careful?"

"He's nutty."

Nellie nodded, as if to say naturally he is, then took a step forward, then another, past the trash cans and down two steps into a cluttered areaway. A cat sat watching her. She watched it back, thinking it's not cats I want, but rabbits. Under the brownstone steps she encountered a little iron grille, which she unlatched. There was a door beyond, no name plate, no bell. No one answered her knock, but from inside she could hear music. The door was ajar, she had only to push it, then she was inside a narrow hallway. "Hello?" she called. "Mr. Harboomsteen?" No reply. She stepped farther in, and went along the hall until she found another door. The music came from behind it. She took a large breath and made a small fist, and rapped. She waited, then rapped again. Someone was moving around beyond the door; she went on knocking until she heard several locks being unfastened. The door opened a crack, and through it she saw part of a face. The face had long hair and a beard; it was a very scruffy face. The eye blinked at her. "Excuse me," she began, talking to the eye, which blinked again. "No one to home," said a voice, and the door shut.

"Please," she called, knocking on the closed door. "Please open." No reply. "Please open the door," she repeated, this time more severely. Then, "Mr. Harboomsteen, I shall not—I shall not go away. I will remain here knocking until this door is open to me." The only response was the music being turned up louder. Accordingly, she raised her voice. "I am a lady, and though I do not always act like one, I nonetheless insist upon being treated as such. Therefore, you will oblige me by opening this door immediately." She was using her starchiest Missy Priss tone, but however starchy, it bore no results. She waited, arms crossed, her face growing redder, then she raised her hand, at the end of which was her large bag, and gave the door a fearful crack. "No more nonsense here," she cried in a louder tone, "do you hear me? Open this door!" The bag swung on her hand, and with the other she felt its contents gingerly, wondering what she might have broken. Then, very quietly, she spoke again.

"Please, Robin? Just for old times' sake?"

He opened the door then, and stood before her. She hardly recognized him, yet she knew that behind the long, unkempt hair and the beard that covered most of his face, it was Robin. He glanced uncertainly at her, more uncertainly at the balloon, then stepped aside as she came in. The shades were drawn, the room was in near darkness.

"Hello, Nellie," he said. She did not reply immediately, but stood looking at him, wanting but not daring to cry. Wanting but not daring to throw herself into his arms. How thin he looked, how pale and drawn, how un-Robin. He returned her look with a jaunty carelessness, and offered her the only chair. She took it, and held her bag on her lap; the insides rattled dreadfully. He moved uncertainly to the far side of the room and turned on a light.

"Welcome to yesteryear," he said.

"Oh, my," she said, staring about her, "oh, my."

It was an incredible sight, that room. It was not large, nor with much of a ceiling, and sparsely furnished: besides the chair only a table or two, an unmade day bed in the corner, a couple of lamps. But it was none of these that caused Nellie's surprise; it was the other contents of the room. Even in the paltry light she could see what it held—not held, merely, but was crammed with: everywhere her glance rested it saw objects she recognized from the long ago past. A museum; Bobbittland revisited. Bobbitt mugs and breakfast bowls and plates on shelves, a Bobbitt rocking horse in the corner, Bobbitt boats and fire trucks, Bobbitt race cars, Bobbitt planes. There was a Bobbitt flying carpet, and riding it, a Bobbitt doll. More dolls tucked amid the toys—Bobbitt the policeman, the cowboy, the knight in armor, the royal prince. The dark walls were covered with yellowed photographs, familiar scenes from the movies: *Bobbitt Royal*, he with his paper crown, *Bobbitt and the Magic Castle, Bobbitt in Love,* the whole history of Bobbitt, that smiling, curly-headed face, gazing out at her with its mixture of wonder and candor, row after row, year after year, growing up.

"I usually charge admission for this," he said dryly, sitting on the edge of the day bed, which dipped and creaked as it took his weight. "How did you find me?"

Nellie told him.

"I've been trying to reach you for a long time," she said.

"I know." He laughed. "I've seen your messages."

"But you didn't bother to answer them," she returned crisply.

"No."

"Why? Why, Robin?"

He shifted his weight; the bed groaned. "I—" He brought his hands up with a hopeless gesture, and let them fall to his lap. "You see how it is with me."

"Yes. I see. I see very well."

"I didn't want you to find out."

"I have already found out everything I need to know about you."

"No, you haven't."

"Indeed I have, and a good deal more to boot." She shook her head determinedly. "It doesn't matter. Nothing matters, except that I've found you."

He slipped her a rueful smile. "Me? Who am I, Nellie?"

"You're Robin Ransome. You're Bobbitt." She glanced at the window. "Do you know . . . what is happening to Bobbitt?"

"I know. But there isn't any Bobbitt, you see."

"Of course there is. I'm looking at him."

He shook his head. "Dear Nellie, what you're looking at is—Well, you know what they call us—'has-beens.' There isn't any more Bobbitt and to tell the truth there really isn't any Robin Ransome. Only Mr. Harboomsteen."

"The names don't matter."

"Ah, but they do, you see," he said sadly. "Names matter very much. You can call yourself anything you want to—Bobbitt, Bobby Ransome, Lord Ransome, Robin—it doesn't matter what, but it doesn't make you any more of a person."

"Everybody is a person."

"I suppose. Except in certain instances." He smiled at her. "I played you a dirty trick, Nellie. I'm sorry. Really truly true."

"If I did not believe that, I would not be here. I have gone to considerable lengths to find you."

He had got up off the creaking bed and was moving aimlessly about the room, lingering over various objects, his back to her. When he turned again he held a teddy bear in his arms; the Bobbitt bear.

" 'Garumph,' said the bear. 'Harumph,' said Missy Priss in her starchiest voice and giving the bear's nose a tweak. 'Oh, my goo'ness,' said Bobbitt, and they all ran down the path together." Robin said the lines in a mocking, self-deprecating way that brought out one of Nellie's fiercest looks.

"Stop that," she ordered. She pointed toward the window and repeated her words. "Robin, do you know the marvelous thing that has happened out there?"

"I haven't been out today. Since you have no umbrella, I assume it isn't raining. Is the sun shining?"

"I am not speaking of the weather. Do you know what is happening all over this city?"

"As you see, I have no television, and I seldom read the papers."

"Robin, you're famous!" she exclaimed. "As famous as ever. All over again!"

"Is that a fact?" Whatever the fact, it appeared of no interest to him. He stood on one foot, then the other, scratching his head. "It's very nice, but I don't want to be famous all over again."

"They *want* you." There were tears in her eyes. "The most wonderful thing has happened."

"Are there still wonderful things?" he murmured, almost to himself. "I doubt it. And I doubt they want me."

"But they do. They *do*."

He shook his head and toyed with the bear. "They want someone else. They want that curly-headed little darling in his shorties and a big white collar. They want that yard-wide smile and a little dance. Look at me, Nellie, take a good look. *This* is me, not *that* one." He sat on the bed again, hugging the bear. He moved to the wall corner, where he sat with his knees drawn up, the bear perched on top of them.

"Nellie—" He faltered, then began again. "Nellie, I told you a lot of stories. They were mostly lies. I did a terrible thing to you—"

"I said it didn't matter."

"It does matter, unfortunately. Will you hear one more story? No, you needn't fear, it's not another fairy tale. I won't make it up this time. It's really truly true. You remember the night we went for the ride in the hansom, through the park?"

"I shall never forget it," she said quietly.

"You laughed and said I was such a boy, such a little, little boy. I said to you, Nellie, I don't want to grow up; I don't care if I never do." He rose suddenly and ran his finger along a shelf of books, until he found what he wanted; he sat with the book on the bed, turning pages in the dim light, then said:

"Listen to this, Nell. 'Peter: I ran away the day I was born

. . . because I heard father and mother talking of what I was to be when I became a man. I want always to be a little boy and to have fun; so I ran away to Kensington Gardens and lived a long time among the fairies.' " He turned some more pages until he found another place and read again. " 'Peter: Would you send me to school? Mrs. Darling: Yes. Peter: And then to an office? Mrs. Darling: I suppose so. Peter: Soon I should be a man? Mrs. Darling: Very soon. Peter: I don't want to go to school and learn solemn things. No one's going to catch me, lady, and make me a man. I want always to be a little boy and have fun.' " He shut the book and set it aside and picked up the bear again. "Any ninny can tell you that that's *Peter Pan*. It's also Master Bobby Ransome. I know *you* think it is. Twenty years isn't such a long time that I can't remember back to that little fellow Vi Ueberroth stumbled across one rainy afternoon having tea and said he ought to be in the cinema. And I wanted to, so badly, I wanted to be a great big movie star. And you know something—I knew I could. I wanted to see my name up in lights over the biggest movie theater in Dublin. Me ma wanted me to come home and be an ordinary little boy. But Aunt Moira persuaded her. After I played with Fedora, I thought, Oh, boy, this is it, this is the most wonderful thing. And so it was. Then I went to Hollywood and Papa Baer and Mama Baer and everyone was so nice, and I thought, Well, Bobby, that's just the way it's supposed to be, and Little Willie, and all the rest. You can't imagine what it was like for me, a poor dumb Irish cluck who'd never been as far as Liverpool and there I was having my feet stuck in Grauman's cement. We were poor, Nellie; I mean *poor*. My dad was a hatter, nothing more; he brushed felt in a hat factory in Galway—not where the castles are and the fine houses, but in the back of a dirty room, brushing felts every day of his life. It drove him crazy y'know? The mad hatter, we called him. Well, now, Papa Baer didn't want folks knowing I was the offspring of a mad hatter, so first off he gives me another father. All made up, a make-believe one—Lord Ransome—and next thing you know I've got a make-believe ma and she's a Lady. Fancy that. Just like in the movie. Little waif adopted by rich folks. They didn't even bother writing a new script. Life imitating art, so t'speak. Course, no one bothered to find out the truth; they took that as the truth. Well, now, I says to myself, this is all pretty swell, it's nice being in Hollywood and doing so well. There we were living in a nice little house, just like I used to dream of, and if it'd stopped right there I guess I might've been happy."

"But you *were* happy," Nellie interjected. "You were such a happy little boy." She gave him a doubtful look. *"Weren't* you?"

"Ah, wasn't I, though? Happy as a cat up a tree. Except I wasn't."

Her look turned to surprise. "You weren't?"

"Never. What I was, was scared. Every blasted minute I was scared down to my socks. From the minute they put me in front of a camera, scared. The worst sort of stage fright you could think of. I like to threw up every time I had to run out on a stage with that yard-wide grin and do my numbers. All those folks out there, watching, and me having to be good. Flop sweat, that's what I had, flop sweat. You remember I told you about that party at Willie Marsh's house. All that Hollywood royalty all over the place and me being taken about to meet everybody famous. I was supposed to be one of them. But I was just scared. They got me up to sing and dance with Willie, with Noël Coward—they were old hands, but not me. 'Oh, he's a natural,' they said, but I wasn't. I *should* have been happy; God knows they liked me. Maybe it was Aunt Moira. . . ."

"What has she to do with it?"

"Auntie? I'll give you an example. You remember the little dog Willie gave to me? I called him Rags."

"Rags. I remember."

"You remember they always gave me a scene where I had to cry. Aunt Moira would come marching into my dressing trailer and she would set me down and say, 'See here now, Bobby, it's about your little dog Rags that you love so much. . . . Well, Bobby, I'm sorry to say it, but Rags is dead. Run over in the street. He's gone, Bobby, under the sod he is.' Well, you can bet I cried. Poor Rags wasn't dead at all, but she made me believe it, and I could cry buckets. Just turn the camera on and let me go. Well, it seemed to me that if telling a little story like that—that poor Rags was dead—to get what you wanted was all right, any kind of story you could tell would be all right. So I started telling stories. And I've been telling stories all my life, to get what I wanted. It's just a way you get into, then you can't get out of it. Then you grow up—no, sorry; take it back—get bigger, and the stories get bigger, become real whoppers, but people still believe them. It's so easy to make people believe, Nellie; the poor fools'll believe anything you tell them."

"I know," she said wistfully. "It's because they want to."

"Exactly. Here's Peter Pan, he says, 'Do you believe in fairies? Say quick that you believe! If you believe, clap your hands!' Everybody claps. 'Oh, thank you,' says Peter, 'thank you, thank you.' And Tinkerbell lives. Except I didn't believe in fairies, I believed in goblins. I had 'em. In my dreams—hundreds of goblins, every sort of creature you can imagine, or that I could. Most kids have bad dreams, I guess, but mine were all movie bad dreams. I used to wake up screaming. Auntie wouldn't put the light on, said I had to outgrow it. Just fantasies, she said. Then in the daytime the bad dreams were gone, but there were other fantasies. I lived off them. It was easy. You can make the dustman believe in fairies and such. It was easier that way, d'you see? I got so I could make anybody believe anything. All I had to do was use my big eyes and my big smile and they'd believe anything.

"And I'd be crazy, mad as my own pa, to tell you that part wasn't a lark. I loved it. There was another, bigger house, and another, and that even bigger, and they came and did it up like a magic fairyland place, and there's my picture on everything in sight, and everybody's loving me, and the President's shaking my hand, and I'm meeting the Queen of England. If the world's truly an oyster, I got the pearl. A whole string of them. That was a fairy-tale world out there, Nellie, darlin', and I was the fairy-tale prince. I thought I would go on and on, and—"

"Live happily ever after?" She gave him a soft smile.

"Sure. Why not? When things get that good you always think they're never going to end. People want you; it never occurs to you that they may stop wanting you. Papa Baer's fat and kind and funny and you think, Papa Baer's my friend, good old Papa Baer. But he wasn't, you know. He was just fat and rich, and he wanted to be richer. Never saw a man who wanted to be as rich as he wanted to be. But you see, the thing was, it was all make-believe, and life isn't that, there's not much storybook in real life. But I never had to make a decision, never had to stand on my own two feet, never had to do anything except turn on the tears or the smile and do what they told me. Everywhere I looked things were pretty, things were fun, things were . . . good. I thought everything, everywhere in the whole wide world was like that. Everybody was saying, Oh, dear, Bobbitt's growing up. I could see how scared they were. They didn't want me to grow up; that meant the end of everything. It wasn't just the studio; it was everybody everywhere. They wanted me to stay a boy. When I saw them frightened, it frightened me. I got the idea that somewhere, out beyond the world I was living in, there was another world—the true one, the real one—and I didn't like it. I didn't want to go there and see. It was like going through the Grimly Wood. I didn't want to see that other world. But then I wasn't a boy anymore, I was starting to become a man, and they didn't want that. They gave me everything except the one thing I needed. I needed to know what that world was like. I needed to know what was really truly true. But I didn't. Then one day it was all gone, everything, overnight. I wasn't Bobbitt anymore, I was just Bob Ransome. It's a terrible thing, Nell, to be wanted and then *not* to be wanted. I think it's better not to have been wanted in the first place. It's like being poor and then rich—better not be rich unless you're going to stay rich. If you stay poor, you never know what it's like, so maybe you don't miss it.

"Well, I said to myself as they showed me the door, that was fun while it lasted. Now what'll I do? But I found I couldn't do anything, except what I'd done. Just the one thing. Only I couldn't do it anymore. Everything had changed, including myself. I never really knew how to act, you know; whatever it was I did was just a natural sort of thing, and if Rags was dead I cried, or if every day was like my birthday I was happy and that was it. But afterward I didn't know what to do. All my friends were grown up now, and they seemed to be getting along just fine—but not me. I still wanted to be a little boy.

"All I could do was sing a little and dance a little and perform imitations, and they put me in nightclubs, but I knew I was a freak, people weren't coming to see me, they wanted to see Bobbitt, but there wasn't any Bobbitt anymore. Bobbitt had grown up, so they went away again. Managers don't pay you when the customers go away."

"But now it's different," Nellie protested. "They want you. They're asking for you. They've been looking for you, too. The newspapers, the television. You remember last year, in the park—the 'Broadway Stars for Children'?" He remembered. She told him of the plan, that he was to headline this year's benefit. "Bobbitt for the children, Robin. You always said you loved the children. You must do it. For them."

He laughed. "It's the same story, don't you see? They don't want me, they want Bobbitt. What they want is their yesterdays, their youth, whatever they remember from then that made them happy."

"You can make them happy now."

"Dear, dear Nell, what a dear girl you are. And a forgiving one. But—" He shook his head. "I don't want to make them happy. I don't want to make anybody happy. I just want to be let alone." He shook the bear so the eyes twirled in its head. "I don't want to be famous again. I don't want to be anything, except Mr. Thingamabob and go to the park and tell stories to the kids. I love kids, Nell, they're really marvelous. I tell them a tale or two, and they love it so, and I pass the hat and I make enough to get along on and that's fine for me." He gazed around the room. "All this is fine for me. The truth is, I like it here. Not much of a place, I know, and this"—jouncing the mattress—"is not a bed of roses, but it's easier."

"There's always something easier than something else." She had got up and now stood looking at him with determination. He recognized the Missy Priss tilt of the chin, the gesture of her hands planted on her hips. He drew farther back onto the bed corner as she moved purposefully across the room, first to one window, where she snapped up the shade, then to the second and the third. The rollers rattled and flopped with her forceful gesture. The sun streamed through the grimy panes, flooding the small place. Robin blinked in the blinding light, shielded his eyes against it, groped finally for his dark glasses and put them on.

"Stand up," she ordered. He stood. She moved about the room, puffing her cheeks and blowing. Dust rose in clouds, their motes sifting into the beams of light, forming dark, murky rays. She took the teddy bear from him and gave it a shake. Dust flew in all directions. She blew along the shelves among the cups and breakfast bowls. She shook the dolls, the clothing. "Dust," she muttered, "and more dust. Nothing but dust." She turned to him. "Robin, is that what you're going to do, live in dust the rest of your life? Because you're afraid? Because if you don't come out now, with me, that's what you'll do. And that's what you'll be." She went and took him by the shoulders and gave him a good shake. "More dust." Then she held him close and reached on tiptoe to kiss him. When she took her face away she was crying, and her voice trembled as she spoke.

"Listen to me, Robin, this is very important. You haven't learned it, but it's something you should know. Darling Robin, you can begin over again. People can. A new start. Everybody should get a second chance, no matter what they've done or haven't done. Maybe not a third or a fourth, but at least a second. It's the one thing people won't be denied. Have your second chance, Robin. It's there. Take it."

"Take it?"

"Take it. Please take it. For me. For the children. For yourself."

"I can't, Nellie. It's nice of you—of them—but I can't. I just can't seem to make anything work."

He sat down again, staring at the buckled floor, his hands shoved deep in his pockets.

"Robin, do you remember?" she said quietly.

He looked over at her. "Remember what?"

" 'If only people wouldn't put their hands in their pockets so much,' said Missy Priss. 'What should they do with them?' asked Bobbitt. 'Why,' she laughed, 'hold someone else's. There's the trick, the whole world holding hands and never letting go.' "

He nodded. "Sure, Nell—it's a good line. Now you just go along and hold hands with all those folks and never let go."

She went to him in a little murmuring rush and knelt and took his hand and squeezed it. "It's your hand I don't want to let go of. 'We must love one another, that's what we must do,' said Missy Priss. That's what I'm trying to tell you, Robin. We must just . . . love one another." She kissed him. He gave her a half-hearted peck and tried to move away. She would not let him go.

"Robin?" she said again. "Robin?" He wouldn't answer, only raised his head and looked around. It had been so long since he had seen sunlight in the room. It brought everything into sharp, ugly relief—the cracked plaster, the unmade bed, the clothes flung about. And the museum; Bobbittland. It was such a little room to hold all those things. Even now the dust that Nellie had shaken up still hung in the air.

He had picked up Nellie's balloon, and sat staring at his own childish image on the front of the inflated rubber. The face looked so ridiculous. His face, but not his at all. Someone else's. A long-ago face. A someone-who-used-to-be face. A yesterday face. He undid the string and let the balloon go and it zoomed around the room, deflating, zipping in crazy circles from corner to corner, growing smaller and smaller, until it fell beside his chair. He reached and picked it up, stretched the rubber out on his knee. He couldn't make anything of the shrunken face; it was hardly even there. Then he began blowing the balloon up. He blew and blew and it got bigger and bigger, bigger than it had been before. Every now and again he would stop blowing and hold it out, watching the face grow larger, the Bobbitt smile stretching bigger and bigger. He blew some more, looked again. *Bobbitt's smile is a yard wide.* He stretched his own lips in a parody of the smile, then blew some more. And blew. And blew. Larger and larger the balloon got, and wider the smile. Until there was a loud pop and he held only the exploded pieces of rubber, then they slipped from his fingers to the floor. "Everybody gets a second chance," he murmured. When he looked at her again he was smiling his own smile.

"What'll we sing for 'em, Nell?"

"Oh, my dear. Then you will?"

"I guess . . . I can try. I guess I could go chasin' rabbits, couldn't I?"

She nodded. "Yes, yes, we'll go chasin' rabbits together."

"But I'll tell you this, Nell—when I get up on that stage, you know what it's goin' to be."

"What?"

" 'Hokum and Bunkum and Bluff.' "

"Oh, my dear. Shall I tell you what it's going to be?" She took his hand and gave it a squeeze. "It's going to be 'For Old Times' Sake.' "

The evening was still and warm. At the east end of the Sheep Meadow stood the open-air stage erected for "Broadway Stars for Children." People had been gathering since early afternoon, staking out places on the ground, spreading their blankets, setting down their picnic baskets. Some had brought tablecloths, which they laid out, with glasses for wine, and candles or little lanterns. It was a special evening. Everybody felt it, everyone was waiting. They were in a holiday mood. Children were everywhere. They, too, waited, eagerly but quietly. The sun dropped, the breeze drifted across the meadow, while people sat in the purple dusk. Overhead the luminous sky was hung with trembling stars as they came out, one by one, then seemingly all together. Over on the side streets off Central Park West, windows were open where old women leaned thin elbows on bed pillows between cans of wilted philodendron, craning to see. They were waiting, too; after all, the show was free, was for everybody. That was part of the fun of living in New York.

Backstage, things moved quietly, orderly. The musicians were getting their instruments from their cases, ready to go onstage. The performers stood in groups, waiting for the overture. The women were gowned and jeweled, the men wore black tie and dinner jacket. In her Missy Priss costume, Nellie primped her side curls in a mirror, waiting for Robin. Rehearsal, which had gone on all afternoon, had been the usual havoc; how they were to pull a show off remained to be seen. She was worried. Robin had been nervous working with the orchestra, had trouble deciding on his key, had thrown out all the suggestions the arranger and orchestra leader had made. Everyone had been kind and friendly toward him, had bent over backward to make him feel at home, to welcome him back into the acting fraternity, but he had kept aloof, was cold and even temperamental, until the others began avoiding him, stood around criticizing his work. He'd even whistled in the dressing room, the worst luck in the world for actors. In the end he'd almost bowed out altogether, and even now Nellie wasn't sure he'd show up.

The orchestra moved onstage, then the conductor, and the overture began in the darkness, then the lights came up, a huge bank of them set out in the center of the meadow, hitting the stage full face, then Bobby Morse, acting as master of ceremonies, got ready for his entrance.

"Break a leg, kid," Gwen Verdon told him.

Out he went and did his introductory comic spot, which had the audience laughing right away. He listed the names of the stars they were about to see, and Nellie took heart from the cheers that rose when Bobbitt's name was announced.

The actors from *The Wiz* opened the show with "Ease on Down the Road" and "Everybody Rejoice." They were followed by Carol Channing, then Zero Mostel. Still Robin hadn't appeared. Doug Henning went on and did his magic tricks; the kids ate it all up. After him came Beverly Sills, who sang her two numbers. Then Nellie heard her own name announced; she and Cyril Ritchard were doing a sketch from *Bobbitt and Alfie,* with Cyril playing Willie Marsh's role as the butler. The lights went down, Nellie took her place in her rocker, her reticule in her lap, the lights went up, and Alfie came out in his butler's costume. Nellie thought she'd never seen such an enormous audience; the faces melted back into the darkness for what seemed a mile. Microphones planted all along the stage apron picked up the dialogue and carried it out to the audience through giant banks of speakers on either side of the stage. "Where's Bobbitt?" she heard a child near the front ask. Where indeed? Nellie wondered, glancing offstage, where the other actors were watching from the wings. Cyril Ritchard took her hand, she rose from her chair, the orchestra struck their musical cue, and they did "Hokum and Bunkum and Bluff" from *Bobbitt Royal*. The applause was very gratifying as they went off, passing Angela Lansbury, waiting to be introduced.

"Has he come?" Nellie asked the stage manager, who growled something and turned to his cue board. Obviously *he* hadn't. She went to the canvas backing at the rear of the backstage area and peered out. There was no sign of Robin. Angela came off, and still he hadn't come. Joel Grey went on, then Lisa Kirk.

Nellie saw the television producer coming across the parking space. He'd been on the telephone; there was no answer at Robin's room. Nellie's heart sank; he wasn't coming after all. The kids from *A Chorus Line* were on, singing "What I Did for Love," which was their only scheduled number, but the applause was so great that the stage manager signaled an encore and they went into the famous high-kicking show finale. Then Pearl Bailey, and then Robert Preston with Jerry Herman at the piano. Following him would be Gwen Verdon, then Robin in the next-to-closing.

Gwen was halfway through her last number; backstage, things were in turmoil. A hurried conference between the stage manager, the director, and the producers broke up, and the stage manager called, "Cut the next-to-closing spot. Get ready for the finale."

"What's happened?" someone asked.

"We got a no-show."

A no-show? In show business there were never no-shows, unless you were Judy Garland. And Bobbitt wasn't Judy Garland. Bobbitt was Robin Ransome, Master Bobby Ransome, who hadn't grown up. Nellie's insides felt like lead. He had let her down again. Then she saw the back canvas ripple, move as someone from the outside felt his way along, looking for the gap. Between the divided flaps a figure appeared, silhouetted against the light. The flaps closed, the figure moved toward the rear stage ramp and came up: Robin.

But what had happened to him? Where was the dinner jacket and black tie they had rented and had fitted so carefully? He was wearing cut-off shorts, striped stockings, a wildly colored shirt, zany hat, and on his back, his nonsense pack.

Confusion prevailed as Gwen Verdon finished her number and the stage manager got ready for his improvised cue to the finale. Nellie rushed to him and said, "He's here—he's come." The stage manager signaled Bobby Morse, telling him to pick up the next-to-closing spot, and Bobby trotted back into the lights and faced the audience. The conductor received this change of cue over his earphones, he struck up Bobbitt's introduction, while Bobby began the rehearsed introduction, building it slowly, carefully. It was the moment they'd been waiting for: Bobbitt at last.

Only it wasn't Bobbitt at all. What came shuffling out on stage into the glare of the lights was Mr. Thingamabob, with his turned-up shoes, his funny hat, and a crazy mask with goggles covering his face. Since he did not pick up his musical cue the conductor cut the opening and the orchestra vamped while Mr. Thingamabob did a little impromptu clog dance. He'd dragged a stool onstage after him, and he sat on it, fiddling inside his nonsense pack, pulling his legs up, just as he used to sit on the mushroom. "Oh, my goo'ness," he began, improvising one of his familiar routines, "lookit all them folks out there." He had a puppet on one hand and was talking to it. But somehow it was all different. Nellie watched from the wings with the others. He looked seedy, shabby, and there were no laughs.

"What's he doing?" they asked.

"Crazy," they said.

Mr. Thingamabob was falling flat on his face in front of all New York. Expecting Bobbitt they had got—who? Most of them didn't even know Mr. Thingamabob, had never heard of him.

"We want Bobbitt," someone called.

Robin got rid of the puppets and took his hoops from the pack and did his juggling act.

"Bobbitt," they called, louder now. "We want Bobbitt." They were doing a clap/chant. "We—want—Bobbitt. We—want—Bobbitt. . . ."

There was an awkward stage pause, while Mr. Thingamabob looked to his right, then his left, then to the conductor. He ducked his head, slid off the mask, and raised his face again, revealing his long tangled hair and bearded face. He spread his hands as if to say, Well, here I am.

"That not Bobbitt," a child was heard to state. Someone booed, then someone else. There were jeers and catcalls.

"Somebody get the hook," Nellie heard the stage manager mutter, referring to the stage hook they used in the old days to yank bad performers offstage.

"Bobbitt" was talking, but you could hardly hear him.

"Get him a mike," the stage manager whispered, and a stagehand ran out with a mike stand and placed it in front of the stool. Robin's voice was suddenly picked up and tossed out through the loudspeakers. It was hoarse and gravelly, and still weak.

"What you sees is what you gets, folks," he was saying, trying for another laugh. Still nobody was laughing. Nellie felt cold waves of embarrassment shooting up her back. Robin was out there dying, and she was dying for him. Not the audience, though; they were hating him.

"That is," he continued, his hand toying nervously with the mike stand, "I used to be Bobbitt."

"Bobbitt growed up," another child said loudly. It started a small laugh.

"Not everyone would agree with you, darlin'," Robin told her. He ducked his head, tried to see out beyond the glare of lights.

"Take off the beard," someone called rudely. "You look like a bum."

"Rootie-toot to you, too." The old familiar Bobbitt line got a laugh, quick but genuine. Robin gave the beard a tug.

"Won't come off," he said. "It's for real." The sound of his swallowing came over the loudspeakers. The orchestra had been vamping through all the remarks, the conductor not knowing what to do. Finally he whispered to the lead men, and they went into the introduction of "Sky High Over the Moon," Robin's first rehearsed number. He missed the cue, and they started again. He began, his voice coming out in a croak. "Sky high over the moon, twice after morning, half after noon. . . ." His face was dead white in the light, and he kept jerking and ducking his head. He mangled his way through the number, and got off his stool. Nellie thought he was going to walk offstage, but he moved to the orchestra, where he borrowed the lead guitarist's instrument, then returned and sat on the stool again.

"We rehearsed that number this afternoon," he said into the mike, "but you really had to be there." His voice was still shaky as he tuned the guitar pegs and plucked a chord or two, and there were more random impolite comments from the audience. They were restless, disconcerted, not understanding what was happening. Was he drunk? Stoned? It was a downhill disaster after all the Broadway professionalism that had preceded it. The other performers were grouped in the wings, standing on tiptoes, trying to see. Nellie clutched her reticule and prayed as Bobbitt began again. Gradually the rest of the stage lights had been dimmed to black, and he stood in a single spotlight, strumming the guitar, singing. Nellie could see he was in terror. His voice cracked several times, he hit a wrong chord, then another. From time to time he would look toward the wings, in panic, but he was imprisoned in the white cone of light. From out there in the audience came coughs and murmurs, more restlessness, talking out loud. Nellie pushed her way through the people blocking the stage entrance, and moved onstage in the darkness.

Robin hadn't noticed her, but he heard a child somewhere near the front pointing up and saying, "Missy Priss." Then he felt her presence as she moved near his stool, standing out of the spotlight, but close. He turned, glanced at her.

"What must we do, Missy Priss?"

"Why, we must put pluck in our hearts, else why did the good Lord put us here? Surely not to chase rabbits!"

Without a break he segued into "Lotsa Pluck," and somehow the hoarseness was disappearing. His throat had relaxed, opened up, his hands stopped trembling, the words came out free and easy. "All it takes is a little pluck, then you add a little luck . . ." and he heard some of the children in the front rows singing along with him. He nodded, started tapping out the beat with his foot. "Little luck, lotsa pluck," he sang, nodding, his smile coming easy now. "Little luck, lotsa pluck," the children sang. The grownups, too; they were all singing along with him. From his side he heard the familiar voice; Nellie was singing, too. "Luck . . . pluck." He glanced at her, they nodded, smiled, like old friends meeting for the first time in years. Then, before he realized it, the song was over. He looked out at the audience in surprise; they were applauding. He grabbed Nellie's hand, pulled her into the spotlight, called back to the conductor, and while she leaned against him, his arms around her waist, they sang "Ditto" together.

"I love you."
"Ditto, I love you, too."
"I need you."
"Ditto. I need you, too."
"Doesn't matter what you say, I'll say ditto . . ."
"I won't let you go your way, I'll go ditto . . ."

And on each "ditto," the audience took it up, joining in as loudly as they could. "Ditto! Ditto!" Nellie's bonnet kept slipping and getting in the way; Robin pushed it aside, making faces, milking the business for laughs.

The applause was even greater. He tried to keep Nellie with him, but she had suddenly slipped away, and he was out there alone again. But what she'd brought him she hadn't taken with her: the applause. He nodded at the conductor and they went into the two remaining numbers they'd rehearsed: "Magic Carpet" and "Really Truly True." He hadn't sung them publicly in almost fifteen years, but somehow, now, it seemed all right. He was there. He had them. They sat quietly out there; nobody stirred, all those thousands of faces, the children watching the Bobbitt they had come to see, their parents the grown-up man they remembered as a child, part of their pasts. They leaned back on their elbows, crossing their feet, with the wide night spaces above them, and the stars, listening. It wasn't the Bobbitt they remembered, because of course he'd grown up, was a man. It was a man's voice they heard, a good, clear baritone. It floated out from the giant speakers, surrounding them, and in its lilt they heard things that made them remember other things, other days, when they were younger, happier, sadder, but they were thinking, We've all gotten older. Everybody does. Fifteen years is a long time. I got older, he got older, she got older, the world got older. Bobbitt got older, too. Somewhere along the line we all grew up. It would be some time before the same realization came to their children. But in fifteen years they would be saying the same thing: We all grew up.

Why, Bobbitt—you grew up. . . .

Give 'em the old schmaltz, Willie Marsh had said. Robin wiped the sweat from his brow and gave them more, gave 'em schmaltz. *They . . .* it wasn't so bad, that *they*. They wanted him. He could feel the strange wonderful thing in him; whatever he bounced off them bounced back.

He finished, heard the applause, then a child's voice speaking out to him.

"Bobbitt . . ."

He looked into the little face down there in the audience.

"I love you."

"Why, thank you, darlin'. Ditto."

The microphones had picked up the exchange; they laughed, they cheered. Now, he thought, get off while the getting's good. He looked to the wings, where the stage manager was applauding with the others, motioning for him to continue. He looked at the orchestra leader, who nodded. Robin winked, whispered a cue, then turned back to the audience. He wiped his forehead, crossed his leg, reset his guitar, struck the first chord, and began softly.

> "Let's take a little cuppa tea, just you and me,
>   *For old times' sake.*

Or maybe yet a glass of wine, yours and mine,
For old times' sake . . ."

It had been so difficult, now it was so easy. Why was that? he wondered. He could see out past all those faces, up through the trees to the buildings, and past them, up into the sky, and past that, it seemed, to years ago, past all the years that had gone between, to a scared kid bouncing out onto the stage of Orpheum and all the Capitols, short pants and scared, giving them the old schmaltz. But scared; always scared. Drowning men, they say, see their past before their eyes; but suddenly he wasn't seeing his past anymore; he wasn't even drowning. It just felt . . . good. So easy, so simple.

"Rememb'rin' all the things that went before,
Memories, we'll have a score or more,
When my hair's gone gray and I can't dance
And you're so big you need long pants . . ."

He could feel the single spotlight growing dimmer, dimmer, the cone narrowing until it held only his face. Judy Garland time. If Willie Marsh were alive . . . This was the real schmaltz. The spot held, his face hung in the surrounding dark.

"It'll still be you and me, a cuppa tea, yours and
mine, a glass of wine . . .
For old times' sake. . . ."

The orchestra completed its last phrase, Robin struck his final solo chord, the light faded altogether, and he stood along in darkness. In the audience, across the whole open meadow, there was not a sound to be heard. Then, in the silence, one voice:

" 'Oo put out th' lights?" Robin said into the microphone. There was an instant audience response to the line. Lowering his guitar to the floor, Robin reached in his pocket. He struck a match and held it in front of his face. It flickered there, one small light in all that huge dark space, dimly illuminating his pale features. Then, as the little flame glowed, someone out there in the darkness struck a match, and there were two, then three, then four. A dozen, two dozen. Fifty. A hundred. It went like that. From everywhere all across the meadow, people were lighting matches and holding them up until, as he looked out, he could see nothing but a sea of tiny flames flickering in the darkness of the spring night, little pinpoints of light, each one held by a single person and behind each light a single face. People he didn't know, would never see again, but in that one moment he saw them. All New York was out there; no, the world. His match had burned out and he moved from his stool, carrying the guitar to the wings, and they were all around him, all the stars, their hands reaching to touch him, their voices jubilant in his ear, and when he looked back, out across the empty stage he could still see the little dots of flame flickering, then dying out one by one. The applause began, swept to a tumult, continued, would not stop.

"There must be a lot of burned fingers out there," he whispered to Nellie. "What do we do now?"

"Why did the good Lord put us here?" she returned joyfully. "Surely not to chase rabbits!" She took his arm and they joined the rest, moving into the blazing lights for the finale. Somehow Bobbitt knew exactly what to do.

Willie

The girl shrieks. She waves her arms and jumps up and down. She shakes the ends of her ten fingers as though they have been scalded. *Oh!* she hollers; *Oh!* The rest are shouting and stamping their feet. It is pandemonium. Still hopping and jumping, the girl flings herself against the man in his After Six dinner ensemble, the gold jacket with contrasting lapels and a colored ruffled shirt, a bow tie the size of a jumbo Hershey bar, he displaying most of his front teeth, she still shrieking and now clutching the check he hands her, making her . . .

"Theeee winnnner of twenty-five thousand dollllars on *The Neeeew Trrrrreasure Hunt!*" the host exclaims, and the show fades for the half-time commercial.

"Rubbish," says Willie Marsh aloud, though there is no one in the room with him. Monday is cook's night out, and he is alone. He intones a reverent grace over his TV dinner: in the center compartment is Salisbury steak with gravy, in the left-hand compartment, carrots and peas, in the right-hand one, mashed potato, at the rear, apple pandowdy. Terrible food, but food interests him little these days; he has no appetite. On a separate plate is a salad, whose vinaigrette dressing Willie has himself ceremonially prepared from a long-standing favorite recipe. Ahead of him stretches another quiet evening— boring, if truth were to be told. Later he will watch himself on television; *Classic Movies* on the educational network is showing one of his thirties films. He will sit in this same chair, the dogs beside him, and relive old memories. The prospect, however, does not please. He would rather some of his friends came and watched it with him, but the phone has not rung in days. He is still in mourning for Bee, and his friends do not like to bother him. Besides, in other, happier days, Monday nights *chez* Marsh were traditionally sacrosanct, a cutting of strings after the weekend's social obligations; it used to be his and Bee's "breathing night"—close, chummy, "pipe and slipper" nights, just Willie and Bee, Bee and Willie. The Marshes at home.

Have it your way with Burger King. The commercial continues: Willie's eye wanders haphazardly about the room. All things being equal, it takes no longer for dust to accumulate in Los Angeles than it does anywhere else. He notes with dismay the clouded mirrors, the grimy chandelier, the unpolished crystal bibelots which in another, better, time had sparkled so brilliantly. The day help are negligent without Bee to oversee them. But Bee is dead.

No, he reminds himself—not *dead*. Rather, she has Gone to her Just Reward, has Passed Over to the Great Beyond, has entered the Gates of Heaven, where she stands before her Maker and Redeemer. Willie is a religious person and these simple pieties offer him a measure of comfort. When, he wonders, will he join her? It would require little for him to oblige the Great Beckoning Finger, if it were to summon him; willingly would he go—Bee is waiting for him on the Other Side.

He does not like thinking of what loneliness compels in people, what deeds it brings them to, what fears it breeds. When Bee had been rushed to the hospital he had suffered his first apprehension, then doubt, then a growing terror. He had confessed to a friend that it was the only time in countless years that he would have slept in the house without her; he begged the friend to occupy one of the guest rooms. Now he sleeps each night without her, but neither pain nor loneliness lessens. She is everywhere, Bee. Sometimes he will turn, expecting to see her, hear the voice, will imagine he smells the inimitable scent of her perfume, her Caswell-Massey soap. Now little stirs him, few things interest him, his senses are dulled. During her Buddha period, Bee often used to say that Life is a Fountain; but to his infinite sorrow Willie Marsh has discovered that life is a rope, a long one, whose frayed end he is most assuredly at.

What he has known best is gone; what he has loved best is gone—and this is not merely, not only, Bee. Out there, beyond the sliding glass doors of the game room where he sits, past the lanai, the pool, down along Sunset and Santa Monica boulevards, is another world, and he does not like it. A new, alien world, into which he seldom ventures. For Willie Marsh, everything, including himself, is old, but what is not old holds little savor. Haunted by the past, hating the present, terrified of the future, he has hung on, but only by his eyeteeth, and those not his own but an expensive dentist's in New York. Out there in movieland are strangers; he neither knows them, nor cares to. They are the new ones, the agents become producers, the office boys become moguls. The William Morris crowd no longer wear the black suit and tie that was once *de rigueur;* they favor mauve jacquard double knits and sport shirts, as though they were going to play golf. Willie Marsh was White Tie and Tails; he represented the quintessential charm and grace, the madcap patent leather toe-tapping jazz-bouncing flask-carrying show business royalty of another era. The elite —Cole Porter, Noël and Gertie, Clifton Webb, Bea Lillie, Fred and Adele Astaire—these had been his cronies, when gentlemen stayed at the Ritz, and were swank with white Charvet scarves and *chapeau claques,* which snapped into a top hat with a flick against the open palm.

With devoted canine attention, two Lhasa apsos wait at their master's feet, hoping for a tidbit. Willie cuts them each a piece of meat and feeds them. In her time, Bee never permitted this, but Willie has a kind heart. His eye travels from the TV screen to the gold urn on the mantel, beneath the portrait of Bee, the famous "Smiling Bee," as it was called in art circles, painted forty years ago in London. The urn contains her ashes.

It had all happened so suddenly, right after the Big Party. It had been exactly fifty years (and two and one-half weeks) since "Little Willie" Marsh had first set foot on a professional stage, and the honors accorded his golden jubilee had been significant. First he and Bee slipped away while he had his face tucked up, the bags removed from his eyes and what wrinkles the surgeon thought might be managed; Bee added to his wardrobe, and brought him back hale and hearty, ready to tackle the round of magazine interviews, the parties and near-public events, all of which culminated in his bronze star being permanently fixed into the glittery pavement of Hollywood Boulevard (in front of the entrance to a trick-and-joke shop), followed by a stupendous party at the grand ballroom of the Century Plaza Hotel, a full-scale Hollywood production with klieg lights, limousines, full television news coverage, and stars stars stars.

There were numerous after-dinner speeches in his behalf.

Shirley MacLaine had introduced the main speakers, whose tributes to "The Grand Old Man of Hollywood" were alternately humorous and touching, Jack Warner for the former, Mervyn Le Roy the latter. It was indeed fitting, yet perhaps needlessly so, that it should be pointed out from the celebrity-studded dais that here was one of Hollywood's greats. Willie Marsh was loved. He was admired. He was a man of repute. He was one of the true gentlemen in a town where few existed. His benevolence and generosity were widespread but not generally known, Mervyn briefly touching on the aged actress Willie was supporting, the medical bills he quietly paid for ailing friends, the hands given in aid to careers of less stature than his own. Willie blushed to hear the accolade. Many of his former screen leading ladies were present to add to the glamour of the occasion: Barbara Stanwyck, Joan Fontaine, Janie Wyman, Loretta Young. "Missy" Stanwyck (when she was still Ruby Stevens) had danced in the chorus of *In Old Montmartre*, of which Willie had been the singing-dancing star, one of his greatest Broadway hits, and the photographers had had a field day shooting them as they kicked up a few steps. Willie's speech of thanks was witty and heartfelt, his words brought tears to many in the room, and *Time* had headlined the story "OLD HOLLYWOOD COMES TO LIFE AGAIN." To cap it all, when the audience rose in tumultuous ovation and refused to sit, he'd sung for them—" 'Ats Off ter Bobbitt," from *Bobbitt Royal*—and then reprised his famous tap number "Gonna Dance Off Both My Feet."

The evening's triumph was only slightly marred by Bee's indisposition, but she went gamely through with it. It was not until they'd arrived home that she complained of chest pains. She'd been put to bed, the doctor called, and the following day she was admitted to Saint John's. The room was a bower of bouquets, the nurses could hardly keep up with the get-well cards, but the simple fact remained that a week later she was dead.

The world agreed, they had been marvelous together, similar in their tastes, their outlooks, and brilliantly complementing each other: Bee a vivacious, clever, moving force in the anthropological structure of Beverly Hills, whose elaborate tribal mores extended all the way across Holmby Hills into Bel Air, even unto Brentwood; Willie urbane, witty, insouciant in the Ronnie Colman—Doug Fairbanks—William Powell tradition. Together they had moved with ease among the glittery, famous movieland aristocracy, of which they were not only accepted but uniquely favored members. If the Marshes were not its king and queen, surely they were an archduke and duchess of Hollywood.

Willie had not got rid of Bee's things; her vanity table remained exactly as it had been during her life, with the lace runner Grandmother Marshuttes had crocheted over a long summer in Mobile, and the tortoise-shell silver-crested combs that had been a gift of Elsie (Lady) Mendl, and the silver oval frames, which held pictures of Bee and Willie, Willie and Bee, in Venice, at Buckingham Palace, at Merle Oberon's Acapulco villa, at the Stork Club. Bee's clothes were still in the closets, her shoes and hats, and her furs remained in storage. He could bear to part with nothing. Since her death he had gone out seldom (twice he had suffered arrest for drunk driving, and in consequence his license had been revoked, which meant he had to be driven), but friends would by appointment wend their way up the hill and pass the evening, cheering his self-imposed solitude with the gossip from The Bistro or Chasen's; or Viola Ueberroth would carry the news being retailed under the dryers at Elizabeth Arden's. They were all willing to hear again the familiar stories about the New York days, the London days, the old Hollywood days. The salad days, as Willie called them; "Salad Days": the title of his still uncompleted autobiography.

The name to begin with had been Marshuttes, William Marshuttes, and as a young actor he had been represented thus in theatrical playbills. Having achieved ill success with it, and following one of Bee's inimitably clever suggestions, he'd taken the name of Ashton Marsh, and together they sailed third class for England, where he laid on the glib British accent he'd been painstakingly rehearsed in, and several months later, after successively disheartening interviews with West End managements (the London successes came later), they returned from Southampton to New York, first cabin on the *Mauretania,* where, meeting the press at the pier, he masqueraded as the new find Ashton Marshmaine. Bee had thought it not going too far for him to sport a monocle, and to complete the picture there were spats and yellow pigskin gloves. Photos made the Hearst rotogravures nationwide and, dapper English actors being then in vogue, Ashton Marshmaine found immediate employment with Jane Cowl, with Ina Claire, with Helen Hayes. When he saw himself nudging stardom, he announced the fraud at an Algonquin cocktail party, dropped the "Ashton" and the "maine," and became something of his old self, William Marsh.

He remained a star for many years on both sides of the

Atlantic, in musicals, revue, light comedy, and in drama. He had been an equally famous luminary in films, until the unlooked-for but somehow inevitable decline. Never mind, Bee told him, your star will rise again. She saw to it. She arranged a talk with Viola Ueberroth, while he was touring endlessly in *The Red Mill,* and after he succeeded in being cast as Alfie in the Bobbitt pictures, he became famous all over again. It was Bee Marsh who had brought Willie and the theater together at the outset. It was Bee who had urged him to lose his Alabama accent. It was Bee who had seen him trained in singing and dancing, Bee who had decreed his education, who herself had schooled him in matters of taste and discernment, Bee who had obtained for them entrée to the proper doors through which he might pass into the most important offices, the most chic apartments, the most envied homes.

Willie has lived in the same house on Cordelia Way since his and Bee's earliest years in Hollywood, a large, rambling, indifferently architectured dwelling encompassing many styles and many changes, mostly her ideas. The house stands high atop Doheny Drive, on an isolated knoll that affords all one could wish for in the way of privacy, being at the end of a cul-de-sac, with no neighbors either side, and affording one a 180-degree view, from the city to the sea. The six-o'clock news has predicted showers, but this summer evening is pleasant, balmy even. Below lies the Strip, then Santa Monica Boulevard, then Wilshire, Pico. Outward and away sweeps the vast panorama of Los Angeles, for once clear of smog: a Santa Ana wind has been blowing from the desert for two days, one of the few natural blessings left to the Southland climate.

From his chair Willie can see Catalina Island, and all the way south to Palos Verdes, where the tourists go to view the talking porpoises at Marineland. He can also see the golden statue of Moroni atop the Mormon Temple in Westwood; the figure glints awesomely in the sun, throwing off visible rays, advertisements for those rich and reverent descendants of Brigham Young whose tithed earnings paid for the figure. Willie himself is a generous contributor to the Catholic cause, and in consequence has been honored with a papal title. (Bee had not thought it going too far to have the small coronet embroidered on all his tricot shorts, an understated acknowledgment of the award.) Privately, however, he wishes the cross of the Church of the Good Shepherd, where they "took from" (their little joke together: it meant the church in Beverly Hills in which they worshiped), were larger, a somewhat more prominent contribution to the view. Still, Loretta Young "took from" Saint Victor's, and you couldn't see their cross past Tower Discount Records.

Soon the sun will be setting, always his worst part of the day. There in the lanai, in those very wrought-iron chairs, it once had been his and Bee's custom to take a late afternoon English tea, a daily ritual. The butler would bring it on a silver tray and they would watch the sunset. Now Bee is gone; so is the butler. Willie hates watching sunsets.

What he has been gradually forced to face—and it has come as the truth always does, slowly but most awfully—is that without Bee he might have been only a mediocrity; worse, a nonentity. With her he's been everything: half a century of stardom was not to be sneezed at. Heigh-ho, he thinks, poking his fork at the carrots and peas, the dollop of gelid mashed potato, the unappetizing Salisbury steak. What can the world be coming to, with such food?

He pushes the portable table and the tray from him; he cannot eat. Gets up, ignoring the television set for the moment, and wanders disconsolately about. What to do? How to get through the evening? He pauses momentarily at the card table in the corner, with the typewriter and his assiduously gathered notes, and the pile of manuscript pages, "Salad Days," long promised to the world. The chronicles of his life and times. His times have ended; his life, not quite. He draws out a page at random, studies his syntax:

```
... at this Coçanut Grove one night
we saw an amazing girl, an unknown
then, one Lucille La Sœur, 𝔁𝔁𝔁 𝔁𝔁𝔁𝔁𝔁
quandom Billie Cassin, of St̶. L̶o̶u̶i̶s̶,  Kansas City
f̶o̶s̶ flashing feet, naughty hips, and
oh, those eyes. Later she became Joan
Crawford, but that night she w̲a̲s just
a girl dancing to win a Charleston cup
in a nightclub. Win she did. How did it
```

feel? ~~to win~~, they asked her. ~~—Oh,~~ Said Joan,
~~Joan~~
~~she said,~~ My little feet may be dancing,
but my little heart is breaking."
She'd had a fight with her beau, a
meatpacker-playboy. Well, that's show
business, " Bee said

Willie slips the page back into the pile and takes up the first page, which bears these words: *"J'ai vécu."*

"I lived; I existed through it all."

Willie leans strongly toward this quotation as the epigraph to his memoirs, courtesy of the Abbé Sieyès, whom he greatly admires. The abbé survived the Reign of Terror and his tenacity saw him safely from the fall of the Bourbons, through the Revolution, to the Restoration. Like the abbé and Joan Crawford, Willie, too, has existed through it all. He is a survivor.

He has survived vaudeville, the microphone, the Depression, three or four wars, CinemaScope, 3-D, television, he has survived the waning of love, popularity, fortune, the loss of hair and teeth, impaired eyesight and hearing, internal disorders, he has survived his own age and that of many others, he has survived even death.

Ah, Bee . . .

My little feet may be dancing, but my little heart is breaking.

It was his impaired hearing that caused him to turn up the volume on the TV, where, on *The New Treasure Hunt,* a black girl was practically in tears because she had muffed her chance at five thousand dollars, and since his sympathies were directed toward the unfortunate girl, Willie did not hear the door chime. The dogs scampered off, barking, but he failed to notice. The cockatoo made him aware that something was happening beyond the range of his hearing. Agitated by the dogs, the bird, in its filigreed cage, was uttering piercing cries as an intruder suddenly appeared in the doorway. Willie at last looked up from the set and stared toward the hall.

"Howdy," called a hearty voice.

Willie could make out only a large hulking shape in the

archway. Alarmed, he dropped his napkin into the gravied meat compartment and half rose from his chair.

"Hope I didn't scare ya. Guess ya didn't hear the doorbell. It's me, Mr. Marsh. Bill Bowie."

"Bowie . . . Bowie . . . I don't know any Bowie."

Squinting, he could make out a faceless young man, rocking on the balls of his feet and punching a fist into his palm.

"Sure," said the young man amiably. "Remember—Friday night—Viola's? You said come for drinks?"

Jesus, Mary, and Joseph. Was he losing his mind? Willie wondered. "You've got the wrong night," he called out. "Tuesday. You're supposed to come Tuesday."

"What?" returned the young man, cupping his ear.

"I—say—you've got the—wrong—night." Ridiculous, shouting this way. Willie consigned *The New Treasure Hunt* to oblivion, while the young man stood in the doorway. A swift stillness hung briefly in the room, then they started toward one another at the same instant, both speaking at once.

"You were supposed to come—"

"I could've swore you said Monday—"

Willie scooped up the dogs, put on his glasses, and watched a giant Buffalo Bill advancing across the room: long hair and a buckskin-fringed jacket, fringed buckskin pants. His large hand was extended.

"—Tuesday," Willie ended weakly. Surely it wasn't the same fellow; this one looked like another person entirely, not the neat young man in the shawl-collared dinner clothes. Nor was he alone. Half obscured by his large bulk, came a girl, teetering in his wake on wooden platform shoes, which clattered on the tiles. Willie hardly knew what to do, juggling the animals and, to his surprise, taking the offered hand. The young man wrung it, and chucked one of the dogs under the chin.

"Hey, boy, hey, boy . . . And this here's Judee," he added, with a nod to the girl.

"Hiyah," said the girl. A cloud of reddish frizzy hair topped her head like an Afro, and her eyes were sooty with mascara and Egyptian penciling. Willie set the dogs down and looked from one to the other. Clearly an impossible situation. What had happened was that last Friday night Viola Ueberroth had given one of her biannual parties, a large affair under a lawn tent. Willie had been persuaded by Vi to renounce his mourning temporarily and attend; he regretted it the moment he arrived: faces, faces everywhere, but so few he recognized. It was while standing at the bar, turning from some people who'd been condoling with him, that he came face to face with the young man. Pleasant enough, he introduced himself, explaining that he was Viola's masseur, and had been invited as part of a contingent of dateless men who could possibly amuse husbandless women. Having scraped acquaintance, and not at all abrasively, he had been complimentary about a number of Willie's pictures. He seemed well informed about them, and it was then that he had mentioned the much-publicized magazine spread, and expressed interest in the collection of art and movie memorabilia, even going so far as to say he would consider himself lucky to inspect it in person. Willie had at first demurred, but remembering that he'd invited some people up for drinks on Tuesday, thought it the considerate thing to include the young man. "Bring a date, if you like," he'd said; and here they were—but on the wrong night.

"Hey, this is quite a spread you got here," said the young man affably. "Even better than in the pictures."

"It's just like living between the pages of *Modern Screen*," the girl chirped, moving past Willie, her large googly eyes gazing around her with the wonder of an urchin at a bakery window.

"I'm glad you like it," Willie said. "But I'm afraid tonight won't do. You see—"

"Aw, say," the young man chimed in, "that's too bad. Boy, are we dumb. Wrong night." He shook his head woefully at his mistake. He looked at the girl and spread his hands wide. "Gee, Jude, watcha think?"

"I think it's terrific," she replied, going to tap the cockatoo's cage.

"See, the thing is," the young man continued, "we got up here, but we can't get down."

"Is your car not working?" Willie asked.

"Naw, see, what it is, we got a ride up. A friend dropped us off. He's coming to pick us up, but not for . . ." He looked at his wrist, where there was no watch, then around him, as if the time might appear and announce itself from any corner.

"I see." It was all really awkward. "Well, uh—Bob—"

"It's—uh—Bill, Mr. Marsh."

"To be sure. Bill." They stood facing one another. Willie abstractedly brushing his pate, the young man slamming his fist into his palm again and grinning. Not knowing what else to do, Willie invited them to sit. The chairs had been resurrected by Bee from the old Turf Club at Santa Anita, four of them grouped around a French lawn basket with a glass top, crowded with glass and crystal ornaments.

"I see you were watchin' TV," the young man said. His cowboy boots were large and colorful, the sides stitched with designs in many hues, the toes squarely pointed and turned up like the toes of a caliph's slippers.

"Yes, that *Treasure Hunt* thing," Willie replied. The girl was silently watching him with her skittish urchin's look.

"Oh, *Treasure Hunt,* uh huh." The young man nodded agreeably.

Willie was still having difficulty recognizing the person he had met before. His hair hung around his face in a long mane. The eyes were clear, if bland, the nose was snub, the face large and square. The round cheeks dimpled when he smiled, which was often. The jawline was outrageous.

"Well." Willie glanced tentatively from him to the girl, and back again. "Well, Bob—"

"It's—uh—Bill, Mr. Marsh."

"Yes, Bill, to be sure—Bill." He stamped it indelibly on his memory, dismayed by the glimpse he caught of himself in the mirror: the bald spot that the public never saw, since he usually wore a toupee, his wash slacks, the canvas sneakers, the shirt that was getting a second wearing; hardly the picture of dashing elegance he had for so long striven to present to the world.

"Honest, I never *saw* so many things," said the girl. "Did *you* ever?" she asked Bill. Bill had never, either. He extracted from his jacket pocket a cloth bag and a pack of papers, sprinkled tobacco, and nimbly rolled a cigarette, twisting the end, which he hung on his lip while he searched in his other pockets for a light.

"Here." Willie handed him a package of matches; Bill lit up.

"'S okay, Mr. Marsh—just Bull Durham," he said reassuringly, as though Willie might think it were something else. He smiled at the match cover and tossed it to the girl. "Look, Jude, how 'bout that."

The girl read the inscribed cover: *"To a matchless person. Sincerely, Bee and Willie."* She giggled. "That's cute. I like it."

"We thought it was fun," Willie said. He hadn't got her name; terribly sorry.

"Judee, with two *e*'s, not a *y*." She held up a pair of fingers to demonstrate, then vee'd them into a peace symbol. Bill was looking around for an ashtray. Willie leaned to bring one closer, straightening quickly as he realized the unattractive sight the top of his head presented. "Well," he said again; obviously the matter was not to be avoided. "I suppose, as long as you're here, you may as well have a look around. How long did you say before your friend . . . ?"

Neither of them seemed quite sure; maybe half an hour? The friend had had to run over to the valley; but he'd be back.

"Well, then . . . Would you like to watch the rest of the show, while I take care of one or two things?" He was already out of his chair, wheeling the TV dolly to a more suitable position.

"That'd shore be swell, Mr. Marsh," Bill said. "Sorry to bother you, though. What a dumb thing . . ."

"Not at all, not at all. I'm working on my autobiography, as you can see, so we'll just hurry through and you can go along and I'll get back to the typewriter. . . ." He pointed to the card table. "I always write at night; the thoughts seem to flow better." He clicked the remote wand. "So"—like a magician, as the picture formed. "I'll be back in a moment." He would slip quickly upstairs, put on his toupee, give the pair the twenty-five-cent tour, and by that time, with luck, their friend would come to collect them. The wrong night, in the name of God. Carrying his dinner tray, he glanced back several times as he crossed the room. They had sat again, eyes already glued to the set; as he went through the doorway the girl gave him a little wriggle of her fingers.

"Bye-bye." She turned back to the screen. "Aw, gee, the show's ending." As shrieks of audience excitement were heard, Willie hurried from the room.

Despite the girl's remark, the show was not ending, but rather just beginning. The couple's attention did not stay long with the television set. The young man waited briefly, then got up from his chair, signaling to the girl, who hurried across to the doorway and looked around the corner. Behind her back she wagged her hand at her companion, who moved to the bar, where he quickly stabbed the buttons on the telephone.

"Hey, you there? We're in." Cupping the mouthpiece, with glances over his shoulder to the girl, speaking in low tones. The girl, meanwhile, stayed by the doorway, keeping watch while her friend listened on the telephone, then, "Sure, fine . . ." Pause. He read off the number from the dial. Another pause. He listened, reported the time from the wall clock, and hung up. He signaled to the girl, and they quickly resumed their places in front of the TV set.

Which was where Willie Marsh found them when he returned a short while later.

"Hey—cowboy," said the young man brightly, eying the togs. Willie had changed into a natty Western outfit: tan whipcords, a plaid Western shirt, tooled leather belt with an enormous silver buckle, and boots not dissimilar to Bill's. Bill slapped his hands on his thighs, spun out two imaginary pistols fashioned from pointed fingers and cocked thumbs, and poked the muzzles in quick rotations. *Choo,* he said as one went off, then *choo* again as he shot the other, then twirled the invisible weapons and neatly reholstered them. "Hugh O'Brian," he said with a sheepish laugh.

"Well, now." Willie rubbed his hands together briskly and gave an affable smile; since his alterations in attire, and with his toupee on, he was of a more amiable disposition. "Where shall we begin, eh?" He looked from the boy to the girl, who got up, and they moved off in a group. Willie took in the room with an expansive gesture.

"Here's what you saw in the magazine layout—the Crystal Palace, as we call it. Or the Crystal Womb. That's a little joke of ours," he explained. "Years ago, Kay Francis was here for the first time. She came in, looked around, and said, 'Heavens, a cwystal woom.'" The girl looked at Willie, then at the boy. Willie explained, "She had an impediment, you see, she couldn't say her r's. So—'cwystal woom.'"

Bill laughed heartily; that was a good one. "Oh, I get it," the girl said finally, melting into giggles. Then, "Who's Kay Francis?"

"She was a movie actress. Very famous. Dead, alas. Now, this room wasn't part of the original house," he said, guiding them to a position where they might have a general view. "We added it on after we bought the place. But it's really the best room—woom?—in the place." The "woom" was wide and spacious, with a high vaulted ceiling from whose central beam hung the large crystal chandelier, dripping prisms. The wide expanse of floor was laid in black and white checkerboard. It was many things, this room. It was rather like a garden, rather like a zoo, rather like a jewel box, rather like a mirror maze. And best of all, when it grew dark, rather like a grotto—a fantasy of gleaming glittering glass and crystal. Mirrors were everywhere—on the walls, on hinged screens behind the two carved religious figures flanking the fireplace, on the column facings which supported the rafters—all cleverly arranged so that the city panorama was distantly reflected, creating a brilliant confusion of images and endlessly repeating figures like a line of Radio City Rockettes.

Willie led them around to view the many collections housed in the room. There was the glass and crystal collection, scores of ornaments grouped on tabletops—obelisks, cubes, eggs, pyramids, animal shapes. There was the monkey collection, white ceramic figures, some with black faces and red noses, some hung on silk tasseled cords from the corner beams, others providing bases for end tables, or half hidden in the profusion of indoor plants. This jungle scheme was further carried out in a large mural on the wall beside the bar, where lions, tigers, and leopards peered from behind green foliage, and a dozen more monkeys gamboled.

"Rather *Douanier* Rousseau, we thought," Willie said, then had to explain who the *Douanier* Rousseau was; one of Bee's clever painter friends had copied the originals, but Rousseau went down the drain as far as the pair were concerned.

Then there was the collection of paintings, "the rare and valuable Marsh collection," as the magazine layout had described it; these were hung along those wall spaces not embellished by mirror. The couple ummed and ohed at the landscapes and still lifes, other modern things which obviously neither of them got the point of. But the richness, the expense, the variety of clever detail in the handsome surroundings were not lost on them.

The slow path of their movements, guided by Willie himself, brought them in a deliberate progression to what he called his "museum," and what the two younger people most particularly had come to view. Here were the sentimental objects of memory that were concrete testaments to that long and illustrious career: a well-worn pair of patent leather tap shoes; a top hat and cane, which had seen service during the long run of *In Old Montmartre;* crossed on a wall two sabers he had swashed and buckled with in *The Scarlet Galleon* and *Quentin Durward;* theater programs; sheet music from his numerous musical pictures, Willie's smiling photograph on each; costume designs. On a specially built stand rested an enormous dollhouse, with miniature furniture scaled to the rooms: the famous Bobbitt house, with authentically costumed figures of the principal characters in the series: Bobby Ransome as Bobbitt, Nellie Bannister as Missy Priss, Mary Astor, Dicky Haydn, and Willie Marsh as Alfie, the butler. In one corner a headless mannequin was garbed in the costume— purple cassock, surplice, stole, and pectoral cross—that Willie had worn in *The Miracle of Santa Cristi.* The prelate's biretta, the square purple hat, was exhibited on a Styrofoam block under a glass bell, while another glass case contained the jeweled crown Fedora had worn as the Holy Virgin in the same film.

While Willie proudly pointed out the various items, the girl said little, trailing along in her floor-length flower-dotted skirt, the ruffled hem dragging on the black and white squares, and peering at the various objects through a pair of granny glasses she had fixed on the end of her nose. The young man, on the other hand, talked and talked. His smile blinked on and off like a neon sign; his teeth, Willie thought, were rather unfortunate; he needed a dentist. His large hands appeared used to hard work; they were dry and callused like a laborer's, even an old man's.

"You know," Willie observed as they moved along, "you don't look like the same person. The other night I could've sworn you had short hair."

"That's a trick of mine. Sometimes I pull it back and put a rubber band on. Most of the time people don't notice the diff'rence."

"I certainly didn't. What a clever trick."

He took them to view the aquariums, one of the room's dramatic focal points, ten illuminated glass tanks ranged on glass shelves, creating the illusion of a wall of undersea life where colorful tropical fish eyed their reflections in the mirrors behind.

"Fish," said the girl redundantly.

"Ye-e-s-s," said Willie brightly, "lots of fish. Fun, aren't they?"

And on the piano, lots of photographs, another collection, silver-framed, an imposing array of Catholic prelates. Two popes, Pius XI and Pius XII, Cardinal Spellman, the Los Angeles diocesan archbishop, and the local bishop, all autographed to Willie and Bee, Bee and Willie. In the center of the wall beyond the piano were a pair of tall carved doors with ornate brass knobs. The doors were closed, and Willie passed them by, neither opening them nor making mention of what lay behind them, but instead directing his visitors back to the center of the room, where they stood awkwardly regarding one another, until the girl suddenly turned with a dismayed expression and asked to use the john.

"Certainly, my dear." Willie showed her to the jungle mural beside the bar. He pressed the nose of one of the painted monkeys and a small door sprang open on a touch latch. She gave him a surprised look, went in, and closed the door. Bill, meanwhile, had returned to the bar and was seated on a stool.

"Shore is a swell spread, pardner," he said as Willie joined him.

"Thank you, Bob."

"It's—uh—Bill."

"Oh—Bill, of course, sorry, same name and I can't even remember it. Bill—Bowman, is it?"

"Bowie. Like in the knife? Bill Bowie."

"That's certainly a Western-sounding name, Bill. Where're you from?"

"Montana."

"Ah, yes, Montana. Gary Cooper came from there, and Myrna Loy, I believe. What's it like, Montana?"

"Big."

"Oh yes. To be sure. Montana's certainly that."

Bill leaned across the black Formica counter to survey the collection of framed photographs over the back bar.

"That's sure a lot of famous people you got there."

"Famous and fleeting, alas. Most of them are dead." It was true: Charles Laughton, Humphrey Bogart, Maurice Chevalier, Linda Darnell, Basil Rathbone, Carmen Miranda, W. C. Fields, the Barrymores; all dead. But, Willie pointed out, many of them had at one time or another been in this very room, sat at this very bar. The cream of the cream of Hollywood had in the old days flocked to the Marshes' game room, where any excuse had been an excuse for a party. Jewels and furs and immodestly exhibited breasts, famous faces, famous names. Here men had traded wives on the spot, women had switched lovers between the canapés and the baked Alaska.

Willie stole a moment to check his appearance in one of the mirrors, and was satisfied. Because his silver-blond toupee was expensive and sat well, it didn't reveal the haste with which it had been attached. He looked dapper and spruce; even though his once-flat stomach was now betrayed by a melonlike paunch, the cowboy outfit gave him a youthful, jaunty air. His eyes were still clear, a gentle but keen gray, with a quizzical, amused air, and his nose was long and authentic-looking. A year-round iodine-colored tan did much to give the impression of health and vigor.

Daintily, gingerly, the dogs had come, their nails clicking on the tiles, to sniff around at Bill's pointed boots. He leaned to pet one of them. "Hey, they're about the teeniest dogs I ever saw." Willie could tell that he was nervous; his pale eyes were restless, they darted away from Willie's, from object to object, space to space, then returned again to confront his host with apologetic mildness. To put him at ease, Willie trotted out the insouciance and stylish wit he was famous for—for years he had been the delight of hostesses for his talents as a raconteur.

The girl was still in the bathroom. Bill leaned back on his stool and called down along the wall to the door in the mural. "Hey, Jude, didja fall in?" There was a mumble and a murmur from within; he sauntered to the door to see what the trouble was. Willie watched him go, the sleeves and shoulders of his buckskin jacket bulging, the fringe bobbing, his legs swinging with an easy cowboy gait. The door opened a crack, there was a brief exchange, and Bill returned to report that Judee needed a hand towel.

From behind the bar Willie took some of the expensive guest towels Bee had ordered at Francis-Orr. Embossed in the corners was the well-known *New York Times* Hirschfeld caricature. Bill handed the towels through the door and returned to his stool.

"Havin' some trouble in there," he confided. "It's her time of the month."

Willie colored in embarrassment; in his day people didn't discuss such personal matters so casually. Badly wanting a drink, he was in a quandary; if he had one himself, he had to offer them one, too. No mention had been made again about their leaving—Willie had already noted the dark marks Bill's boot heels left on the white tiles; they would be difficult to clean up. He was reminded of lately occuring events which would have made Bee blush, had she known, other boots and other marks, the results of scuffles and fracases. Since Bee's death he had, out of loneliness, on occasion entertained some vaguely Hollywood types, hardly savory ones, and there had been several "incidents." One morning the cleaning woman had arrived to discover one of the mirrored screens smashed, and there was blood, too. Willie had a black eye and a swollen lip, and he doubted she believed the story that he had walked into the screen by mistake. But those were the sort of things that happened since Bee was gone.

Still, he prided himself on being a hospitable host, no matter the circumstances, and all at once he heard himself asking, "Would you care for a drink, Bill, while we're waiting?"

"Ah'm not much of a drinker, Mr. Marsh—"

"Willie. Call me Willie." He disliked being called Mister by younger people.

"Uh—Willie," repeated the young man, though the name did not come easily to him.

"Perhaps a little wine?"

Wine would be fine, he said. Willie opened the bar refrigerator and brought out a half-gallon jug of Gallo Chablis.

"Hey, look at all the champagne," Bill said. The top shelf held nearly a dozen bottles, Cordon Rouge, of which Willie usually kept a large supply on hand, but not for casual drop-ins. He shut the door quickly and poured the Chablis into a goblet, one of Bee's good Baccarat. He snicked the rim with his fingernail as he handed it over; the ring held, then died in the room.

"Hey," said Bill.

Willie took one of the Baccarat double-old-fashioned glasses and mixed himself a large Scotch and soda, then filled the ice bucket from the refrigerator. He closed the door quickly again, set the bucket on the bar, and added cubes to his drink.

"Say"—Bill was peering across the bar at the pictures again—"is that Fred Astaire?" Willie nodded, and pointed out several others: Jean Cocteau, Jack Dempsey, Edna Ferber, Cecil Beaton, each signed: "To Bee and Willie" or "To Willie and Bee." There was a photograph of Willie side by side with Serge Lifar on a piano top, another with Helen Morgan on a sound stage, another with Somerset Maugham, standing on the terrace of a villa. "South of France," Willie explained. Bill nodded. One with Carl Van Vechten, with Franklin and Eleanor Roosevelt, with Fiorello La Guardia, Coco Chanel. Bill nodded and nodded.

The girl finally came out. She clopped across the floor on her wooden platforms and stood dolefully beside Bill, blinking shyly at Willie behind her granny glasses. She looked shabby and bruised and a little tender; Willie felt sorry for her as he would for a cat kept out in the rain. He finished his drink quickly and made himself another, and Bill rang the rim of his glass for the girl—Willie had forgotten her name again—and held it against her ear. She had obviously burned her bra or didn't own one; her breasts sagged under the print halter whose knot she kept tugging at nervously behind her mop of hair.

"How come everyone calls you 'Little Willie'?" Bill asked, smiling crookedly at him across the bar. Willie swirled the cubes in his glass, drank, then smiled modestly.

"That's an old, old story," he began expansively. "Goes back to before I was an actor. A recitation I used to do when I was a boy. I—hem—became kind of famous for it, and the name stuck, so on so forth."

"Recitation?"

"We used to do what they called parlor pieces in those days." He set his glass down and stepped out on the checkered floor to offer his famous impression of a small boy coming onto a stage before an audience of which he is terrified. With appropriate gestures he recited:

> *"Little Willie in the best of sashes*
> *Fell in the fire and was burnt to ashes.*
> *Later on the room grew chilly,*
> *But nobody thought to poke up Willie."*

Bill slammed his large hand on the black Formica counter. "Hey, that's darn funny, y'know?"

Willie went behind the bar again. "It was just this little thing I learned for company. People were always saying, 'Do Little Willie,' and after a while the name stuck."

"Darn funny," Bill repeated. He seemed to respond to each of these anecdotes in precisely the same way, a quick bright laugh that grew slightly hollow; he would nod and sometimes crack his knuckles, and the eyes continually swerved. The girl, who had perched herself on another stool, said nothing. Her lips were full and ripe and the top one overhung the lower with a curl that could be taken for either cuteness or petulance.

"How you feelin', Jude?" Bill asked.

"Okay."

"Are you not feeling well? Would you like to lie down?" Willie offered solicitously.

"Naw, naw," Bill said, "it's nothin' like that. It's—you know." He winked at Willie again, and put his arm around Judee and gave her a little hug.

"I need a Tampax," she said forlornly. Then, "You don't possibly have . . ."

"No, no, I don't," Willie answered quickly.

"We'll get Arco to stop at Turner's when we go down the hill," Bill told her.

"What do you suppose has happened to your friend?" Willie asked.

"Danged if I know," Bill said. "He'll be 'long."

"Would you care for some wine?" Willie suggested; she nodded. He brought out the jug again.

"Look, Jude," Bill said, pointing to the gallery of pictures, "Tallulah Bankhead. Signed personal." The eleven-by-fourteen glossy of Miss Bankhead was inscribed to "Darling Bee and Willie," etc. Judee had seen the actress on *The Lucy Show;* one up for the host.

"Here's a funny one, if you like Tallulah stories," Willie said, pouring wine, then mixing himself another Scotch. "Bee and I used to play bridge a lot with her, and we were always looking for a good fourth. She'd met this fellow, name of Vinson, I think, up at San Simeon—the Hearst ranch, that is—and she discovered he was a good partner. When the game was won she tossed her address book at him and said, 'Dahling'—she called everybody 'dahling,' you know—'dahling, put your name down for me and we'll play again sometime.' He did, and when she saw he'd written it under *V* she asked why. Because his name was Vinson, he said, and she flung the book back at him. 'Don't be tiresome, dahling, I can't remember V—put it under *B* for Bridge. *Bah* hah-hah-hah-hah!' "

Bill chuckled appreciatively. "Hey, that's a terrific imitation."

"We were quite good friends." He pointed to one of the gallery pictures, a large group gathered onstage, all smiling broadly for the camera. "A Sunday night benefit at the Winter Garden. They were all there that night—Tallulah, Lynn Fontanne, Helen Hayes, Merman. Ruth Gordon, Jane Cowl. Most of them had been my leading ladies."

"Honest?" said Bill with evident interest. "Did you really work with Lynn Fontaine?"

"Font*anne*," Willie corrected mildly. He tapped a manicured nail under one of the faces. "And there's Bee herself, between Lynn and Lenore Ulric. Right up there among the greats."

His host went on pointing; Bill seemed to see Bees everywhere. An original framed *New Yorker* cartoon by Peter Arno showed a crowd of people clustered around the entrance to a nightclub, from which were emerging two heads; said one curious onlooker to another, "Dunno, it's either a raid or Bee and Willie."

Under glass and handsome black-and-gold-bordered mats were:

> *Little Willie with the best of sashays,*
> *And Bee in a bonnet of Lilly Daché's,*
> *Hither, thither,*
> *To lyre or zither,*
> *Lots of dither,*
> *Bee and Willie go.*
> *But every Russian, Lett, or Hessian,*
> *Must ask himself poor Willie's quession,*

> *Like Hamlet in his hamlet, see?*
> *. . . To Bee or not to Bee?*
>   COLE PORTER

And:

> Please do not you think me harsh
> If I say of Willie Marsh
> He must mind his q's and p's
> And all the p's, I think, are Bee's.
>   DOROTHY PARKER

There were sketches and caricatures by James Thurber, Covarrubias, John Held, Jr., the latter making reference to "the Bee's knees." Another, a few scrawls on a cocktail napkin and signed "Dali," showed the head of an enormous bee, wings fluttering, and covered with glittering jewels. The bee's face was similar to that in all the other drawings, and under it was printed "The Queen Bee."

Judee touched Bill, her features screwed into a plaintive, waiflike expression. "When's Arco going to get here?" she murmured. Bill reassured her that Arco would be along. She took a chair, diddling her wineglass nervously, while Bill lunged to peer at one of the paintings hung in an elaborate gallery arrangement along the broad length of an unmirrored wall.

"Hey, who's this guy stuck with arrows?"

"Ah, the Saint Sebastian?" Willie went to stand beside Bill. "Bee picked that up in Italy." The picture portrayed the near-naked gnarled figure of the saint, bound to a tree and martyred by many arrows. "It's Quattrocento."

"Huh?"

"That means it was painted in the fifteenth century."

"Oh. Hey, that's *old*."

"We think so."

Bill's busy eye darted about the room, again flicking speculatively to the pair of closed carved doors, finally lighting on the jeweled crown under the glass dome, Fedora's crown.

"Did you by chance see us in *The Miracle of Santa Cristi?*" Willie asked.

"Aw, sure—sure, I saw that one."

Willie took up from the table a framed Kodachrome still and handed it to Bill. It showed Fedora costumed as the Virgin Mary, wearing a blue headdress bordered in gold, flowing white robes gathered by a gold girdle at the waist, and on her brow, the identical crown that was in the glass dome.

"Did you know we're on TV tonight?" Willie remarked.

"No kidding? What in?"

The Player Queen.

"I missed that one. I saw *Mozambique* once, though."

Madagascar.

"Right. *Madagascar*. Ever see *Madagascar*, Jude?"

"No." She sounded disconsolate as she ran her fingertips over the glass tabletop.

"Listen, why don't I go call, how's that? Could I use your phone, Willie, see if I can track Arco down?"

"Certainly, my boy." Aware that the girl was watching him, Willie replaced the picture on its stand and turned to her.

"Would you care for some music?" he offered.

"Okay."

"What kind do you like?"

"'S up to you. Pink Floyd?"

Willie laughed as he crossed to the pickled and bleached armoire where the stereo components were hidden. "Afraid we're not very modern here. Anything else?"

"I don't care."

He thumbed through some albums on a shelf, slid one out. "How about some Broadway show music?" She said that would be okay; he put on *Call Me Madam*. Bill was talking in low tones on the telephone. Taking his drink along, Willie joined the girl, who had wandered out into the lanai. Her large, softly bulgy eyes popped out with the entranced wonder of a child. Willie thought they indicated a hyperthyroid condition.

"Gee," she said, "it's really nice, huh? Real movie star." She looked around at the wrought-iron furniture grouped on the bright green Astroturf, the luxurious chaises by the pool coping, the cabaña at the shallow end of the pool, at the other, the diving board, and a fountain with a nude female figure pouring water from an urn into a large stone shell, whence it in turn flowed into the pool.

"If you look just there," he said, pointing, "you can see Catalina."

"No kidding? Where?"

He took her to the end of the pool and pointed again to the island, whose low lines could be discerned against the far horizon.

"That's the first time I ever saw it," she said.

"Really? Where're you from?"

"Here. Right down there, as a matter of fact." She indicated some buildings in another direction. "See that gray roof in front of the big blue building? The Shermart?"

Yes, Willie knew the market.

"That's where I come from," she said. "The Shermart."

"I don't understand."

"My mother left me in one of the aisles." She made a little face, then added, "In a shopping cart."

"You mean she forgot you?"

"No. Just left me. Between breakfast foods and cake mixes."

"Your mother *abandoned* you?" Willie was shocked.

She nodded. "I'm an 'agency baby.' That's what they called us. I've had about six foster mothers." It didn't seem to bother her. She straightened her legs and unconcernedly clacked her shoes together. Willie was dumfounded, revolted that a parent could do such a thing to her own child, flesh of her flesh; and between the breakfast foods and cake mixes!

"I was Miss Pacific à Go-Go," the girl remarked wistfully. "I used to spell my name with an *i*, I dotted it with a circle, I thought it was pretty, but Arco didn't like it."

"Who is this Arco?"

She peered at him over the rims of her glasses. "That's who we're waitin' for, Arco."

"I see."

"I think you're real nice, Mr. Marsh." He insisted that she, too, call him Willie. "And I think you're real lucky," she pronounced solemnly. Her face was curiously round for her thin body, with an almost schoolgirl plumpness, and she waved her babyish hands at everything she saw.

"Lucky how?" he asked, trying not to sound patronizing.

"All this. Being rich and famous. Having a lovely home where people can come to, and you give them wine, and everybody acts nice. You're really very fortunate."

"Why . . . yes, I suppose I am. Thank you, Judee." He was both surprised and quite touched at her little speech. For all her present discomfort, she seemed an amiable sort, obviously not very bright, but his heart went out to her, having been so callously disposed of by her parent. Her nails were painted a dull brown color, and her lipstick didn't match. When she turned to look at the view again he noticed a series of ugly red lines down her thin back, exposed by her low-cut halter; they looked as if they must be painful.

He glanced through the open doors to the bar, where Bill was still talking on the telephone. "Where do you live now?" Willie asked Judee; she flagged her hand eastward. "Over there, on Fountain. Gee, I bet if you had a telescope you could see right into the mayor's office from here."

Well, practically, Willie pointed out; at night you could see the lights of Dodger Stadium at Chavez Ravine, and the illuminated buildings of the Civic Center.

"I won't be sorry to be leavin' Hollywood, though," Judee went on, with a philosophical sigh. "It's time anyway."

"Oh? Are you going away?"

"First Hawaii, then—um—I think it's Fiji or some-place. . . ." She trailed off indecisively.

"What will you do in Fiji?"

"We're supposed to live there."

"You and Bill?"

"Unless he gets in the movies. He wants to a lot, but Arco says that's degrading to the human spirit. He says Harmony will be better."

"Harmony?"

"Harmony's this island. Arco's going to buy it. . . . It's a—a atoll? He calls it Harmony, or is it Concord? He changes the name a lot, but as soon as we get the money we're going to buy it and live there. Very sim—simplistically and in tune with nature."

"That sounds like an interesting proposition. What does your friend—Arco, is it?—what does he do?"

"He's our guide. Hollywood's just been a stop in our life cycle, and now it's time to move on."

"I see. And Arco is buying this island?"

She nodded gravely. "It's some kind of real estate deal."

"I should think it was."

"We got this friend, his name's Gary, he's a rock singer, in Nashville, a recording star, he's going to be a key investor." She seemed to have perked up considerably, and Willie listened obligingly as she explained. They had a plan, she said, a master plan, there was a road to be traveled, Arco was their guide, they would travel it, at the end lay peace, happiness, true contentment. They wanted to save humanity, they wanted to save the children, they wanted to restore the race, they wanted to protect the environment. Pollution; the factories and chemical plants were polluting the water, it was unsafe. "Do you drink bottled water? You should; costs more, but it's worth it." She chattered on. Women in fur coats were a menace, so were gun clubs, hunters, and bankers. The world was to be given back to the people.

"Sounds like an interesting idea," he said agreeably. "You and Arco?"

"Oh, no; there's to be lots and lots, all of us who need a home. Arco calls us the 'newly lost.' We're to eat breadfruit and coconuts and fish and build grass huts and live by the fruits of our labors." The island, she explained enthusiastically, was to be an example, a model to astonish the world. On she went in magpie fashion, mostly about Arco, who was in turn described as macho and charismatic and will-compelling; such terms as "persona" and "mystique" came up several times. He seemed to have had a varied career, including a little movie acting experience as well as pumping gas on Sunset Boulevard.

"Don't tell me it was Arco." Willie chuckled. She looked blank. "Arco—Arco gas?" She hadn't got the joke; Willie let it go by as she went on, speaking of Arco with a mixture of zeal, admiration, and profound reverence; he was friend, protector, leader, and both temporal and spiritual teacher. Here the key word seemed to be "izzat." Judee wasn't exactly sure what that meant or how it was to be applied, but Arco had lots of "izzat," and was trying to inculcate it in his disciples.

"You've really got to get to know him. He's very sensitive as a person. He really knows what people are like. I mean he's the one person I ever met who really seems t'make sense, y'know? I mean he's really got his act together." Her hands flitted unceasingly, touching her glass, feeling the sisal matting of the diving board, smoothing her skirt, poking her hair, caressing her arm, her forehead.

"Where do you know him from?" Willie asked.

"He met me in this go-go place where I was dancing. Topless, y'know?" To demonstrate, she gave a little shake to her shoulders, setting her breasts jiggling. "And he just took'n brought me home. I've been there ever since. He likes my boobs."

"I—uh—I gathered you were sort of Bill's girl."

"Oh, I am, too."

"Too?"

"Sure, Arco and Bill, I'm both their girls. Bill likes my boobs, too."

"I see. . . . You mean you all live together . . . ?"

"On Fountain. Over a garage. It's just one room, but Arco's got it fixed up like you'd never know it was a garage—like a sheik's tent, sort of. You know, you really ought to put Bill in one of your movies, Mr.—Willie, he's terrific. I mean he's talented. Gino says he's got more talent than Burt Reynolds, if he could just get a manager and the right part."

"Who's Gino."

"Gino? *Arco!*"

"They're the same person?"

"His name's Michael Gino Archangelo—you know, like archangel?"

Michael the archangel. He sounded impressive, Willie concluded. The girl seemed less shy now; traces of a smile had crept into her dour expression. She had a gay, elfin sort of humor that struck a responsive chord in Willie, and she was plainly awed both by her surroundings and by Willie himself.

Bill came out just then, carrying his glass, the wine jug hooked on his thumb over his shoulder.

"He's on his way," he announced, striding over. "He's gonna make that little stop f'r ya, Jude—don't worry. I brought the wine along, Willie—thought it'd save a trip inside."

"Very considerate. Please be careful with those glasses, though." Usually he used the plastic ones for poolside purposes.

"Well, Jude, we finally got to see William Marsh's house." Bill had dragged up a chaise and plunked down on its foot, leaning to give Willie a friendly pat on the knee. "It's a swell spread, pardner," he repeated. "Is this Beverly Hills?"

"Actually, no, we're West Hollywood. Beverly starts just on the other side of Doheny. We're BBH, here." He chuckled at his little joke. "Barely Beverly Hills. Look," he said, pointing in still another direction. "You can see the Mode O'Day sign."

"Mode O'Day?"

"Brassieres."

"Oh. Brassieres."

Judee giggled. "They must be close to going out of business these days." Everyone enjoyed a laugh at her sally. Bill had filled her glass, then his own, recapped the jug, and set it aside.

Willie raised his drink and they all clinked together. "Here's to crime," he toasted. Judee giggled.

Bill spoke up quickly. "Hey, Jude, Willie's glass's almost empty. Whyn't you hop in an' fix it up?"

"Want me to?" she asked Willie.

"That'd be fine, Judee, thank you."

Bill watched her as she bore Willie's glass away. "She's really nifty, a nifty gal, the Wimp."

"Wimp?"

"Nickname. It's what Arco calls her—you know, wimpy? Sort of—well—just girlie. Judee's really girlie."

"How did she hurt herself?"

"Hurt herself?"

"Those marks on her back."

"Naw, she didn't hurt herself. She just gets banged up sometimes." He winked. "Sometimes she just gets banged." He stretched, then looked around, clearly pleased to be there. For all his impressive size, he seemed diffident, engagingly awkward, and Willie suspected that his hearty manner hid an innate shyness. Though he flashed it too often, his smile was winning and he seemed to embody characteristics that Willie admired: simplicity, naturalness, and a disinclination to talk about himself, which Willie found an admirable trait, especially among would-be actors.

Judee came back with Willie's drink. "Thank you, m'dear," he said tasting. "Mm—you've made it awfully strong."

"I just did it half and half," she explained. "Isn't that the way?"

"Drink up," Bill said. "Y'only live once." Judee took her glass and sat beside Bill on the chaise, and they remained quiet for a time, touching each other, listening to the water splashing in the fountain. It was calming and pleasant, and Willie felt satisfied, relaxed; could he say happy even? In some indecipherable way the pain had been momentarily assuaged, he realized he wasn't thinking of Bee so much. Maybe it was just having young people around him, even if they weren't particularly bright or stimulating.

Bill turned to him, smiled, drew his imaginary guns with cocked thumbs and said *choo . . . choo*. His smile faded; he grew serious. "You know somethin', Willie? I'm really glad I came tonight."

"I'm glad, too, Bill." He eyed him for a moment, then: "Why did you?"

"Huh?"

"I say, why *did* you come tonight instead of tomorrow?"

Bill's grin grew sheepish. "I told you—"

"I know what you told me, but it's not *quite* the truth, is it?"

"Well, by golly—" He slid onto the chaise again and sat facing Willie. "By golly, I'm glad you brought that up. I've been wantin' to get it off my chest. I plum lied to you," he said emphatically, rolling another cigarette from his Bull Durham sack.

"That a fact?"

Bill's expression and tone grew solemn. "Yes, sir, plum lied. Y'see, I used to park cars at Chasen's, and once I saw you go in, and I thought, He's stuck-up. Just another movie star. Don't get me wrong, Willie, you're really a very human guy, but that's just the point."

"What is?"

"Well, see, I mean, after all, William Marsh doesn't invite a guy like me over every day of the week. But when you did, I thought, I'm just goin' to catch that fella with his pants down."

"To coin a phrase."

"I wanted to see you like you really are, y'know? Look, you didn't have to go up and put your Western duds on, and your toupee, just for us—I mean that was really terrific, takin' a little trouble, puttin' yourself out. Most people wouldn't of bothered, right, Jude?"

"Right."

"That's the trouble with bein' a star, Willie. Nobody that goes to your pictures ever gets to see the real you, because you're always playin' a part. But tonight me 'n' Jude, we got to see the real you, and that's why it'll be an experience I'll never forget."

Willie was touched. The young man's evident sincerity, his ingenuousness as he confessed his little plot, was most ingratiating. "Bill, that's one of the nicest things anyone ever said to me."

"It's true." He reached over and gave Willie a locker-room punch to the shoulder.

There was the glint of moisture in Willie's eyes. "I'm very glad you came the wrong night. I'm glad you're here, both of you. I was prepared to spend a pretty lonely evening." He paused, giving consideration to some private matter, then said, "As I mentioned, I'm on television later. *The Player Queen* is a particular favorite of mine—Fedora, you know—and I was thinking, perhaps you and Judee would like to stay and watch it with me. You might enjoy it—it's a fun picture."

"Do you have color?" Judee asked.

"I do, but it's in black and white."

"Hey, I think that'd be terrific," Bill put in. "I really do, but we'd have to ask Arco, see? Arco's sort of the boss. Tell ya what—when he gets here, if he says we can watch, then we'll watch; how'd that be?"

"Well . . . Yes, certainly; Arco, too, if you think he'd enjoy it."

"Aw, he'll love it," Bill said. "He's really artistic. You'll like him. He's the most terrific guy. He's a big person, y'know? Bi-i-i-g-g-g. He's really got a lot of heart, Arco. And a brain, too. He knows more stuff."

"You make him sound like a paragon."

"Para— Huh?" Bill didn't know the word.

"A model of excellence and virtue."

"Yeah, sure; see—that's Arco, right, Jude?"

"Right."

"And, Willie, there's somethin' I want."

"Oh? What would that be?"

"I want cher t'give me a real genuine autographed picture, signed by you pers'nal. I'm gonna start a collection, just like you got."

"I'd be happy to, Bill."

"And there's somethin' else, too."

"What is that?"

"Well, you showed us all your things, the whole room, but there's one thing we didn't get to see."

Willie's face lighted up. "That's true, I didn't. It's not something I generally show, unless particularly asked."

"Well, sir, we're askin'," Bill said brightly, "me and Judee are a-askin'. We'd like to see that there lil ol' trinket."

Trinket? Had he heard wrongly? Willie was puzzled. "Which trinket?"

"That mirror Fedora gave t'you, like it said in the magazine."

Oh.

Willie hid his disappointment; the mirror wasn't what he had meant at all; there was something else he'd decided he wanted to show them. "Ah, you read about the mirror, did you? Yes—belonged to Catherine de' Medici." He pronounced it in the English manner: "Deemedeesee." "Incredible piece of workmanship. Cellini himself did the goldwork." He rose. "Come along, then. . . . Uh, Judee? Bill?" They were still sitting opposite each other, a fixed look passing between them. At the sound of their names they came suddenly aware, and both jumped up.

"I can see you two are really—shall I say?—in love." Willie chuckled, leading the way; neither replied. Willie staggered slightly as he crossed toward the lanai, and Judee giggled. "I told you that drink was strong," he said, coming again into the game room. He raised his glass to the portrait over the mantel, in another toast. "We've got comp'ny, dearest Bee." He stopped them at a table, where they set down their glasses. As he guided them to the mysterious pair of carved wooden doors, Bill gave Judee a surreptitious nod behind Willie's back.

"I don't show this to just anybody," the older man continued, "but since I can see that you're both—well—sensitive, I think you'll appreciate it. Would you just slip your shoes off, please?" Judee looked questioningly at Bill, who shrugged, and they slid out of their footgear, which Willie ranged against the baseboard to the left of the closed doors. Then Willie laid his hands on the brass knobs and drew the doors open wide.

"Holy—"

"Precisely." Willie weaved as he stood aside to expose the room. "As you can see, this is our very own chapel."

It was indeed a chapel, apparently perfect in every detail: the walls covered in scarlet damask, a red, luxuriously piled wall-to-wall carpeting, the moldings and ornate carvings enameled and gold-leafed. Beyond a gilded railing, an altar, draped with an embroidered linen cloth; on it a thick leather-bound Bible and a cofferlike box. Behind the altar, cemented into the floor, rose a tall free-standing wooden cross. Above and behind this, canted away from the wall at an angle, gazing down on the cross, was a life-size portrait of the Virgin, holding the infant Christ in one arm, the other hand raised in the traditional annunciatory gesture. High up on the adjoining wall was a large round window of stained glass. In a corner stood an electric organ.

Bill stared in amazement. "What is it?" he whispered.

"It's a Wurlitzer," Willie whispered back.

"No—I mean the chapel. What's it for?"

"For the worship of God, Bill." Willie turned unsteadily to a panel on the rear wall and began to flick rheostat switches. Immediately the room was theatrically illuminated. A spotlight hit the cross, another the stained-glass window from outside, casting shards of broken color everywhere; a third fell on the altar, a fourth on the painting of the Virgin. He adjusted this beam until it satisfied his esthetic sense, then drew his guests onto one of the two padded seats flanking the doorway. "Lovely, isn't She?" he asked ardently.

The Mary painting was softly sentimental, a fuzzy nimbus around the head, the expression one of benign mawkishness, the eyes seemingly looking in different directions.

"Rather tender, we thought," Willie continued in a hushed voice. "It's Quattrocento, too. How do you like the cross?"

"Terrific," Bill returned in the constrained whisper the nature of the place seemed to dictate.

"It was made from one of the cedars of Lebanon. Brought from the Holy Land by a Knight of Malta during the Crusades. Notice the wormholes. Bee had the altar cloth embroidered

294

by nuns in the Lowlands. They do such fine needlework in Bruges. You might care to see the work closer." He admitted Bill and Judee through a small wooden gate in the gilded railing, and lifted a corner of the altar cloth. "You see, *every single* stitch placed *just* so." He dropped the cloth and smoothed it, then his hand passed on to the cover of the Bible. "This is an interesting item—thirteenth century; it once belonged to Cardinal Richelieu." Bill nodded soberly, but the cardinal seemed to make no impact on him; his eye was on the wooden coffer. Fashioned of ornately carved wood, it was heavily bound with brass and iron bands, secured by a trio of small gold locks. "That," Willie pointed out, "came from the monastery of Mont Saint Michel. It's reputed to be over eight hundred years old—we've had it carbon-tested at UCLA. It once contained the gold hoarded by the monks, and was kept in a secret hole in a stone wall. All the brasswork, as you can see, is repoussé."

Repoussé held no interest for Bill, but its present contents seemed to. "What's in it now?" he asked.

"Aha—what indeed?" Willie said with an enigmatic smile. He made no immediate explanation, but beckoned them to a small picture hanging on the rear wall. It might have been an illustration from a ladies' magazine, showing a conventionally prettified figure of Christ, sitting on a garden bench, garbed in pristine white, surrounded by hollyhocks and other storybook posies, while a little girl in a pink dress and Mary Jane shoes looks innocently up at his neatly bearded, benevolent face. The child's question formed the caption: *"How did you hurt your hand?"*

"How *did* he?" Judee asked, peering closer. "Was he gardening?"

"Uh—no, m'dear; the wound in his hand is one of the Stigmata, from the Cross, you see. They nailed him and he died and now he's come back into this lovely garden, you see, and here's this little girl and—"

"I don't get it," she said.

"Hey, that's pretty funny," Bill said.

"Oh, I don't think it's supposed to be," Willie replied. Bee had unearthed the picture in a secondhand shop in Glendale; they had liked the sentiment. "Let's pray, shall we?" Willie suggested suddenly. He brought them to a gilded railing, where four small benches faced the altar. The embroidered pads gave spongily as, under Willie's gentle urging, they knelt. Placing himself between them, he crossed himself, clasped his hands, and bowed his head in prayer. The other two glanced at one another, shrugged, then did the same. While Willie's eyes were thus lowered, Bill allowed his gaze to return to the wooden box. Willie's breath came in dry bursts through his open mouth until at last he lifted his head. Relieved that his praying business was concluded, Bill made a move, followed by Judee, only to have their arms firmly grasped as they were held in place.

"Holy Mother, hear us, these your sinners," Willie began intoning, clasping his hands again and gazing reverently up at the painting behind the cross. "Accept our grateful thanks for Thy blessings and forever keep us in the paths of righteousness." He stopped, and Bill felt obliged to say "Amen."

"Amen," Judee repeated.

"Not yet." Willie gave an impatient shake and continued.

"Hear us, O Holy Mother, receive this our thanks for Thy guidance and succor and know that Thou hast ever a home here on Cordelia Way." Bill refrained from stirring again, only glancing furtively at Willie, whose cheeks had taken on color and whose voice trembled fervently. "And bless, Holy Mother, the soul of our departed Beetrice Larson Marshuttes, that Thy Son hast seen fit in His wisdom to take from us. Give her rest, that she may know life everlasting and keep her safe until this, Your servant, may join her in Heaven. And bless this night, for in Thy holiness Thou hast seen fit to bring me companionship and good company, for which I thank Thee. Bless also this young man beside me, Bill—uh—" he faltered only momentarily—"Bowie, and Judee—uh—"

"Lutz," she supplied.

"Lutz, and bless them with the happiness they deserve, and send Thy light to shine upon them."

Here Willie reached out and placed his warm, moist palm on the crown of each one's head; Bill could feel the hand trembling as it pressed down with the weight of increasing emotion. "Let them know they have a friend in Jesus, and in this Thy humble servant. Amen."

"Amen," Bill added quickly and leaped up, smoothing back his hair, which had become disarranged under the blessing. Rising, Judee turned to Willie. "I didn't know these houses came with chapels in them."

"They don't, my dear. We had it specially built."

"Does the organ play?" She went to push one of the keys. "Gee, broke, huh?"

"You have to turn it on, you see, it's electric. Do you play?"

"A little."

Willie clicked the switch, then invited her to the organ; she shook her head, hung back reluctantly.

"I only know one piece. *You* play."

"Shall I? Just to give you an idea of how it sounds?" He took the bench, opened the music on the rack, flexed his fingers, and struck the keys; Judee jumped as a thunderous chord set the room vibrating.

"Wow, that's terrific!" she exclaimed, sliding beside him. Without his glasses Willie was having trouble reading the complicated notes, his vision clouded by the drinks. "It's called *The Epiphany Triptych*," he said over his shoulder to Bill. "Lovely, isn't it?" He struck a number of wrong notes, but he played loudly and flashily, pulling the stops and furiously working the pedal bars with his feet, nodding in tempo, while Judee clacked the toes of her platforms together.

The music swelled and boomed resoundingly against the ceiling and walls. Judee had placed her small hand on Willie's shoulder; he found the physical contact strangely comforting. Playing, he'd glanced back several times at Bill, who now seemed to have disappeared. After several more bars, Judee took away her hand and slid from his side. Willie was only vaguely aware that she'd got up altogether, and when he looked over his shoulder again, he saw her moving to Bill, who had reappeared smiling in the doorway. Willie's spread fingers stopped abruptly on the keys, the music ceased, the chords echoed, then died away, and in the sudden silence Bill stepped aside, saying:

"Willie, meet Arco."

Willie did not rise immediately, but remained on the bench, looking at the figure who had moved into the chapel and now stood between the other two. A beam of light struck him from above, throwing his features into sharp relief. Pale face, bright eyes, dark beard and mustache, both neatly trimmed, and obviously calculated to offset the receding hairline of a closely cropped poll. He glittered—his eyes, his teeth as he showed them, not in a smile, but something more like a grimace. What did he remind Willie of? Something he'd seen—a painting? Hardly the paragon he'd expected, which to Willie implied a certain physical stature. Next to Bill, Arco looked quite small; was, in fact, only a little taller than Judee, slight and taut and possessed of an almost palpable energy that seemed all at once to leap out from him.

Willie cleared his throat, then rose, left the organ, and approached. Offering his hand politely, he found the newcomer's strangely warm, an unresponsive, almost soft grip of bones with hardly any feel of flesh to them.

"Good evening—and welcome," Willie said.

"Good evening, sir." Arco looked around, taking in the chapel and its appointments.

Bill draped an arm companionably over his shoulder. "How's that for some cross, huh? Where'd you say it came from, Willie?"

Willie again supplied the information about the cedars of Lebanon, the Knights of Malta, not failing to mention the wormholes in the wood. Then there was the matter of the altar cloth and the fine embroidery of the nuns of Bruges— Bill wanted Arco to be shown that—and the Bible that had belonged to Cardinal Richelieu, and the coffer from the monastery of Mont Saint Michel, which had once held monks' gold. Looking at it, Arco repeated Bill's earlier question.

"What's in it?"

Willie gave a modest laugh. "Not gold, I assure you. But a treasure of even greater value than gold. The treasure of the house, as you might say."

Judee, who had been strapping on her platform shoes, stepped forward with sudden urgency, touched Arco's arm, then leaned to his ear and asked, "Arco—didja bring it?"

"Hm?"

"The"—she glanced at Willie—"you know. Tampax?"

"Oh, sure, Wimp." He led her through the doorway and pointed to a zippered shoulder bag which had been casually dropped by the entranceway to the game room. She carried the bag to the mural, where she touched the monkey's nose and went inside. Willie turned to Arco, who was studying the photographs of the church figures on the piano top. His thin, dark lips curled slightly, and he ran the tip of his tongue along them.

"Care for a drink?" Willie offered.

"If you're having one, sir."

"I'll get the wine." Bill headed outside to bring in the jug. Arco glanced back at the chapel.

"Who says Mass?" His tone was quiet, and slightly sardonic. His look swung to Willie questioningly, his brows lifted; they were black and so perfectly arched they might have been plucked. The Latin regularity of his features was marred by a too-large nose, and a random scattering of brownish moles accented the pallor of his skin. Willie volunteered that the archbishop himself had several times held private family services in the chapel. Glancing at the photograph of His Holiness John XXIII and the personal signature beneath, Arco made a minute adjustment to the frame, then followed as Willie led the way to the bar.

"Really an amazing place, Mr. Marsh," he said.

"Willie," he corrected, going behind the counter and offering Arco a stool. "It's fun, isn't it?" He took a towel and polished the Formica and emptied the ashtray. "Well. I've been hearing a lot about you, Arco."

"Not all bad, I hope?"

"To the contrary. Your friends think quite highly of you. I understand you're off to the Pacific one of these days."

A faint crease furrowed his brow. Had Judee spoken out of turn? Willie wondered.

"One of these days," Arco returned easily.

Bill came in with the jug. He slung it onto the bar and took the stool next to his friend. "Hey, Arco, guess what— Willie's on TV tonight. He wants us to stay and watch. Can we?" As Willie turned to the refrigerator for ice, Bill and Arco winked at each other.

"Sure, why not. If Willie's agreeable to having guests."

"Consider yourself a guest, Arco. You'll probably want something to eat, but I'm afraid you'll have to take pot luck— it's cook's night off."

"Whatever."

Arco turned to Bill and said, "Run out to the car and get my cigars, will you?"

"Sure thing, Arco." Bill hurried to fetch them.

"We have cigarettes," Willie offered.

"I prefer a cigar," Arco returned evenly. Willie poured him a glass of wine, and as he sipped, his eye darted around the room and finally back to the open chapel doors. "I have to admire such—what shall I call it?—such devotion? Your own chapel, archbishop, pope—you must be well connected up there." Drinking, he pointed a finger to the ceiling.

"We all have our faith, I suppose. Are you a churchgoer?"

"No. Not at all."

"I see. I didn't used to be. I was raised a Baptist."

"A Baptist? What happened?"

"I come from Alabama, and we were hard-shell as could be. I was dunked in the Tombigbee River to get my name. This ol' preacher fellow, he wades right out in the water with me and turns me ass-over-teakettle and holds me under while he baptizes. If I'd had a longer name I'd of drown'd, Ah swear."

"Goldarn, Willie," said Bill, returning with the cigars. "You got a Southern accent."

"Sure do, boy, jes' a good ole Alabama cracker, thass me."

Arco slid a Tiparillo from the pack and waited for Bill to light a match for him. "Why'd you turn Catholic?" he asked, puffing.

"I became converted. Even as the Apostle Paul."

"Oh? Yes. Saul into Paul. Were you struck blind on the road to Damascus?" Arco's voice sounded carefully, even purposely, modulated, as though under a self-imposed discipline. Willie noticed a somehow affected attempt to disguise a regional speech pattern. The soft tones emerged not from the chest, but through the large beak of a nose, with a nasal, adenoidal quality.

"Not exactly," Willie replied to his question about Saint Paul on the road to Damascus.

"How then?"

"I . . . was made to see."

"That's not a bad thing, depending on what you see. What did you?"

"I saw God."

"That so? What does he look like? Old man, beard, all that?"

"I don't mean I saw *Him*—but I saw His *spirit*."

Arco nodded agreeably. "I understand. How did all this come to pass?"

"Well, it's a rather personal thing. I don't know that you'd enjoy hearing—"

"No, no—I really would. I'm always interested in hearing how people find God."

Willie flashed him a searching look, which Arco returned blandly, deliberately softening the intent expression in his eyes. Judee had come out of the powder room, and was lingering at the end of the bar, as though waiting for Arco to notice her. He waved her to him, put his arm around her waist, and gave her a friendly little shake.

"Feeling better, Wimp?"

"Uh huh. I'm okay."

"Good girl." He bussed her cheek, slid his hand down and gave her rear a squeeze, then patted the stool beside him. "Put it down—Willie's going to tell us a story."

"More wine, Judee?" Willie asked, playing host.

"Sure, okay, fine."

He brought down another goblet from the shelf, then

opened the refrigerator door for ice. Judee blinked at the stock of champagne. "Ooh, look at all the shampoo."

Willie's hand froze on the door. "Uh—champagne—yes. Perhaps you'd prefer some of that?"

"I *love* shampoo."

"Why, then, shampoo it shall be. Grand idea." He brought out a bottle and handed it to Bill to uncork. They carried their drinks to the furniture grouping in front of the fireplace, two matching Chesterfield sofas with floppy down-filled cushions; they had come from the boudoir of Marion Davies's beach house. Bee had bought them at auction. Bill peeled the champagne foil, undid the wire, then worked the cork out.

"It didn't pop," Judee exclaimed in disappointment.

"Good champagne rarely does, my dear," Willie explained.

Bill displayed the label. "That's Cordon Rouge, Jude." He held up a goblet and rang the crystal rim. "Hey? Hey?"

"Baccarat," Willie said, settling the dogs into the chair with him. "Bee always liked Baccarat. The—hem—'crystal of kings,' they call it."

"All right, everybody, quiet. Willie's going to tell us a story." Arco leaned back in the corner of the sofa, his arm around Judee, who was curled up beside him, her knees drawn up on the cushion.

"Well," Willie began, "it's not something I generally tell. . . ." This, however, was hardly a fact; he had been telling the story for years; of all his many anecdotes it was his favorite, since it concerned the most important experience of his life. "Well," he began again, "The Conversion of Willie Marsh, as I call my tale. This goes back some years now. I was in Italy, doing a film. Since Rossellini, one felt the whole rebirth of the Italian picture thing. Magnani—like an Italian Fedora in those days. Lots of the studios were making movies abroad then. Bob Taylor had done *Quo Vadis* for Metro. Ty Power did *The Black Rose* for Fox. They made *Three Coins in the Fountain* with Clifton Webb—you probably remember the song. So on so forth. Well, Bee and I went over to film *Miracle of Santa Cristi*—perhaps you saw it?" he asked Arco. "Fedora was in it? And Lorna Doone?"

"No. I didn't."

"It doesn't matter. What's important is what happened to me. Here, inside." He touched his breast lightly, then dipped the finger into his glass. "Truly the most glorious experience of my entire life. Bee had gone down to Capri to visit Gracie Fields, and the company was shooting on location in this little hill town called Rocaillo, about eighty kilometers outside Rome." He paused to drink, stretching his withered neck out like a turtle. "I was playing the part of Bishop Bruggiatti and on this particular morning—it was a fine Italian spring day—the production manager had arranged for us to eat our lunch in a *trattoria* on the piazza where we were working. At one end there was this beautiful fifteenth-century church. Have you ever been to Italy, Arco? No? You should—divine place. Anyway, there I was in my bishop's robes—the same costume you see over there"—he pointed to the clerically draped mannequin in the corner— "with that same pectoral cross and chain on my chest. I'd ordered a bottle of Soave and was just sitting there with Lorna Doone. Lorna had a home-movie camera she always carried around with her, and she was shooting away, when I saw this woman coming down the steps from the church. Typical peasant type—old, short, squat, with a black dress and stockings, and a black square of cloth over her head, bits of gold screwed in her ears, so on so forth. Halfway down she seemed to stumble, then fell backward onto the steps.

"Since I was first to see her fall I got to her before anyone else. I knelt over her and looked at her face: white as paper; eyes staring straight ahead, practically bugging out of her head; white foam oozing from her mouth."

"What was wrong with her?" Judee asked, wide-eyed.

"I was sure she was having an epileptic seizure. I pried her mouth open—her breath was incredibly rank—and I reached in and pulled her tongue out from the back of her mouth, where it was stuck. A lot of people had crowded around and everybody was making suggestions. Except Lorna—she just kept grinding away with her camera. Gradually the woman began to relax. Her eyes lost their glazed-over look and I could see she was coming out of it. Someone brought water, which I tried to get her to drink. She took a little, choked, then said, 'Padre,' and then she said, '*dimmi, dimmi,*' which of course means 'tell me,' or 'say to me.' I didn't understand what she wanted. Then I saw that my pectoral cross was swinging in an arc in front of her face and her eyes were following its path. I was astonished. The poor creature believed I was actually a real priest. Without a moment's thought I pulled the crucifix from my neck and gave it to her to kiss, making signs of the cross above her, and then I recited the Latin blessing, which I'd had to learn for my part in the picture. Imagine my horror when I saw this expression, this look of divine peace, come over the poor thing's face, and she died."

"She was dead?" Judee echoed.

"As a doornail." Willie crossed himself reverently at the memory.

"Jesus," Bill said.

"Exactly. I felt so embarrassed—I mean I wasn't a priest, just a layman, and here the woman had expired thinking she'd had the last rites. And what authority did I have to administer them? Bee was most interested when she arrived back from Capri and I told her what had happened, but it wasn't until Lorna had her movie film developed that Bee really was struck by the truth. Remember, Lorna had shot the whole incident, and when we got back to Rome she ran the film at Cinecittà. When it was over Bee asked Lorna if we could be alone and she had them run it again. She made me look—really *look*—at that poor ignorant peasant face, and then I realized how the spirit of God makes itself known to the heart of man. Bee had seen how moving the old woman's simple faith was, and the power of what my costume and prop cross represented to her. Well, it so happened that coming from Capri to Naples she'd spent time on the ferry with a Monsignore de Dominicus, who was then secretary to one of the papal legates. They took the train together up to Rome. And through Bee I later got to meet the monsignore. She'd already told him about the old woman's dying and how moved we'd been by her faith, and at week's end we were both taking instructions. Bee's idea, of course. We'd met Cardinal Spellman in New York and naturally he was delighted when we cabled him our intentions.

"Before you knew it we'd had an audience with His Holiness, and in no time we were in the fold, so on so forth." Willie set down his glass and gestured with both arms to the portrait of Beetrice Marsh. "And we embraced the Faith with all the ardor, all the passion of—well—school children. Simple Sunday-school children."

He fell silent at last, dropping his head and staring into his empty glass.

"Uh—gee, that's fantastic, Willie, it really is. Isn't that fantastic, Arco? Arco?" Arco's mind seemed elsewhere; Bill leaned and gave his knee a knock. "Hey, buddy—"

Arco came suddenly aware. "Yes." He raised his glass to Willie. "That's quite a story, Willie. You have my congratulations."

"Thank you."

Willie's mind was slightly befuddled; he peered over at

Arco, trying to read his expression. Was he mocking him? He couldn't tell.

"I envy you, Willie."

"Nobody should envy anybody else."

"No, no, I do. I freely admit it. You've got it all, haven't you?"

"I have my share."

"Ohh, I'd say you got a good deal more than your share. I admire a man like you."

"Why is that?"

"You represent all the virtues. You are faith, hope, and charity."

Willie ducked his head modestly. "Well, if one has it, I think it should be . . . shared, shouldn't it?"

"Certainly."

Arco suddenly snapped his fingers at Bill, a sharp, incisive sound, and pointed to Willie's glass. "The gentleman needs a drink, Bill. Don't make him tend bar in his own house." Bill obediently took Willie's glass to the bar; Arco jerked his head toward him as he went. "Used to be a bartender, Bill did."

"That a fact?"

"He wants to be in the movies. You think he's got a chance?"

"Why, I'm sure he does—"

"You ought to put him in one of your pictures, Willie."

Willie was flattered that someone should still think of him as "in pictures."

"It's not like the old days, you know; one doesn't just 'put' people in the movies. Today they have to know what they're doing."

"He's taking classes."

"Classes is not acting; classes is learning. And contrary to popular belief, Lana Turner was not discovered on a soda fountain stool at Schwab's. It takes work and the breaks and the right part, and even then, who knows? Who knows what it takes to make it?"

"You like being a movie star?" Arco asked.

"Like it?" Willie considered the question. "Certainly. Why?"

"I think it must be a rotten life. A whore's life."

"Perhaps. I think only those who've been through it really know what it's like. Yes, I'd say I enjoyed it. We had a good life; it brought us a lot."

"You talk like it's over."

Willie shrugged, his eye wandering to the portrait of Bee. "What's left? Done it all. Seen it all. Been it all. What's left?"

"Was it worth it?"

"Pays well, even though the work's not steady."

Arco nodded appreciatively. "How'd you get to know the Pope?"

"He knighted me."

"For what?"

"For aid and comfort to Holy Mother Church."

"I see. And since you found . . . religion, do you forgive your enemies?"

"Ah, no, Arco."

"Why not?"

"I'm far too busy forgiving my friends. Thank you," he said to Bill, who brought his refilled glass, then remained standing until Arco indicated that he sit.

"Do you love God?" Arco asked Willie.

"Of course. He's divine." He giggled suddenly, and choked on his drink.

Arco moved to examine the pictures on the wall. "A lot of paintings you have, Willie. Been collecting long?"

"Quite a while." Willie heaved himself from his chair, moving unsteadily as he crossed to Arco. "That's a Tchelit-chew."

"I know."

"Are you interested in art?"

"Arco's an artist," Judee piped up. Arco's head turned and he glared. She subsided with a little pout, helping herself to more champagne.

"Are you indeed?" Willie asked Arco.

Arco puffed on his cigar. "Not really. I used to be, once."

"Why'd you give it up?"

"Too hard. Couldn't stick it. Frankly, I don't like being alone that long—you've got to be alone to work." His tone was confidential, easy, winning. "I showed some sculptures a couple of times, down on La Cienega."

"Did you in fact? What sort?"

"Living sculptures. Me." He explained that what he had tried to produce was a new kind of art, in which he himself had figured as principal subject. Once he had lain for ten days in an open coffin while people came to look at him, not moving, merely lying there, eyes wide, staring at the ceiling. Another time he had been a living crucifixion; had stood nude with arms outspread before a cross. "The Living Martyr," the piece had been called.

Humorously, Willie asked, "Did anybody buy you?"

"They were just attention-getters. Statements. What I call

living metaphors. All of life's a metaphor, really, if you can grasp and understand it."

Though he seemed to be trying to say something, in Willie's inebriated state the implication remained obscure to him.

"Don't s'pose I can. Sounds interesting, however."

Arco had moved again and was looking at the Saint Sebastian picture.

"Quattrocento," Willie observed.

"*Quat*trocento?" Suppressing a chuckle, Arco examined the picture more closely, then shook his head. "I think you got taken on that one."

"Why?"

"It's a copy. Some art dealer hooked you."

"It doesn't really matter, does it? We like it."

"Patron saint of pinmakers—did you know that?"

" 'S that a fact?"

"If there's any fact in religion. Doesn't seem worth being made a human pincushion, though."

"Are you against religion, Arco?"

"Certainly not. It's the opiate of the people. Whatever turns you on is okay by me."

"I think perhaps you are anti-establishment."

"Not at all," he returned mildly. "I like order, peace, and continuity. I am not a violent person." Unnoticed, his cigar ash fell on the floor.

It was then that a strange look passed between the two men. Even in his slightly befuddled state Willie felt an instantaneous awareness; he thought of the look as that of strangers who recognize some unspoken but telltale sign, a sudden fine comprehension that identifies each for the other, as the lawman knows the felon. In some way Willie felt he had been discovered, that he had been caught out. Then the moment passed, and Arco resumed his easy, bantering tone.

"Violence is for those who can't afford peaceability," he continued, moving along the wall of pictures. "Plutarch says perseverance is more prevailing than violence. That's why Avis tries harder—"

"Plutarch, eh? Most people don't have Plutarch at their fingertips. You've been to school, obviously."

"Most everybody's been to school at one time or another."

"Where'd you go—Harvard?" He giggled at his joke.

"Arco went t' the seminary, di'n't ya—"

"Goddamn you." Arco whirled and confronted Bill angrily. "Why don't you learn to keep your mouth shut?"

"I was just—" Bill broke off and heaved his shoulders.

Judee leaned and whispered in his ear. The blood that had surged into Arco's face receded as he turned to Willie.

"Yeah—I went to the seminary for a while."

"Well well well. Did you take orders?"

Arco laughed. "They gave them but I didn't take them. I took up tap-dancing instead."

"You don't strike me particularly as the religious type."

"I'm not."

"What is this word your friend Judee mentioned—izz— izzat?"

"Judee talks too much, too." He threw a dark look over at the girl curled up on the sofa, but when he turned back to Willie his expression was bland, almost benign. " 'Izzat' is a Hindi word. It means a man's personal dignity and honor. I think that's more important than any formal religion. I believe that a man's izzat can bring him greater happiness and fulfillment than kneeling down and worshiping plaster saints. They might as well be calves of gold. And all that glitters . . . is bulla shitta. That'sa whatta my mama done tolda me—"

Judee jumped up from the couch. "Hey, that's my song. 'Blues in the Night.' "

Arco seemed uninterested in pursuing the topic, but went on looking at the paintings, apparently knowledgeable about each of the names—Berman, Bérard, Perlin, Bemelmans— arriving eventually at the mantel, and the portrait over it. He stepped back to scrutinize it, and Judee came up and put her arm through his.

"It's a John," Willie explained to Arco.

"So I see."

"John who?" Judee asked.

"Augustus John," Willie told her, then to Arco: "It's rather famous, you know. They call it the 'Smiling Bee.' "

Judee was standing on tiptoe, looking. "I don't see a bee anywhere."

Willie laughed. "No, no, my dear, her name is Bee. Beetrice *Marsh*." He used his index finger to remove the dust along the bottom of the frame, then switched on a narrow light attached at the top which threw the portrait into full illumination. Against the turbulent background of mauves and bitter greens sat a woman, with softly marceled brown hair, chin in hand, one slender finger resting along a cheek as she leaned slightly toward the viewer, dressed in the fashion of the twenties, with a large rope of pearls around her neck.

"Beetrice Marsh herself," Willie announced, stepping back and extending his arm dramatically. "We were having a bit of a holiday in Venice that summer, staying with the Porters —Cole and Linda, of course—I believe that Scotty Fitzgerald was along, too, and we caught John—Augustus—up one afternoon in the Piazza San Marco with the Baroness d'Erlanger and Princess Aspasia, and John said Bee absolutely must sit for him." Willie did not deem it necessary to mention that it had not been the painter's idea, but Bee's, and that he had charged an exorbitant fee.

"You can get a better view of it from here," he said, moving back to the sofa. Arco and Judee came and sat beside Bill and they all looked at the picture together. Willie rattled the ice cubes in his glass, then dropped his head. "It was all very sad."

"How's come?" Bill asked.

"She's dead, you know. Very unexpected." He pointed to the urn. "That contains her ashes."

Judee looked closer. "Is it—?" She broke off uncertainly.

"Full? No, she was quite a small woman."

"No, I meant is it real gold?"

"No, my dear, only gold-washed. We didn't want anything ostentatious."

Bill said, "She—uh—must've been a wonderful person."

"That she was, William," Willie nodded his head for emphasis. "A *won*derful person."

"And a kind person, too. You can see it in her face."

"The kindest person I've ever known."

"Something in the eyes, a—uh—"

"Depth?"

"Ri-i-ight. Depth's what I meant. Really *deep*. Huh, Arco? Sort of a depth of—uh—"

"Character?" Willie suggested.

"Ri-i-ight. You can see she's got character."

"*Had,* m'boy."

"Had. Sorry."

Arco said nothing, but sat stroking his beard, listening to the conversation.

"I miss her dreadfully, you have no idea. Not a day passes but I don't think of her, don't pray to the Holy Virgin to keep her safe for me."

"I guess most guys aren't so lucky."

"No, no, they're not, I'm sure." Willie hiccuped, dug for his handkerchief to wipe his eyes with. "I'm just glad she got to be here for our golden jubilee."

"Golden what?" Judee asked.

"Our fiftieth anniversary."

"Gee," she said reverently, "that's a long time."

"That's beautiful, Willie, honest," Bill said. "Shit, fifty years."

Judee pushed her fingers in her hair and massaged her scalp. "Most folks don't stay married that long these days. My father and mother never even got married. I guess fifty years must be some kind of record, huh?"

"What's the matter, Willie?" Arco had spoken up finally.

Looking as if he'd choked on something, Willie was staring open-mouthed at Judee, who was patting her hair into shape again. He closed his lips and touched them with his handkerchief. "What's that you say?" he finally managed.

She dropped her head and gave her frizzed hair a good fluffing. "I was saying fifty years married must be some kind of record. . . ."

Aghast, Willie looked from her to the portrait, then back again, and his words came out in a hoarse croak. "Beetrice Marsh was not my wife," he pronounced indignantly.

"Not your wife?" Bill echoed stupidly.

"Certainly not. Beetrice Marsh was my mother."

Judee's head snapped up, her eyes roundly bulging. "Your *mother?*"

"Yes, of course. My mother."

There was a moment during which nobody said anything. Only the gentle snoring of the dogs could be heard. Willie looked at the three of them, looking at him. "My mother," he repeated, raising his eyes to the portrait. "God bless her."

"Oh. Sure," said Bill.

"Oh. Sure," said Judee.

Arco said nothing.

Willie coughed, and shifted in his chair. "Beetrice Marsh was the most wonderful mother a boy could hope for. And I accept Judee's error as the greatest compliment. The greatest in the world. 'Every good boy loves his mother, loves her first before another.' That's what Bee always used to say." He was forced to use his handkerchief again. "There was a rumor for years that she was my sister, but nothing could be further from the truth. Bee was mah l'il ol' mama. Oh, sure, she talked 'southren' and I guess while you could take the girl out of the country, you couldn't take the country out of the girl, but she was a grand person. The most famous mother in Hollywood. In all show business," he added, wiping his eyes again.

"Your mother," Bill echoed dumbly, shaking his head. "I'll be jiggered." Arco still made no comment. Judee clambered down to the end of the sofa and leaned to Willie, wriggling her fingers at him.

"Gee, sweetie, don't *cry*. . . ."

"I'm sorry." He sniffed and blew his nose. He pocketed his handkerchief and raised his glass to the portrait once more. "Well, dearest Bee, here's to crime." He tilted his head back and drank, long and fully. The dogs stirred; Judee giggled; nobody said anything.

"Well," Willie offered finally, mastering his emotions, "why don't I just pop out to the kitchen and see what's in the refrigerator that I could give you? Meanwhile, you all just make yourself at home."

"Fine, Willie." Arco pressed his hand on Willie's shoulder; again there was that strange warmth emanating from it. Bill and Judee were on the sofa, talking. He waved to them as he pursued an erratic course through the room, heading for the kitchen. "His *mother*," Bill echoed. "Ssh," said Judee. She giggled again.

When he returned Willie was surprised to find the game room empty. Outside, darkness had fallen. He was more surprised, and a little shocked, to discover a trail of hastily doffed clothes, leading to the lanai. He went out to find everybody in the pool. Judee was nude astride a float, while Arco, also naked, lounged along the pool steps, half in, half out, and smoking a cigarette. The odor of pot drifted across the water. Bill's tanned bulk was stretched full length on a second float, midway between the two. He lay on his stomach, and there was a narrow white band where his bathing suit would have been, but he, too, was naked.

"Hey, Willie, ol' pal, we're 'bout outta champagne," he called cheerfully. "How's 'bout 'nother bottle?"

Willie maneuvered through the maze of wrought-iron furniture and went inside again. Heading toward the bar, he realized he was quite drunk. Hardly a new condition, and he knew well enough how to handle himself in the circumstances, but he had misgivings; already he was thinking perhaps he'd made a mistake asking them to stay. He should have let them leave, and watched *The Player Queen* by himself. Still, he was having a good time, wasn't he? At least he wasn't alone. He brought an unopened bottle from the refrigerator, then found some of Bee's second-best glasses, stored in the back of a cupboard. He proceeded outside, and as he bent to set down the champagne bottle, his toe touched something. He heard the sound of glass shattering, and looked down to where someone had set one of the Baccarat goblets: it was snapped at the stem.

Bill circled on his float. "Oh, heck, did it break?"

"Yes, it did," Willie said curtly, bending to pick up the pieces. He started as a wet face suddenly emerged at the coping and Arco grinned up at him.

"Sorry, man. I guess I shouldn't have left it there." His eyes seemed brighter, his smile more of a leer.

"It's all right," he said, trying to appear friendly. "After all, it's just one more worldly possession. We all have too many of those, anyway."

"Some of us do, anyway."

Willie brought the dustpan and brush from behind the barbecue, finding that Arco's close scrutiny made him feel absurdly ill at ease. He dumped the broken pieces in the trash can. "People can get cut that way," he said when he came back.

"I said I was sorry."

Willie could see that Arco meant it; or perhaps it was only that he wanted to believe it. Suddenly, and with no apparent reason, it had become important that Arco like him. He said, "I'm sure you are."

"Hey—psst—c'mere." Arco beckoned him to the pool's edge with a confiding gesture. "You want to drop?"

"Pardon?"

"We all just dropped half a dot—y'know, acid? There's a half left if you want it."

Willie cleared his throat. "No, thank you. I'll abstain on that, if you don't mind. I want to watch my movie with a clear head."

Arco laughed. "Oh, sure, sure. We're all going to watch it. What's to eat?"

"Well, there are some hot dogs, and I've made a salad—"

"Terrific, man." In only a brief while his cultivated speech seemed to have undergone alterations: the careful diction had disappeared; in its place was a kind of street jargon, hip, cool, jazzy. His arm still hung on the coping and Willie noticed a colorful tattoo on the knotted deltoid: an ornate letter Z circled by what looked like a snake eating its tail.

Willie adopted a casual, pleasant tone as Bill and Judee paddled their floats over. "It's all right, just an accident, nothing really, the glass can be replaced." Judee began shrieking as Arco upended her from her perch, and there was a lot of good-natured splashing while he appropriated the raft. He flopped onto it backward, with no attempt at modesty as he paddled to the deep end of the pool, where his pale form became half obscured in the shadows. Willie filled two of the cheaper glasses with champagne, and when he handed them to Bill on the raft he noticed that his shoulder bore the same tattooed emblem as Arco's, the Z circled by a snake. Bill maneuvered out into the pool and paddled over to join Arco, where the rafts paired side by side, also the two heads; Willie could see them, the fair handsome one, the dark not-so-handsome one, also side by side. He absently touched his toupee, then turned to Judee, who was chattering again.

" 'S really a treat," she chirped gaily. "I just love shampoo." Drops of water clung to her lashes, lending them an odd, sparkly effect, creating a kind of jeweled fantasy face. Coyly, demurely, even flirtatiously, she clambered out, stretching naked along the stonework and squeezing her kinky-wooly hair between her fingers. She rolled onto her stomach, propping her head on her hands and staring up at the sky. The red lines on her back were more obvious, and there were yellow bruises on her thighs and buttocks. "Gee," she said, "d'ya think it's gonna rain?"

"According to the news, it's supposed to."

"The stars just went in, all of a sudden. Like they turned off a switch or something."

Scanning the sky, Willie was surprised to discover it had clouded over; there were no stars. At the end of the pool Bill and Arco lay on their rafts; Bill's deep baritone floated across the interval, his words unintelligible. In the watery light his body was golden, while the other one's was pale and marmoreal, as if it seldom saw the sun, or even daylight.

"Hey, what're you fellows doing over there?" Willie called genially. Arco's laugh was muffled, and Bill glanced back over his shoulder, but neither answered.

Judee said, "Isn't he terrific?"

"Bill?"

"Oh, Bill, too. I mean Arco. I never had sex with anyone until him—can you believe it, a virgin at sixteen? He's really fantastic. Better than Bill."

"Uh—" Willie thought a moment, not caring particularly for the turn in the conversation. "How old are you now, if one may ask a lady?"

"Seventeen. How old're you?"

"Uh—that is a question I do not choose to answer."

"What sign are you?"

"I'm a Libra."

"Oh, Libra? Gee, I don't think I know any Libras. Arco's Taurus—they're terrific. Bill's Leo—they're terrific, too. I'm Aquarius—y'know, the water-bearer?"

"Yes, I know the water-bearer."

"Don'tcha believe in astrology?"

"Not particularly. I tell fortunes, though."

"Oh, gee, honest? Cards or what?"

"I read hands."

She stuck out her palm. "Do it, do it. Hey, gang—Willie's going to read my fortune."

He took her hand and turned it toward the light, so he could see the lines. He traced several with his thumbnail, and pointed out the various areas of the hand as Bee had explained them to him during her palmistry phase.

"Oh, I know all that stuff." Judee giggled impatiently. "Tell me if you see a trip somewhere. Like to the South Seas— Fiji, y'know?"

Well, yes, he thought possibly there was. He found the lines muddled and obscure, with little revealing about them, but he dreamed things up, evoking the inevitable stranger entering her life, happy prospects, the trip she sought, and anything else he could think of to give her pleasure. She beamed, then crowed excitedly, "Hey, gang, c'mere—this guy's fantastic."

The rafts were now empty; Bill and Arco sat side by side on the diving board, still engrossed in their conversation.

"Look at them, aren't they gorgeous?" Judee called to them again. Bill waved, handed his glass to Arco, then stood on the tip of the board and dived.

Judee applauded. "Doesn't he make you want to cream? That body—Arco says it's absolutely the Greek ideal. Oh, God—Arc-o, be careful!"

Having carelessly set the glasses on the diving board, Arco was bouncing up and down. One by one the glasses moved to the edge, then fell into the pool.

"It's okay, I'll get 'em." Willie watched Bill deftly execute an elegant surface dive, his thighs flashing in the turquoise light as he submerged, his body gone quickly dark as he traveled downward. Arco continued jouncing on the board and Willie, suddenly embarrassed by the display of nudity, bent down to dust the toe of his boot.

"Honest," Judee said, "wouldja b'lieve that thing? Everytime he takes it out I want to stick my head in a gas oven." She made a comical face, screwing up her features and widening her mouth into a downward grimace, the Greek

313

mask of tragedy, through which she poked her pink wet tongue; Willie laughed in spite of himself. Meanwhile Arco had sprung off the board in an awkward, leggy dive, and came up looking for Bill, who surfaced behind him, holding the glasses aloft.

"Got 'em!" Together the pair made their way to the coping, where Bill set the glasses down, then they got out of the pool.

"Towels in the cabaña," Willie called to Bill. As he passed, the light played across his bare back and flanks, and Willie noticed red marks and bruises similar to Judee's; some were almost welts. Dripping, Arco had taken Judee's place on the chaise, ignoring Willie's mild remonstrance that he wait for a towel.

"It's okay," he said breezily. Judee took his right hand and presented it for Willie's inspection. Without touching it, Willie looked at it for a long moment. Like Arco's body, it was slim and well made, rather delicate, like a woman's. The nails were long and carefully manicured, the fingers spatulate; the mound of Venus was pronounced, indicating an active sex life. When Willie finally took the hand in his own, it again felt curiously warm, which was strange, since Arco had just come out of the pool. Willie bent it back so the lines showed more clearly. He studied them for some time, aware that Bill had come up from behind with a pile of towels, another nipped around his waist.

"Well?" Arco's eyes, bright and watchful, snapped with nervous concentration. Willie peered into them, then down, then suddenly dropped Arco's hand, pressing it quietly from him and crossing himself.

"Sorry . . ." he muttered, and stood.

"What d'you mean, sorry?" Arco demanded with a perplexed expression. "Something wrong with it?"

"No no no, not at all." Willie caught himself rubbing his palms on his thighs. "It's really silly, isn't it? Judee, I think you're right—it's going to rain." He pretended to be studying the sky. Scowling, Arco jumped up and leaped out into the water.

"Jeez, Willie," Bill said, "you oughtn't to of done that. Why wouldn't you read it?"

"It doesn't matter, really. It's all rather medieval, fortune-telling. No basis in fact whatever." Bill turned away, then took a running start and dived back in the pool, clearing the water with beautiful strokes which quickly brought him to the far end of the pool, where Arco hung on the corner. Then, together, they started swimming back toward the shallow end.

"Arco must be a city boy," Willie observed to Judee.

"From outside Detroit. Howdja know?"

"He's not a very good swimmer. And he dives badly. Bill should give him lessons. . . . He doesn't seem to get much sun, does he?"

"He can't go in the sun—it's bad for his skin. He *never* goes in the sun. Arco, Willie says you should have swimming lessons," she called as he swam by.

Arco stopped and stood waist-deep, his brows still knit. "Oh?"

"I simply said I thought you probably came from the city," Willie explained, "and hadn't much opportunity to swim."

"That's right," Arco returned coolly, wading over to the coping. "Just a poor city boy. They didn't hand out swimming pools in Hamtramck."

"That's where—Hamtramck," Judee said, gulping from her glass.

"Detroit, pops. Where the Polacks come from. Us wops needed a passport to get in."

Judee laughed shrilly, the others joined her, excluding Willie from the moment.

"Why don't you drop your duds and take a dive, Willie?" Arco suggested. Their eyes locked again and Willie saw that he was being dared.

"Sorry, no swimming. I've got"—he couldn't say "gout"; it sounded like an old man's disease—"respiratory troubles," he finished weakly.

"Gee, that's too bad." Arco's sympathetic expression flattened out into mere careful watching. Watching and waiting; this was the impression Willie had.

Then Arco reached from the water and tickled Judee between the legs. "Pussy pussy."

She shrieked with laughter; Willie looked away in embarrassment again.

"C'n I have some more shampoo?" Judee waved her empty glass.

Willie picked up the bottle. "Feel free at any time."

"Put it down," Arco said sternly. Willie's mouth dropped, and he set the bottle back on the table. "Ask again," Arco ordered Judee.

"Please-Arco-may-I-have-some-more-shampoo?" It seemed a sort of child's ritual between them.

"Yes. Then you may take six giant steps." She held her

glass out to Willie; he filled it, and she went marching nude around the pool.

"Hey, let's see your medals," Arco said casually to Willie. "What are they?"

Willie held out the cluster of gold medals on a gold chain around his neck. "This one's Saint Genesius, patron saint of actors, this one's Saint Christopher, that's for travelers. And this," showing a third, "is Saint Dympna."

"That's a new one on me."

"Oh, she's very helpful—patroness of those suffering from nervous distress. This medal has been touched to her relic."

"Where'd you get it?"

"Sent away for it. In *TV Guide.* You mail a coupon."

"I see." Arco appeared interested. He got Willie bending forward from the chaise so he could examine them closer. There was also a gold heart and two keys. "What're they?" Arco demanded.

"A present."

"What're the keys?"

"To my heart."

"Jazzy."

"*I* thought so."

Arco extended his empty glass and Willie tipped the mouth of the bottle to it. From inside came the sound of the telephone. Before he could move to answer it, he found himself being grabbed around the wrist and drawn from his seat. The strength in the small hand, the thin arm, was enormous.

"No—no," he murmured in panic, realizing Arco's intent, but the force was irresistible. The phone continued ringing; he could do nothing. He was dragged to the edge of the pool, forced to step awkwardly around Judee, his protest rising to a quaver, then a cry as he was yanked off balance and tumbled into the water. He glimpsed the pale loins and dark pubic hairs, as first he was submerged, then forcibly held under. The blood was pounding in his throat and ears while a merciless hand bore down on him, he felt a swirl of current and saw Bill's legs thrashing toward him, then sudden release. He shot to the surface, choking.

"Hi, pops." Arco greeted him with a grin. He was holding something in his hand; Willie realized it was his toupee. When he tried to grab it Arco first dangled it out of reach, then flopped it onto his own head, and paddled backward.

"Hell, Arco," Bill shouted, "whadya want to do that for? In all his clothes?" Fuming and sputtering, Willie waded to the steps and bent to wring the knees of his trousers. Judee

316

came running around to help him up, while Arco stood arms akimbo, ludicrous under the wretched toupee. Inside, the phone rang and rang.

"Damn," said Willie. "Damn."

"You okay?" Bill asked. Willie was already stripping off his soaking shirt, fighting down the urge to order Arco from the house. His clothes, his toupee, his boots, the broken Baccarat goblet. No, he told himself, it wouldn't do any good to get mad; better to take it as a joke.

"All right, Arco," he said, wagging a playful finger. "I'll get you for that."

"You're on, pops." Arco tossed the toupee, which whizzed through the air and fell sopping on the deck. Judee retrieved it and stroked it as if it were a pet. The phone stopped ringing, began again.

"Please—*someone* answer the *phone!*" Willie hurried into the cabaña, removed his wet things, and sat shivering on the bench, huddled in a monogrammed bath sheet. Outside he could hear them laughing.

"Did someone get the phone?" he called through the louvered door.

"They hung up," Judee said.

Willie was angry; he hated missing calls. "Bill, would you check the time? I don't want to be late for the TV show."

"Right, Willie."

Silence.

Whispers.

Giggles.

He finished drying himself and put on a robe. He opened the door, then as an afterthought stuck on the little cap that hung from a peg. Along with the cap he stuck on a smile as well, slid his feet into a pair of Japanese *zoris,* and came padding out.

Bill was sprawled on one of the chaises, wrapped in his towel. Arms behind his head, staring at the sky, Arco lay on the diving board, occasionally making it jiggle as he kicked his feet. Siren-like, the girl lounged in the fountain shell, singing, dangling her legs, too short to reach the pool. Willie headed for Bill, and took the adjoining chaise.

"Hey, that's terrific," Bill said of his robe. "Where'd you get it?"

"Bee bought it for me in Marrakech," he said shortly. It was a striped djellabah, with braid around the cuffs of the short sleeves and the low-cut neck.

"And the cap—Morocco, too?"

"No, it's from India. Gypsy Rose Lee gave it to me." The cap was small and round, with small squares and circles of mirror stitched into colorful embroidery.

Willie wished Judee would get out of the fountain; it was badly balanced and could easily be upset. He angled his head away as Arco walked from the diving board onto the grass and stood on his hands.

"It's okay, Willie," Bill said consolingly. "He was just having some fun." He moved beside him, put his hand around his shoulder, and gave his arm a squeeze, then three or four little shakes. "Arco's a real pal. He don't mean nothin'."

Willie stared at his thin arm, saw goose flesh form, lifting the sparse hairs that grew there. He thought for a moment, then turned to Bill. "Listen to me. Your friend Arco—"

"Yes?" Bill persisted.

"Your friend Arco is going to be in a lot of trouble one day."

"Why?"

"He has a very bad hand."

"Aw, c'mon, Willie, you just got finished saying that don't mean anything. It's a lot of crap."

"Nevertheless. I saw it. He's a dangerous person and I'd advise you to be careful unless you want to get in trouble."

Bill started away; Willie caught him by the arm. "Don't say anything, please," he cautioned.

"You think I want to get my head knocked off? Heck. You never seen him when he's really angry." He strode off to where Arco and Judee were horsing around in the fountain. She screamed, he yowled, Bill dashed forward as the stone shell tipped, pitching them into the water while the shell struck the coping, bounced, and dropped like a cannonball into the pool. As it settled to the bottom, water from the broken fountain pipe shot into the air against the darkened sky. Willie ran behind the cabaña to turn the valve off, then hurried back. Judee was climbing up the pool ladder while Arco stood looking at the cracked coping. In the glimmering light his flesh was pale as a piece of marble statuary, as if his veins had been opened and drained of their blood. Bill sat beside Willie and hung his heavy arm over his shoulder again. "Hey, pardner, c'mon—you're so nervous. Relax, okay?"

"Okay."

Drunk, he still felt tense, stiff as a board, as if he might shatter, break. He drank from his glass in long gulps, thinking what did it matter, he might as well be plastered. He leaned and whispered into Bill's ear.

318

"I want him to go."

"Why, Willie?" Bill asked gently.

"I don't . . . like him."

"Why?"

"He scares me."

"Hey, man." Bill exerted a greater pressure, gripping Willie's wrist with his other hand, making encouraging little movements. "Hey, man . . . hey, man." Uncomforted, Willie lifted his face to the darkened sky as the first drops of rain spattered the pool. In the yellow garden lights the nude figures looked bizarrely unreal as the palm trunks reached their swaying shadows across them to bleed again into the darkness. Their leaves trembled and whispered, and Willie imagined for an instant that the sound was like the whisper of the wings that death flies on; he felt afraid.

"Hey, man," Bill said, cradling him, "hey man . . ."

The room, for the moment, appeared deserted; but that was only the room, and only Willie's way of looking at it. In the dimly reflecting planes of mirror it seemed he could make out the truer sense of the place, those remembered figures and images, woozy and half-realized fantasy shapes, that once had brought it life, where people, music, conversation, flowers carefully arranged, food lavishly provided, gave it breadth and sweep and animation; but all these, he saw, were only shadows of that past which had died with Bee's death, were gone, never to come again. He hiccuped, then glimpsed a quick flash of movement, and looked to see the girl's elfin face—her name was forgotten again—peer down at him.

"Hi, sweetie. Feelin' better? Gee, didn't it rain some?"

As far as Willie Marsh was concerned, the last two hours or more had been a washout even before the rain began. His plan for the group to watch the TV broadcast of *The Player Queen* on *Classic Movies* was spoiled, since Bill remained out in the lanai barbecuing hot dogs, while Arco wandered around the room making a careful inventory of the memorabilia, and Judee, in a terry-cloth robe from the cabaña, curled cutely like a movie ingenue on the sofa, interrupted the picture a dozen times with questions and comments. A fire smoldered in the grate; the logs were damp. Bill popped in at polite intervals and caught a look, though Willie could tell he wasn't greatly interested. Arco had called him, and they initiated a game of darts while the hot dogs overcooked. They ate, finally, watching the last reel, a form of silence which might have passed for boredom, and even Willie had found himself unabashedly yawning. So much for *The Player Queen*. The rain ended, a quick summer storm, but it leaked and dripped from every palm frond, and night fog had rolled in from Santa Monica, reducing the glimmering city view to a murky blur. When Willie turned off the set Judee wanted to put more records on. She patted his mirrored cap and told him he sure used to be a handsome fellow when he was young, and took Arco to dance, her platforms clattering like sabots, he moving lithely, balletically, the way a cat would; too feline, Willie thought, for a man.

Spread across the glass-topped coffee table was the litter of the improvised meal, with the half-chewed ends of hot dog rolls and mustardy napkins and smears of red ketchup and curled watermelon pickle. Wet horseshoe-shaped marks had crushed the nap of the velvet chair seats that someone had thoughtlessly lounged on in a damp towel, and the dogs had torn apart one of the velvet sofa pillows, in which Arco had playfully tucked their rubber toy.

Idly, dizzily, Willie again wished that they would go, but no one took the hint of his elaborate yawns. Bill clumped back and forth to the bar, bringing more champagne and other drinks; Willie didn't know what they were, didn't care. A good deal more pot had been smoked; the room still reeked of cannabis. More pills of undisclosed prescription had been swallowed. After a while the other two stopped dancing and disappeared, he had no idea where. Then Bill, too, was unseen for a time; Willie wasn't sure, but he had an idea they were investigating other parts of the house. He felt too weak to remonstrate; everything seemed vague, remote. It was almost as if a spell had been cast over the place, though whether of enchantment or evil he could not tell. Vague currents of emotions swirled through the room, intangible feelings whose sources he could not trace or identify.

The girl came clattering back on her platforms, swinging her hips in a campy trollop's slouch she called her "trash walk," one hand on a hip, the fingers of the other spiraling her frizzed mop of hair. "Ya look all strung out, sweetie—are ya depressed?" She stopped and tickled him; he cried out sharply, moved back. He hated being tickled; it was painful to him.

She sat beside him, touching his hand. She smelled of a familiar scent: she had been upstairs at Bee's vanity table.

"You're using a dead woman's perfume," he told her.

"Ooh," she squeaked in her child's treble. "I don't like to

think about death. It makes me all squirrely inside. I like to think about living; it's so much nicer, isn't it?" She cuddled closer to him, as though for her own comfort.

"Yes. Yes, it is," he agreed solemnly. Someone approached across the floor, a large, loping hulk, heels scraping on the tiles.

"Ah, Bill, where've you been?"

"We wuz jes' havin' a look at the pitchers in the dinin' room. You havin' a good time?"

"Cert'nly am."

"Sure?"

"Sure."

"Really sure?"

"Really sure." In his djellabah and embroidered cap Willie felt a little exotic, raffish even.

Bill flipped out and pointed his finger pistols—*choo choo*—gunning down his image in a mirror, reholstered them, moved away again. On the TV screen was a silent graphic shot of a family group; the caption read: "Parents—do you know where your children are tonight?" Judee flopped off the Marion Davies sofa and went to join Bill and Arco at the aquariums. Willie closed his eyes, the room turned inside his head. Why wasn't Norma Shearer here tonight? Irene Selznick? Bill Holden, Roz, Junior Fairbanks? Where were Willie Wyler, Billy Wilder and Audrey? "Sing something, Judy," he murmured, meaning Garland, but it was the two *e*'s who giggled.

Opening his eyes again, he saw their blurred heads clustered together, dark against the brightly lighted fish tanks, with blue-green and gold reflections tossed to the ceiling and back again, subaqueous figures in an undersea cave, their faces now in profile, now turned away, huddled, ostensibly watching the fish, and they might have been fish themselves, undulant, slow-moving in the room, and brightly decorative. Willie envied them their easy rapport, their casual interchange of affection, their . . . trio-ness, no point of which could be breached by him, for that would make a square.

"Ol' square," he mumbled, resetting the embroidered cap on his head.

"Hey, Willie—c'mere." Someone was asking the names of the fish; he rose unsteadily and went to supply some: zebras, white clouds, sailfin mollies, blue tetras.

"No piranhas?" Arco had heard of a man who kept piranhas in a pool in his garden, "and if you stick your hand in all you'd get back is a mess of bones."

Willie paused uncertainly, weaving in the light, watching

with a stuporous expression. Drunk himself, he found it difficult to tell just how high on drugs Arco was. "Piranhas can be dangerous. Wouldn't recommend them for around the house."

Arco was half turned away, the marblelike planes of his face absorbing light from the tanks as he watched the fish with fierce concentration. It came to Willie then, the image he had been seeking. Arco reminded him of one of those Zurbarán figures of churchly piety that the Prado Museum is full of, those darkly brooding, saintly figures which seem to glow with an inner incandescence, a trick of the painter's art. Arco had the look of the ascetic whose intensity of expression verged on the fanatical, an almost holiness of purpose; was it merely about buying an island in the Pacific in order to go pick coconuts?

His eyes trailed a fish as it lazed through a pink stone castle, fanning the silvery membranes of its tail. Now he slid aside a pane of glass on the top of the tank, his hand flashed, dipped into the water, and he scooped up the fish and brought it out squirming in his palm.

"Hey, Wimp."

"No," Willie said. "Put it back."

"Sure sure, just want to see something." He held the fish out to Judee, who stared uncomprehendingly. "Eat it, Jude."

She gave a nervous little laugh; her hand fluttered to her breast.

"It's alive, Arco—"

"I know. Swallow it. I want to see something."

"Put it back," Willie protested again. Without looking, Arco fended him off with his elbow.

"Do it, Wimp." His voice was quiet, level, but with a core of steely authority. He held the quivering fish closer, and her eyes started. There was a moment's indecision, then she put her head back and opened her mouth wide. Arco slid the fish inside. She closed her mouth, and clutched her throat as she swallowed. Then her smile returned, her eyes danced, and she flung herself away, holding her stomach and screeching shrilly as she turned round and round.

"Ooh—Arco, I can feel it—it's wriggling." Her hand moved upward and downward, examining the sensation. "Ooh! Ooh!" she cried in little spurts of newly discovered joy. "It's jumping around. What a trip!"

"See?" Arco said. "Anytime you want a trip, call me."

"Oh, Arco, you're such a crazy person!" She found a glass and took to washing the fish down in gulps of champagne.

Eventually she and Bill drifted away and began dancing in the far, shadowy corner, she lolling languorously against him and dragging her shoes noisily, neck arched in a white line, pelvis thrusting in and upward at him, he moving with a pathetic lack of rhythm and the proverbial grace of the bull in the china shop. Willie feared for his bibelots.

Weaving, swaying, he watched Arco as he passed along the wall, reviewing several paintings—the Buffet, the Cadmus drawing, the Bemelmans gouache of a nun's face under a starched wimple and flying headdress—then moving farther along to take in the carved figures mounted on square pedestals on either side of the fireplace.

"Where'd you get them?" he asked, flopping into a chair.

"They came out of the MGM auction. Church figures. Very old."

"Quattrocento?" Again, the mocking insinuation.

"We really don't know, but they've been authenticated by the museum. They probably came out of some cathedral in Italy. We think they're very beautiful. *Gl'Italiani sono grandi amanti della bellezza.*"

" 'Italians are great lovers of beauty'—yes, pizza parlors with plaster flamingos on the lawns." He crossed his knee and made himself comfortable, lighting up a fresh joint and inhaling the smoke.

"Why did you leave the seminary?" Willie asked.

"Discipline, man, discipline. I mean they've got the whole thing worked out. They didn't like me much."

"Why not?"

"Said I was a troublemaker." He inhaled deeply, held the smoke down, his face growing red as he talked on his stifled breath.

"Why?"

"Asked questions. All the time I was asking questions. And they had no answers."

"The Church has an answer for everything."

"Oh?" He swung his leg over the chair arm and dangled it indolently. "Possibly they do. 'You must believe,' they said. 'Believe what?' I asked. 'What we tell you,' they said. 'How can I know it's right?' I asked. 'Because we tell you,' they said." He smoked in silence, taking deep drags, his puffs eating up the tobacco, and when he had finished he wet the end of the roach and popped it into his mouth. He swallowed it, winked at Willie. "Better than live fish." They both turned as through the chapel doors a sudden blast sounded from the organ, setting the crystal ornaments on the tables to rattling.

This was followed by some tentative pickings at the keys, then a few bars of a song, then the sound of Judee's sand-papery voice, singing.

" 'My mama done tol' meee' "—*bump*—" 'when I was in knee pa-a-ants' "—*bump*—Each *bump* was an accented chord, played slightly off key.

"Ridiculous," Willie muttered, struggling to rise; his feet had gone painfully to sleep. "That's not proper music for a chapel."

When Judee had completed the eight bars, she began again. " 'My mama done tol' meee' "—*bump*—" 'when I was in knee pa-a-ants' "—*bump*—

Arco got up, clapped Willie on the shoulder, silencing his protests. "What's the difference?" he said, steering him to the bar. Bill appeared, then joined them. Arco jerked his head toward the chapel.

"What's the Wimp doing in there?"

"Havin' fun."

Arco turned to Willie. "See? Havin' fun, that's all. No harm." Passing it off, he sat the still muttering Willie down on a stool and poured him a Scotch and water. Willie didn't take it, so Arco placed his fingers around the glass and held it to his lips. Willie drank.

" 'My mama done tol' meee' "—*bump*—

Arco cupped his hands and shouted, "Cool it, Wanda Landowska."

Judee paid no attention, started over. Arco's look darkened.

"It's quite all right, really," Willie said. "If it amuses her. She's young; maybe she'll improve." He drank, and twirled the cubes in his glass. "Heigh-ho. *'Si jeunesse savait, si vieillesse pouvait,'* eh?" He gave Bill a broad wink. Arco's frown remained.

"What's that mean?" Bill asked.

" 'If youth but knew, if age but could.' "

"Could what?"

"He means if he could get it up," Arco snorted. Willie seemed suddenly to have wilted; his hand fell into his lap, he slid sideways against the bar. Arco signaled to Bill, who tried to prop him up. "You okay, Willie?"

" 'Kay," Willie mumbled, opening his eyes. " 'M okay."

"Listen—remember what you said you were gonna do f'r me?"

"Do? Do?"

"Doo doo doo," Arco muttered under his breath, drumming his fingers on the bar.

"You're gonna give me that autographed pitcher, huh? T' start m' collection, pardner?"

"Picture . . ." Willie mouthed wordlessly, blinking at him. He sat up, suddenly aware again. "Yes. Course. I 'member." He went to a box on a shelf, slipped out an eight-by-ten glossy, brought it back to the bar and showed it. "This will do?" He went behind the bar and opened a drawer. He found a pen among a jumble of things and began writing across the bottom of the photograph in a wildly florid script: *"To Bill . . ."* "Last name? Forget it . . ." Bill gave it again. *"Bowie. Handsome is as handsome does. I have nothing but the highest faith in your star. Affectionately, Willie Marsh."* He slid it along the bar to Bill, who held it out and read the words.

"Goldarn, that's right nice. I really 'prishate it."

"S'all right, m'dear."

"Don't call him your dear." Arco's words came out in a tightly controlled threat.

Willie shrugged. "Jus' 'n expression, that's all. Doesn't mean anything."

"Fuck it doesn't." Arco's voice had gone suddenly ugly. He grabbed the photograph; Bill tried to take it, but Arco held it away. "I'm not going to hurt it," he said, keeping it at arm's length and studying it. "Long time ago, huh, Willie?"

"It was taken by a studio photographer."

Arco laughed harshly. "Man, you haven't worked at a studio in—how long's it been?"

"I'm . . . semiretired."

"Bet your ass you're retired. Washed up, is what you are." He made a motion as if to tear the picture in half, then laughed again and handed it to Bill. "Okay, jasper, stick it up in the bathroom where you can look at it every morning while you crap." He snapped the words out crisply; Willie stared in amazement, trying to accommodate the swift, volatile alteration of personality. Arco hunched his narrow shoulders, looking like a small but dangerous animal. His hand shot suddenly out, collaring Bill and pulling him to him. He grasped his face between his hands and forced it in front of Willie, who cowered back on his stool. "You see him, Willie? You see him? You want to know about him? He's bad, Willie. You watch out for Bill Bowie. He's a killer."

"Aw, c'mon, Arco—" Bill protested, trying to extricate himself, but the small, strong hands held him fast.

"He's a killer, Willie," he repeated. "You want to know what he's come here for? He's come to rob you. That's right —rob you. It's a fact." He suddenly released Bill, who jerked away, rubbing his head where Arco's fingers had gripped him. Arco leaned and placed his hands on Willie's knees. "But don't you worry, Little Willie. Arco's here. And you know why he's here, Willie?"

The older man shook his head, understanding nothing of it.

"He's here to save you, Willie," he said, bringing his face closer and speaking very softly. "Arco's here, and he'll save you. From what? Ask me from what, Willie."

"Fr'm what?" he said blandly.

"From yourself, Willie. I'm going to save you from yourself." He reared back on his stool in a wildly uncontrolled burst of laughter, then slapped Willie's knee again. "Hey, man, don't look so scared. Where's your sense of humor?"

Willie looked around uncertainly. "You said . . . rob me."

"I meant your izzat, Willie. You mustn't ever let anybody rob you of your izzat, see. It's all a man has."

"You mean—all a joke?"

"Sure, just a joke." The ugly menace had disappeared and in its place was the shining smile, the sparkling eyes. Relieved, almost pleased, Willie grinned from one to the other as Arco leaned back cozily and drew Bill to him, his small pale arm circling his waist. Judee reappeared, singing. " 'My mama done tol' meee . . .' " She put her hands behind her head and did a stripper's grind. "*Bump!* What's all the ruckus, gang?" she asked. "It's not gonna be one of *those* nights, is it?"

"Jesus, don't you know another song?" Arco whirled on her and raised his hand; she ducked past him with a frightened look and moved behind Bill for protection.

"C'mon, c'mon, no fights t'night, huh?" Bill pleaded.

Arco laughed. "Wimp, if you're going to do that number you've got to learn the bridge." Then suddenly they were all laughing again; it seemed to be a game they were playing. Willie didn't understand, couldn't keep up with it all. He slumped against the bar, closed his eyes, ran his fingers over his forehead. Someone whispered something; someone else giggled. There was complicity in the room. He didn't care; let them have their fun, their childish games. Crazy people, they were all crazy people. He shrugged; he was beyond the games, outside it all, just trying to be a good host. He opened his eyes, looked around at the mess. Styleless, graceless, witless. He glimpsed his face in a mirror: scarlet spots had sprung on his cheeks, circles like those painted on a toy soldier's face; his nose seemed larger, redder, a toper's nose. He became aware of Bill standing behind him, massaging his shoulders and neck.

"How's that feel?"

He nodded and let his head loll.

Arco was playing darts. Willie watched for some moments, then clinked his glass on the bar. "How izzat, Arco?"

"Hm?" His hand stopped in midair; he glanced at Willie, who wiggled his fingers playfully.

"How izzat? I said. How izzat?"

"Izzat?" His brow furrowed again, the dart poised beside his head.

"Yes, izzat? How izzat—you know izzat."

"Willie . . ." Bill began warningly.

"No no no," Arco said easily, "it's okay. He's just joking, aren't you, Willie?"

Willie winked at Judee. "Jus' joking. Izzat okay?" He swiveled on his stool, back and forth. Then, " 'I'd like to get you on a slow boat to Fiji,' " he sang, wagging his head idiotically.

"What's that supposed to mean?" Arco tossed a dart lightly; it struck the cork board with a thunk.

"I hear you're goin' to Fiji, tha's all." He sang, tapping rhythm with two fingers on the bar top: " 'I've got an island, in the Pacific . . .' "

Bill flashed another glance, shook his head; Willie snickered wetly and continued: " 'And ev'rything about it is t'rrific.' T'rrrific. I'n that right, Arco? I hear the island's ab-so-lutely terrific. Fish and poi and all that crap."

Arco said nothing, tossed two darts in quick succession. Willie continued his needling. "Two kinds of people in the world, Arco—the haves and the have-nots. That puts you on the other side, don't it? The have-nots?"

"Guess it does, Willie." Plunk; another dart.

"And there's another kind. Givers and takers. You're not a giver, Arco, you're a taker, no matter what you pr'fess t' these poor be—benighted . . . izzats." Arco's dart whizzed through the air, struck the board. Watching his reflection in a mirror, Bill gathered back his hair and secured it with a girl's ponytail elastic he had taken from his pocket, and slicked the loose ends over his ears. Willie drank his drink. Then, giggling again, he said:

"I understand you're an actor, Arco." Arco looked at him; Willie smirked over his glass. "That true?"

"Right, Willie. To be or not to be, all that crap."

Willie laughed stuporously. "Pretty good, kiddo. 'To Bee or not to Bee.'" He pointed to the framed Porter lyric on the wall. "Story of my life. What movies you been in?"

"Lots."

"Which ones?" Willie persisted doggedly, swaying on his stool. Arco snapped his fingers. "Hey, Wimp, get my bag over there." She clopped across to get the shoulder-strap bag, carried it back, and he took it onto his lap, unzipping one of the side compartments.

"Naw, naw—" Bill began, leaning across the bar with his hand. Arco knocked it aside and began laying out pictures on the black Formica.

"Come here, Willie, have a look at these."

"Aw, Arco . . ." Bill whined.

Willie only smiled inanely, shrugged, remained on his stool.

"Willie. Here." The two words snapped out like a dog's command were sufficient to bring the older man to a position where he could view the pictures.

"Aw, c'mon." Blushing, Bill protested, tried to cover them with his hands, "He don't want to see those."

"Sure he does, jasper." Arco's voice had a coaxing allure in it. Judee giggled, and inched forward; Willie could feel her warm breath on his neck. "He's old enough, aren't you, Willie?" His fingers gripped the back of Willie's skull, directing his look. "Here's some stills from our latest flick. See? Arco, Bill, and Judee. Hot stuff, huh? You can see why they call him 'Pistol Bill,' the hot rod. Ladykiller, y'know? Really shoots 'em with that."

"Very interesting. Judee, you're extremely photogenic. Bill, too. Sorry about that nose, Arco, it looks like it might get in the way of your work." He glanced again at the trio of nude bodies in the pictures, then turned away.

"You ever seen a skin flick, Willie?" Arco asked.

"Cert'nly."

"I don't mean soft-core—I mean the real hard stuff."

"Cert'nly. I'm not a child, you know."

"That you're not, Willie, that you're not. Are you still young enough to get it up? *Si vieillesse pouvait?* Tell you what I'll do. If the price is right, I'll let you have your pick—either one."

Willie stared at him, shook his head, not understanding.

"You can have either one—or both, if you can manage it. How's that? Up to you." He seized the back of Willie's head again and forced him to look, first at Bill, then at Judee.

"They're both up for grabs, Willie. What d'you say—Judee the Wimp or Pistol Bill?"

"Arco, knock it off."

"Shut up, jasper. Well, old-timer, what about it? Hot stuff or not?"

"Bill, I really think—" Willie tried to extricate himself from Arco's grasp.

"If I say so, they've got to." Staring in the mirror, Willie saw the grim smile, saw him watching; lowered his eyes. "That's how it works. Right, Wimp?" She murmured something and ducked her head. "Right, buddy?" Bill only shrugged helplessly. "Jasper, I'm talking to you."

"Right," he mumbled in an embarrassed tone.

Arco wandered away to the card table and picked up a manuscript page of "Salad Days."

Willie waved his arm. "Leave that alone, please."

"Say, this stuff's go-o-od, Willie, you know that?" From his mocking tone, Arco didn't think it good at all.

"You'll get them mixed up. M'autobigraphy . . . Put 't down—" He had difficulty getting off his stool, spun, and fell against the girl. Arco came back, resuming a measure of geniality. His former fierceness had melted again; he was sunny as morning. Willie sat, leaning his head on his hand. Someone had turned up the music. Judee was dancing by herself. Bill was watching Arco, as though for some cue. Nothing more was mentioned about their leaving. Again there were little fleeting currents ebbing and flowing, whose tensions Willie couldn't follow. His hiccups came back. Judee made him put his hands over his head and hold his breath. Then she got him to take gulps of water; he continued hiccuping. Arco and Bill had begun Indian wrestling. It seemed impossible to Willie that that small, wiry arm should be possessed of such strength. It held its own for some time against the larger one, the two hands tightly clutched, fingers laced, trembling with vibrations that shot all along the tendons and muscles. At last, the greater strength prevailed as Bill's shoulder hunched forward, slightly shifting the angle of torque, and Arco's arm quivered, then surrendered under the pressure. With gasps they unsprung their grip and fell back at opposite sides of the bar, panting. Judee clapped and bounced and leaned to kiss Bill's ear.

"Ver' good, m'boy," Willie congratulated Bill.

Arco's eye wavered thoughtfully between Willie and Bill. Then, as if just noticing, he musingly said to Bill:

"What's the rubber band for, jasper?"

"Hey, you know. Keeps the hair out of m'eyes."

"I don't like it." The words came out in a muted snarl.

"Okay, okay." He undid the band, shook his head, and the blond locks fell about his face. Arco leaned back on his stool, scrutinizing the effect like an artist studying his model. Something seemed to displease him. "Christ, you're a mess," he said contemptuously.

"Aw, c'mon, buddy, knock it off."

A pause; then, quietly: "What? What's that?" he questioned with subtle menace. "You telling me to knock it off? Knock what off?"

"Never mind." Bill fell silent.

"No. I *do* mind. I mind a *lot*. Let's talk about it. What is it you want me to knock off, jasper? Mm?" Bill said nothing; Arco's fingers gripped his arm. "I asked you a question, jasper, I want an answer. Remember? *I* ask, *you* answer."

I think we ought to go," Judee interrupted quickly. "I think we ought to go right now. Before—"

"Before what?" Arco's eyes dared her to move. She sat again, biting her lip and hugging her waist. "You know what I think, Willie?" Arco continued, with a mixture of elaborate deference to the older man. "I think we've got a troublemaker here. Here we are, having a nice time, and this jasper wants to make trouble."

"Come on, Arco," Bill protested, "f'r chrissakes. What'd we come here for?"

"Shut up." Releasing his arm, he gripped a handful of Bill's hair, then slowly sifted it through his fingers, examining it.

"You know what I think . . . ?" It began as a casual, off-hand notion. Bill tried again to free himself, but Arco's fingers dug into his hair and held him. "I think . . . we ought to . . ."

Bill's eyes rolled fearfully, the look of a trapped animal. "C'mon, buddy—"

"No, no, wait. I think we ought to—"

"Jesus, Arco, not again."

"Yes . . . I think so . . . Definitely . . . I definitely think we ought to cut your hair." Bill balked and reared back, pulling Arco from his stool. Long strands of hair hung from his fingernails. Taking the scene as another joke, Willie laughed foolishly. Judee seized his arm with fearful intensity.

"Got some scissors, Willie?"

Willie pointed to a drawer in the back bar. Arco yanked it

out, upturned its contents on the bar. Tools fell out—screwdriver, hammer, pliers, boxes of tacks and nails, a roll of electrician's tape, and among all of it, a large pair of shears. Arco took them up, making test snips in the air. "Yes," he said mildly, "they'll do." His face had flushed. He breathed through his open mouth; his eyes gleamed.

He handed the shears to Judee, who pulled away.

"Take them."

She read his expression and took them.

"Bill?" He spoke the name lightly, Bill's features drew taut, the muscles in his jaws jumped as he slowly came and stood submissively in front of Arco, who pointed downward. Bill knelt slowly, as a dog does, resistant to unwelcome training.

Willie put out a protesting hand. "No. You can't."

"Be quiet."

"Not in m'house . . ."

"It may be your house, sir, but they're my kids. They do what I tell them." He nodded to Judee, who whimpered and pouted as she came to him.

"Arco—do I have to?"

Without replying, he crossed his arms over his chest and waited. She made a few tentative snips at the ends of Bill's hair and looked up timidly. Arco shook his head.

"More."

With a little sigh she began in earnest, working neatly, sliding the ends of the hair between her second and third fingers and shearing them off blunt.

"I didn't say give him a styling," Arco told her coldly. "I said *cut it off.*" He snatched the scissors, pushing her aside; he bent over Bill, who remained mute, kneeling in a penitential attitude, hands clasped at his loins, presenting the broad nape of his neck and the blond crown of his head. Snip snip, went the scissors, their steel blades glinting in the light. Willie was quivering with fascination; he seemed to view the scene through a glaze, his vision smeared by drink and emotion. His arms and legs began to shake, and he seized his thighs to quiet them. It was ceremonial—dreadful, wasteful, sadistic, but nonetheless ceremonial. Once only Arco paused, glanced sideways at him, then returned to his labors. There was the hoarse sound of his nasal breathing; the only movement from the kneeling figure came as, hair falling on his shoulders, down his back, his fingers unclasped and he grasped his thighs, the tendons in the backs of his hands working as he clutched himself. Then it was done. Arco stepped back, Bill raised his head. Willie turned his eyes away from the look of passionate submission he read there. Arco tossed the scissors onto the bar.

"Get up," he ordered. Bill rose and stared at the hair littering the floor. His hands came up to feel the damage. His hair, brutally hacked, hung unevenly. In silence he used the scissors before a panel of mirror and began evening the ends. The others remained seated on their stools. Nobody said anything.

Someone had been playing with the light switches, and dim beams cast random pools of illumination in the grottolike darkness, glinting among the chandelier prisms, striking the crystal and the murky mirrors. Willie finished his drink, made himself another, and crossed the room to sit down on the sofa. The portrait of Bee smiled down, caught in the golden rays of the gallery lamp over the frame. Willie closed his eyes, rested his head back. When he opened them she was still there, smiling. He wished she would go away; wished they would all go away.

"You got yourself in, Billyboy," the portrait seemed to say, "now get yourself out."

Bee was always saying that. He began talking back to her, something he had rarely done while she lived, muttering words, phrases, to which she listened, smiling, always smiling. Spectrally, out of the darkness, Arco once more materialized. Willie dropped his eyes, with an uncomfortable flutter of his lids. He was half sprawled on the sofa; Arco took the chair on his right, then Judee came and slid into the one on his left. She leaned to pat his hand. He was still muttering, talking disjointedly.

"What's that you say, old-timer?" Arco asked. Willie couldn't remember. His mind was not working properly. Thoughts came and went, elusively; he tried to catch the tail of one and attach it to the head of another, and failed. Still he talked, rambling on about Bee. There was something he wanted to say—to tell them. He couldn't say it very well, but it was there, had been there, and it wanted to come out. It came out in scarcely cogent, half-realized spurts . . . dribs and drabs. He'd gone past his limit. Too many Scotches, trouble thinking . . . difficult. But . . . wanted to say it . . . Held his glass up to the portrait with a glazed, mouth-drooping expression.

" 'S Bee. Queen Bee. Lady Bee. She ran the hive. Buzz buzz buzz. All the other bees swarmed, Bee sat and waited for the honey. Honeybee. Honey Bee. Hi, honey Bee." He shook his head dumbly, wiped his wet mouth, wiped his hand on his robe. "See, it was this way. Mama, she said let's get out of here, let's us get out of Al'bama. We got. Little Willie 'n the bes' of sashes. All dressed up for show biz. Mama knew how." He waved his glass foolishly at the picture. "Di'n'tcha, Mama?" His bleary eye skewed to Arco, then to Judee, who sat quietly observing him. "Tell you something. Smart lady, Bee. Knew how to get th' world by the tail, twist it up, and tickle its ass. Ver' religious person. Not originally, y'un'er-stand. Recent vintage. Tell you a secret. . . ." He drew in a deep breath and held it, his head weaving, mouth agape, eyes blank on the picture.

"What's your secret, Willie?" Judee asked.

He blinked at her. "Nice Wimp. Sweet Wimp. Dumb Wimp. Poor dumb bitch. Mother left you in a shopping cart. Mine never lef' me for an instant—not one. On the road, she traveled with me. Took a suite, she had the next room. G'night, Billyboy, come to tuck me in, safe an' sound. 'L'il Willie in the best of pajamas.' *With* monogram—here." He stabbed his left breast. "Alexander Shields, silk pajamas. Bet you never saw silk pajamas. I wear 'em. Bee picked 'em out. Bee picked everything out. Pick pick pick." He tugged at the gold chain around his neck.

"What're the keys for?" Arco asked again.

"Told you—key to my heart." He sniggered.

"Secret heart? What's the secret, Willie?" Arco prompted from his chair.

"Secret? . . . Yes, secret, Mama Bee. Buzz buzz." He pursed his dry lips, seemed to gather himself together into a semblance of momentary lucidity. "Was this way. I once had a passion. Not a perf'ctly grand passion . . . nor necessarily normal one . . . but for someone who hadn't had any passion at all it was enough. Sweet are the uses of perversity, as they say." He hiccuped. "But Bee—buzz buzz buzz—could not approve. Wouldn't have it. I had to lie, cheat, make up things. But a ride on the Grand Canal by moonlight . . . gon-dola . . . what's blacker than a Venetian gondola? I sneaked around in gondolas, she pretended not to know. But she did. Said it would kill her. I gave up the passion, of course. Had to, for her. But. Here's the secret. She did it to make sure that for the rest of her life—and after—*now*—that wherever I might love, whomever, I would feel guilty."

He seemed to have collapsed in upon himself, a small shriveled nut-brown figure, ridiculous and pathetic in his robe and mirrored cap, clutching his glass. His nose ran, and his eyes. He maundered on, alluding to escapades, license, thrills of his youth, all of which had received the cold water Bee had dashed on them; she had been like a fireman, extinguishing every threatening flame. Though she wore no apron she had kept him on tightly tied strings. And . . . "And"—he shrugged again, hopelessly—"when Bee was at the door, love flew out the window. Why should a person feel guilty about love? Can you explain it to me?" He leaned forward, entreating them. Judee shook her head mutely, softly crying; Arco observed him with a sleepy, half-lidded look.

"That's too bad, old-timer," he said at last. "She really had you by the balls."

Willie nodded sorrowfully, and put his index finger up to make a point. "But, you see, long before she died she made sure that there'd always be a lady in th' house. Hostess, as 'twere."

"Who?" Arco asked.

"Laguna Lil." He raised his glass again. "Here's to crime, and here's to Laguna Lil."

"Who's Laguna Lil?"

"Told you. Lady of the house."

Arco came suddenly alert. "She home?"

"She's *always* home."

Arco glanced at Judee. Willie had struggled up from the sofa, draining the dregs from his glass. Approaching the mantel, he let his hand caress the funerary urn. "Hi, dearest. Dearest mum. Mummy. Mommee. Here's your l'il Billyboy, drunk again." He looked over at the others. "Bee di'n't approve of drinking. Mama"—looking at the portrait, then at the others, wobbling backward to make the introduction— "that's Judee with two *e*'s, you can call her the Wimp, ever'body does, and tha's Arco. Watch out f'r Arco, Mama," he added slyly. "He's tricky."

"Aw, c'mon, Willie." Arco had risen and was grinning at him, his voice gently coaxing as he came toward him. "Hey. Hey, listen. Bill was telling me about this present you got," he began.

Willie stood weaving, holding his empty glass, blinking and peering at him. "Present?"

"Some—uh—" He was trying to remember. "Mirror? I think Bill said Fedora gave it to you. That right, Bill?" Bill didn't answer. "*That right,* Bill?" he snapped out.

"Yeah. Right." Bill looked over from the bar, where he sat smoking a joint.

"La Fedora," Willie mumbled, his *zoris* making light clapping sounds against his bare heels as he moved away from

Arco to the armoire. He adjusted the volume, then began dancing by himself.

"Willie?" Arco came after him, his voice soft, casual, yet insistent. "This mirror . . ."

"Mirror, mirror, on th' wall . . ." He was making drunken, outlandish, dipping circles. "Who's the fairest . . ." Withdrawing from Arco again, he continued executing a series of turns, holding the glass away from his robe, his feet describing erratic patterns on the tile squares. "Mirror, mirror, on the wall . . ." he began again.

"Right." Arco followed, motioning curtly to Judee, who closed in from the other side, and together they moved with Willie across the floor.

"Who's the fairest—"

"Of them all. You are, Willie." Judee tapped his shoulder and he stopped. Hands clasped behind her, she raised herself on tiptoe and demurely pecked his cheek with her lips. "You're cute, sweetie," she told him. "I'd sure like to see this mirror."

"Mirror," he repeated dumbly.

"You got it around?" Arco had appeared suddenly before him; Willie drew back, then waved his hand airily.

" 'S in the safe."

"Oh, yeah?" Arco said interestedly. "In the safe?"

Willie danced a few more steps. "Locked up. V'expensive." They followed.

"I bet it is. Where's the safe, Willie?"

"Around." He moved away; they came after him.

"Around where?"

Willie shrugged and wagged his head again. "Here there, up down, over under, in out." His head protruded on his withered neck, he peered at Arco with a sudden roguish look before dancing off again. "Jus' around . . ."

"Wouldn't you let us have a look?" Arco pursued him.

Willie stopped suddenly and they collided; Willie eyed him with an angry stare. *"No."* The word popped out abruptly, defiantly. He wheeled, spilling his melted ice cubes, then did a ludicrous little step, slid on the wet tile, and fell. Miraculously, the glass remained unbroken.

"Hurt yourself?" Arco knelt solicitously at his side.

"I'm . . . awright." He angrily yanked his arm away, rolled over, squatted, then came abruptly to his feet.

Arco got up and pressed close to his side, still grinning. "Don't you want to show us the mirror?"

Blinking, Willie brought his face close, then pulled it back.

"Just realized who you look like," he said, giggling foolishly. "Know who you look like, Arco? Jolly Roger."

"Who's Jolly Roger?"

"You know. Pirate flag. Skull 'n' crossbones. That's what you look like—skull 'n' crossbones."

"Sure, sure, Willie. But don't you want to show us the mirror?"

"Show and tell," Willie said. "I'll show you mine if you show me yours. Judee—bring it here and show me. Hear that, Mama, l'il Willie's talkin' dirty. Right durty, ain't ah, Mama?" He lapsed into a broad Southern dialect. "Mama and Tallulah both wuz Al'bama girls. Sen'tor Bankhead wuz a friend of Granddaddy's. Hello, dahlings," he said in the Bankhead parody, trailing off into the famous laugh. "*Bah* hah-hah-hah-hah. Bee, darling, Judee, dahling, fellow dahlings, it's sho-o-owtime. Le's bring her on—ol' Laguna Lil."

Arco muttered something unintelligible, then motioned Judee with his head. She closed in on Willie again and wound her arms around his neck. "Hi, han'some." She pulled him close and danced with him. She whispered in his ear; he giggled. She brought her mouth around and kissed him lightly; he kissed her back, then stared blankly at her, as if at a stranger. "Your face keeps changing," he said. "Everything keeps changing." She murmured something, and touched her lips to his again, forcing them open, inserting her tongue. The dance became a struggle, they scuffled together. He pulled his head back, she closed on it with her mouth; he tried to free himself, while her arms tightened around him, still moving in the dance. He thrust her from him and shrank back, wiping his lips. "Get away from me, you little freak!" As she came at him again he whipped up his hand and slapped her. He stepped forward, with some blind intention in mind, then staggered back. His momentum propelled him in reverse across the floor, narrowly missing a table, then a chair, until he had got to a small coffee table which somehow passed between his spraddled legs and under the skirt of the robe. He stepped over the table without touching it, and falling back onto one of the sofas, looked around with a smug, pleased look. The cushions collapsed under his weight, he laid his head back, and passed out.

He awoke; came to; opened his eyes, at any rate, looking into the maze of mirror reflections. He sat up from his slouched position and gazed around. He seemed to be caught in a jungle whose green-black foliage had suddenly come alive, moving and swaying. From somewhere a bird sang; not the cockatoo— was it a mockingbird? What time was it? He couldn't see the clock. The rain dripped from the gutters and rattled tinnily in the throats of the downspouts. A gauzy mist was spread in mysterious splendor over the flats below, through which the city lights gleamed, fewer now, and more dimly. Between it and him, the jungle: palmetto, elephant ear, aralia, sharp spiky plants, the orange heads of bird-of-paradise. The pool light had been turned off, the water lay silent and unstirring, a slab of glistening obsidian. Then, among the foliage, he made out—what?—beasts moving? Candlelight flickered in the lanai, and on one of the chaises he saw a form. The thick arms were thrown back over the head; tanned skin and a band of flesh untouched by the sun. This was only partially visible, for over it, kneeling between the spread legs, was the curve of a back. It moved, too. It settled closer, the back tensing. He heard low animal cries, muttered obscenities. Along the yellow canvas-duck upholstery lay a hand, palm up, the fingers spreading, stiffening, clenching, opening again. The head rolled to one side. Murmurs, whispers, cries. Two of them, but they were not alone; there was a third one, standing in the shadows; watching.

Willie closed his eyes against the explicitness, lay back in lassitude, trying to shut out the scene. It stung him, fascinated him, disgusted him, heated, chilled him.

Beasts.

Animals.

He heard his knee joints crack as he tried to rise, working his way finally to his feet and staggering in an oblique path toward the doorway, where he braced himself and hung swinging back and forth on the aluminum frame.

"Get out!" he hissed at them. "Get out of here! All of you!"

Arco smiled lazily, while the girl crossed her arms over her breasts, moving aside as Bill reached for a towel and tucked it around his waist. With an adroit leap, he was off the chaise and close to Willie, who drew away.

"Hey, c'mon, pardner, don't act that way. We thought you was asleep."

"Wasn't asleep. Want you to go. All of you. Now. What do you think this place is?" He felt his knees buckle, struggled to hold himself upright.

"We think it's terrific, pops," Arco said easily, reaching for his jeans and sliding his bare legs into them. "We were just having a little busman's holiday," he continued, his face popping out of his T-shirt. "That's how we make our living, y'know. You got to watch free of charge. Most people have to pay."

"That's a thought, Willie," Bill said jovially. He tried to touch Willie, who pulled farther away, then turned and went inside. Bill came after him.

"Hey, babe—hey, babe, don't act like that, huh? Okay? Honest, Willie, I'm real sorry." He looked ridiculous with his shorn head, his stupid, happy-go-lucky smile.

Trying to draw himself up, Willie confronted him where he stood, his voice sneering, his hands gesticulating wildly. Bill was a clod, a yokel, a bumpkin, he was coarse, deceitful. He would never make it as an actor—not even as a human being. He was common, he was cheap, was filth. Bill's face flushed red; then redder, first with sheepish embarrassment, finally with sullen anger. He grimaced—not smiled—the thick, larded cheeks lifting and making his eyes smaller, squintier. His boyish innocence had disappeared and he seemed suddenly malicious. Yet he let the accusations fall in silence. No one spoke. Wind riffled the palms, whisked the surface of the pool, died.

Arco, suddenly placating, made a move toward them. "C'mon, Willie—"

"Who are you?" he demanded loftily. "I don't know you."

"Sure you do, Willie." This was Bill, but altered. "This is m'friend Arco." He reached and brought Arco past him and placed him before Willie, towering over him from behind. There was sudden menace in the movement, in the sound of his voice, which had suddenly gone soft and babyish. "Arco, wantcha t'meet m'friend Willie."

"Sure, sure, we met. Hiya, Willie." He made a quick motion to Bill, who walked out into the lanai and started dressing. The girl lay watching from the chaise. Arco smiled insinuatingly at Willie. "No harm done, man."

"No," he said, sinking suddenly and wearily onto the sofa and putting his head back. "No harm done." He looked at the tables and the food mess among the crystal ornaments. "Someone will clean it up." He closed his eyes, his burst of anger seeming to subside. Arco waited a moment, then came and sat beside him. He began stroking one of the dogs and toying with its ear. Willie reached and took the dog onto his lap.

"I wouldn't hurt him, Willie," Arco said gently.

"I'm sure you wouldn't. It's cold." He looked at the embers of the fire. Arco was snapping his fingers over the sofa back. Bill's face appeared.

"Mind if I have one for the road?" Arco inquired.

"Feel free at any time."

He got up and went to the bar. The girl wandered casually in and took his place on the sofa.

"Gee," she said, smoothing her skirt, "some night, huh? Crazy. Everybody's crazy tonight."

He turned and looked at her. Bill was laying another log on the andirons. No one said anything. The room seemed terribly quiet, empty. Willie thought about what it would be like when they had gone. His eye wandered to the portrait.

"Mama."

"Huh?" The girl stared at him.

"That's m'mother."

"I know," she said sympathetically. "And she's dead."

He nodded; let her touch his arm, caress it.

" 'Little Willie in the best of sashes,' " he said.

"Do it, Willie," Bill said, fanning the embers.

Willie giggled, then staggered up and began his act. " 'Little Willie in the best of sashes—' "

" 'Fell in the fire and was burnt to ashes,' " said Bill, lowering himself comfortably into a chair. Arco was getting cubes from the refrigerator. Judee smiled. Willie smiled back.

" 'Later on the room grew chilly,' " he said.

" 'But nobody thought to poke up Willie.' "

They finished together, and laughed together, and suddenly it was fun again. Arco had gone into the bathroom, and Judee was putting on more records, and Bill was making Willie another drink, and everyone had forgotten about the blow-up. Bill was sorry and Willie was sorry; everybody was sorry. Never mind; it was only a momentary thing. Then Bill and Judee were dancing, and Willie, holding the dogs, watched, content that no one was leaving.

"Laguna Lil," he mumbled, suddenly sitting erect. They didn't hear him, or his gleeful anticipation as he got up again, put down the dogs, and did a nimble tap step across the room.

" 'My little feet may be dancing,' " he crooned as he went, " 'but my little heart is breaking.' " He took one backward look, then went through the entranceway and disappeared. The dogs watched him go, then came back, curled up, and went to sleep, their noses on Judee's thighs. Presently Arco came out of the bathroom and looked around. "Where'd he go?"

"Dunno."

"Holler."

"Willie?" No reply. Bill shouted again; the name echoed

in the room and died away. Arco had moved to the wall and was tipping pictures on their hooks to peer behind them. "What're ya doin'?" Bill asked.

"Lookin' for the safe."

"How we goin' to open it?"

"He'll open it."

"How?"

"I said he'll open it. He'll open it."

Arco backed away from the wall, staring up, thinking. He went to the armoire. He knocked against it; the record arm jumped, and scratched across the disk. The cockatoo ruffled its crest and screamed.

"Fucking bird." Arco swatted the cage and it rocked violently on its stand, while the cockatoo flapped its wings. Arco continued past the fish tanks and the open glass doors, where the rain leaked through the grommeted weepers in the canopy. He crossed to the far wall and felt behind the pulled-back curtains. At the end there was another picture. He angled it away and looked up and under.

"Shit."

Moving quickly, purposefully, he recrossed the room to the bar, looked down around the shelves, then went into the wine closet behind the counter. Bill had sunk down on a stool, and sat swiveling, studying with dissatisfaction his reflection in the mirror. Judee came and leaned onto his lap, caressing his cheek. "Billy, poor old Billy," she crooned softly. She kissed him, and as their mouths parted Bill looked past her frizzed head, toward the chapel.

"Holy God!"

"What?" Judee nuzzled his neck.

"Look." He lifted her head and pointed. "The painting—see it?"

"What?" Judee said; she didn't see anything wrong.

"It moved. I just seen it move."

"Aw, Billy," she giggled, then sat bolt upright. "Oh, my God . . ."

She had seen it, too. The life-size figure in the painting behind the cross cradling the infant Jesus had come suddenly, miraculously, to life. The hands were moving, extending the child out into the light. The head became animated, then the body, the shoulders surging gracefully, the drapery softly rippling.

Judee moaned, and Bill cursed quietly. Arco came out of the wine closet and his eye followed Bill's pointing finger.

One hand of the figure still extended the Infant, while the

340

other hand made languid beckoning gestures. The three crossed the room, staring up at the moving form in the white robe, with the blue, gold-bordered headdress, the cloth wimple beneath, the gold girdle. The arms brought the child back to the curving bosom and gently cradled it there, the head gazing down at it, holding the pose in perfect tableau.

As the three came to the chapel doorway and stared, the figure raised its head and spoke.

"Hello, dahlings, how's tricks?"

"Jesus—Willie!" Judee fell against Bill, shrieking with laughter.

The figure flourished its draperies and bent in formal greeting. "No, dahlings—Laguna Lil." He stepped down from the bench he stood on, revealing the painting of the Virgin behind, then moved past the altar, came through the gate, carrying the child, floating past them out into the game room. The blue headdress lifted, fluttered, as a gust blew through the open doors, and the sparkle of a gold sandal showed at the hem of the gown. Majestically the figure moved to the center of the room, where it made obeisance to the portrait, then gravely curtsied, first to Bill, then Judee, then Arco, turning slowly in a circle in a parody of a formally devout attitude.

"Here she is, dahlings," came the Tallulah drawl. "Laguna Lil in person." A brief dip to the painting. "Hello, Bee, dahling, it's Laguna Lil again. And the little one." The Jesus figure was held up to the picture; a life-size doll with blinking eyes. "Here he is, dahling, the little tot himself, Jesus-Billyboy. Why don't I marry him off, dahling?" The voice rang out bitter and sarcastic.

The others stared in silence as the face, garishly made up, with long fluttering eyelashes, penciled brows, cheeks powdered and rouged, a painted mouth, peered around the circle, the scarlet lips turned up in a burlesque smile. "That's it, you see, dahlings, that's what she did to Billyboy. Married him off. Her only begotten son, and she married him to Laguna Lil. She did, dahlings . . . a shotgun wedding. Pistol Willie. *Bah* hah-hah-hah-hah." The Bankhead sheep laugh echoed in the room, and the head angled coyly, campily.

" 'My mama done tol' me'—bum bum bum bum bum *bump!*" With lewd pelvic thrusts, the swathed figure flounced in a stripper's walk, fluttering fabric from head and arms, extending the gold-sandaled foot. " 'When I was in knee pants'— *bump!* Well, hardly knee pants; more like knee skirts. I'll give you th' bridge to that song, Wimp. . . . 'A woman's a two-face . . . a worrisome thing . . . leave ya t' sing . . . blues

341

in th' night.' You see how it is, darlings; she couldn't let her Billyboy go, so she married him. To Laguna Lil. 'My mama done tol' me—Son . . .' " The hand lifted the skirt of the gown and let it fall. "Like it? Fedora's. From the movie. But not Mary, you know, not the Holy Mother. Bee's the holy mother. This is Laguna Lil . . . that's what we call her. Billyboy and Lil get married and Mama's happy, aren't you, Mama? Buzz buzz buzz. And . . . Mama lets her Billyboy wear . . . well, you see what it is." Holding the skirts out, the figure drifted to the glass case that contained the silver crown, took it out and placed it on his own head. "Divine, isn't it?" He moved back and held up the photograph of Fedora, dressed as the Virgin in *The Miracle of Santa Cristi*. The costumes were identical, yet one was a travesty. "Tallulah would have adored it. Bee did, and . . ." The hand came up in a delicate but hopeless wafting gesture, settling the crown more securely on his head. "All because a woman died in an epileptic fit on the . . ." The voice faltered as the figure collapsed to its knees before the portrait. ". . . steps of an . . . Italian country . . . church." He lowered his head, the crown slipped, he caught it and tossed it like a quoit onto the arm of the doll, then laid both aside. He hiccuped, blinked, stared blankly around, his gaze eventually coming to rest on Arco, who was watching the scene with detached amusement. The clock chimed. The sound held, died; there was an infinitesimal pause, a moment's beat as when an actor goes up in his lines and needs prompting. Then, in the silence, Arco's amusement vanished, to be replaced by a fierce expression, as if he were assuming another role. Again his pale face darkened, his languor was transformed into galvanized action, and with a furious half-laugh, half-cry—"Blasphemy!"—he threw himself at the collapsed figure. Tearing away the blue, gold-bordered drapery, he stared down at Willie's crumpled face, macabre and ludicrous in its woman's make-up, and raised his arm in violent menace.

"You're not going to hurt me, are you?" Beneath the long lashes the eyes peered up at the bright ones above. "Are you?" There was the palest color of something in the query, as if hurting him were not totally beyond question, or even beyond desire. Instead of striking, Arco grabbed at the gold neck chain and yanked; Willie's torso bent forward under the strain. Judee pressed forward, weird giggling sounds coming from around the small fist she had doubled up at her mouth. Arco leaned over and used both hands to snap the chain, catching the medals and keys as they fell. Sorting them, he dashed back across the room to the chapel, where he banged through the gate and began fitting the keys at the locks of the wooden coffer on the altar.

"No—" Willie had half turned, his arm raised in supplication. Bill came from behind and restrained him until Arco rushed cursing from the chapel, struggling under the weight of the box. Eluding Bill, Willie staggered up and grabbed at Arco as he came. "Give me that." Arco shoved him away and set the opened box on the table.

"There's no mirror in here. What the fuck is this anyway?" He held a small white object, perhaps three inches long. He grabbed Willie's arm and shoved the object under his face. "What is it?"

"A . . . holy object." Clutching the draperies about him, Willie struggled forward. "Give it to me—"

"Lemme see." Judee took the thing from Arco and examined it. "Looks like some kind of bone."

"Yes, a bone." Willie reached out to her. "Please? Let me have it?" Arco knocked his hand away and seized the object from Judee; Willie started whimpering. "It's a bone from the foot of Saint Trebonius. A holy relic. You shouldn't touch it, it's holy, holy—"

"Shit!" Arco flung it away and Willie scrabbled across the tiles to retrieve it. He cupped it in his hand, crooning and pressing it to his chest. "Mama . . . ?" The mocking Bankhead laugh broke out once more as he rose and began the bump-and-grind step again, lurching about the room. " 'My mama done tol' mee'—*Bah*-hah-hah-hah-hah, dahlings, you see, it's all a joke, just a joke."

Arco advanced on him. "What d'you mean—a joke?"

" 'S a fake—one of Bee's ter-rific ideas, dahling." He sauntered away, reverting to his natural voice. "I don't even know if it came from a foot, let alone Saint . . . whoever." He pointed toward the chapel. "Everything's fake. Cedars of Lebanon? Not at all. A man from the studio prop department made that cross. California cypress, not cedar. No Knight of Malta. Box is a fake, too. No monks of Mont Saint Michel. Bible— no Cardinal Richelieu. Fake, see? Movie props; make-believe. Bee—busy bee—she did th' embroidery. No nuns of Bruges. It's a movie set. And the painting. Not Renaissance, not Quattrocento, not a bit of Quattrocento. Done by a painter in Laguna, friend of Bee's. Laguna Lil, see? It's all a joke, see, just a joke. Bee's joke." He was laughing, then harder, clutching himself, laughing so he couldn't stop; it rose up out of him in squalls of high-pitched mirth. Holding his stomach, he tumbled back on a sofa. "Joke—see the joke?"

Arco struck him. Three violent blows, but punctuated by precise pauses between, lifting the hand and holding it a moment, watching, and striking again. Blood began to run. The dogs cowered, then fled. Willie stared wildly up at him, waiting each time for the next blow. Arco was coolly, almost indifferently, angry; it was as if the scene had been rehearsed between them. Willie slid from the sofa to the floor and knelt there. Arco raised his foot, paused; Willie waited, was toppled backward by the blow planted on his chest. He clasped himself, rolling sideways; there was blood on the tiles. Judee was screaming and laughing, inane sounds coming in gurgles from her throat. Willie crawled, the skirts of the white gown draping themselves along his thin form in graceful, bloodied folds. He stumbled to his feet, sweeping the clothes around him in a whimsical parody of maidenly modesty, and the draperies rippled and whispered as he fled.

It became an absurd, almost comical chase. Out through the doors he went, across the lanai, to the pool. He would run, trailing his ridiculous costume, his features grotesque in their make-up, laughing, sobbing, turning, stopping, waiting. His breath came fast, his body trembled with excitement. The others ran after him, shouting, laughing, crying out, past the diving board, the broken fountain, with cries and pantings, more stops, waits, opposing moves around a chaise, until Willie collapsed again and Arco was on him, yanking his head up so his neck arched like a bow.

"Punish you." Hot, fierce, demanding. Willie's eyes gleamed, apprehensive yet enticed.

"Punish, how?"

Arco whistled on his fingers, sharp urgent blasts, until the others came. It had all become a game, of course, they were laughing or appeared to be, Judee was tickling Willie's ribs and making him scream with mirth, then pain, then he was being lifted vertically to his feet, and as he started to fold again, with a quick neat movement Bill bent beneath him, caught him on his shoulder like a potato sack, and carried him with giant strides back into the house. They brought him across the game room to the doors of the chapel—laughing, everyone was laughing—and inside. No, Willie cried out, laughing and gasping, too, when he saw what the joke had become; let him go now, he cried out, it was enough, but no, it wasn't, there was something else yet at hand, something more to be done, and then, suddenly, no one was laughing at all.

Out of darkness, into light—a little. From somewhere, far, far away, he could hear the clock striking; counted the notes It was two; or he thought it was. He found it strange, almost dreamlike, coming out of that place where he had been, the void where seemingly he had floated as though above the earth, not soaring, but hovering. The promise of nightmare, but happily he had awakened before . . . The light struck him from above, hitting him across the plane of his forehead and bare shoulders. Bright, hot light stung his eyes, but through the glare he could see into shadows where figures moved, silent, devious, nefariously occupied. His body hurt; he did not mind it. His jaw ached; he didn't mind that either. His hands, feet, felt numb, but somehow even this seemed fitting. Everything as it had come about seemed to him oddly fitting. Strange, but where he was was where he had wanted to be. He had imagined himself here, had wondered what it might be like, what feelings he would experience, what thoughts and emotions. Now he was here, in pain, but with it a suffusing tranquillity.

Someone giggled. Seated cross-legged below him, leaning across her knees, the girl looked up with her soft, bulgy eyes, staring, not moving. Oh, her expression said, oh, he was a funny sight.

"Wha'? Wha'?" he murmured, his mind cloudy again.

"Hi, sweetie," she said. "How're ya? You okay?" He nodded, coughed, swallowed. From out there in the darkness he heard the sound of booted feet moving; again a shadow passed. The girl turned.

"He's come to."

The feet sounded louder; a figure appeared in the doorway. He recognized it as Bill, or something that seemed like Bill.

Uncomprehendingly, Willie looked first at his right hand, then at his left, bound to the wooden crosspiece with black tape. Wound about his middle, crisscrossed over his chest, securing his torso to the upright column was some sort of plastic lamp cord. His knees were bent, his ankles also taped. Below his feet was the altar with its embroidered cloth. He lifted his eyes again, and through the open chapel doors, across the white and black squares, above the urn on the mantel he saw the portrait.

The famous Bee smile.

Then Arco came.

From his position of preeminence, Willie looked down on him. The younger man returned his gaze, his eyes no longer sparkling; through Willie's blur their light seemed dimmed, in their vaguely querying expression. They regarded one another silently for some moments. Willie laughed weakly; after all, it was only a joke. Yet between them across the sharply angled space, a little more than a dozen feet, there hung a question; unspoken, unanswered.

"It's Gethsemane time, gang." Arco made a clownish leer, pantomiming a microphone and speaking into it like Walter Cronkite. "Good morning, ladies and gentlemen. We are here high atop Golgotha, overlooking the holy city of Jerusalem. Let me tell you, it's quite a hike up here, folks, but the view is magnificent. If you look to your left you can see the Wailing Wall, and just over there is Pilate, washing his hands. As you see, he's using Camay, and afterward, Vaseline Intensive Care Lotion. And just there is dear Mary Magdalene, on a coffee-break with the Virgin Mary. And here, you lucky people, on the cross, you see before you Mary's son, and here's the son's naughty drag, for which we will not cast lots." He tossed up the draperies which had been stripped from Willie's body, leaving him naked, except for his undershorts, white tricot boxers, with a coronet embroidered on the thigh; his papal crest.

"How's it going, old-timer?" Arco asked good-naturedly, stepping fully into the light.

Willie shook his head, croaked out four words. "Get me down now."

"Not yet."

"Wha' we waiting for?"

"For you to tell."

"Tell. Tell what?"

"Where's the safe, Willie?"

"Safe . . ." He remembered something about the safe.

"The mirror's in it," Arco explained. "We want it."

Willie's shoulders shook as he laughed again. "Mirror? You . . . want . . . mirror?"

"We got a guy. He'll pay five g's for it."

"Worth more."

"Doesn't matter—it's enough to get us where we're going."

"Hula skirts? Tropical shores? Won't get you to Redondo Beach. Arms are going to sleep."

Arco's voice was soft, gentle even. "Where is it, Willie?"

346

He closed his eyes; lights danced behind the lids. He rested his head back. "Can't tell you."

"Can't or won't?"

"Suit yourself."

"Willie, you can come down or stay up there, but if you come down you've got to tell first."

"Mean . . . I have a choice?"

"That's what I mean. What it's all about—everything's a choice. Up or down."

"Up."

"Suit yourself."

"Metaphor?"

"Hm?"

"This . . . one of your . . . living metaphors?"

"If you like."

"I don't." He watched the figure below. "Significance escapes me. Who'm I s'posed to be? Jesus? That what you have in mind?"

"Whatever turns you on, babe."

Willie choked, gagged, hiccuped.

"He needs a drink," Judee said.

"Get him one," Arco ordered. Judee clopped away on her wooden shoes, Arco following.

Bill paused in the doorway. "You better tell him, Willie."

Willie chuckled; the joke was outrageous. He shook his head again.

Bill said, "He's going to hurt you, Willie." He, too, went away.

Judee came back with a glass of water and ice. She dragged over a bench to stand on and held the glass to his lips. He drank greedily. She rubbed an ice cube on his forehead.

"Wha's happening?" he asked her.

She shrugged. "I'm pretty ripped, sweetie. You better do what he says, though." Willie was laughing again; she didn't understand why. He started to tell her, then decided not to. He emptied the glass and she took it away. He held his breath as she had suggested, and the hiccups subsided. He felt more sober. He closed his eyes, wondering how long they would leave him there before they let him down. His wrists hurt, the circulation was stopping in his legs. His vision blurred, then focused, blurred again. Beyond the light, the uprights of the door seemed to bend and waver like reflections on water. Someone moved in front of the fireplace. Willie blinked, felt a chill when awareness seeped in on his dazed state.

347

"Bad cess to you, Arco," he called defiantly through the open doorway.

Arco was dropping manuscript pages, one by one, onto the burning logs.

"You can stop it, Willie," Arco returned.

Willie clamped his mouth shut, staring unbelievingly as page after page was fed to the flames. Then Arco began dumping in whole sections; smoke poured out into the room.

"*Gl'Italiani sono grandi amanti della bellezza, non è vero?*" Willie called.

"*Vero.*" Arco's hand moved methodically, transferring the pages from the crook of his arm to the fire.

"Liar!"

"*Sì, caro.*" The destruction went on.

What did it matter? Willie thought. A lot of silly stories. It was true, he could stop it, could be taken down. He could tell them where the safe was, let them have the mirror, get them out of the house. His eye went from the flames to the gleaming portrait. "Mama," he said. He did not smile back at her. Out of the vague swarm of thoughts that came to him—and there were few he seemed able to hold on to—there was one: in all his life he had never risked anything, chanced anything, dared anything. Bee had made the decisions, forced the hands, seen to the arrangements, ruled the roost. He had been a kind of wind-up doll with a little steel key in his back: bow, move, twirl, sing, dance, amuse. Hardly a life; hardly a man. He sorrowed for both, but not for his autobiography. Salad Days, when he was young and green. He was older, wiser, tireder now.

He would not tell.

In they went, page after page. Judee dragged up a chair and sat watching, giggling moronically as she recited, "Little Willie in the best of sashes fell in the fire and was burnt to ashes . . .' " Willie closed his eyes, but could not keep them shut; the sight was too fascinating. The ruin of the manuscript took time, the hearth blazed, flames roared in the chimney. Then at last it was done. Arco's hands were empty. He dusted them in a neat, decisive gesture, and looked across the room to the cross.

" 'Later on the room grew chilly, but nobody thought to poke up Willie,' " Arco said. He did not laugh. Willie eyed him silently as he came and stood in the doorway. "You ready to tell now?" Willie closed his eyes again, wilted against the cross. Arco left.

When Willie reopened his eyes he could scarcely believe the sight that presented itself. "No—no—" A cry escaped him before he could prevent it.

"What about this?" Arco was asking sardonically. "Is this a fake, too? This another of your jokes?"

"They're her *ashes!*"

Arco had lifted the gold urn from the mantel and was cradling it in one arm; in his other hand was the lid, which he wrenched away. It rolled, then fell flat with diminishing metallic reverberations on the tiles. "Maybe it's just cigar ashes. Maybe it's not Mama at all." He brought forth a handful of gray matter and held it palm up before him. Drifting currents lifted a small puff and they sifted to the floor. Then he tossed the rest in a flurry up in the air.

"In God's name—it's my mother!"

Arco was scooping out the ashes with his fingers and letting them sift across the yellow velvet of a chair, across the Marion Davies sofas, across the coffee table. Then he stepped to Judee and drew an ashy X on her forehead and made the sign of the cross.

"*Pox vobiscum.* That's Latin, Willie," he called, advancing back to the chapel. "Where's it at? Tell, or there won't be anything left of Mama come the dawn."

Willie shook his head. "No."

"It's your funeral. Sorry, I mean your mother's. To Bee or not to Bee, all that crap." He came in through the gate and stood at the altar, where he tilted the urn, letting the ashes pour from the inverted mouth. When the vessel was empty, he raised it over his head and hurled it against the stained-glass window. The lead mullions gave way, and the glass shattered in an explosion of color. Willie moaned and averted his head.

"Watch me, Willie." Arco's face was paler than ever as he stood below, fists planted defiantly on his hips. Then an arm shot out, he pointed upward, the blood surging back into his face in a new outburst of fury. "Look, you sick prick, I know you. I *know* you! I've seen you everywhere. In every city I've been in I've seen you and your stinking kind, with your goddamn fancy cars and your goddamn fancy jewelry and your goddamn fancy women. You've got it all—you think. But you listen to me—you're not going to keep it all, you hear? None of you people!"

"We earned it—"

Arco raised his hand and slammed it down on the altar. "I don't care who earned what! You've got it! You got your share and you got my share and his and hers"—pointing at Judee and Bill—"and we want ours. That's what we came for. To get ours."

"Then . . . it wasn't just . . . ? You had it all figured out.

"I got everything figured out." He moved closer; his words spilled out in a harsh rush. "Listen, old man, I'll do things to you. I'll frighten you. I'll hurt you. You understand? Hear me? *Hear me?*"

On the cross, Willie's body trembled. Spittle had gathered in the corners of his mouth. He favored Arco with a thin, mocking smile, then, in an effort at lightness, said, "Somebody bring me a drink. Scotch, not too much ice."

"Sure thing." Arco stalked rapidly from the room, going first to the bar for the Scotch bottle, then to the table for Willie's glass. "Here's ice, Willie." He picked up one of the crystal cubes and dropped it in the glass, then another. He poured Scotch over them and held it out. "Here's to crime, Willie." He raised the glass over the table, then released his fingers. The heavy double-old-fashioned glass slipped, struck the tabletop, and shattered. He circled the table, taking up one crystal object after another and letting it drop—obelisks, eggs, animals, cigarette box, ashtrays. He turned and grabbed up another glass and sent it crashing against one of the mirrored screens. The cockatoo screamed in its cage, the dogs scampered under the piano.

"Yes, Willie?"

"No."

Arco whirled, rushed to the bar, and with a violent gesture swept the remaining glasses from the shelves, then the liquor bottles, which he seized by their necks and threw one after the other, crashing, out onto the floor. Next the refrigerator door was hurled open and with two or three quick movements he had cleared the shelves of champagne bottles. He tore the photographs from the wall and scaled them out into the room, where they fell helter-skelter. Then he was among them, tearing out the signed pictures from under the shattered glass and throwing them into the fire.

"Everything, Willie, everything goes."

No reply.

Lamps went over, and tables, chairs, the remaining mirrored screen striking the floor with a crash; jagged shards flew in all directions. Arco scrambled around until he had retrieved several of the crystal eggs, and assuming a pitcher's stance, he lobbed them at the fish tanks. The glass panels shattered, water sluiced forth in cascades, carrying rainbows of fish,

350

flopping, grasping, dying on the tiles. The dogs ran to investigate, then retreated as the rest of the aquariums broke. When they were empty, Arco dragged them from their shelves and heaved them through the panes of the sliding doors. Wind sucked the curtains out in pale gauzy flourishes.

The cockatoo had not stopped screaming. Arco lunged at the birdcage and with a vicious yank tore it from its stand. The bird flapped wildly, its wings striking the wires, then, as the door was held open, it flew in crazed circles around the room until it blundered through a broken window and sailed low across the pool, and up into a palmetto tree.

"Tell."

Arco's breath came in frenzied pants as he stood in the chapel doorway, looking up at Willie. There was no answer. Turning, he rushed to the wall and snatched down one of the sabers and began attacking the sofa pillows, the sharp edge slicing through the fabric and sending feathers up in clouds. Then, brandishing it aloft, he began hacking at the chandelier, ducking his head after each swipe, as the crystal prisms rained around him. He had signaled to Bill, who took down the other saber, and together they ran about the room, slashing at everything in sight, coming at last to the cathedral figures at the fireplace. With a wild swing of his blade, Bill struck one of the heads, spattering chips in all directions.

"Plaster?" Arco looked across the room. "Jesus, what a fake."

"Movie magic," Willie muttered.

They toppled the statues, and half crouched over them, wielding their blades with alternate strokes, like woodsmen, chopping; one of the heads rolled onto the floor. Its fellow soon followed, then, in turn, the arms and legs, until the dismembered trunks lay piled one on the other like a pair of decapitated corpses amid a pile of broken chips, over which hung a small cloud of plaster dust.

Exhausted, Arco flung aside his saber and threw himself into a chair, gasping with exploded passion, clutching his stomach. Bill stumbled toward the chapel, dragging his saber, the point scraping on the tiles. He stared up, dazed, at Willie on the cross, the same sheepish but crooked smile puffing up his cheeks and making his eyes small. With his uneven teeth and chopped hair, there was something macabre, dangerous, about him; utterly unlike the simple, abashed cowboy who had arrived at the door—how many hours ago? He lurched into the chapel and lolled over the altar railing, his mouth slack and wet.

"You better tell now, Willie. He's damn mad." Willie closed his eyes, heard only the voice. "He's gonna hurt you, pardner. You don't know him when he's mad. . . . That out there"—he gestured haphazardly at the vandalized room—"heck, that's nothin'."

Willie opened his eyes and stared out at the wreckage, his gaze moving across the sea of broken glass, the toppled cage, the watery floor where fish were still expiring in nervous agitation among sodden pillow feathers. A back draft in the chimney blew ashes up in a black gust, and they settled about the room, mixing with the grayer ones that were the remains of Beetrice Marsh.

"It . . . doesn't matter," he said weakly. "Give me something . . . to drink . . . ?"

"No." Bill went away, leaving Willie alone in the chapel. He could see their heads together in connivance beyond the back of the sofa. Someone had turned the records over: Mantovani and *Music for a Rainy Night;* appropriate. In its fetters of black tape and plastic cord his body began trembling, shaking uncontrollably. The circulation had left his arms, his legs, and he could feel his heart throbbing; nothing would quiet it. Sharp pains shot through his head. He looked at the empty place on the mantel, and the portrait above.

Whatever had happened still seemed fitting, cause and effect. Whatever had brought him to this bizarre place he now occupied seemed to him some logical proper conclusion. Here was the crux of it, the crux become cross: his place of torment. It was a joke—a bad one, but still a joke, wasn't it? They'd put him up here to embarrass him, make a foolish old man more foolish. The living metaphor. Decide. Decide to come down. He knew he would not. Not of his own volition. He would never tell them. It was the biggest joke of all.

He looked at the face staring back at him, the famous Bee smile. Her eyes, averted as though by personal delicacy from the litter of shattered mirror and glass, were directed at him, a confrontation which said only—almost wistfully—that this was none of her doing; she had no part in it.

You have got yourself in, my Billyboy, you must get yourself out. She sat in unperturbed quietude, in another age, almost another century, with no hair out of place, oblivious to the havoc, while maintaining the prominence that had always been hers in life. "My Billyboy's a churchgoer again," she used to tell people proudly after his conversion. "I can die a happy woman." She had wooed him into the hands of the Jesuits, who sternly and valiantly wrestled for his soul. They had won, although he would have preferred the Franciscans, who were more indulgent; but in religion as in life he was not to know clemency.

Smile, dearest Bee.

Then suddenly, for the first time, he realized it was no joke; there was nothing to smile about.

He had chosen his final role; and for once it was to be his own choice, not hers. That would be the metaphor. Whatever prospect it held, he would offer nothing except mute defiance. He would let them hurt him, his defiance would be meant not for them but for her, whom he had never defied. For her he had denied himself everything, every vestige of any sort of life he had really wanted. Now, naked, he would divest himself *of* himself. And of her. This was a thing he could do in a way that only he could do it; without Bee. It was between him and Arco. Or between him and God.

"See me, Mama, see me now." But could she? See him? He doubted it; doubted she wanted to.

In front of the fire the girl bent, dragging some sort of sack—a pillowcase?—which she was filling, like a dispossessed creature looting the ruins after a bomb blast. With a squeal of glee she stood, placing Fedora's rhinestone crown on her head. She tramped back and forth in front of what mirrors remained intact.

"Look—look, Fedora—see? I'm Fedora."

Jazzy, bopping, balancing the crown, she came picking her way through the glass, and moved into the light of the chapel. "Hi. How ya doin'? You okay, sweetie?" He tried to laugh, then coughed and swallowed. He felt he was choking. He managed to clear his throat with dry hawks, and spat from the corner of his mouth. *"Scusi,"* he said to her, vainly trying to wipe his chin against his shoulder. The crown slid again; she caught it and turned as rapid footfalls were heard. Arco reappeared, his pale face skeletal, almost devoid of flesh, the delicate bones fiercely modeled in the light. He came with purpose. He wore pink rubber cleaning gloves from the kitchen and his paired hands cupped a vessel of some sort, like a votive offering, a glass, containing an amount of clear liquid that gleamed in the light. His voice was soft but quite clear as he told Willie what it was.

"Acid, Willie. From the car battery. You better shut your eyes." He came forward, holding the glass away from his chest, motioning the others to safety. Together Bill and Judee retreated to the wall, watching in fascination. "Acid, Willie, hear me?" he went on. "It won't do your face any good." He opened the gate and stepped through, extending the glass. "It's your last chance, Willie. You want to tell now?"

"No." He made no attempt to protect himself.

"I'm going to throw it, Willie," Arco told him. "On the count of three. One . . ." Glass poised, he waited. "You want to tell?" Willie made no reply.

Arco pronounced warningly, "Two, Willie." He brought the glass nearer and upward, standing to one side to avoid the liquid's splashing on his own body. "Tell." Willie remained silent. Arco waited another moment, then brought the glass closer. He held it suspended for another moment, and whispered, "Three, Willie." His hand described a quick, neat arc, the glass tipped, and the viscous liquid flew upward into Willie's face.

"It burns," he screamed, his head writhing as the liquid splattered and ran down his cheeks. *"It burns!"*

"Does it, Willie?" Arco made a little swagger, mocking and tinged with disgust.

"Oh, God," Willie cried, "God, how it burns!" His body tore against the slack of the restraining cords, his wrists yanked at the tapes. Arco let the glass drop, and crossed his arms on his chest, watching clinically as the liquid slid down Willie's bare chest. Some of it dripped on his feet, and fell on the rug. Willie groaned.

"Judee." Arco's voice cracked out, and as if by habit the girl stirred, then came from the wall. Pointing at the feet, he drew her through the gate. "Lick them."

"Lick them?" She tried to pull away; he held her, pushed her forward.

"What I said—lick them."

"Jesus—it's *acid*," she protested as he forced her closer to the feet. He waited another moment, then released her with a low chuckle.

"Does it hurt, Willie? Does it hurt bad?"

"Yes! Yes! It hurts!"

"You lying son-of-a-bitch. You know what it is? Pickle juice." Reaching behind with his foot, he kicked open the gate and passed from the room without looking back. Bill and Judee were breaking up, falling over each other with laughter. Watermelon pickle juice.

"Oh, Willie," Judee said, watching him and shaking her head. "If you could've seen your face. Honest, you had me fooled. I really thought it was burning."

Bill had left for another conference in the game room. He

and Arco sat together on the sofa. Arco stripped off the rubber gloves, puffing another cigar, and Willie could hear the angry rise of his expostulations. Then he moved diagonally toward the bar and came back with a sheaf of darts in his hand. He began throwing them at the portrait over the mantel. One struck Bee's cheek. Another her neck. A third her bosom. Willie winced, but he watched as if hypnotized. Arco threw another; it struck the canvas, pierced it, and the point was embedded in the wall behind. He had to stand on a chair to retrieve the darts; on a level with the picture, he drew on his cigar until the tip glowed red, and he pressed it into Bee's eye; smoke curled; he did the same thing to the other eye, there was more smoke, and when he stepped down, Bee stared out from dark, sightless holes. He moved away again, returned, this time with the saber. He touched the sharp point to the top of the canvas, then slashed the fabric, which flopped out of the frame. Then the portrait fell, struck the mantel, and tumbled to the floor. He turned and looked to the cross. "I'll do the rest of them the same way." He was moving along the wall, slashing canvases, one after the other, and he threw them at the fireplace, where the varnished canvases caught, flamed, sizzled, smoked.

The famous and valuable Marsh collection.

Tossing the saber aside, Arco collected the darts again, made a bundle of them, then divided it into two separate bundles, handed one to Judee, and advanced with her into the chapel.

"Throw a couple," he told her.

She giggled, then shrieked at the notion. "Oh, Arco, you're crazy!"

Willie looked down on them. They would throw the darts all around him, trying to frighten him. It no longer mattered. He had denied himself everything, shed everything, every vestige of his life, his personal respect; his "izzat." Even his sense of himself, of his mother. The mutilation of the portrait had sickened him, yet he did not feel guilty—it had also given him an exquisite thrill. He realized now how he had hated that painting, the "Smiling Bee." And yes—he had hated her, too. But that he had realized only then, in that very moment.

I hate you, Bee, he had thought. *I have hated you all my life.* He was laughing then; painful waves of uncontrollable mirth shook his body, racked him. Arco looked up suspiciously.

"What's so funny?"

"What . . . you . . . asked . . . me. Before. What it's like. Movie star. Bullshit. Want to know that? It's a crock."

"What?"

"Said . . . fifty years . . . it's . . . a . . . crock." His words astonished not only Arco, but himself as well. It was a terrible admission to make; yet, for him, at least, it was true. He could say it. Arco grinned delightedly.

"Glad you've seen the light, Willie. Now tell." Willie only shook his head.

"Tell, Willie," Arco repeated threateningly, holding a dart aloft, "or I'll do it." The sharp steel point made delicate, tentative passes in the air.

"Do it," Willie said. He would not tell. He had repudiated his mother, himself, his career; he had only his God now. "Do it," he said again; he would not tell. But of course they wouldn't; it was still part of the game, another joke to frighten him. Then the gray striped feathers revolved in the light as the dart left Arco's hand and struck Willie in the thigh. He grunted, but made no sound.

"Go ahead," Arco ordered the girl impatiently, and she nervously raised a dart. Her hand trembled, drew back. Arco nodded at her. The feathers made a slight whir as they passed through the air, and the point stuck Willie in the side, just under the rib cage. She gave a little squeal. The dart held for a moment, then slipped out and dropped on the rug.

"No points, Wimp. You really got to get—it—in—there." His hand made another arc, a dart flew from his fingers, striking Willie above the groin. His pelvis convulsed, and the blunt impact of wood and bone could be heard as his coccyx struck the cross behind him. "See," said Arco, "*in* there."

"Like—that?" Judee threw another; it caught Willie in the other thigh, where it dangled. Points of red showed, and minute tricklings of blood.

"Not bad," Arco said, "but still no bull's-eye."

"Saint Sebastian," she said, giggling. She threw another.

"I bet pinmakers all over the world are saying their blessings tonight." Arco's hand came up again and the last dart left his hand. When Judee had thrown her remaining one, Arco came through the gate and stared up at the victim on the cross.

"We can keep this up all night, if you want," he said dispassionately. "With a little practice, Judee could get real good." He withdrew the darts one by one and clutched them in his hand, their bloodied points glinting redly. "You want them again?" He waited for an answer, gave half the darts to Judee.

"He wants them again."

They took their turns, and one after the other the darts sailed through the air, striking and penetrating the drawn, withered flesh. Still Willie made no cry, only an occasional whimper. Then there was a third round. Arco was right: Judee was getting better.

Bill had appeared from somewhere out of the darkness, dragging the saber with him; he stared up with a stupefied expression.

"Jesus, what a freaking sight." He fell to his knees, his arms upraised, gripping the saber hilt and swashing the air with the blade in exaggerated amusement. "Oh, Jesus, Arco, what a sight. Groovy, man. I'm gettin' off on it. Christ, Arco, you are warped."

"As the twig is warped, so grows the tree, babe. Don't give him any more to drink."

Willie's face dripped perspiration: the make-up slid from his lips and eyes and ran in garish rivulets along his chin and jawbone. He seemed unaware of what had happened to him. Arco and the girl had gone away; Bill remained, making gashes in the damask wall upholstery and tearing away the fabric in huge pieces whose ends trailed on the carpeting. Then he, too, left and Willie hung there, the darts still sticking in him. He saw the girl go past to turn on the radio. She slid out of her halter and danced across the black and white tiles, her breasts jiggling. "How I started, sweetie," she called. "Topless, y'know." She laughed, then was past his line of vision, but he could hear her at the bar, telephoning. Bill had shouted that he had the munchies and was going to raid the kitchen again. Willie's head dropped, and he stared down at the feathered barbs hanging from his flesh, the growing dribbles of blood. Music came from the radio. "California dreamin' is becoming a realiteeee . . ."

Arco returned another time, carrying a lighted candle. He came through the gate and stood at the base of the cross, where he tilted the candle sideways. The hot wax dripped on Willie's bare feet. His toes moved, separated, curled; he did not cry out. Arco watched him carefully, as if testing him to determine the limits of his endurance.

"Pray, Willie," he said softly.

"Yes. Our Father, who art in heaven—"

"You don't believe."

"I do."

"You're a fraud. The cross you hang on is a fraud. Your God is a fraud."

"I believe. I do. I do." The old man mumbled, muttered,

wincing as the wax fell. "Want to believe. Trying to . . . want to . . . want to . . . Dear God, help me believe. Mother? Mama? Want to believe." He was crying. Tears welled up under his closed lids and rolled down his cheeks.

"Try Dial-A-Prayer, Willie."

Bill came back in, spooning baked beans from an open can. He slumped down on the bench, eating, watching the wax fall, drop by drop.

"Where's the Wimp?" Arco asked over his shoulder.

"On the phone."

"Get her in here."

Bill shouted; they waited; he shouted again. Finally Judee came, doing her trash walk, trying to balance the crown on her head. From her other hand the Jesus doll dangled by one arm. "Hi, gang, I was placin' obscene phone calls." She did a funny little duck, made one of her outrageous faces. "No, no, I'm just kiddin'. I was talking' t'Gary in Nashville."

"Come here."

Her smile faded as she passed through the gate. He held the candle out to her. "Do it," he ordered.

"Oh, let him down anyways," she said, looking up at the sight on the cross. Wax was piling up on the tops of Willie's insteps, with ugly red marks around them. "Do it," Arco told her again. He shoved the candle at her and went through the gate.

"Oh, Arco, honest . . ." She lowered her eyes, the lashes fluttering, as she held the candle the way she had been shown, dripping the hot wax. "Honest," she said prissily, "this is getting all over the carpeting. It's just silly, if you want to know the truth. Whyn't you tell, sweetie, huh? Whyn't you just whisper it to me?" He shook his head. She was staring at his shorts, the expensive tricot fabric now spattered with blood. She touched the embroidered coronet above the hem of one thigh. "What's it mean?"

Willie chuckled with soundless mirth. What indeed? Grace and favor from His Holiness, but it wouldn't help him now. He didn't want to think about it. "Countess Mara," he said; his joke was wasted on her.

"She royalty?"

"Neckwear, dear."

"Huh?" She still didn't get it. She continued her task the way Arco had instructed her, watching Willie's toes jerk and curl as the hot drops struck them. "Makes ya twitch, huh?"

" 'My little feet may be dancing . . .' "

"Huh?"

" 'But my little heart is breaking . . .' "

She didn't get that either.

"Joan Crawford," he explained; the name meant nothing. When she felt sure the other two had disappeared again she blew out the candle and put it on a bench. She sat the doll beside it, and stole to the organ and began playing softly.

" 'My ma-ma done tol' me' "—*bump*.

"Water," Willie said.

Looking back over her shoulder, she traced the whispered word with her eyes, shook her head. "He'd get mad." She indicated the ceiling with her chin. From overhead came the noisy vibrations of heavy boot treads, and the sounds of their ransacking could be heard as they threw open doors and marched from room to room.

" 'When I was in knee pants' "—*bump*—" 'A woman's a twoface, a worrisome thing—' "

"Judee? Please?"

" 'Who'll leave ya t' sing—' "

"Please?"

"I guess with a little practice I could get that bridge right."

In the game room the radio station had signed off. Only a dull intermittent buzz came between the organ phrases. The sounds had crept inside Willie's head, they seemed to ring and leap with electrical shock, and behind his lids pinwheels of light whizzed and whirled, bright hot sparks flying off in all directions, blazes and showers of light, fireworks. His eyes opened again, softly metallic globules of moist transparency floated past his vision, while all the time the blood flowed from a dozen wounds. He was weaker. He moaned. He prayed. He waited for a cold Hand to touch him, to end it; it did not come. His expiation was slow, painfully slow; he saw how angry Arco could be.

They returned lugging a giant gilt frame, the canvas backto; Willie recognized it without seeing the front. It had by Bee's decree hung in his bedroom, her "later" portrait for which she had sat to the Laguna painter; Willie despised it and at her death had banished it to a closet.

Under Arco's direction it was leaned against the doorframe, and another Beetrice Marsh gazed complacently out. Older, old, gone to fat, her hair dyed a reddish blond and screwed into a fashionable cap of curls, her chins choked by a triple strand of pearls, the flesh of one wrist plumply bulging between diamond bracelets, her eyes half hidden in fatty creases as if they had seen too much of the world, the wrinkled cheeks rouged and powdered, the too-red painted smile revealing a smug self-satisfaction. Her jeweled fingers held, almost coyly, face up on her ample lap, a hand mirror. *The* mirror; Willie wondered if they'd noticed. Arco hadn't, apparently. He stood looking up again, his hands flatly extended in a gesture of offering, ceremonially, like the figure in an Egyptian frieze; Willie's eye fell not on his face but on his palms, remembering the lines he had read. No need to warn young Bill, he was a part of them; even in horror a kind of togetherness. Arco blinked in the light, looking for a clue, the hint of solution to the mystery between them.

"Tell."

No reply.

He went away again and returned with a tin can: starter fluid from the barbecue. He squirted a stream of fluid onto the wax covering Willie's feet and ignited it. The fluid blazed up, coldly blue, and made a flashing sound, then quickly died out. He used more, touching flame to it and standing back. As soon as the fire had evaporated in flame more was squirted from the punctured top of the can and reignited. The wax melted, the fire seared in quick painful spurts, and they took turns in a new sport of tossing lighted matches at him. The fire leaped higher, up his shins, to his knees, his thighs, higher. They seemed to revel in his screams. They were kids in a playground, taking turns on a ride.

They tired of the sport and went away again. Willie hung on the cross, his cries dying to whimpers. He desperately wanted something to drink. Finally Arco let Judee bring him another glass of water. She stood on the bench and held it to his lips and he took it greedily; much of it dripped down his front. Then his kidneys gave way. She jumped back. Fastidious Willie was disgusted; the body's natural processes had always made him squeamish.

"I'm sorry," he said.

"Like, man, when you gotta go you gotta go. It's okay, you can clean it up." She'd taken the Bible from the altar and brought it to a bench, where she sat comfily, a coed in the window seat of a dorm, her granny glasses perched on her nose, studiously turning the pages and occasionally perusing them.

"Hey, listen to this," she said once, "it's really terrific." She read:

" 'For yet a little while, and the wicked shall not be: yea, thou shalt dil—dil-i-gently consider his place, and it shall not be.' Oh," she said fervently, mulling over the words, "I hope so. Honest." She continued:

"'But the meek shall inherit the earth; and shall delight themselves in the abundance of peace.'" She held the book on her lap and said to Willie, "See? That's what we're gonna do." She continued in her childish, winsome voice. "'The wicked have drawn out the sword, and have bent their bow, to cast down the poor and needy, and to slay such as be of upright conversation.' See, that's just like Arco says; it's all right here."

She glanced toward the doorway and went into another fit of laughter. "Oh, Arco, honest—you're such a crazy person. Look at you."

He came as a priest, wearing the purple cassock, the lace surplice, the stole, the square purple biretta. One hand lay reverently folded on his breast over a pectoral cross, while the other bore a small jar. With mock reverence, he made the familiar sign.

"Ego te absolvo . . ."

Willie wrenched his head away.

"Unction, Willie," he said soothingly. "Ease. It's here. You want it?" Willie shook his head, raised it higher, so he would not look.

"Extreme, Willie," Arco said significantly. "Last rites, understand? The real article, not what you gave that poor slob in It'ly." He stood on the embroidered pad of the bench, touched his thumb to oil in the jar. The liquid felt cold on Willie's lips as the mock priest applied it. "For 'your sins, Willie, I forgive you"—crossing the oily liquid over his lips— "the lies this mouth has spoken. I forgive you your false cross, your false reliquary, your false chapel, I forgive you your false beliefs. *In nomine Patri et Filii et Spiritus Sancti.* Amen."

On the cross, Willie shook his head violently back and forth. His tongue slid out, tasting. It was the salad dressing; vinaigrette. The purple-robed priest dipped his thumb again, and applied it to Willie's nose, his eyes, ears, uttering words of forgiveness with each application, speaking of vanity, falsehood, lust, gluttony, then stepping down again and pouring the remainder over the bare charred feet, whose toes twitched unceasingly. The mixture dripped onto the embroidered cushion, ran down the leg of the bench onto the red rug. Arco said, "That's the best I can do f'r you, Willie . . . unless you want somebody to pray for you. Read him something from the good book, Wimp." He went away again.

Judee read: "'Behold, thou art fair, my love; behold, thou art fair; thou hast doves' eyes within thy locks: thy hair is as a flock of goats, that appear from Mount Gilead.'" She smiled up at Willie. "Isn't that the most beautiful? I had no idea."

Her eye returned to the page, her finger following along under the words as she read. " 'Thy lips are like a thread of scarlet, and thy speech is comely: thy temples are like a piece of pomegranate within thy locks. . . . Thy two breasts are like two young roes that are twins, which feed among the lilies.' " She giggled. "Gets sort of sexy, huh? 'Until the day break, and the shadows flee away, I will get me to the mountain of myrrh, and to the hill of frankincense.' " She had a good deal of trouble with "myrrh" and "frankincense."

"That's enough," Arco told her, returning with Bill. He brought them together to the altar railing and made them kneel, speaking in Latin to them.

"Jesus, Arco, I can't do this," Bill protested. "I'm Baptist, see? This's a Cath'lic church."

Arco's face grew red; he raised his pointed finger to the ceiling and brought it downward. "On your knees!" he roared wrathfully. "Pray for the poor old bastard! Pray, you fuckers, pray, pray!" He danced around, holding up the hem of his cassock, then moving between the other two, shoving their heads down, slamming the palms of his hands onto their backs. "Pray! Pray, you fuckers. Pray like you never prayed before!"

"Our Father who art in Heaven," Bill began. He got as far as "forgive us our—" but couldn't remember if it should go "debts" or "trespasses." Judee looked up past her shoulder at Arco.

"Pray!"

"Now I lay me down to sleep," she piped in her thin voice. "With a bag of peanuts at my feet!" She collapsed on the carpet, laughing.

Willie watched Arco go, hiking the purple cassock up about his shins, bobbing and weaving, the biretta rakishly canted, the skirts swirling, swooping, a stoned goblin priest waltzing in dreamlike circles into darkness, into nothingness, and then all there was was the disembodied laugh. Willie's chin fell weakly onto his chest again, and he fainted.

He came to, how much later he didn't know. The dogs snored at the foot of the cross. Out past the lanai the sky had become lighter. Then from far away, traveling as through a tunnel, came the hollow reverberations of the clock: a single chime. Half past—what? The light hurt his eyes, but through its moted haze he could see into the dark shambles of that bright and glittering room: Warsaw under siege. The shock of pain had sobered him considerably. He thought surely they must let him down now.

Out of the darkness the girl came. He recognized the silver brocade dress: she'd been going through Bee's closets.

"Hi," she said softly, the metallic threads gleaming as she moved into the light. She modeled it for him, a grotesque, camp mannequin. "Swanky, huh? Don't cha think it's me? Very fifties?"

"Yes—very you, my dear," he replied weakly. He looked down at her with traces of a sad, wry smile. The dress had cost eight hundred dollars; Don Loper had created it for Bee for a party. It had a train. One dress dragged from among many out of a closet, out of another time. He could even recall the party—Master Bobby Ransome had performed for the guests. Willie had thought it an ugly dress then; on the girl now it looked merely pathetic.

"Keep it."

"Gee. You're really swell."

"Don't mention it."

She held the skirt out and examined it. "Was it hers? Bee's? I mean"—she said it shyly—"your mother's?"

"Once."

"I always wondered what they did with dead people's clothes. You ought to give them all away—you've got tons of them up there." She thought an instant, then innocently, as if it were perfectly natural: "Do you ever wear them?"

"Sometimes."

She turned to the portrait leaning against the doorway: now she would notice the mirror; but she seemed not to. "Look," she said, "same dress." She scrutinized the face, then said with a child's candor, "She doesn't look like a very nice lady, y'know?"

"That was no lady—that was my wife."

"You loved her anyway, huh?"

"Every boy . . . loves his mother," he replied dryly. Talking was difficult; the words came hard. "Every . . . good boy, that is."

"I don't know," she said speculatively. "Maybe a person's better off being an agency baby. But then, blood's thicker than water, I guess." She glanced down at the stains on the carpet.

"Maybe." He gagged, made retching noises, fell silent for a moment. Then, in a blurred tone, he asked, "Which market did you say?"

"Market?"

"Your mother left you . . . shopping cart . . ."

"The Shermart."

"Yes. Shermart. I remember." His voice cracked. "Mostly shop Beverly Hills. Jurgensen's. Gourmet."

"You c'n afford to, sweetie, you're rich." She pouted charmingly. "You've got it all. We got nothing."

"You have . . . an island . . . don't you?"

"I think that's just a dream of Arco's." Her voice was wistful; she pulled a frayed silver thread from the front of the dress. "I don't think it'll ever really come true. I don't think dreams ever really do come true."

"They do if you're not careful. Or if you're unlucky."

She regarded him solemnly. "I don't understand. Did your dreams come true?"

"Many times. A surfeit of dreams come true."

"Like bein' a big big movie star?"

"Like that."

"I guess it's everybody's dream." Her look became quizzical. "Is there something you'd rather have been?"

"I suppose not. My cup was ever full, and I drank and it still was full. I often wished that cup would pass from me."

"But what would you rather have been?"

"A floorwalker in the porcelain department of the biggest department store in Mobile, Alabama."

She had seated herself at the organ and was again playing.

" 'My mama done tol' me' "—*bump!*

He managed a sound which might have passed for a laugh. Why, she wondered, was he laughing when he was in so much pain? "What's funny?"

"I was thinking . . . what my mama done told . . . me."

"What?"

" 'Don't forget your rubbers, Billyboy.' " Each word was costing him strength. "Judee . . . little Judee with two *e*'s . . . can you get me down? Please?"

" 'When I was in knee pants' "—*bump!*

"Please . . . ?"

" 'My mama done tol' me—Son-n-n!' "

"Please, Judee . . . ?"

Bump. She wouldn't hear him. The carpet grew more red, a darker one, from the blood. The dogs, as though knowing what and whose it was, daintily avoided it, sat staring up, mute and motionless.

The girl talked over her shoulder as she worked the pedals,

monotonously playing the keys. "I thought you were terrific in the movie, Willie. Fedora was really a big star, huh?"

"Yes . . . biggest of them all . . ."

"That was funny, when she threw the apple to the queen." She thought a moment. "Joan Crawford—didn't she used to be a movie star?"

"Will always be a movie star, Joan Crawford. Judee . . . can you . . . take those things out of me?"

"The darts? Oh, gee, I don't think so. Arco . . ." She thought a moment and looked at him curiously. "He said you wanted to get hurt. Did you?"

"Get hurt?"

"No, *want* to. He said you liked it."

"People like different things. Judee—listen . . . I'm going to die. . . ."

"Ooh." She gave a little squeal and waved her fingers as if drying her nail polish. "I toldja—I don't like that word."

"In the drawer, there in the altar—my rosary. Give it to me."

She found the chain of beads in the drawer and climbed up to put them in his hand, hanging them over his fingers, which twitched as they touched the pendant cross.

"Upstairs," he told her, "in the front bedroom—a dresser. There's money in the third drawer. . . ."

Her face lighted up; she glanced toward the doorway and put her finger to her mouth. He shook his head.

"For Masses. Have a Mass said . . . for my soul, will you?"

She nodded, batting her eyelashes at him. She was sucking her fingers, like a baby. "I got this darn hangnail." Her lips curled; she blew him a kiss. Then she blurred before his eyes, he watched the gleam of silver, heard her platforms rattle over the vinyl, and she was swallowed up by the darkness. He was growing steadily weaker. It was all a joke, but he was going to die of the joke.

Sometime later Arco reappeared out of the darkness. Had he shrunk? He looked somehow smaller, less ferocious; even light of heart.

"How's it going, pops?" Willie stared down at him, saying nothing. "Some big house you got here. Been through every room; can't find it." No reply. "Y'know? The safe?"

"Safe." Willie echoed the word with grim mirth. "You haven't looked, Arco."

"You bet your ass I've looked. Tell me—you're way up there, what d'you hear from God, Little Willie?"

"God?" he echoed stupidly.

"You still believe in God, Willie?"

"I . . . believe."

"Then have him make a miracle, Willie. Have him get you down from there."

"Doesn't . . . matter."

"You're right, Willie. Nothing matters much, does it? I'll make you a trade. I'll trade you your life for that mirror— how's that?"

"Cheap at . . . half the price." His laugh was little more than a croak.

"You don't want to die for a mirror? Or do you want to die for God? Which?"

"Don't want to die. . . ."

"Course you don't, Willie; nobody does, when you finally get down to it. You don't know what's over there, on the other side, do you? That's the trouble; no one does. Hamlet's problem. Maybe God's not even there, huh? Did you ever think of that? Do you really believe in Him?"

Willie considered the question, but made no reply.

Judee had returned, stood hugging herself and whimpering. "Arco . . . ?" she murmured. "What's going to happen? What if he dies? It'll be murder. We'll go to prison."

Arco gave a raspberry laugh. "Wimp, you're in California, the land of nuts and fruits. They're used to this sort of thing. You can get out in seven years, with good behavior."

"How come?"

"They parole you. It's the law." He turned back to the figure on the cross. "Last chance, Willie. You want to tell?"

Arco watched him closely.

The old man's head moved, changed its angle so he could look down. The attenuated tendons of his body gave him the look of an El Greco figure, the martyr in the flesh. He was demonstrating some kind of pitiful bravado; it was foolish, capricious, lacking any consequence whatever, yet it was an admirable, dogged sort of pluck, the determined truculence of the aged. His mouth opened, there were salivating clicking sounds behind his teeth. He worked his jaws and lips and tongue, finally pushing his dental plate forward. The double row of teeth emerged grotesquely and fell on the carpet.

"Ith thith," he lisped.

"Yes?"

"I—defy—you."

Arco's look was mildly curious; he examined the face at length, almost tenderly. "To the death, Willie?"

"Yeth."

Arco shrugged lightly, as though the matter were of small concern to him. "I'll say this—you've got guts." He stood looking up and what Willie saw through his clouded vision was the grinning face of the buccaneer's flag. Arco peered out past the chapel doors. Yes, the sky was getting lighter; somewhere a mockingbird sang, louder, more brashly. He shouted for Bill, then went out again.

Later, it was lighter still. They returned together, all three. With a watchful attitude, the girl dropped onto the organ bench in the silver dress, while Bill lounged against the doorjamb. "Heck, I sure am sorry 'bout this, Willie," he said. "We was havin' such a right nice evenin'."

Arco had come with tools: a hammer and a box of nails. "You've been wanting this right along," he said, not looking up, but climbing onto the bench and proceeding with his work.

"Hail Mary, full of grathe," Willie prayed, when he saw what the intention was. "The Lord ith with me."

The hammering shattered the silence, sending shocks along the wood of the cross, and the screams that came with it enraged the cockatoo in the palmetto tree. The rosary slipped from Willie's fingers.

"Blethed art Thou among women."

The girl hugged her knees and shivered in horrified fascination as the hammering continued.

"Jesus," Bill said, awed. "What a freaking sight."

"And Blethed ith the fruit of Thy womb, Jeethuth."

The hammering went on. Arco worked nimbly, like some crazed carpenter, holding the nails between his teeth before driving them with the heavy steel head.

"Holy Mary, Mother of God, pray for uth thinnerths now and at the hour of our death amen."

"A-*men*," Arco said.

Judee called the dogs to her, and took them on her lap, cuddling them and fondling the silky hair of their ears, as, with a dishcloth, Bill sopped blood from the carpet and drew arcane images across the slashed damask, his sweeping movements causing the small picture on the back wall to tilt across its hook. Nobody noticed. Bill was engaged in his task, Arco in his, the girl watching while the brown body jerked and wrenched in frantic spasms, stretching and loosening the cords so it sagged in the middle. Yet he remained hanging upright; the head jerked back at every thudding shock, the skull striking the upright with a hollow sound. The cries grew more feeble, became moans, ended.

"What he wanted all along," Arco said. He flung away the hammer, got down, and stalked from the room. The victim moaned, rolling his eyes to the side, then at Judee. Seeing what he required, she picked up the rosary and put it back into his twitching fingers, whose tips fumbled the chain of beads. He was mumbling frantic snatches of prayers.

In his burning head was one idea, one single notion. He would go to his reward, he would sit on the right hand of God, he would see the pearly gates, angels with halos, gold harps, white feathered wings, he would be possessed of the peace that surpasseth all, life everlasting, the promise of Christ, the Resurrection and the Light.

Or would he? The vision he had conjured with its attendant images separated into a sort of double vision, trembled, then dissolved, like a desert mirage, leaving only darkness in his mind. The rosary again slipped from his hand, the crucifix glinted on the red rug. "Forget . . . the Math," he murmured.

"Forget the Mass?" the girl repeated, incredulous. "Why?"

"I don't believe," he whispered, not to her but to the portrait. "I never did. . . ." His words trailed away in a wondering tone; on his lips was a weary, rueful smile, touched by some private irony. He did not speak again.

Arco had come in still wearing his habit, and was listening. "See," he said, his face alight with passion, "I knew it." With a wild rush he kicked open the gate, and, the purple cassock sweeping around his legs, he sprang onto the bench, reaching on tiptoe to clutch the naked, quivering shoulders in a fearful grasp, and planting his lips on the old man's. The two mouths remained pressed together, then Arco pulled away and released him. *"Ciao, caro,"* he said, and stepped down, panting.

"You kissed him!" the girl exclaimed, with a little shudder.

"Shut up, Wimp," he told her angrily. Then, more mildly, "It was the kiss not of passion but of peace." His voice had grown soft, almost meditative, as he surveyed the effect of his deft carpentering. It was the final agony. It could not go on; it had to end. But the old man was stronger than he looked, the light would not go out, the spirit would not be quenched, and what breath was left was given up only reluctantly. Arco eyed him with both regret and a mute respect. Then, with a rush, at last, everything went lax. Willie lost control, his stomach churned and heaved; his bowels loosened. He suffered the final humiliation in mortified silence, lifting his chin away, and his eyes.

He died shortly afterward.

They looked upon the cadaver, the wildly staring eyes, the indignantly arched nostrils, the rictus of the mouth gaping in shocked protest, and Michael Gino Archangelo appeared to be satisfied. As a final touch he had taken Fedora's crown and tilted it onto the bloodied head.

Outside, dark nocturnal shapes had taken on a pale, wan reality. Early traffic moved along the boulevards. The fog had lifted but in its place a skein of acrid smog was already being spun out over the flats. The Mode O'Day sign had gone off, and buildings assumed their unremarkable, commonplace shapes in the dull but persistently growing light. The feeble early sun drew upward. It would not be a lovely day.

It was inevitable that before leaving, one of the three should have noticed the picture askew on the back wall, and the safe hidden behind it. They scrambled among the wreckage, searching for the second key that had hung on the dead man's neck. Inside the safe they found what they had been hunting, the Medici mirror. The corpse watched them remove it, examine it, gloat; it would bring them five thousand dollars. It would take them to the South Pacific. It would save mankind.

They had found one unbroken champagne bottle and one Baccarat goblet. The cork exploded, hit the ceiling, and bounced; foam spurted in all directions. "Ooh," the girl cried. "Be careful, you'll get it on my dress." She crouched to hunt under the furniture for the cork: a souvenir.

They celebrated, clustered around the piano. The girl felt the bubbles popping against her nose; then she was crying.

"Why," she said, looking at the cross, "that nice old man—he didn't even say goodbye."

Salad Days

The Beverly Hills Hotel, a mock-Spanish pile of pink stucco shaded by awnings, is situated on Sunset Boulevard between Beverly Drive and Benedict Canyon. Across from it is a small public park with green sloping lawns and seasonal floral plantings under rows of stately Washington palm trees. High-salaried nurses sit there on benches rocking babies in rubber-wheeled carriages and reading paperback novels. It is a common sight, and one that Barry Detweiller saw one noon-time in 1957, passing in his rented car on the way to an appointment at the hotel. He drove under the porte-cochère, where he received from a red-jacketed attendant a numbered parking ticket, passed through the portico into the lobby, where busy bellboys with pillbox hats and chin straps were wheeling luggage across the floral carpeting, turned right, then took the first left, into the Polo Lounge. The dim room was already filling for lunch, and men relaxed at the bar be-fore the East-Indian-style gold-leafed mural, drinking whiskey sours, or sat at the semicircular banquettes, holding important conversations on plug-in phone extensions. They wore suits with narrow lapels and pink shirts, some blue, or even white. The women's skirts were cut at midcalf and their hats were bell-shaped, with touches of veils or narrow feathers. Barry gave his name to the headwaiter, who led him out into the sunny patio, where a table had been reserved in a quiet corner under the arbor. Scarlet bougainvillaea climbed the pink walls, there were red and yellow hibiscus and white star jasmine. The tablecloths and napkins more or less matched the stucco.

Barry had been sent by *Life* magazine to Hollywood to do a story on the popular Bobbitt movies, and their star, Bobby Ransome. Last night there had been a party in honor of the child phenomenon, given by Willie and Bee Marsh. Barry had already done several studio interviews with Little Willie concerning the upswing in his professional fortunes, and the actor had stated for publication that he never could have done it without Bee. It was the first time Barry had been to the Marsh residence on Cordelia Way. The party had been enormous, with many famous people present. Bogie and Betty were there, Frank Sinatra, Judy Garland, Audrey Hepburn, Rosalind Russell, Hedda and Louella. There was a mambo band by the pool, in which gardenias and candles had been floated, and a dance floor laid over the lawn. There was a striped tent with strolling musicians playing personal requests, the waiters wore military braid on their mess jackets, the buffet was flanked by silver candelabra with fifteen-inch candles, and épergnes filled with grapes and peaches from the Farmer's Market. People said that Bobby's cheeks looked like those peaches. In the center of the buffet was a stupendous ice sculpture, a reproduction of the crown the child star had worn in *Bobbitt Royal*. Later, guests were invited to view the recently installed private chapel, while Bee lectured at length on its various features: the cross that was made of cedar wood from Lebanon, brought across the Mediterranean by the Knights of Malta; the Quattrocento painting of the Virgin; the coffer containing a bone from the foot of Saint Tribonius; the Bible that had belonged to Cardinal Richelieu; the altar cloth embroidered by the nuns of Bruges. On the game room piano were silver-framed pictures of Pius XII, the cardinal, the archbishop of the diocese, and the local bishop. Bee declared that now that her Billyboy was safely in the bosom of the Church she could die a happy woman; Willie replied that he never would have done it without her showing him the way. Though Barry Detweiller had admired such filial devotion, he found Beetrice Marsh grossly overbearing, the cliché of the stage mother. Her humor was waspish, her urges willful, she was loud, brash, and extremely clever, but far too old to be as giddy as she appeared. On the other hand, he had found Willie to be exactly what he'd expected—generous, considerate, charming, and a witty raconteur. "The Grand Old Man of Hollywood."

He rose as they now approached across the dining patio.

Willie looked dapper in a light-colored striped business suit with a vest, and two-tone shoes. Bee wore a flossy print, a hat not only with net but a feather as well, and dark glasses with white frames. A brightly contrasting handkerchief was attached to her lapel, waitress style. Her bosom, squashed upward and together so it looked like a baby's bottom, was more emblazoned with scatter pins than a general's with insignia. She wore gloves and earrings and a necklace. She wore several bracelets. Barry had the impulse to tell her to go home and take off any three things.

She said how exciting it all was, waiting for Willie to pull out her chair and seat her. She took up a good deal of room at the table, laying her things about as she began talking—her pocketbook, a pack of Kleenex, and several parcels. One of these was a zippered cloth case of watered silk. She showed Barry what it contained: an ornate oval hand mirror. After lunch Willie was driving her to Laguna to sit for her portrait; a young man she'd discovered and who had, she declared, a lot of talent. The mirror would be resting in her hand in the picture. It had once belonged to Catherine de' Medici, and was the work of Cellini; Fedora had given it to Willie. This, as Bee confided *sotto voce*, was not the original, however, but merely a cheap copy made as a prop for one of Fedora's lesser successes, *The Mirror*. The real one was safeguarded in a vault in the Bank of America, while this counterfeit was kept in a wall safe to fool potential burglars.

The waiter brought menus, orders were taken. Barry wanted only a salad and Willie suggested the Niçoise. The ingredients were wheeled out in a bowl on a cart—tuna fish, black olives, hard-boiled eggs, filet of anchovy, small cold potatoes. The butter lettuce was the palest green, with yellow and white hearts, and Willie had made sure the leaves were individually patted dry after being washed, and saw to the elaborate preparation of the vinaigrette himself. The trick, you see, he said, was a pinch or two of dry mustard, and one or two of sugar.

It was during the mixing of the dressing that Bee Marsh, subsiding at last, permitted Willie to speak at length. He was in a reminiscing mood—he was commencing his memoirs, to be called "Salad Days"—and he lingered lovingly over earlier times, more pleasant ones, when they had called Twentieth Century-Fox "the country club," and a working star thought nothing of taking off in the middle of the afternoon for a golf game; when the San Fernando Valley had been walnut groves and Santa Monica rice paddies; when there had been no freeways and people were driven by their liveried chauffeurs in Duesenbergs, when there had been no smog and the sun shone bright and unceasingly, when lawns stayed green without benefit of sprinkling systems, when polo matches were played at Will Rogers's ranch and Gable danced with Lombard at the Trocadero.

Looking about him, Barry noticed several recognizable industry figures at other tables. Among them were a producer, a columnist, and several actresses of note. It happened that at the opposite end of the arbor sat an elderly woman in navy blue, talking quietly with a companion. Willie had singled her out as someone whose name Barry knew, but whom he had never seen in pictures. She did not wear dark glasses; she was in the shade and there was no need of disguise. Nobody recognized her, with the exception of Willie, who had pointed her out, and few would have remembered her. She had appeared in several early films for Derougemont, and her name had been in lights above the title on theater marquees all over the country. Her pictures were mostly forgettable, and though her name had been set in a star on Hollywood Boulevard, no one paid attention to it as they walked over it. Now no heads even turned to glance at her: one of the Talmages, and formerly one of the biggest stars in movies.

Although neither she nor Barry nor Willie Marsh realized it, the day of Hollywood was already nearing its end. The mastodon was groping its way to the boneyard to die. The old guard was fearful of becoming the rear guard. A Presence lurked in town. Television studios had been built, NBC in Burbank, CBS at Beverly and Fairfax. Long a tradition in the courtyard behind Paramount's Marathon Street gate, the goldfish pond had been torn out to make room for a parking lot. Mayer was gone from MGM, Zanuck was reported leaving Fox for independent production, Jack Warner was said to be contemplating the sale of his studio. De Mille was then in the process of cutting his last movie. None of this, however, was discussed. What was talked about was the old, forgotten actress. Signs of the times, Willie said. Bee protested. No, she maintained adamantly, once a star, always a star. For once, Willie disagreed with his mother, and then recounted to Barry a story which he hoped proved his point.

It had been back in the late thirties, before Fedora had left Hollywood prior to the war. She had completed her last film and one Sunday she called Willie and asked him to take her for a drive. He picked her up at her house in Pacific

Palisades and they drove south along the Coast Highway. It was a gray, foggy day, the sort of weather Southern California often sees in June, and there were few people on the beaches. When they got to Santa Monica, Fedora said she wanted to stop and have a picnic on the sand. They parked and went into a delicatessen, Tashkent's Select Kosher Deli, as it was called. After examining the glass meat cases, Fedora ordered bagel sandwiches with lox and cream cheese, hard-boiled eggs, and soda pop, to go. Opening two root beers, the proprietress, Mrs. Tashkent, peered up through her green celluloid eyeshade at Fedora and said, "Say, ain't chou a movie stah?" Fedora shook her head; no movie stars today. "Shuah, you're a movie stah," persisted Mrs. Tashkent, coming around the counter for a closer view. "I know you're a movie stah. Ain't chou?" Again shaking her head, Fedora retreated to a rack of magazines, waiting for Willie to bring the food. Little Mrs. Tashkent was not to be put off; she eyed Fedora from under her eyeshade, ruminatively tapping a fingernail against a front tooth, trying to decide who this "movie star" might be. "Listen, mistuh," she asked Willie, "she's a movie stah, isn't she? I know I've seen her, I know I have. Seen her in . . . pictures."

"I shan't tell you," Willie said sweetly, "unless you pay me a dollar."

"A dolluh?" Mrs. Tashkent was shocked. "A dolluh's a lotta money these days for just a movie stah." She peered closer at Fedora and as though reading the riddle of the Sphinx, she asked again, "Please, ain't chou a movie stah?"

"Yes"—Fedora finally acquiesced—"I'm a movie star." As if to say: Yes, dear little Mrs. Tashkent lady, for you I'll be a movie star. If my being a movie star makes you happy on this gloomy June day, I'm a movie star.

"Yeah," said Mrs. Tashkent dubiously, "but are you a *poimanent* movie stah?"

Laughing, Fedora went out, and as Willie followed her, Mrs. Tashkent touched his arm confidentially and leaned up to him. "No kiddin', mistuh, what's her name?" Willie whispered in her ear; Mrs. Tashkent nodded, his words at last satisfying her. "I thought it was." Willie went out, and before the screen door closed he could hear Mrs. Tashkent shouting to the rear of the store, "Irving, guess who's just in fa' lox and bagels—Verree Teasdale!"

"And don't forget me," Willie called through the screening, "Adolphe Menjou!"

They took their picnic onto the fogged-in beach, where

they walked along, Willie waiting for Fedora to decide on a spot, which turned out to be the farthest point from any visible object—from the lifeguard tower, the trash can, the street, the pier. The sand was flat, moist, well packed. There were no footprints other than their own trail behind, and those of the sea gulls. The wide strand had a clean, just-raked look, pristine, unmarred by litter, and not another soul was to be seen. They could actually make out the individual silvery particles forming the fog; they touched their skin in minute glistening globules, cold and damply soothing. From the car Fedora had brought a light lap robe, and in a suddenly capricious mood she flung it around her head and instantly became a peasant woman, stretching out her hand and groaning, "I *hon*gree. Plees, you geeve oldt lady foodt, yais?" The great face became Duse, became Bernhardt, became the movie Fedora. She flung herself against Willie, twining her arms about him, embracing him, then arching away with the impassioned expression of the classic tragedienne, breathless, pulsating, panting, eyebrows scooped, yearning at an imaginary adoring audience, accepting its homage, the entire history of acting written across her brow. And in men's trousers, too; what a sight, thought Willie Marsh.

Then they heard it, the far-off sound of a military band rising above the waves. Beyond the pier the fog had rolled in so they could see scarcely twenty feet in front of them, but, unmistakably, there came the beat of martial music. Fedora seized Willie's hand and dragged him along, running across the beach to the street, following the sounds, brass and glockenspiel, drums and fifes, tubas, then they stopped, astonished, as out of the swirling fog came a full marching band, high school kids in outfits like movie theater ushers, their shining instruments playing "Stars and Stripes Forever." A befrogged drum major in his furry shako bowed to Fedora and Willie; he was followed by a pretty drum majorette, in short skirt, with shapely thighs, full breasts, and blond hair. A pretty thing, the vision of the all-American girl, with red lips and white teeth and a confectionery smile, as she spun her silver baton with its white rubber-tipped ends. Up in the air the baton flashed, and when it came down Fedora darted to catch it, then twirled it before her, strutting spectacularly, doing high kicks with her long legs, back arched, singing with a heavy Russian accent, "Oh, the mon-kee wrapped hees tail ar-round the flag-po-ole," and with a mighty toss sending the baton into the air again, out of sight into the fog, waiting, looking for its return, the brass section ducking it, the French horns scattering, the percussionists shielding their heads against its descent. It dropped and the drum majorette ran to retrieve it. "Hurry up, Cookie," someone called from the departing column, and the girl smiled and waved, then ran to take up her position again. Fedora watched them go, her face alight like a twelve-year-old's, breathless from her act as the band disappeared again into the blurred white and the music faded away in the distance.

"Such a pr-retty girl," she said of the blond majorette. "You know—she really ought to be in the movies."

ABOUT THE AUTHOR

Thomas Tryon was born in Hartford, Connecticut. His earliest impulse was toward painting—and after graduation from Yale he attended the Art Students League. Thomas Tryon has played many roles in television, on stage, and in films; perhaps his most famous was the title role in the film version of *The Cardinal*. In addition to *Crowned Heads,* he has written *The Other, Harvest Home,* and *Lady*.

"The rich fabric of Tryon's tale
makes delectable reading."   —PLAYGIRL

LADY

by Thomas Tryon

C2592 $1.95

Against the rich nostalgia of a small New England town in
the '30s and '40s, this spellbinding novel unfolds the story of
a wealthy and beautiful widow whose enigmatic past weaves
an ever-tightening web of suspense around her and those who
love her.

They call her Lady. Lady—who lives in the big house on
the other side of the Green. Lady—who is the special friend
of young Woody, who lives across the way. Lady—who is
kind and fair and generous, except when she hides herself
in the darkness of her memories. Lady—who lives in agony
with her terrible secret until she no longer can.

Also by Thomas Tryon

HARVEST HOME   2-2999-8 $1.95

It was almost as if time had not touched the village of
Cornwall Coombe. The quiet, peaceful place was straight out
of a bygone era, with well-cared-for Colonial houses, a white-
steepled church fronting a broad Common. Ned and Beth
Constantine chanced upon the hamlet and immediately fell in
love with it. This was exactly the haven they dreamed of. Or
so they thought. But for Ned and his family, Cornwall
Coombe was to become a place of ultimate horror.

THE OTHER   2-2684-0 $1.75

At the center of this terrifying novel are the handsome
young twin sons of an old and respected family—Niles and
Holland Perry, complicated, secretive boys, bound together
in the intense fidelity of twinship. In their strange, imaginative games, the dark-natured Holland dominates. Yet it is
Niles, gentle and loving, who is gifted in the strangest game,
an almost mystic game of empathy with all living creatures,
which their adored grandmother Ada learned as a girl and
has taught them.